Telson
CHABAD of Rani
895-7256

PLAN B

A Novel of Suspense and Deceit

ELI SHEKHTER

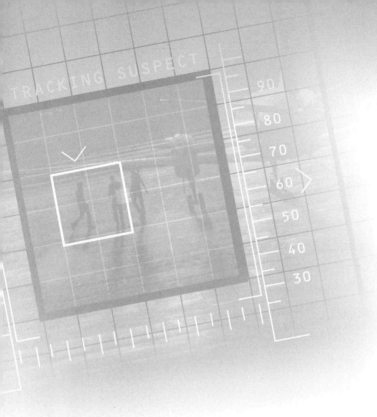

ELI SHEKHTER

PLAN B

A Novel of Suspense and Deceit

Author's Note

The tragic events of 9/11 are seared into our memories forever. This book is in no way intended to trivialize or show disrespect to the thousands who perished in the attacks. Rather, it is meant to draw attention to the incredible evil of terrorist groups and their leaders, and to portray a scenario where these villains are subdued—allowing the free world to live in peace. *Be'ezras Hashem* may we see that day soon, with the coming of Mashiach.

Copyright © 2005 by I. Weiss

ISBN 1-931681-78-3

All rights reserved. No part of this book may be reproduced or transmitted in any form or by any means (electronic, photocopying, recording or otherwise) without prior written permission of the copyright holder or the distributor.

Cover design by Deenee Cohen
Translated by Debbie Shapiro
Edited by Elky Langer

Distributed by:
Israel Book Shop
501 Prospect Street
Lakewood, NJ 08701

Tel: (732) 901-3009
Fax: (732) 901-4012
Email: Isrbkshp@aol.com

Printed in Israel

Prologue

Eight forty-six AM.
A Boeing 767 flying directly above the Hudson suddenly swerved to the right and started flying toward downtown Manhattan. Straight ahead: the World Trade Center, a maze of tall skyscrapers dwarfed by the Twin Towers.

The streets of downtown Manhattan were crowded with people hurrying to work. No one was paying attention to the airplane flying along the Hudson River. The airplane decreased its altitude as it flew over the upper class residential district of Battery Park, causing the windows to rattle.

The plane lowered its altitude still further. As the noise grew in intensity, curious pedestrians began looking skyward. It was a clear day—yet they still rubbed their eyes in disbelief at the sight of an enormous jet flying directly toward the World Trade Center's north tower.

The seconds passed quickly. Much to the onlookers' horror, the plane remained on course, rapidly approaching the upper floors of the north tower. What was wrong with the aircraft? Was there anything the pilot could do to avoid a head-on collision?

Half an hour earlier, the supervisor at the navigation tower in Boston's Logan Airport had started feeling panicky. Five times, he had tried to contact American Airlines Flight 11. There had been no response. The plane had flown off course fifteen minutes before. This wasn't usually a cause for concern—a quick call to the pilot always put the airliner back on track. But not this time.

The supervisor tried to contact the pilot again. The plane had already flown off his radar screen, and he didn't even know where it was located. This time he added SOS, so the pilot would realize that the situation was desperate. But there was still no response.

The supervisor was at a complete loss. In his entire career, which spanned over two decades, he had never dealt with such a strange sequence of events. He hesitated for a moment before pressing the red emergency button on the panel above his head.

Minutes later, his phone rang. "Joe Winterman speaking," a voice boomed into his ear. Joe, a four-star general, was in charge of the nearest military base.

"There's a problem with American Airlines Flight 11," the supervisor began. He briefly related the strange sequence of events.

"Continue trying to contact the plane," Joe ordered. "And keep your line open, so we can stay in touch."

As the supervisor hung up, relieved to have the responsibility out of his hands, Joe went to work. After taking a few seconds to consider his options, he lifted his telephone to make another call—this one to Ed Greene, another four-star general and a good friend.

Joe actually outranked Ed. But this was only a matter of protocol—they were close friends, and treated each other as equals. Joe sketched out the recent events for Ed, and the two men started discussing their options.

They had finally decided to order two F-16 jets to approach the straying airplane—hoping the aircraft would follow the jet escorts and land safely in one of the nearby airports—when another call came in from the supervisor.

"I found the aircraft, though the pilot still isn't answering me."

"Where is it?" Ed asked.

The supervisor's voice grew hesitant. "This is going to sound strange, but—I think it's heading toward New York."

New York? Joe didn't like the sound of that. "What do you think?" he asked Ed.

Ed was silent for a moment. "The plane was hijacked," he suggested hesitantly.

"I agree. I'm ordering the F-16s to keep the plane in sight."

"Fine," Ed agreed. "But something is strange about this. Why aren't the hijackers making themselves known? They usually inform us that they've hijacked a plane and then warn us that they'll hurt the passengers if we try to stop them."

"Yes. The whole situation is very unusual."

Ed could hear the strange note in his friend's voice. "Tell me what you're thinking, Joe."

"I think that we had better obtain approval to shoot the plane down. It looks as though we should prepare ourselves for the possibility."

"Yes," Ed managed to say. He knew he had to agree, though he never imagined that he would be the one to order American soldiers to open fire on a civilian plane containing American passengers, as it flew over American soil.

Ed picked up the phone to contact Air Force headquarters in Washington, DC. Headquarters agreed with his decision and tried to contact the President, to receive the necessary approval.

The people on the street watched with disbelieving eyes as the plane flew straight into the upper stories of the northern tower. For a moment the plane seemed to disappear, swallowed by the enormous building. Then reality returned as burning debris cascaded from the point of impact. The huge hole in the building quickly filled with thick black smoke and tongues of fire.

The 911 emergency switchboard was flooded with calls. They all reported the same terrible accident. A huge airliner had collided with one of the towers in the World Trade Center, and the upper floors were on fire.

Sirens filled the air. Hundreds of firefighters started pouring in from every direction, the first fire truck arriving within three minutes after the collision. The firefighters, dressed in their protective flame resistant suits, began the long trek up the steps, passing panicky office workers who were trying to leave the building as quickly as possible. They continued to nurture a faint hope that there would be some way to get through to the people on the upper floors, and somehow bring them to safety—despite the fire that was raging out of control.

Scores of newspaper reporters and cameramen congregated both within and without, intent on taking pictures to capture the immensity of the tragedy. A deafening roar overhead made them stop for a moment.

Every gaze swung skyward—where another airplane was heading straight toward the southern tower.

It took only seconds for the realization to sink in. The reporters on site immediately changed their description of the collision from "accident" to "terrorist attack."

The moment of collision was caught perfectly on tape, as the stunned reporters could only watch helplessly.

The southern tower began to collapse an hour later. Within moments, the enormous building had turned into tons of debris, covered by a thick cloud of heavy smoke. The thousands of people still standing nearby fled down the streets, in an effort to escape the flying debris. They could not stop thinking about the people still trapped inside.

The United States would never be the same after the events of that fateful day—September 11, 2001.

Forty-five minutes after the second plane crashed, another plane had collided with the Pentagon.

The FAA froze all flights. Pilots in flight were instructed to land at the nearest airport. The navigation control towers informed the pilots that any plane seen flying off course would be shot down without warning.

What the public didn't know was that there were still two more hijacked airplanes which remained unaccounted for. The Air Force pilots patrolling American airspace were given instructions: shoot them down on sight! And so the search began for the missing airplanes.

An F-16 pilot, Jerry Lowell, was the first to catch sight of the missing Boeing 767. In the bright sunlight, the words "United Airlines" sparkled against the body of the gray plane.

Jerry fought to keep his voice steady as he keyed his microphone. "There's a Boeing 767 one hundred and forty degrees to my right," he reported. "It's headed toward Pittsburgh, Pennsylvania."

"That's the plane," his commanding officer confirmed.

Without waiting for further instructions, Jerry pulled his plane to the right. He was now flying one thousand feet above the civilian plane. Jerry accelerated the F-16's speed, and within less than a minute he had passed the Boeing.

When the plane was about two hundred feet in front of the Boeing, he pressed the navigation stick down. The F-16 lowered its altitude until it was flying directly in front the Boeing 767.

Jerry slowed the jet to five hundred and fifty miles per hour, the same speed as the Boeing. He tipped the jet's wings up and down, the international sign to follow him.

"Aircraft in view, please identify, over," he said into his radio.

There was no response. The plane continued flying straight. It was as if the Air Force jet was invisible.

The two planes were flying dangerously close. Jerry decided to try another approach. He turned his F-16 sharply to the right and flew two miles away from the Boeing 767. Then he made another sharp turn, this time to the left, so he ended up flying straight toward the suspicious jet.

The Boeing continued to ignore him.

Jerry decided to try one more thing. He flew ahead of the civilian plane so the pilot would lose sight of him. Then he turned around and flew on a collision course straight toward the Boeing 767. When he was about six hundred feet away, he pulled on the navigation stick and made a quick ascent, barely missing the civilian plane.

Incredibly, the Boeing made no acknowledgement of his presence.

"They won't give in," Jerry informed his commanding officer. "I have tried everything in the book, but they continue to ignore me."

"Get behind the Boeing in shooting formation," the officer ordered in a shaky voice.

Jerry forced himself to remain calm as he obeyed orders. His actions were mechanical. Over the years he had been taught that the key to success was discipline, and now he realized that this was of utmost importance if he was to succeed now. He was going through the motions like a robot, while his conscience was screaming at him to disobey.

"I am flying directly behind the plane," Jerry reported into the microphone attached to his helmet. His mouth was dry, making it difficult to speak.

This is it, Jerry realized. He was about to murder forty-five innocent civilians. He was about to shoot down a plane carrying American citizens as it was flying over American soil.

But what choice did he have? Jerry knew what had happened to the World Trade Center. The alternative was far, far worse.

"Prepare to fire," his officer instructed him.

Jerry armed his gun system, automatically obeying orders even as the tears began to course down his cheeks. He closed his eyes momentarily before pressing the button that would send a missile straight at the civilian aircraft.

"What's going on?" a sharp voice asked over his radio.

Jerry's eyes flew open, and he stared in shock out his cockpit window. The plane was no longer flying in front of him. It was heading downward, in an uncontrollable dive. As Jerry watched, transfixed, the airliner struck the ground—and exploded.

His commanding officer spoke again. "What happened to the airliner? Did you shoot it?"

"No," Jerry said, bewildered. He checked his weapons system. No, he hadn't actually pressed the button yet. "I don't know what happened, but—the airplane suddenly crashed."

"Any survivors?"

Jerry looked downward at a scene of devastation. "No," he said quietly. "I can't imagine that there are."

"Come back to base," his commanding officer ordered.

Relieved that he hadn't actually had to pull the trigger—though horrified at the airliner's tragic end—Jerry turned his fighter plane around and started flying back to his base. What had happened to the airplane? Jerry couldn't imagine—and he suspected that he would never know.

The Secret Service agents guarding the White House discovered the second missing airliner. It came descending through the sky, heading on a collision course with the White House.

The agents on the roof alerted their colleagues inside of the impending disaster. Fortunately, the President was away. But for them, they knew, there was no escape.

They remained at their posts on top of the building's north wing, trying to control their terror as the enormous airplane approached the building's western wing. It was too late for the Air Force to do anything—even if they shot the airplane down, the resulting crash would hurl it straight into the White House, raining debris upon the entire area.

The plane was seven hundred feet away from the building when it made a sharp turn to the east and started gaining altitude again. The Secret Service agents watched, openmouthed in amazement, as the airliner disappeared from the horizon.

One

Teheran, Iran, 1979

The last rays of sunlight were filtering through the huge picture window as Rachamim Roji stared unhappily at the empty street. The day was already coming to an end, and he had not sold a single item from his exclusive clothing store.

Rachamim's upper class Iranian customers—including several members of the royal family—had stopped venturing out into the lawless streets, afraid of being caught in a protest rally against the Shah and brutally lynched by the undisciplined mob. The royal family and their friends preferred to remain safely cloistered inside their homes in a relatively quiet area of the city, protected by a ring of the Shah's loyal soldiers.

Rachamim heard a muted roar—the sound of thousands of voices emanating from the city center. The individual words were indistinguishable, but he had no doubt that they were shouting their rallying cry: "Down with the Shah!"

These protests had become an everyday event. The brutal Savak, the Shah's secret intelligence organization, was slowly losing its iron grip on the country. Fiery tapes of Ayatollah Khomeini's speeches aroused the workers to rebel against the Shah, even at great personal risk. The tapes were distributed everywhere, despite the fact that it was illegal for an Iranian citizen to have one in his possession. All government efforts to stop the sale of these tapes had been fruitless. Khomeini's devoted followers had succeeded in smuggling hundreds of thousands of his tapes into the country.

The charismatic leader had used these tapes to arouse the masses to rebel, demanding the overthrow of the secular government and the start of a fundamental religious regime. Despite relative economic success, the Shah's use of the brutal Savak to repress both his real and imagined enemies had led the masses to clamor for a change. Khomeini knew that the time was ripe for his rebellion to succeed.

Still staring out the window, Rachamim noticed Muhammad Meshhadi lowering the metal bars that protected the display window of his jewelry store, right across the street. Rachamim glanced at his watch. It was ten minutes to five, and Muhammad never closed his store before seven. Did Muhammad have inside information? Was something going to happen in this area?

Leaving his store, Rachamim crossed the narrow street. Muhammad nodded briefly at his friend, but didn't speak as he finished lowering the metal bars.

"Where are you going so early?" Rachamim asked.

Muhammad turned. "I am going home, and I advise you to do the same. The mob will be here in a few minutes."

Rachamim was startled. Muhammad had always been the optimistic one, assuring him that despite the angry mobs, the Shah would remain strong and in power. It was Rachamim who remained skeptical, expressing his fears about the current situation in Iran. While the Shah, Muhammad Riza Pahalavy, was popular among the wealthy secular sector and those who weren't interested in Shiite rule, many had become disenchanted by the Savak's brutal repression. The Shiite majority were actively seeking a return to Islamic rule.

Muhammed had always dismissed Rachamim's concerns. But now, it seemed, the tables had been turned.

"What brought this on?" Rachamim asked his friend.

Muhammad busied himself with locking his door, unwilling to look Rachamim in the eye. "The Shah has left the country," he muttered.

Rachamim gasped in shock.

"He knows what he has been unwilling to admit to us. Khomeini has succeeded in fulfilling his promise. Tomorrow morning, he will arrive here on an Air France flight. The French are disgusting," Muhammad hissed in hatred. "I wonder what Khomeini promised them in return for their assistance?"

Muhammad kept muttering about the treasonous French, but Rachamim barely listened to his political explanation. He knew his friend had to justify his own lack of foresight. Muhammad had laughed at Rachamim when the latter had suggested that Muhammad transfer his money and possessions to a Swiss bank account.

"I need cash to expand my business," Muhammad had said, ignoring the changing political reality. "People are panicking and willing to sell everything they own for a tenth of its value. Once the situation stabilizes, I'll become a millionaire."

He had tried to convince Rachamim not to sell out. Rachamim, however, refused to listen. "A bird in the hand is worth two in the bush," he retorted.

Muhammad had purchased most of Rachamim's possessions at a tenth of their real value. Muhammad knew that Rachamim had transferred the cash to a secret bank account in Switzerland. Now, Rachamim suspected that Muhammad was regretting his decision.

"The first of February will be remembered in history as the day Iran lost its freedom," Muhammad said gloomily. "The Shah has already escaped the country."

"And that's exactly what we had better do. We must run away, escape, leave!" Rachamim blurted out.

They could hear explosions in the distance. From past experience, they could recognize the sound of rubber bullets and smoke bombs. The gunshots were even louder than usual.

"What are you waiting for? They're coming closer! Close your store and let's get out of here!" Muhammad urged him.

Rachamim ran across the street and started yanking down the iron bars covering his storefront. The shooting was coming from Teheran's center, west of the commercial district. He would have to pass through the eastern side of the city to reach his home in the suburbs. He hoped the area was clear. Being a Jewish businessman was more than enough reason to be lynched by the rioting masses.

Rachamim quickly finished lowering the metal bars in front of his store, and the two men hurried to the parking lot at the corner. Rachamim and Muhammad were close neighbors, and Rachamim drove Muhammad to work each morning. Muhammad had never learned to drive—he had given up after failing the driving test for the seventh time.

Sitting in his car, Rachamim glanced at the lowered bars covering his store windows. He had a gut feeling that this was the last time he would ever see his store. He noticed the tears in Muhammad's eyes, and he realized that Muhammad must be feeling the same way.

Muhammad noticed Rachamim's glance. "Yes, you did the right thing by selling your property," he admitted for the first time. "I was stupid and used all my cash to buy real estate, which I'll have to leave here. If only I had listened to you." Tears began to trickle down his cheeks. "If I had listened to you, I would still have something. Now, I only have these three diamonds that I took as I left the store."

Muhammad showed him a small velvet bag containing three sparkling gems. "This is everything I own. If I don't survive, I am giving them to you as a present."

Rachamim didn't know what to say. He had known Muhammad for over forty years. They had grown up together on the same street, and later, they had moved into the same neighborhood and opened businesses across the street from each other. He had never heard Muhammad be pessimistic about anything. Now that their futures hung in the balance, Muhammad was finally admitting that his world had been built on quicksand.

They left the business district. The sound of gunfire and rioting lessened as they moved further from the center of town and the royal palace. Rachamim drove without speaking. Both men were contemplating their futures, which didn't seem promising.

Every once in a while, armed soldiers stopped them to check that they weren't Muslim fanatics attempting to enter the residential area reserved for the elite few who were friendly with the royal family. Rachamim suspected that it wouldn't be long before these soldiers paid dearly for their loyalty.

Rachamim stopped in front of Muhammad's home. Instead of leaving, Muhammad remained seated and looked Rachamim squarely in the eye. "What will you do now?" he asked.

"I don't know," Rachamim said helplessly. "I'll decide tomorrow. Maybe, if everything calms down, I'll go back to the store."

"Are you out of your mind?" Muhammad asked in disbelief. "If your store isn't destroyed tonight, it will be tomorrow night—or it will be confiscated by Khomeini! Didn't you hear what I said? The Shah is gone! Prime Minister Shapour Bakhtiar is trying to keep the government going, but it's just a matter of time before Khomeini takes over completely. How do you think you will fare under Islamic rule?"

"So what are you going to do?" Rachamim asked. "Will you try to escape?"

Muhammad's wife had passed away recently, and the two of them had had no children. It would be easy for him to run away—he had just never thought it would be necessary. For his part, Rachamim would have left long ago, but he was afraid to take his two small children on such a dangerous journey.

"Why haven't you escaped?" Muhammad countered.

Rachamim hesitated before answering. He knew how much pain Muhammad felt over his lonely, childless state. "It would be difficult for me to travel with my family," he said finally.

Muhammad remained quiet as he opened the car door and stepped out. He looked at his silent, empty house for a long moment before turning around to face Rachamim. "I don't know what will happen tomorrow. I don't know if we will ever meet again. I want you to know that I admire you. I hope you will survive somehow."

Muhammad slammed the door behind him. He did not look back as he walked up the path to his home.

Rachamim parked his car in front of his house and quickly walked inside. His wife Naomi was busy cooking supper. The moment she heard the front door open, she greeted him with a big smile.

Naomi had been worried about him. The telephone lines in the business district were down, so she had been unable to speak with him during the day. His two children, Yosef and Yechezkel, jumped gleefully into his arms, happy to see their father home so soon.

Rachamim hugged his children and quickly told his wife why he had come home early. Her smile faded as he described the Shah's abandonment of his country.

"I'm going to *daven maariv* now, and then I'll be right back," he concluded.

Naomi nodded. "Pray for us," she whispered.

Rachamim returned to his car and drove to the nearby synagogue. He wanted to pray one more *maariv* in the ancient synagogue where his ancestors had prayed for generations. Would Khomeini allow the synagogues to remain open? Would his children be able to attend their religious schools? What would happen to the vibrant Jewish community under Islamic rule?

The synagogue was packed. Those who planned to escape prayed for their journey to be successful; those who were to remain behind prayed that they would able to continue in the traditions of their forefathers.

Muhammad was panting from exertion as he cautiously approached the dark, neglected corner behind the Teheran flea market. Unable to find a taxi willing to take him even part of the way, he had raced through the side streets of Teheran for over half an hour. Though there was still the sound of errant gunfire from far off, the streets here were empty.

Muhammad carefully looked around. Such meetings were dangerous, even during better times. Now they were even more dangerous. Muhammad was shivering with fear as he ducked behind a large trash container.

A sudden noise made him whirl around. A figure was crawling out of the trash container. "It is I," a familiar voice reassured him.

Muhammad remained wary as the figure walked around the trash container to where he was standing. With his right hand, Muhammad fingered the automatic pistol kept securely hidden in his pocket.

Though he had worked with Abdullah for the past ten years, Muhammad had never been privileged to see his face. Abdullah always appeared dressed as a religious Muslim woman, with a heavy veil covering his face so only his eyes showed between the veil and hair covering. Abdullah was his main jewelry supplier, providing him with exclusive merchandise for his store. Clearly, the distrust went both ways: Abdullah did not trust Muhammad enough to reveal his face, or even his last name.

"Why are you so frightened?" Abdullah asked. Muhammad could see the man's eyes glaring at him from behind the filthy veil.

"I'm not frightened," Muhammad retorted defensively.

"Follow me!" Abdullah commanded. He turned around and started walking through the maze of alleyways behind the ancient marketplace, while Muhammad followed closely behind.

The two men entered a small alleyway, where an ancient Ford van was parked in the middle of the street. The street was so narrow that there was barely room for pedestrians to get through. Abdullah had to press himself against a wall to sidle past the truck, and he waited while Muhammad did likewise. Muhammad was heavier than Abdullah, so it took him twice as long to get past the truck. He also tore his expensive suit in the process.

Another van was parked further down the street. It was such an old model that Muhammad could not identify its make. The back was covered with a dark canvas tarpaulin. Abdullah went around to the back and climbed inside, waiting for Muhammad to follow suit.

"That van is protecting us," Abdullah explained, pointing to the old Ford van blocking the sidewalk. "If we have any unwelcome visitors, it will give us enough time to escape."

Abdullah pulled down the tarpaulin, cutting off the dim light provided by the lone street lamp. It was completely dark inside the van. Muhammad remained standing until Abdullah grabbed his hand and guided him to an uncomfortable seat on an upholstered chair that did not provide protection against the broken springs inside.

"What would you like to buy from me today?" Abdullah asked.

"I need your help," Muhammad admitted.

"Oh, I see. So you want me to smuggle merchandise in the opposite direction. Instead of smuggling merchandise into Iran, you would like me to smuggle you out of the country."

Muhammad tried to stop the surprised gasp that escaped his lips.

"Surprised that I guessed what you want? I receive at least ten such requests daily. You would be surprised to know that there are many people willing to give up everything they own to be able to escape Iran before the Shah is overthrown."

"Are you assisting everyone asking for your help?" Muhammad asked hesitantly.

"It depends," Abdullah said coldly.

"It depends on what?"

"It depends on the price," Abdullah responded calmly.

Muhammad was afraid to ask any more questions. He realized that if it depended on the price, it could not be a token sum. Everyone knew that Abdullah never put himself into danger for paltry sums. Throughout the years, he had only dealt in high profit merchandise.

"The Shah's airforce commander asked me to smuggle him out of the country," Abdullah added. It was clear that the price was not low.

"How much are you asking for?" Muhammad finally asked.

"One hundred thousand American dollars." Abdullah spoke as if it was nothing.

"One hundred thousand American dollars?" Muhammad repeated in disbelief.

Abdullah smiled. "Yes. You have heard correctly. Many people are willing to pay much more than that. I'm only asking for such a minimal amount from you because of our longstanding friendship."

Minimal amount! Muhammad could feel the blood rising to his head. "I'm going to have to think about it," he finally managed to say. His three diamonds were valued at about one hundred thousand dollars. He was planning to use that money to start a new life. If he paid it now, he would be left with absolutely nothing. Perhaps it would be better to live in wealth under Khomeini than to live in poverty in a different country.

Muhammad stood up, ready to leave.

"Don't move," Abdullah ordered.

Frightened, Muhammad stood perfectly still.

"You can obtain this service without paying a single cent," Abdullah continued coldly. "You still haven't heard all your options."

Muhammad felt a strong arm grab his shoulder and guide him back to his seat. In the thick darkness he couldn't see who had grabbed him—but he did know that it wasn't Abdullah, whose voice was coming from a different direction. Breathing heavily, Muhammad tried to control his sense of panic.

"What service can I provide instead of paying the money?" he asked, licking his dry lips.

"There are others I want to smuggle out of the country. Do you know anyone with small children who is interested in leaving Iran?"

"Small children?" Muhammad repeated.

"That's what I said," Abdullah said impatiently.

"But why—" Muhammad began in bewilderment.

"That's my business," Abdullah retorted briskly. "I don't like it when people ask me unnecessary questions."

Muhammad knew that well. During most of their business dealings, Abdullah had barely said a word. He always found a way to evade answering Muhammad's questions.

"There's my neighbor Rachamim and his family. I know he would leave if he could. But I don't think he has a hundred thousand dollars in this country. And besides … he's Jewish."

"Jewish?" Muhammad could detect a note of excitement in Abdullah's voice. "That's even better."

"But how can you take small children on such a hazardous journey? It could be extremely dangerous."

"Once again, you're worrying about my problems," Abdullah snapped. "The only thing I want you to do is convince him to join you in your escape."

"And then you'll take all of us for free?" Muhammad asked in disbelief.

"*When* he agrees to join you," Abdullah stressed, "then yes, I will take all of you for free. Go now, and convince him that all will be well on the journey out of the country. I'll come to your house in four hours. If you have succeeded in convincing him to join you, then we will go together to retrieve his family before setting out on our journey."

Muhammad could feel a light breeze as Abdullah opened the van door. He knew better than to ask any more questions. He jumped out of the van and followed Abdullah through the maze of alleyways back to where they had met. Then Abdullah suddenly disappeared down one of the narrow alleys.

Two

Afghanistan, 1979

As darkness fell upon the capital city of Kabul, five thousand Soviet soldiers crept up on the Tapa-e-Tajbeg palace, where Afghanistan president Hafizullah Amin had his seat of power. The soldiers, ostensibly sent by the Soviet Union to support Afghanistan in case of attack, were actually the first part of an invading force that was intended to bring Afghanistan completely under Soviet control.

President Hafizullah Amin had no reason to distrust the Soviets. The two countries were on friendly terms, and Amin relied on the Soviet Union for military, technological and economic aid. But what Amin didn't know was that the Soviets were displeased with his rule. Amin took help from the Soviet Union, but he wanted to lead the country himself. He refused to recognize that Soviet aid came with a price tag attached.

And now, on December 27, 1979, Amin would be paying the ultimate price.

An explosion destroyed Kabul's communication system, planted by Soviet infiltrators several days before. At the same time, President Amin and his guests suddenly came down with an apparent case of food poisoning. The real culprit: the Russian-born cook, who had been a gift to Amin from the Soviets. The man was actually a KGB agent, who had patiently bided his time until contacted by his masters. Now, as Kabul was rocked by explosions and the sound of gunfire, the President lay incapacitated, unable to lift a finger in his country's defense.

Armored vehicles began driving from Kabul International Airport to various locations on the outskirts of the city, where Afghan army divisions had been stationed. The heavy tanks, C-72s, were among the newest makes on the market. They made the earth shake as they moved ponderously through the streets of the capital.

That night, the Soviet tanks managed to occupy the military and strategic centers of Kabul: Pul-e-Charkhi, the Qargha Division, the Rishkhor Division, the police force of the Ministry of Interior, the television and radio station, and the presidential palace.

Afghan soldiers, tricked by their Russian advisers, had been told days before to turn in all live ammunition and substitute blank rounds for a training exercise. The Soviet advisers had prepared for the invasion in other ways, as well. Batteries had been removed from vehicles, ostensibly for repair; fuel had been siphoned off from tanks because of an apparent fuel shortage; and many officers had been told to go on vacation. As a result, the Soviets were met with almost no resistance.

By morning, Kabul was under Russian control. The victorious invaders installed their own puppet regime, whose leaders answered only to the Soviet rulers. With their hold on the capital city firmly in place, the Russians now turned their attention to the rest of the country.

Thousands of Soviet troops poured into Afghanistan. Armored tanks accompanied infantry divisions and quickly overran the cities of Kandahar and Jalalabad. With city after city falling to the invading armies, the Soviets were confident that the country would soon be completely under their control. The vast countryside remained unconquered, but the Soviets anticipated little resistance from the primitive inhabitants of the wilds of Afghanistan.

They were wrong.

The fervently religious Afghans were fiercely opposed to the atheistic invaders. It did not take long for the Mujahadin, the Afghani rebel movement, to fight back. The rebels joined forces in the Pakistani city of Peshawar, just thirty miles from the Afghan border.

"We cannot give up," said a tall, well-built young soldier. His clothing was elegant and tailored, in marked contrast to the rough, homemade uniforms of the other men. "With Allah's help, we will get rid of the Russians."

"Who are you?" Muhammad Omar interrupted. Muhammad, the leader of the rebelling Pathan tribal clan, stared belligerently at the strange soldier, who clearly was not a native of Afghanistan.

The young man proudly rose to his full height. "My name is Osama bin Laden."

Omar did not yield an inch. The two men stood examining each other for several minutes, waiting to see who would be the first to look away.

Omar finally spoke again. "You did not answer my question. Your name is meaningless to me. What brings you to us? What has given you the right to speak to those who have suffered the invasion of their country?"

At that, another man hidden in the shadows came slowly to his feet. Omar's eyes widened with recognition, and he bowed his head in respect.

"You know who I am, Omar," the third man said in a resonant tone.

"Yes, Abdullah Azzam," Omar said, his voice reverent.

Azzam turned to face the rest of the rebel leaders, who had been silently watching the confrontation. "I bid you to welcome my student, Osama bin Laden, who has given up a life of luxury and wealth to help the cause of Afghanistan and Islam. Please, hear what he has to say."

Murmurs from the surprised leaders died away as bin Laden began to speak. "My wealthy parents live in Saudi Arabia. I had everything I could possibly want in my parents' home. I gave up all the pleasures of this world to come here and help you in your struggle."

His sincere words made a deep impression on the listeners. Omar softened. He was beginning to like this stranger's arrogance.

"Why Afghanistan?" he questioned the young man.

"Here in Afghanistan it will be possible to build an Islamic country. My heart tells me that the Soviet invasion is a decree from Allah. Allah wants the youth of Afghanistan to train for war! He sent us the Russians to use as targets so we can hone our fighting abilities."

"Interesting," Omar said thoughtfully. "And after the Russians are defeated?"

"Once this war is over, our soldiers will be the best trained forces in the entire world," bin Laden exclaimed. "No nation will be able to stand up to them. Our brave men will bring the light of Islam to the entire world!"

Omar liked the young man's strong stance. As a member of the most radical party in the Afghanistan Islamic movement, he appreciated bin Laden's way of thinking. Not only did bin Laden bring a strong vision—he also brought wealth. And that meant training and arms for his men. Omar sensed that with this young man's support, he would be able to obtain the necessary means to force the Russians out of country, and ultimately bring Afghanistan under Islamic control.

"How will you be able to assist us?" Omar asked.

"I can supply you with money and connections," bin Laden said confidently. "You will have access to highly advanced American weapons. I have the right contacts. Through my family's connections in Saudi Arabia, I am able to negotiate with the Americans."

Hedad! Hedad!" The men rejoiced at these words. Without proper weapons, their chance of victory against the heavily armed Russian forces was almost non-existent. Osama bin Laden had given them hope for true victory.

Omar nodded slowly. "Very well," he said, lowering his voice for bin Laden's ears alone. "Let us meet, you and I. There is much to do."

Omar could see that while most of the men were pleased with this turn of events, several leaders of the opposition party were unhappy with bin Laden's overconfident promises. They sat together at one end of the cave, whispering among themselves. Omar would have to move quickly to cement their unified front and bring the recalcitrant leaders to accept bin Laden's involvement. Only by working together would they be able to succeed.

After the meeting had ended, bin Laden accompanied his revered teacher, Abdullah Azzam, back to the tiny room where he had made his home in Peshawar. He listened intently as Azzam eloquently spoke of global jihad and the importance of training Muslim militants who were fully dedicated to their cause. The struggle in Afghanistan, he assured his rapt listener, was the first step on the path to fulfilling their ultimate goal of restoring the Islamic Caliphate to its former glory, and removing all Muslim lands from foreign dominion.

The charismatic Azzam had lectured in several universities, but it was through his tapes that he extended his reach deep into the Muslim world. Osama bin Laden had heard Azzam speaking via his tapes, which circulated among the students at King Abdul Aziz University. Those fiery speeches had made a deep impression upon the wealthy youth, and he had pledged to dedicate his life to achieving Azzam's goals: an absolute return to the values of Islam, which would protect the Muslim world from the dangers and decadence of the West.

The Islamic Revolution in Iran had electrified bin Laden to the possibility that an Islamic government could succeed in returning the rule of Islam to the Muslim world. Working with Azzam, though from a distance, bin Laden began to help him gather his forces, bringing together true believers where they could be trained to effectively fight against the Western enemy.

"Find people in Iran who are committed to Khomeini, to true Islamic rule," Azzam urged him. Through his many business contacts, bin Laden was able to accurately identify those who were most dedicated to their cause. They were delighted to be given the opportunity to join Azzam's fledgling organization.

Along the way, however, bin Laden was dismayed to discover many Muslims who had lost their belief in the golden future of Islam. His astonishment at their eagerness to leave Iran, rather than celebrate Khomeini's return, soon gave way to steely determination. When these Muslim traitors turned to their contacts in the Iranian underworld—many of them, as it turned out, Azzam's underlings—to help them escape from Iran, bin Laden conceived of a diabolic plan.

He would help to pave the way for the Islamic revolution, by recruiting true, dedicated believers to Azzam's cause. He would help the parents escape ... but he would keep the children.

Children as young as six years old were smuggled out of Iran and into Azzam's training camps in Pakistan. Azzam knew how to indoctrinate these youngsters with his beliefs. The children became the most dedicated, passionate fighters, eager to lay their lives on the line for the glory of Islam.

Bin Laden's work in Iran came to an end when the Soviets invaded Afghanistan. He knew he had to be in the center of it. Afghanistan, according to Azzam, presented a golden opportunity. It was here in Peshawar that the rebels gathered, and it was here that bin Laden met personally with his role model.

As the weeks passed, the two men forged a close relationship. Azzam provided the vision and fiery commitment that caused men to pledge their lives to their cause, while bin Laden, with his money and connections, developed a streamlined, organized fighting force that could effectively strike at the invaders. Together the two secured the confidence of Muhammad Omar, who supported them in their leading role in the struggle against Russian control.

Three

Teheran, Iran, 1979

Yechezkel watched his mother sitting on her armchair, listening worriedly to a special radio announcement. His little brother, four-year-old Yosef, was already sleeping, but Yechezkel couldn't bear remaining with him in the lonely dark room. He joined his mother in their luxurious living room, hoping she could somehow assuage his anxiety.

Recently he had started feeling threatened. He could sense the tension in the streets and at home. He did not understand why everyone around him was constantly worried and uneasy. He had heard that Khomeini was planning to come to Iran and of the danger that it posed to the Shah. But what did that have to do with him? His eight-year-old brain could not comprehend the connection between his parents' nervousness and current events.

Although he was very young, he still realized that his parents were not telling him the full extent of the danger. They simply asked that that both he and his younger brother recite *Tehillim* often, and beg Hashem to guard His nation.

Yechezkel heard the radio announce that Ayatollah Khomeini's plane had just landed at Teheran International Airport. In the background, they could hear the jubilant cries of the masses as they greeted their leader from his French exile.

Naomi's anxiety grew. Yechezkel noticed that his mother was extremely pale, which served to intensify his own fear. He stood up and took a seat next to his mother, on the chair's armrest. She tried to reassure him by gently stroking his hair, but he could feel the trembling in her hands.

Naomi twisted the dial, searching for more positive news. "Air France Flight 039 from Paris to Teheran landed this morning at Teheran International Airport," the announcer reported. "The plane carrying Ayatollah Khomeini was joyfully greeted by thousands of admirers jubilantly waving Iranian flags." Yechezkel noticed a tear slide down his mother's cheek.

Sounds of gunfire could be heard in the background. The state-controlled radio station, loyal to the Shah, was being defended by the Shah's loyal soldiers. Incredibly, the announcer ignored the sounds of violence and simply moved on to the weather forecast.

Naomi turned off the radio, too nervous to keep listening. The house fell into an uneasy silence.

"Where's Abba now?" Yechezkel whispered.

"I don't know." Naomi jumped up in a sudden panic. "Why hasn't he come home yet?" She pushed Yechezkel aside to reach the telephone. Her fingers shook, making it difficult to dial the synagogue's number.

The telephone rang ten times before she hung up. Naomi bit her lip, then tried again. But again there was no answer. She let the phone drop back into its cradle, unable to hide her growing anxiety.

The doorbell rang twice. Naomi's eyes brightened at the sound. Rachamim always rang the bell twice before entering the house. She could hear the key turning in the lock, signaling that her husband was home.

Reassured now, Naomi stood stroking Yechezkel's hair, waiting for her husband to join her in the living room.

He appeared in the doorway. "Good evening, Naomi," he said in a low voice.

"Good evening," she replied quietly. She walked over to the large dining room and started setting the table.

Rachamim took off his jacket and hung it on the mahogany coat rack before entering the dining room.

After serving him a plate of food, she sat down opposite him. "Why aren't you eating?" he asked, when he saw that she had not prepared anything for herself.

"I'm not hungry. I just had a cup of coffee and piece of cake," Naomi said evasively. That had been in the morning, but she didn't feel like eating.

Rachamim did not pressure her. He took a few bites of the chicken and then pushed his plate away. "The food's delicious," he admitted, "but with the present situation, I've also lost my appetite."

Rachamim stood up to turn on the radio. The announcer's voice was trembling. Rachamim recognized the voice of Prime Minister Shapour Bakhtiar. "All citizens should remain calm. Business will be proceeding as usual in Teheran. I will continue guiding the present regime in governing the country," he promised.

Bakhtiar added, "Since Iran is a Muslim country, the government will take Muslim law and the Koran into account."

"A wasted effort," Rachamim muttered. "Bakhtiar is a moderate Muslim, and the radicals won't listen to him. The Shah thought that by appointing a Muslim to run this country, he would be able to appease the masses. Now that Shah is gone, this idiot is trying to remain in control of the government. He should disappear before it's too late."

Naomi did not respond at first. There was a look of terror in her eyes. "And what's going to be with us?" she asked, her voice desperate.

"What will be with us?" Rachamim repeated her question. "What will be with all the Jews?"

"So what should we do?" she asked. "Should we pick ourselves up and try to escape?"

"We should have tried that a week ago. Now it is impossible. The airport is surrounded by the fervent masses, thousands of fanatics who are drunk with victory. They would never let us through."

"Is there any other means of escape?" Naomi asked. "What were people saying at *maariv*?"

"Some plan to leave, others are staying here," Rachamim returned. "Either choice is risky. The escape route is extremely dangerous." Rachamim glanced at Yechezkel, who was sleepily curled up in his mother's vacated armchair. "I can't imagine bringing children along on such a journey. As far as staying here goes ... we just don't know what Khomeini will do. All we can do is pray, and hope."

Rachamim fell silent. The two of them remained seated in the dining room for the next hour, contemplating their seemingly hopeless situation. They knew there was nothing they could do. Even getting up from the dining room table did not seem worth the effort.

At ten-thirty that evening, a light knocking came at their front door. Naomi, who had nodded off into a light doze, woke up with a start. Rachamim stared, frozen, in the direction of the door.

"What is it?" Naomi asked.

The knocking continued. Rachamim stood up and walked hesitantly toward the door. Naomi stood stiffly from her chair and hurried after him.

"Be careful!" she hissed, as Rachamim stood on tiptoe to look through the peek hole in the door.

"It's Muhammad," Rachamim said, surprised. "I wonder what he's doing here?" When they had said goodbye that afternoon, Rachamim had been certain that Muhammad was planning to escape that evening.

"Are you sure that you're doing the right thing?" Naomi asked, as Rachamim started turning the key in the lock. "Isn't it dangerous to open the door at this hour?"

"Muhammad would never do anything to harm me," Rachamim reassured her. Still, his hands were shaking as he pulled the door open.

Muhammad entered the house quickly, slamming the door behind him. It was clear that he was deathly afraid. "I will be running away tonight," Muhammad whispered.

"I thought you might," Rachamim said. "But how? The airport is in the rebels' hands. Did you find another way to get over the border?"

"I was not planning to take a plane out of here," Muhammad murmured into his thick mustache. "I found someone willing to guide me over the border in exchange for one of my diamonds. He's going to smuggle me into Turkey."

"When are you leaving?" Rachamim asked. He was puzzled by Muhammad's visit.

"Soon." Muhammed took a deep breath. "Would you like to join us?"

Rachamim stared at him in disbelief.

"Yes, I am willing to include you in my plans," Muhammad repeated.

"But—my children! How could they survive such a dangerous journey?"

"The guide knows about your children. He is not concerned. Apparently he has done it before."

Rachamim stared at him with open suspicion. There was something strange about Muhammad's behavior. Why was he making this offer, which would only endanger his own escape?

Muhammad added, "Obviously, you'll have to cover the price of the diamond that I'm paying the smuggler."

The cat has been let out of the bag, Rachamim thought. Now he understood Muhammad's seemingly generous offer.

"The smuggler asked for a certain price," Muhammad explained. "The price is for guiding us over the border. He emphasized that it made no difference to him how many people would be going. It's all the same price. So, are you interested in joining me?"

"Perhaps," Rachamim said slowly. "How much are you asking for the stone?"

"Twenty thousand Iranian rials." The answer came in a monotone.

"What? It can't possibly be worth so much. Are you trying to make a profit off of me?"

Muhammad said coldly, "Your family consists of four people. I don't think that's too much money for helping such a large family escape in such difficult times."

"That's the smuggler's concern, not yours," Rachamim pointed out. His eyes narrowed in suspicion. Muhammad's behavior was becoming exceptionally odd. Neither did it make sense for a smuggler to agree to a single price, no matter how many people were in his group. Something strange was going on.

Muhammad shrugged. "It seems that the price is too high for you," he muttered, as though to himself. "I'll find another family willing to pay an even higher price to escape."

"It's not just the money," Rachamim said patiently. "I could have left weeks ago, if I had wanted to. I still feel the journey is too dangerous for my children. And your concern is solely for your money. You haven't said anything to convince me that my family would survive this journey."

Muhammad, opening the front door, didn't reply. A cold wind blew in through the doorway. "May you be in peace, and may Allah guard over you wherever you may be," he concluded.

"The same to you," Rachamim said mechanically.

He watched Muhammad step outside, and automatically began closing the door after him.

"Wait!" Naomi called.

She rushed to the doorway. Muhammad stopped short, turning back to look at them inquiringly.

"Did you tell them how old our children are?" she asked breathlessly. "Are they sure they can take us all safely?"

Muhammad hesitated, clearly fumbling for a reply.

"I can see that you did not," Rachamim said sharply. "I'm sorry, but I'm just not willing to take the risk. You haven't convinced me that it is worthwhile."

"But, Rachamim," Naomi said imploringly, "I'm afraid to stay here. What will happen to us?"

Rachamim didn't know what to say. Naomi had a point. This might be their last chance to escape.

Perhaps he should go alone and bring his family out once he found a safe haven? Although that seemed like the sensible thing to do, he knew that the possibility of being smuggled over the border might not come again. He had to grab the chance now, while they still had the opportunity. Once the fanatics gained control of the country, the borders would be hermetically sealed and it would be impossible to leave—ever.

By now, Muhammad had stepped back into the house, closing the door behind him. "This is not a discussion that should take place in the open," he muttered, his nervousness clearly apparent.

Rachamim stared at his friend. "I know you too well, Muhammad. You're hiding something. What is it?"

Muhammad squirmed slightly. "You're right about the price," he finally admitted. "I was trying to foist it all on you. Tell you what, we'll split it evenly. But please join me in my escape. I can't possibly pay it all on my own!"

All at once, Rachamim was convinced. "All right," he said abruptly. "We'll come with you."

Muhammad gave a relieved smile. "You're doing the right thing. Trust me."

Rachamim did not share his sense of relief. He was about to say farewell to his place of birth, to leave the graves of his ancestors, without knowing if he would ever come back to see them again. He would have liked to visit the cemetery one last time to see his parents' graves. But that was impossible.

"I'll be back in another two hours," Muhammad announced, as he walked out the door for the second time. "Pack a few essentials, some food and your valuables. Nothing heavy. Remember, much of the way will be on horseback, riding up and down the steep mountains dividing Iran from Turkey."

Muhammad was already standing outside when he suddenly remembered something. "Don't forget to take warm clothes. It's cold in the mountains." He quietly closed the door behind him.

"Okay, that's it." Rachamim took a deep breath. "We're leaving Iran tonight."

Although it had been her decision too, now that she was faced with the reality of leaving her home, Naomi started to cry. "I've invested so much of my life here," she sobbed.

He gave her a pained look. "So have I," he sighed. "And what about all the time and energy I put into the business?"

Leaving Iran would be difficult for both of them. Only through mutual support would they be able to overcome this trial. "I'll miss the synagogue here," he went on. "I'll miss the Rav's daily shiur. And what will be with the graves of our ancestors? I will never be able to come back here to visit them."

Watching Naomi's face, Rachamim realized that every word was like a knife stabbing into her heart. But he knew that she had to face reality.

"We must remember that this is Hashem's decree, and that's the way it must be." He took a deep breath, feeling a lightening of their heavy burden. "Remember, Hashem is righteous, and all His deeds are righteous."

Four

Afghanistan, 1979

The Soviet rulers in the Kremlin ignored the international protests that erupted after their brutal takeover of Afghanistan. They knew the United States was distracted by their own problems. It was an election year, and President Jimmy Carter was hard-pressed to defend himself against his Republican challenger, Ronald Reagan. The people of the United States were particularly upset about the hostages being held in the American Embassy in Teheran, who had been captured nearly a year before. So while the United States was concerned by the apparent growth of Communism and Soviet control, there was little they could actually do—aside from public protests, which the Russians simply ignored.

The well-oiled communist propaganda machine swung into action. The television showed pictures of Afghanistan citizens praising the Russian action. They described the difficulties they had faced before, and how the Soviets had managed to organize the country and make things run smoothly. The propaganda even succeeded in swaying several Western political analysts, who accepted the Soviet argument that Afghanistan's citizens were tired of the chaos resulting from each individual commander doing as he saw fit. The people of Afghanistan wanted a central government that would act responsibly, and the Soviets were promising to deliver it.

The truth hit the Soviets a few weeks later when the streets of Kabul turned into death traps for the invading Russian soldiers. The rebels attacked from all sides. The situation was even worse in the mountainous regions. The tribes residing there took every opportunity to assault the Russian forces. While the Mujahadin suffered enormous casualties in their struggles with the well-armed Russians, they made up for it with their brutality and passion for their cause. The Red Army's morale plunged.

In the mountainous regions, the rebels took advantage of the thousands of natural caves and curved mountain paths. The topography gave them a definite advantage over the Russians. The caves provided natural shelter to the rebels, who were familiar with every twist and turn, while for the Russians, these caves were death traps.

The quarreling tribes united under the banner of the Mujahadin, who had announced a jihad, a holy war, against the invading Soviet forces. Any male between the ages of twelve and sixty was recruited into the rebel army.

Osama bin Laden remained at the forefront of the struggle, ensuring that money and arms continued to flow to the Mujahadin forces. While many soldiers continued to fall in battle, the tide inexorably began to turn. Soon the rebel fighters began to hope that the situation really would change, and the Russians would be forced out of Afghanistan.

But then the Russians played their ace card: they began employing combat helicopters, using one of their most advanced weapons to fight the primitive tribes. The Mil Mi-24, popularly known as Hind helicopters, were equipped with machine guns and missiles. A helicopter would suddenly appear on the horizon, spraying the Mujahadin fighters with heavy fire, and then disappear quickly before the surviving Mujahadin fighters could retaliate.

To the soldiers operating the helicopters, it made no difference if there were innocent bystanders or small children among the fighters. On more than one occasion, the helicopters had massacred groups of children because they assumed that some Mujahadin fighters were hiding in their midst.

This brutal tactic achieved its goal. Several population groups refused to allow the Mujahadin to enter their region. They rightfully suspected that association with the Mujahadin would result in attacks by the Russian helicopters.

Over the next few years, the Mujahadin were forced to decrease their operations. Morale dropped significantly, and once again the tide turned—this time, in favor of the Soviet invaders.

Toward the end of the summer of 1986, the rebel leaders gathered in the Tora Bora Mountains to work out a plan of action to renew the fighting and raise their morale. The weak candlelight inside the cave emphasized the sadness reflected in their eyes. The helicopters had destroyed the rebellion. The number of deserters grew from day to day.

The Pathan Mujahadin leader, Muhammad Omar, painted a dispiriting picture. "The morale among our men is at an all time low. They feel, and rightly so, that the Mujahadin has no means to protect them from the highly advanced Soviet helicopters, which seem to appear from nowhere. We must find a way to get rid of these helicopters."

A tall young man stood up. No longer a youth, he had been seasoned by the battles of the past six years. Osama bin Laden had fully participated in the fighting, and he was now a full-fledged warrior for the Afghan cause.

"I can overcome them," he announced.

Everyone stared at him. There was suspicion and even some hatred in those eyes. Back at the beginning, he had promised to provide the rebels with advanced American weapons. The rebel leaders grudgingly admitted that he had indeed come through on his promise. If it weren't for those weapons, they would have been wiped off the map long ago.

Still, all of bin Laden's wealth and contacts had been powerless against the Soviet helicopters. Many of the leaders illogically blamed him for their recent losses. While Omar still supported bin Laden, others had become less enamored of the wealthy Saudi leader.

"How can you overcome them?" one man demanded.

Bin Laden answered in a calm voice. "The Americans have developed a missile, called the Stinger, to be used against these helicopters. They claim that these missiles are extremely effective against low flying aircraft."

"Thank you very much for your excellent lesson," Omar said impatiently. "We know all about the Stinger." Everyone had heard about the Stinger, a tube-like missile small enough to be carried by the soldiers and designed to be incredibly accurate. But the missiles, the latest in American technology, were not among the weaponry being offered to the Mujahadin fighters in Afghanistan. As much as he relied on bin Laden, Omar was skeptical that the young man could bring the Stingers to the rebels.

Bin Laden's face glowed in the dim candlelight. "I am able to obtain those missiles."

Everyone stared at him in amazement.

"Liar!" someone yelled from the depths of the cavern. *Liiii...aaaaar* came the echo from the opposite end of the cavern.

The guilty party was a young leader from the south, nicknamed "the Lion" for his fierce independence. His eyes seemed to be on fire as he pointed a threatening finger at bin Laden.

Omar refused to get involved in the argument between the two youths. He waited for bin Laden to repute the charge made by the young leader.

Bin Laden stared straight into the Lion's eyes. "Who's the liar?" he asked.

The Lion stood his ground. "You!" he retorted. "You're providing us with worthless illusions. Tell the truth! Are you working for us or for the enemy?"

In response, bin Laden removed a large package wrapped in brown paper from between the folds of his wide cloak. Since he was so tall and his cloak so wide, he had managed to keep the package hidden, despite the fact that it was over a meter long.

Very carefully he started removing the brown wrapping paper, enjoying the curious stares of his colleagues. The last layer was lined with tiny plastic bubbles, designed to protect the contents of the package. He finally held what appeared to be a tube—a missile that was compact enough to be carried over the shoulder.

"Here is the famous Stinger," he announced.

Murmurs grew around the cave as people jostled closer, eager for a look at the American missile. Just then, a sound penetrated into the cave—the roar of a Soviet helicopter patrolling the area.

"Now is the time to prove the missile's efficiency," bin Laden exclaimed. "Follow me!"

Bin Laden quickly made his way to the cave's opening. The leaders followed him, though they were careful to remain out of sight.

They could hear the roar of whirling propellers as the helicopter approached the cave. In just another moment, they would be able to see the aircraft flying over the opposite hill. The pilot would illuminate the area with high-powered lights, and then he would notice them standing there.

Bin Laden placed the missile on his shoulder and stood fearlessly in the cave's opening. The helicopter appeared over the horizon, and strong lights swept the ground ahead of the aircraft. Still bin Laden waited patiently for the perfect moment, when the infrared missile would be able to accurately seek its target.

The rebel leaders inched back further into the cave as the helicopter drew closer. They watched bin Laden poised and waiting, listening intently to the warbling sound of the seeker on the missile. Just as the helicopter's lights pinpointed the cave's opening, bin Laden finally pulled the trigger.

The missile shot out of its holder, leaving a trail of sparks and burning a few hairs of bin Laden's beard. The infrared seeker headed straight to the Hind's turboshaft engines. The rebel leaders watched, mesmerized, as the missile impacted the helicopter—and exploded.

The deafening sound sent them fleeing into the cave, as debris rained down outside. Bin Laden retreated just far enough to avoid the flying debris, but he stayed near the entrance where he could watch the burning, mutilated helicopter spinning helplessly through the sky as it nosedived toward the earth.

The rebel leaders cautiously approached the entrance of the cave, in time to see the helicopter impact in a huge ball of fire. A burst of stones and dirt flew up where the fireball hit the ground.

"That's all that remains of the Russian helicopter," bin Laden announced in satisfaction.

That was the last opposition to bin Laden's leadership.

Five

Teheran, Iran, 1979

The faint tapping came at Muhammad's door less than an hour later. Abdullah stood there, right on time for their second rendezvous.

"Well?" Abdullah demanded.

"I was successful," Muhammad stated, feeling a tinge of pride. "My friend and his family are willing to join us."

Abdullah's eyes gleamed in triumph. "Wonderful. You have done well."

"So, are we ready to leave?" Muhammad asked hopefully.

"We will be leaving within the next hour," Abdullah replied. "I will need your help along the way, though, to keep your companion calm and reassure him during the trip. Oh, and I will need your help with one more thing …"

Muhammad paled as Abdullah described the part he was required to play. His hands were shaking as he took a package from the disguised smuggler.

"Don't be so worried," Abdullah said in a mocking tone. "If the plan succeeds, you will be privileged to receive something that would make many army generals jealous. You will have escaped from Iran without paying a cent."

Muhammad nodded mutely. He was wondering what in the world he had gotten himself into. He just hoped that he, at least, would come out of this alive.

It was nearly midnight when the passionate voice of Ayatollah Khomeini was heard over the radio.

"*Salaam Aleikhem*," began the charismatic religious leader, in his first speech on Iranian soil. Khomeini thanked everyone who had gone out into the streets to protest against the "Shah's corrupt government." He described the Shah and his followers as heretical sinners. This speech was a sign to the masses that the government was now in Khomeini's hands.

"The radio station is now in Khomeini's hands," Rachamim told his wife and children.

He allowed himself only a moment to listen to Khomeini's words. There was very little time left. Muhammad was expected back in half an hour, and they needed to finish packing their belongings.

Rachamim and Naomi went through their possessions, choosing and discarding them one by one. It was especially difficult for them to decide what to do with those items that had sentimental value. Should they leave them behind, lost to them forever, or should they take them instead of other, more essential items? The decisions had to be made quickly. In the end, they decided to take nothing of sentimental value except for two wedding pictures.

At twenty minutes past midnight Rachamim stopped packing. Naomi glanced at her watch. "We have another ten minutes before Muhammad and our guide arrives. I want to take a few more items."

"Whatever we haven't packed, we'll just have to leave here," Rachamim responded. "I want a few minutes of quiet to speak with the children before we say farewell to our home."

Eight-year-old Yechezkel and four-year-old Yosef understood the importance of this moment. The two boys sat fearfully at their father's knee.

"We are about to leave this house forever," Rachamim told them. "We are about to depart on a dangerous journey, and we have no idea what the future holds in store for us. I do not know how we will manage on this trip. We must trust our heavenly Father to guide us to safety." He realized that these were harsh words for children so young, but he hoped they would recall them and perhaps gain the courage to survive the hardships that they would have to endure.

Rachamim took a deep breath and forced himself to continue. What he was about to say would take every ounce of his emotional strength. "However … if it is Hashem's will that we do not manage to make it to the place that we are traveling to, and if, G-d forbid, it is decreed that we are separated during this journey …"

"*Nooo!*" Naomi, listening in horror to her husband's words, let out a bloodcurdling scream. "Do you really think I might become separated from my children? In that case, let's stay here!"

"If we remain here, they will definitely take our children away from us," Rachamim pointed out. "They are trying to make the country into a fundamental Islamic state, and they know that as long as the children are being raised in our home, they will never be able to make them into good Muslims."

Naomi gulped for air, but she remained silent.

"If, G-d forbid, it is decreed that we become separated," Rachamim repeated to his sons, "I want you to always remember that you are Jews. It's possible that you will be sent to a non-Jewish home. From this day on, you should always leave a small amount of food on your plates, so if you are forced to eat non-kosher food, you will remember that the food is not kosher. Every time you leave food over, you'll recall that I had asked you to do that so you won't forget that you are Jewish."

Rachamim stopped speaking and looked straight into his children's eyes, to see if they understood his request. The tears coursing down their cheeks were a clear indication that they realized the importance of his words. They had grown up overnight.

Rachamim straightened up. "One more thing." He removed a twenty-rial bill from his pocket. Placing the money on the table, he wrote a word on each side of the bill. Then he folded the bill and tore it down the middle, and handed each of his children half the bill.

Each of the boys looked at their half bill with a mixture of curiosity and fear. They noticed that their father had written the Hebrew word "*Echad*, one," on each side of the bill. There was also a number across the bottom of the bill, which was torn in half.

"Each of you must keep the part of the bill that I handed you." Rachamim's face was fiery with emotion. "If the day ever comes when we are separated, or if one of you is separated from his brother, guard the bill carefully. The word *Echad* written on each of the sides will remind you that you belong to a nation that believes in One G-d and that you are Jews. The fact that the bill was torn in half will push each of you to look for the other half, to search for his brother.

"On the bottom of the bill is a number torn through the middle. That is the number of my secret bank account in Switzerland. Over the last few years, I've transferred most of our wealth to that account. You need the entire number to open the account. If, G-d forbid, you are separated, make sure to keep this information secret. Don't tell a soul about it. After Hashem will reunite you, and you bring the two sides of the bill together, you will be able to use the money in that account. Divide it equally, and take advantage of it to rebuild your lives as Jews."

Rachamim paused. He had a deep, gut feeling that his words would come true. He sensed that despite every precaution they might take, the children would eventually be taken away from him.

Rachamim gazed at the two youngsters. They were curled up together in the corner. Yechezkel was trying to reassure his younger brother, who was crying hysterically.

Rachamim was proud of his older son's sudden show of maturity. "*Ribono shel Olam*," he murmured, "if it is decreed that we be separated, at least keep my two sons together." Yechezkel, he was certain, would make sure his younger brother did not break the golden chain of his religion.

There was a sound from outside, and then someone knocked lightly on the window facing the backyard. Rachamim went over to the window and cautiously moved the curtain to the side. It was impossible to see a thing. Very carefully, he opened the window and stuck his head out.

"Look over here," he heard someone whisper. He turned his head toward the source of the voice. In the inky blackness, he could make out a dark figure hidden among the decorative shrubs.

"Are you ready?" the voice whispered.

Rachamim could not identify the speaker. "Muhammad?" he asked, pitching his voice low.

The figure moved forward, out of the shadow cast by the foliage and closer to the source of light. Rachamim immediately recognized Muhammad.

"Are you ready?" Muhammad asked again.

"Yes."

"In just a few minutes, a truck will stop in front of your house. Its back doors will be closed, but not locked. It will remain in front of the house for four minutes, and not a moment longer," Muhammad emphasized. "In those few minutes, you and your family are to jump into the back of the truck."

Muhammad did not wait for Rachamim's reaction. He slithered back into the bushes and disappeared.

Rachamim closed the window and returned to the hall. He was surprised to see that Naomi was still busy packing. She had taken advantage of the few moments he was speaking with Muhammad to stuff another suitcase with their belongings. Rachamim briskly tried to stop her.

"Enough! We are about to leave. We can't carry anymore."

Naomi stood up to face him. Her face was covered with sweat and tears.

"It's a waste of time to pack so much," he continued gently. "We can't carry so many things."

"And what about that picture?" Naomi pointed to an enormous painting hanging in the living room. It was a portrait made of the two of them on their wedding day. She was dressed in a beautiful wedding gown that sparkled from many jewels sewn in the skirt. He was wearing a dark suit. The expressions on their faces reflected the joy in their hearts.

They had been so happy then. The life ahead of them appeared promising and rosy. He came from a relatively well-to-do family that had made its money by importing French shoes to Iran. She was the only child of a wealthy businessman, and her father was one of the leaders of the Jewish community in Teheran. Her parents owned an exclusive clothing store in the center of the city, which had been in their family for generations. All the wealthy residents of Teheran bought their clothes in her family's store. Her father had connections with the royal family, and he used those connections for the benefit of the Jewish community. Her parents wanted only the best for their daughter, and when Naomi married Rachamim, her father promised to help him open up a similar business.

Rachamim forced his mind to return to the present. "You know we can't take the picture with us," he told her. She could hear the pain in his voice. "It's much too big. How will we be able to carry it?"

She knew he was right. With the tears still coursing down her cheeks, she turned around and slowly left the room, silently carrying the burden of pain.

Rachamim followed her into the other room. "It's time to leave," he whispered. "Muhammad will be here in just a few minutes."

She did not move. She was staring at the large chandelier hanging from the ceiling. It was a present from her late mother. She had given it to them on the day they had moved into this house.

Rachamim couldn't allow himself to be overwhelmed with nostalgia. He had to remain connected to reality. The children were frightened, and he sat down on the floor next to them and hugged them tightly. He would have liked to offer them reassurance, but there was no time for that. He stood up and pulled the two children close to his heart. "We must leave the house now," he told them quietly.

Without waiting any longer, he picked up the two heavy suitcases and began walking to the front door. His family trailed after him. Before leaving, he stopped for a moment, placed his right hand on the *mezuzah* and recited a short prayer. His two children and Naomi followed suit, begging Hashem to guard them from all evil.

Instinctively, Rachamim locked the door behind him, though he knew it was pointless. After all, he would never be coming back to this house. What difference would it make if someone broke in?

"I ask all citizens to return to their normal lives. The government will continue running normally under my leadership." Shapour Bakhtiar's voice was heard booming over the radio in the ancient truck.

Rachamim woke up from a light doze when the driver turned on the radio. Bakhtiar's speech did not interest him. The idiot was standing on the edge of a cliff, and even the tiniest wind would send him toppling.

The truck stopped in front of a neglected looking gas station, the only one on the road. The driver jumped out of the truck and exchanged a few words with the attendant, who had run out to assist him. The attendant spoke with the driver as he filled the gas tank. When he finished, the driver handed him a few bills and jumped back into the front seat. He turned on the ignition. The truck gave a few heavy groans and started moving again.

Rachamim peered out the grimy windows in the back of the truck. He could see the first rays of dawn. They had managed to travel quite a distance, and the terrain had changed completely. Instead of cities, there were endless sand dunes and emptiness as far as the eye could see. They had left the mountains surrounding Teheran and now there were just monotonous stretches of sand.

They had traveled for several hours without being stopped for a security check, which gave Rachamim a sense of confidence. The driver seemed to know how to avoid the main roads where the army had set up checkpoints.

Perhaps, he thought, the political situation might actually be for their benefit. The country was in such a state of chaos that the army was completely disorganized. The soldiers had no idea what they were supposed to do, and preferred to remain secure in their army camps. Knowing the Iranian mentality, Rachamim assumed that the commanders had decided to wait until the situation stabilized, so they would know which was the winning side. Their chance of stealing into Turkey seemed plausible.

Rachamim curled back up into the heavy quilt that Naomi had brought from their home, hoping to get some more rest. The children snuggled closer to him.

This was very different from his usual mode of travel. Every time the truck passed over a bump, it rocked wildly from side to side, rudely waking the children. But they were so exhausted that they immediately fell back to sleep—until the next bump. He appreciated that they did not complain. Despite their youth, they understood that their father had no control over the situation.

Daylight filtered in through the grimy windows, and the passengers began to awaken. As the morning wore on, the scenery changed again.

Now they were back in the mountains. The truck slowly climbed the curving mountain passages and then raced down the steep hills.

Rachamim stood up, poured some water into a cup and washed his hands. He washed his children's hands, and started praying together with them. Muhammad must have been envious, because he also started prostrating himself in prayer.

They traveled up and down the steep mountain passages. The temperatures dropped as they gained altitude. They snuggled close together to protect themselves from the fierce cold.

Toward evening, they turned into a rundown parking lot with an ancient sign in Persian and Turkish prominently displayed above the gate, advertising a dilapidated restaurant. Another rundown truck and two outdated cars were also parked there. The driver parked his truck directly in front of the main entrance. It was freezing cold outside, but the restaurant's door was open wide.

Rachamim peeked through the window. The restaurant was filthy and illuminated by a few gasoline lanterns hanging from the ceiling. The customers were seated on wobbly stools that looked as if they would break momentarily.

The driver went around to the back of the truck and told the passengers that he had stopped to eat. "I'll be here for a while," he explained. "It's been a long time since I've tasted my childhood favorites." Apparently he had grown up in this region. "It would be a pity not to take advantage of this opportunity."

Rachamim decided to pray *mincha*. While he and Yechezkel prayed, Naomi recited *Tehillim*. They finished, but the driver had not yet returned. Rachamim glanced at his watch. They had been there for over half an hour. He turned around to ask Muhammad if he knew why the driver was taking so long.

Rachamim was surprised to see Muhammad on his knees, praying like a strictly observant Muslim. Rachamim knew Muhammad well, and this was definitely not his usual behavior. Several times he had seen Muhammad partake of alcoholic beverages, although it was forbidden by the Koran. Rachamim knew that he smoked American cigarettes, and Muhammad often laughed derisively at Muslim law. Praying did not fit into his normal pattern of behavior.

Muhammad was extremely serious after finishing his prayers. He looked around until he noticed Rachamim staring at him. "Where's the driver?" he asked.

"He hasn't returned," Rachamim replied. "He's still eating."

Muhammad wondered aloud if he should go into the restaurant to call him. He looked out the window.

There were three men sitting inside the dark restaurant. The gasoline lanterns hanging from the ceiling had gone out, and the customers were crowded around a single candle. Muhammad and Rachamim were unable to identify the people sitting inside. "I'll go down to see if our driver is also sitting there," Muhammad announced.

Muhammad jumped out of the truck before Rachamim had a chance to stop him. He went over to the left-hand window, the one closest to the table where the three men were eating, and peeked inside. The driver was sitting with a group of men who were dressed as Kurds. He could not hear them talking. He noticed that they were bent over a map.

"He found some friends," Muhammad explained upon his return. "He's speaking with them." He refrained from telling Rachamim that the group was obviously in the midst of planning something.

"If you already endangered us by leaving the truck, shouldn't you have told him that it is getting late and that we had better get going?" Rachamim asked with obvious impatience.

"No," Muhammad stated. "We're in a region populated mostly by Kurds."

Muhammad did not have to say any more. Every Iranian knew the history of the Kurds. They were a pursued nation that had never obtained independence. For hundreds of years the Kurds, under the rule of Iran, Iraq or Turkey, had fought for independence. All these attempts had been brutally subdued, sometimes at great cost to human life. The Iranians had also spilled much blood in repressing the Kurds. No Iranian would dare show his face in this region.

"Are you trying to tell me that we are now in Kurdistan?" Rachamim asked fearfully.

"Yes, but why are you so frightened? You're a Jew. They'll see that immediately and they won't harm you. After all, you are also a member of a pursued nation," Muhammad added bitingly.

Rachamim remained silent as Muhammad peered out the window. The driver was arguing with the waiter about his bill. It looked as though they had come to an agreement. The driver stood up and went around the table before warmly hugging the men he had dined with. From the way they took leave of each other, Muhammad could tell that they were close friends.

The driver jumped into the truck and started the motor without even bothering to make sure that the passengers were in the back. For the next twenty minutes they drove along a paved road before turning off onto a dirt path. The driver raced down the dirt road while the truck rocked violently back and forth. After that, the truck groaned noisily as it climbed a mountain, leaving behind a cloud of dust. Rachamim could only imagine what would happen if it started raining and the dirt turned into mud.

Once again, they drove the entire night. Before dawn, the driver stopped the truck on a mountaintop and walked around to the back of the truck. He opened the back door and, speaking Persian, said, "You can get out and stretch a bit. I have to catch a few hours of sleep."

Muhammad was the first to accept this offer. Jumping out, he stretched his arms and breathed in the fresh mountain air. He appreciatively studied the scene that spread out below them. They were atop a huge mountain, and the green expanse below them was dotted with colorful Kurdish tents. The greenery was a result of the hard work and diligence of the peasants living here, who took advantage of every sliver of land for either grazing their sheep or agriculture. Muhammad could see the young shepherds guarding their herds of wooly sheep. The peaks surrounding them were so high, they appeared to be kissing the heavens.

Rachamim, Naomi and the two children also left the back of the truck. They, too, were amazed at the magnificent beauty surrounding them. Shaking his head in wonder, Rachamim murmured, "How wondrous are your ways, Hashem."

"Isn't it beautiful?" the driver asked. He was smiling at their astonishment. He was used to the view, but each time he smuggled people across the border, he enjoyed watching their amazement.

"I grew up in this region," the driver added, "and most of my childhood was spent in these mountains. We would drink in the sparkling clear air. And in the evenings..." He closed his eyes in nostalgia. "In the evening, we would gather together, all of us shepherds, under one of the apple trees and sing softly deep into the night. Those nights were so wonderful that today I still miss them."

He suddenly stopped himself. "I'm sorry to have burdened you with my memories. You're from the city, and of course you've never experienced such things, so you'd never be able to comprehend what I'm talking about."

"Not at all," Rachamim said sincerely. He enjoyed listening to the driver's words. This was the first time he had ever heard firsthand about such a different lifestyle.

"We're going to have to wait here until it gets dark," the driver said, abruptly changing the topic. "It would be too dangerous to cross the border in daylight. We got here faster than I thought we would, and as I told you before, I'm going to take advantage of this break and catch up on my sleep."

"Where's the Turkish border?" Muhammad asked.

The driver turned up his nose. "The Turkish border is very far from here."

"What do you mean?" Muhammad demanded. "Aren't you supposed to be taking us to Turkey?"

"Well, yes," the driver conceded. "What you call the Turkish border is actually quite close. That is not the real Turkish border. The Turks had the audacity to make their border within the region that rightfully belongs to the Kurds."

"I'm sorry," Muhammad muttered in embarrassment. "I wasn't planning on making a political statement. That problem has nothing to do with me."

"You don't have to apologize," the driver sighed. "You're not the first to make such a mistake. I realize that it's not your fault. The Turks and Iranians have had control over our land for so long that the world has almost completely forgotten that this land belongs to us."

There was a tense silence after the guide finished speaking. Both Rachamim and Muhammad had no idea what to say. Naomi and the two boys were standing inside the truck, looking down at the three men.

"We'll have to stay here for the next ten hours," the guide continued, ignoring their little disagreement. "You can spend the time relaxing, or maybe you want to prepare some food for breakfast. We're very close to what you call the Turkish border, and we'll cross over as soon as it gets dark.

"It will take us a few hours to cross." The guide looked at the boys in the truck, and he frowned slightly. "This is as far as the truck can go. I'll be bringing horses for the trip over the mountains. I just hope your children can make it." His voice was tinged with doubt.

Six

The Stinger changed the tide of the battle in Afghanistan, and in the end, determined the outcome. The Russians furiously complained to the Americans that they were assisting the rebels. The Americans blandly explained that a small supply of Stinger missiles had been stolen, and had somehow found their way to the rebel forces. The angry Soviets knew this was a complete fabrication, but they were helpless to stop it.

The supply of Stinger missiles continued to flow steadily to the Mujahadin fighters—thanks to the efforts of Osama bin Laden, their acclaimed leader.

It was midnight in Kuwait City. An American undercover agent, known only by his code name, Fire Dragon, entered the Black Swan, an illegal club that sold alcoholic beverages against Islamic law. He nodded in greeting to his associate, a tall Muslim with a full black beard whose head was covered by a large traditional turban.

"We require more missiles," bin Laden told the CIA agent.

"I have already given you over a hundred," Fire Dragon pointed out.

"And they have been used for their intended purpose," bin Laden returned. "We used each of those missiles to down Russian helicopters. We finished our supply two months ago. For a while the Russians were hesitant to send their helicopters unprotected against our ground forces, fearing that we had more missiles. But when they saw that we had not downed a single helicopter in the last two months, they started attacking us again."

Fire Dragon nodded. He had been closely following the war in Afghanistan, and he knew bin Laden was speaking the truth.

"How are the missiles working out?" he asked.

"Wonderful!" bin Laden replied enthusiastically. "Most of the missiles hit their mark. We have downed nearly one hundred Russian helicopters. The pilots are afraid of us now, leaving the area open for our guerilla forces to strike their troops." Bin Laden's face was glowing with enthusiasm as he continued. "People are growing encouraged. Once again we have new recruits joining our fight to free Afghanistan."

Fire Dragon calmly removed an elegant pipe from his suit pocket and filled it with expensive Cuban tobacco. He continued looking through his pockets until he found a gold-plated lighter and carefully lit his pipe. Another transgression against Islamic law.

Bin Laden moved away slightly, trying to hide his discomfort and anger. Alcoholic beverages and smoking were being freely enjoyed inside a religious Muslim country. Someday, he vowed to himself, Kuwait would enforce Islamic law. Instead of decadent Western leadership, in its place would be leaders loyal to the laws of Islam.

"Why should I give you these missiles?" Fire Dragon asked. "How will the United States benefit?"

Bin Laden didn't hide his annoyance from the American. "You may recall, you were the ones who contacted me first," he said coldly. "I know the United States wishes to stop the Soviet invasion and Communist threat." His eyes narrowed. "Do not make me beg for favors. We are doing your work for you. We are the ones bleeding and dying. All we ask for is the weaponry that will enable our success."

Fire Dragon nodded. Bin Laden was right, of course, but it didn't hurt to stress the favor that the Afghans owed the United States.

"Jeff Redstone," bin Laden said suddenly.

The color drained from Fire Dragon's face. Bin Laden had just stated his real name, and that was considered highly classified information. There had been a serious security leak. He knew he had to leave Kuwait immediately.

Bin Laden ignored Redstone's reaction. "I can assure you that the missiles will benefit the Americans no less than it will benefit the rebels."

Redstone had a hard time focusing on bin Laden's words. How had the rebel leader discovered his real name? Bin Laden enjoyed watching the American agent's discomfort. He knew the man was trapped.

"Don't worry," bin Laden reassured him, accurately guessing his train of thought. "I am not planning to harm you. We are brothers in arms. As long as you supply us with the material, I will make sure that you are safe."

Redstone nodded mutely. The message was clear. He was safe—as long as he kept supplying bin Laden with the missiles.

"Okay, the deal's closed," the CIA agent muttered. "We'll meet in Paris in two weeks, and I'll give you the details then."

"Leaving Kuwait so soon?" bin Laden asked, with a malicious smile.

Bin Laden watched in satisfaction as the American flushed angrily, then turned and walked hastily toward the door. He remained seated, ordering a glass of fresh orange juice. "With Allah's help," he whispered, "one day I shall succeed in fulfilling my life's dream, for which I was sent to this world." His eyes shone with a strange, otherworldly glow.

The next time the two met it was in a nightclub in Paris. Located in a Parisian slum known for its high crime rate, the place served as the perfect location for shady business dealings and confidential meetings.

Jeff Redstone hesitated for a moment before entering the dim hall. His eyes searched through the thick screen of cigarette smoke, but it was impossible to make out anything more than a few feet away. With a sigh, he made his way toward the bar in the center of the room. He hoped bin Laden wouldn't keep him waiting long.

"I see that you arrived at the right place," he heard a familiar voice speaking behind him. Redstone turned around at the sound of bin Laden's voice. But while the man standing behind him was tall, he was also clean-shaven.

"Don't you recognize me?" the stranger asked.

Redstone was shocked. "You shaved your beard?" he gasped.

Bin Laden shook his head. "Let's go outside for some fresh air."

Redstone gladly accepted, pleased to get free of the stuffy air in the club. "Why did you shave your beard?" he asked again. "You don't believe in the Koran anymore?"

"Not at all. Come, I'll show you." Bin Laden opened the back door of a green Mercedes waiting at the curb and sat down. Redstone saw that there was a chauffeur sitting in the front seat.

The car sped away the moment Redstone closed the door behind him. Bin Laden took out a pair of scissors and started cutting away the mask that was covering his face. It was so closely fitted that it had fooled even Redstone.

"This wouldn't fool you during the day," bin Laden explained, as he pulled away the mask, "but in the dark, and especially in that smoky club, this mask fits tightly enough to hide my beard."

"So," bin Laden sat back in his seat, "did you manage to get the goods that I requested?"

"Yes," Redstone replied softly. "I managed to get them, but it wasn't easy. My superiors forced me to sweat before I was able to convince them that you are right."

"Good things never come easily," bin Laden noted coolly.

"The CIA is willing to provide you with a large shipment of missiles," Redstone responded carefully, trying to avoid letting his irritation show. "But they will expect to see results before they send additional cargo. They asked me to make it very clear to you that you should not expect an open check."

"Don't worry about results. The CIA is invited to come and watch the Russians bleed to death. Just imagine," he continued, pointing a finger at Jeff, "what a hero you'll be when the Russians are forced to flee Afghanistan."

He's right, Redstone realized. *These missiles will make the difference and I'll be looked upon as a hero.* But it's also possible, Redstone knew, that someday his good friend Osama bin Laden might turn around and use those weapons against the United States.

"The missiles are now on board a ship making its way to Karachi, the capital of Pakistan," Redstone said. "The ship's called *Sea Lion*. It's a Liberian ship and should be arriving in Karachi the day after tomorrow. There are seven crates of missiles on board. It's up to you to arrange for trucks to take the cargo from the port. The Pakistani customs officers who will be on duty when the ship arrives have been well bribed. They won't ask any questions."

"Wonderful," bin Laden said enthusiastically. "My drivers will be waiting for *Sea Lion* to arrive."

Bin Laden picked up an expensive black leather briefcase from the car's floor and handed it to Redstone. "Here's a million dollars for you. This money is yours, for your own private use. It's not part of the official payment. To pay for the goods, we'll transfer the money to your government through the special Swiss bank account that was opened specifically for this purpose, as we agreed upon previously."

Taken aback, Redstone was about to say something, but bin Laden pressed the button to lower the partition separating them from the driver. "Take us to our first stop," he told the driver.

Redstone sat silently, wrestling with his conscience as the driver maneuvered his way through the streets of Paris. The car stopped on one of the main thoroughfares next to Champs Elysee. "I would imagine that you are familiar with this area of town," bin Laden said.

The driver got out of the car and politely opened the door for him. Redstone got out quickly, intent on getting to a safe place—far away from bin Laden—as quickly as possible. But, bin Laden noted, he took the briefcase with him.

Americans will sell their souls for money, bin Laden noted with distaste. He would use that knowledge well in his fight to achieve his ultimate goal.

Bin Laden managed to arrive in Karachi before the ship reached port. From the meeting with Jeff Redstone he drove straight to Charles De Gaulle airport and boarded a Pakistan Airlines flight to Karachi that was departing that same night.

In Karachi, he immediately arranged for seven drivers and several dozen armed escorts to take the goods from the harbor. For such a sensitive job, he would only trust members of his organization who were native Arabs.

As usual, bin Laden was extremely well organized. By the time *Sea Lion* anchored in Karachi, seven semi-trailers were waiting just outside the port. Bin Laden and several dozen experienced soldiers from his organization remained concealed in the shadow of one of the many warehouses scattered throughout the area, observing the goings-on in the harbor. Bin Laden did not rely on the fact that the customs officers had been bribed. If something were to go wrong, he was ready to use force to gain control of the shipment.

The customs officer on duty took out his radio and called the head truck driver to notify him of the ship's arrival. The line of trucks drove directly to the harbor's back entrance, which someone had made sure to leave open—supposedly by mistake. They entered the harbor and pulled up in front of *Sea Lion*.

An ancient crane was waiting next to the ship. The sailors on deck quickly tied the first crate to the crane, which lifted it off the ship and placed it directly on the first semi-trailer. The driver hurriedly secured the crate to the back of his truck and jumped into the driver's seat, then drove away to make room for the next truck in line. This action was repeated seven times.

The trucks left the harbor together. Once they were out of the harbor, however, they separated and took seven different roads. An armed car escorted each of the trucks as it made its way toward the mountainous desert bordering Afghanistan.

All the crates arrived safely. Inside hidden mountain caves and ravines, the goods were divided into smaller containers and loaded onto camels.

The following night, concealed by darkness and pelting rain, the missiles were smuggled through the Tora Bora Mountains across the border and into Afghanistan. The Soviet soldiers, hiding in their shelters to stay warm, never noticed a thing.

The first round of missiles downed seven Soviet helicopters. The pilots, certain that the rebels had used up their missile supply, were reckless. It was a major blow for the Russians.

Over the next 28 months, Stingers shot down hundreds of Soviet Hind helicopter gunships and MiG fighter jets. Without helicopters to provide coverage for the Soviet ground forces, the rebels were able to annihilate entire units of Russian soldiers.

By the end of that year, the Russians announced that they would be pulling out of Afghanistan, bringing over a decade of Afghanistan oppression to an end. On February 15, 1989, the Soviets retreated back to the Soviet Union.

Just as bin Laden had promised Redstone, this defeat eventually brought about the destruction of Moscow's totalitarian dictatorship. Soviet communism, which had existed for seventy years, entered its death throes on the day the Russian army left Afghanistan.

Afghanistan, however, never recovered from the Soviet oppression. The tribes that had joined together to battle a common enemy began fighting among themselves for control of the government.

Eventually the warring groups formed into two opposing factions. The first group, the Northern Alliance, originally had the upper hand, but in 1996 they lost control to the second group. The second group, led by Muhammad Omar, the Pathan leader, immediately instituted Islamic law throughout Afghanistan.

The new rulers of Afghanistan were called the Taliban.

Seven

All of Rachamim's worries returned full-force as he stared at his innocent young children. "Haven't you taken children before?" he asked the driver fearfully.

"Yes," the driver said doubtfully, "but they weren't that young …"

"Don't worry," Muhammad interrupted him.

Both men turned to stare at him.

"It will be fine," Muhammad insisted. "You will see."

"Are you such an expert?" the driver asked, annoyed. "Exactly how many times have you done this before?"

Muhammad flushed in embarrassment. His eyes flashed, but he somehow managed to bite back the angry words that were undoubtedly at the tip of his tongue.

The driver turned away, and Muhammad, muttering to himself, stomped off to the side of the road, where he stood staring down into the valley.

The driver ignored him. "I'm going to have to leave you for a while," he said to Rachamim. "I need to get some sleep, and I have to contact the person who will be bringing us the horses."

"You're going to leave us alone here?" Rachamim demanded. The driver seemed friendly enough, but there was no reason for Rachamim to trust him. What if he abandoned them atop this lonely mountain?

"There's nothing to be afraid of," the guide reassured him. "No one is going to come here. No one even dreams that you are here. Obviously, you're only safe if you remain on this mountaintop and don't try to leave."

"Are you taking the truck with you?" Rachamim asked. He was happy that his wife had gone back into the truck and hoped that she would remain there until the driver returned, so she would never realize that he had gone.

"No," he replied. "I'll be leaving the truck here with you. I'll take a footpath down to the first tent, and then my brothers will assist me in getting what I need."

The man turned around and began racing down the footpath. Within a few seconds, he disappeared from their view.

The hours passed slowly. Muhammad spent the time taking walks along the cliffs, while Rachamim and his family recited *Tehillim*. Towards evening, Rachamim and his family finished reciting the entire *Tehillim* for the second time. He began preparing to pray *mincha*.

"I hope our guide wasn't caught," Muhammad said.

"He might be resting somewhere," replied Rachamim, trying to sound optimistic. "After all, he had been driving for over twenty-four hours without a break."

The sun was about to set over the mountaintops. Rachamim apologized that he had to cut the conversation short, before it was too late for him to pray *mincha*.

As the sun sank below the horizon, Muhammad took a radio out of his pocket. "This is a short wave radio," he explained to Rachamim. He turned the instrument on, but they were only able to hear static.

"The surrounding mountains must be getting in the way of any transmissions," Muhammad commented. He looked around, although it was difficult to see anything in the dusky darkness. "I think I'll climb to the top of this mountain. Maybe there I'll be able to hear something."

"Don't do that," Rachamim argued. He was frightened. "You're not familiar with the region. You might fall off one of the cliffs. Also, the driver warned us to stay put."

"I'm also worried about our driver. Why isn't he back already? He should have come back ages ago. We must find out what's going on, and it's preferable to do that as soon as possible, while there's still some daylight," Muhammad retorted. "If we don't take action immediately, we might end up stuck here the entire night, and tomorrow discover that we have walked into a trap."

Rachamim reluctantly admitted that Muhammad was right. It did not seem reasonable to continue sitting there, doing nothing. He was also worried by the driver's disappearance. Then again, how would listening to the radio help Muhammad discover the guide's whereabouts?

Muhammad was just trying to make himself feel better, Rachamim realized. But he couldn't blame him.

Muhammad started climbing the mountain. "I won't go far," he called back. "I'll stay in sight."

When Muhammad was about fifty meters away, he stopped. Rachamim watched him turn on the radio. He also noticed something strange. He realized that Muhammad was speaking into the radio.

So, it wasn't a radio! It was a transmitter! Muhammad was contacting someone.

A wave of panic threatened to engulf him. Rachamim had been suspicious of Muhammad from the start, but he had allowed his greater fear of Khomeini's regime to lull his other doubts. Now, though, it was clear that he had made a big mistake in entrusting his fate to Muhammad. Would his innocent family pay the ultimate price for his error?

"Where's your friend?" he heard someone calling from behind. He turned around and saw the driver standing just a few feet away.

"He's contacting someone!" Rachamim blurted out.

"Who? What are you talking about?" The driver looked puzzled—and more than a little alarmed.

Rachamim swung toward Muhammad, who was now climbing back down. Unaware that Rachamim had seen anything, Muhammad greeted the driver with a show of relief.

"Where were you all day?" Muhammad asked.

Instead of responding, the driver stared at him with open suspicion. When he finally decided to speak, it was in a very quiet voice. "We had to wait for darkness to be able to continue. My friends are bringing the horses now."

"I understand," Muhammad stuttered, taken aback by the driver's open hostility.

"Now it's my turn to ask you something," the driver continued. "What were you doing up there on the cliff?"

"I just wanted to hear the news report. I tried to do that here, but I was only able to hear static. You can ask him about that." He pointed to Rachamim.

The driver did not reply. He just continued staring at Muhammad. Muhammad clearly felt uncomfortable. "The high peaks around here were interfering with the reception, so I wasn't able to hear the news report," he tried to justify himself. "I had to climb higher up in order to be able to hear something."

"Really." The driver looked skeptical. "Maybe I can have a look at your radio."

"Take it, please." Muhammad removed a radio from his back pocket and handed it to the driver.

Rachamim saw that this wasn't the same radio Muhammad had used before. The other radio was larger and had a metal frame, while this one was compact and made of plastic.

"That's not the radio you used!" Rachamim exclaimed.

The driver stiffened. "What do you mean?"

One look at Muhammad's guilty face was proof that Rachamim was right.

"What did you do?" the driver demanded.

There was a clatter of hooves as several Kurds crested the mountain, leading small, wiry horses. Muhammad jumped back as the driver took a step closer to him.

"We won't need those horses," Muhammad shouted. "I have a better way to get us across the border, a way that will not endanger the lives of the children."

The driver took another menacing step.

"Don't move," Muhammad yelled. Rachamim stared in shock as his friend flourished a pistol that he had pulled from his pocket.

The driver stopped. "What do you want?" he said, his voice shaky. The Kurds coming up behind him stopped short, clearly puzzled at the situation.

"Wait a few minutes and you'll see," came the harsh reply.

They heard a noise in the distance. The men turned around to look for the source of the noise, but it was hidden by the darkness.

The noise grew louder. It sounded as though something was kicking the air. Within a few seconds, a dark form appeared above them, concealing the moonlight.

"A helicopter," the driver muttered in fear.

"Yes, it's a helicopter," Muhammad said, confirming the driver's words. "It doesn't belong to who you think it does. It's not connected to the rebel forces."

The driver stared at him. "How do you know the helicopter's identity?"

"Because I asked it to come," Muhammad declared. "Did you think that I was about to rely just on you?"

The helicopter descended until it hovered just above the ground. Four figures jumped out and surrounded them, pointing machine guns in their direction.

"Raise your hands above your heads," the leader of the group barked in Persian.

Once their hands were raised, the leader gestured one of his men to check that they were unarmed.

The helicopter landed about eighty feet away, on a small patch of flat land. Its landing lights illuminated the area, and they were able to see another figure standing next to the helicopter. He must have jumped out to direct the pilot in this dangerous landing.

The guerilla checking for weapons ignored the helicopter and continued examining them. All he found was an automatic pistol in the driver's pocket. The fighter spent a few minutes admiring the pistol before placing it in his belt. "This is mine," he announced to his friends-in-arms.

"They're clean," the fighter declared as he finished. The other three guerillas tightened their ring around them.

"Come on, let's *go!*" the leader screamed to the group, while the guerillas gestured menacingly with their weapons, forcing them to walk toward the waiting helicopter.

Naomi and the two children were roughly pushed out of the truck by one of the guerillas. Rachamim's heart nearly burst at the sight of his family. Yechezkel was holding little Yosef's hands. He was behaving so courageously despite his youth.

As they reached him, Yosef started to sob. Rachamim gently stroked his hair. "Don't worry, my little angel," he said softly. "You'll see. In the end, everything will work out for the best."

The children hung back, frightened by the whirling propeller blades, but Naomi urged them on. Every step was dogged by the menacing guerillas.

They were forced into their seats as the helicopter started gaining altitude. Rachamim watched the ground drop away beneath them. The whirling rotor made it too noisy to talk without shouting, so he contented himself with smiling reassuringly at his children, who gradually calmed down.

Three fighters remained near the small group, while the other two retreated behind Rachamim's seat, toward the rear of the helicopter. It was cramped inside, and Rachamim shifted uncomfortably on the metal seat.

"What's that?" he heard one of the fighters say in Persian.

Rachamim tried to see what the man was looking at, but there were no windows in the rear of the helicopter. The man was peering out in front, next to the pilot.

"Americans!" he heard the man say. "Quick, take cover!"

The children screamed as the helicopter dropped in a steep dive. Naomi clutched the sides of her seat, her eyes wide in horror. The bottom seemed to be dropping out of their world. The standing guerillas had fallen off-balance as the helicopter had dived, and several were still picking themselves up off the floor.

"What is it?" he heard Muhammad shout.

"Americans," the nearest guerilla said tersely. "Shooting at us. Hold on, we're moving again."

This time the floor slanted the other direction, as the helicopter climbed upward. The floor vibrated and the seats shook with the pilot's frantic maneuvers.

"Watch out!" a voice shouted behind him.

Rachamim braced himself, but the danger came from an unexpected direction. Something crashed into the back of his head. Stars momentarily filled his eyes. He tried to shake his head to clear his vision, but the pain brought a rolling blackness in its wake.

Rachamim realized that he was going to pass out. The pain kept intensifying, and he could barely hold onto consciousness. Somehow, Rachamim managed to pull his scattered thoughts together. He had to get one last message to his children.

"Yechezkel," he managed to scream in Hebrew, so his captors would not understand. "Yechezkel, take care of your younger brother, Yosef, and remember what I told you before we left home."

And then the world went dark.

Eight

Yechezkel gradually became aware that he was trembling from cold. He opened his eyes to what appeared to be a cave, though he quickly realized that it was actually a cellar. The ceiling was raw stone, and only a tiny lamp illuminated the cavernous room. He fingered the heavy blanket covering him. It was filthy, and barely offered him protection against the freezing weather.

What had happened to the helicopter?

Yechezkel thought back. He had been fighting to keep his balance on the vibrating helicopter when he had heard his father shout. Turning his head, he watched in terror as his father's head dropped to the side. His eyes turned to his mother, just in time to see her also slump in her seat.

He had tried to pull himself erect—but he never made it. The last thing he could remember was a terrible pain in the back of his head.

"I see you're awake," a voice said in Persian.

Yechezkel turned toward the sound. A man with a long black beard was standing about ten feet away from him, his fiery eyes protruding from his bony face. He was dressed in a filthy robe that Yechezkel realized had once been white.

"You must be hungry," the man continued, speaking gently despite his cruel appearance.

Yechezkel realized that his stomach was rumbling from hunger, but his biggest concern was his thirst. His mouth was so dry that it was impossible to swallow.

"I'm sure you'd prefer to drink something before eating," the man added.

"Water, please," Yechezkel requested in a hoarse voice.

The man removed a dirty canteen from his belt and held it out.

Yechezkel hesitantly raised his arms to take the canteen. At home, he would never drink from someone else's cup without washing it out first. Now he was about to take a drink from a filthy canteen that had been used by a total stranger.

His thirst overcame his disgust. He slowly opened the canteen and brought it up to his lips. He took one swallow of the refreshing water and then quickly drank the entire contents before returning it empty to the stranger.

"Would you like some more?" the man asked when he realized the canteen was empty.

"Yes, please," Yechezkel answered weakly. He was still thirsty. He had no idea how long he had been sleeping.

The man left him alone for a few minutes and returned with a full canteen. It was dripping wet. He must have taken the water from another, larger container. He handed the canteen to Yechezkel. This time, Yechezkel returned it half full.

The man did not pressure Yechezkel to eat. He remained sitting quietly opposite him.

Yechezkel closed his eyes and tried to clear his head. He had so many questions. But would the stranger be able to answer them?

"Where are my parents and younger brother?" he finally asked.

The stranger stared at him in puzzlement. "I don't know."

"What do you mean, you don't know?" Yechezkel was beginning to panic. "How did I get here?"

"I found you outside my hut," the man explained. "I decided to adopt you as my son."

"I don't need to be adopted!" The young boy sat up in anger and fear. "I have parents who love me, and I love them. I have a family. I also have a younger brother, and I am responsible for him if something happens to my parents."

The man lowered his gaze and spoke in a pain-filled voice. "I don't think you have parents anymore, or a younger brother."

Yechezkel jumped up and made a fist. He did not think about how ludicrous it appeared—an eight-year-old boy threatening a grown man. He was too angry, upset, and scared to think things through.

The man did not respond. He continued sitting opposite him, staring at the floor, making no move to protect himself.

Yechezkel faltered.

"I am sorry that I have to tell you this," the man finally said quietly. "But I think it's important that you should know the truth."

"What truth?" Yechezkel asked, fighting back the tears that suddenly welled up in his eyes.

"I think that … you should realize that …" The man was having trouble getting the words out. "The truth is that I'm almost certain that your family was killed. You are the only one who survived the helicopter crash."

"A crash?" Yechezkel whispered. He tried to think. Was it the crash that had caused him to black out? He couldn't remember a crash. What had happened?

"Where was the crash?" he asked.

"It crashed here in this valley, not far from my home. I think the Americans shot it down."

Yes, that sounded right. Yechezkel could remember someone shouting about Americans shooting at the helicopter. "Why were the Americans here? Where am I?"

"You're on the border that lies between Iran and Afghanistan," said the man.

Yechezkel tried to visualize where he was, but he had never really liked geography, and his knowledge of Afghanistan was foggy at best. The only thing he could remember was that it is a mountainous country, primitive, and divided among numerous tribes.

"You're on the Afghanistan side of the border," the man continued.

Yechezkel's parents had been trying to escape Iran, so Iran must be an evil country. But they had been trying to reach Turkey, not Afghanistan. "I still don't understand. Why would Americans want to shoot down the helicopter?"

"The Americans were doing some type of a military exercise, and the helicopter got stuck in the middle. The Americans didn't want anyone to realize what happened."

The Americans. He recalled his father's disappointment in them. "They threw the Shah to the dogs," he had often said. His father had often commented how the Americans appeared to be friendly with the Shah, but never actually did anything to help him when the rebellion started. "They just stand there," his father would fume, "without even lifting a finger to help all the innocent people who are suffering as a result of the rebellion."

The youngster seized on that thought, eager to place the blame for the sudden destruction of the life he had known. The Americans were the cause of all his problems! All at once, he was consumed with a hatred for America and its people. They had destroyed his family. Because of them, his family had had to flee. Because of them, the helicopter was shot down and his loved ones were murdered.

His eyes welled with tears of pain and anger. "I will revenge my family's death," he mumbled to himself. "Those people who took away my father, my mother, and my younger brother will pay a heavy price for their evil deeds."

Yechezkel did not notice the pleased smile that flickered on the man's lips. He had just taken the first step in planting the seeds of hatred against America in the young boy's mind.

The indoctrination had begun.

"Stand at attention!" called the camp commander.

The recruits rushed out of the cave that served as their training center in the Tora Bora Mountains, lining up in two straight rows. They waited as their commander strode between them and came to a halt.

"In another few minutes, we will have the honor of hosting our beloved head commander," he proudly announced. "The Sheikh himself, Osama bin Laden, has just informed us that he will soon be arriving here to see for himself how we have prepared for jihad."

The group of excited young cadets started clapping their hands. The name Osama bin Laden electrified them. From the time that they were small children, they had been taught that Osama bin Laden was the personal messenger of their prophet, and that his words were divine.

Bin Laden understood the soldiers. He knew how to plant an intense hatred for America deep in their hearts. Each of these young men had suffered difficult lives, and they placed the blame squarely on America. They believed that the Americans were trying to control the world, and that the United States government had no qualms about destroying countries, families, nations—and their childhood.

A division of soldiers proudly riding horses suddenly appeared from one of the surrounding ravines. They were dressed in white cloaks and were fully armed. They quickly surrounded the group of cadets and pointed their M-16 rifles at them. Bin Laden's personal bodyguards were the only members of al Qaeda permitted to carry American rifles. The other soldiers had to manage with outdated Russian M-47s.

The division commander dismounted from his horse and walked between the two rows of cadets. "Throw your weapons to the ground," he ordered.

The cadets were quick to obey. The ground thundered as the weapons came crashing to the earth. The commander ordered two of his soldiers to walk among the cadets, checking to be sure that no one had disobeyed. When he was sure that all the cadets were unarmed, he took out a short wave radio and reported that the area was clean.

Bin Laden appeared from a different ravine in the mountain, riding a white Arabian horse. He was surrounded by a smaller group of armed bodyguards, also riding white Arabian horses. All the bodyguards had long unkempt beards. Bin Laden only allowed devout Muslims to join his personal circle of bodyguards.

Many of the cadets had never actually seen bin Laden before. But they had all seen pictures of him and recognized him immediately. They jumped to attention, awestruck by the erect figure of their idol sitting before them.

Without saying a word, bin Laden got off his horse and started walking slowly between the rows of cadets, carefully examining the faces of each and every one.

"What's your name?" he asked, stopping in front of one of the cadets.

The cadet was so excited that he could barely speak. "Ishmael," he murmured.

"Come with me," bin Laden instructed, speaking gently.

Bin Laden turned and started walking toward the cave, while the cadet followed closely behind. Bin Laden's personal bodyguards trailed after them, but stopped short of entering the cave. Once inside, the cadet was surprised to find himself alone with bin Laden.

"I don't want anyone in the world to know what we're going to speak about," bin Laden commented. "Now, Ishmael, tell me something about yourself. I have an important task that needs to be fulfilled, and I wish to ensure that you are the right one to do it."

The youth swallowed hard, and nodded. "I was born in Iran, before the revolution," he began. He lowered his voice. "I was born a ... a Jew."

The cadet dropped his eyes in shame. He knew how bin Laden felt toward the Jewish people and Israel. He would have preferred to leave out this horrible detail of his distant past, but he did not dare be anything other than fully truthful. Somehow, he was sure, bin Laden would recognize that he had hidden part of his background.

Bin Laden remained silent, and Ishmael finally looked up. He was surprised to see that bin Laden looked kind and gentle, despite this revelation about Ishmael's background. He felt reassured and was able to go on.

"I don't remember much about my childhood. I only recall that my father's name was Rachamim, and my mother, Naomi."

"Do you remember your Jewish name?" bin Laden softly asked.

"Yes. My Jewish name was Yechezkel, and I had a younger brother named Yosef. Everyone in my family was killed when we tried to escape Iran. Our helicopter crashed. The evil Americans shot it down for no reason," he hissed.

Bin Laden clearly appreciated this outburst of hatred. "Tell me about your escape," he pressed him. "How do you know the Americans downed the helicopter?"

"I remember, when we were flying in the helicopter, the pilot started shouting. He said the Americans were shooting at us. He tried to avoid them, but they must have managed to shoot us down."

Ishmael paused and took a deep breath. He was re-experiencing the pain. "A few days after the crash, the man who rescued me brought me to the spot where the helicopter had been shot down. There was nothing there. We could see signs of the fire and of the crash, but the helicopter itself was gone."

Ishmael had relived these memories every day for the last twenty years. He was able to make it through those difficult first days in training and the hours of harsh, endless practice and exercises because he was obsessed with the thought that he was preparing himself to avenge the death of his family.

"I started looking through the sand," Ishmael continued. "The man who had rescued me helped me in my search." Ishmael closed his eyes, trying to picture the events of two decades ago. "I hoped I would find some souvenir of my family, but the only thing I found was a piece of metal about the size of the top of a tin can. I thought the metal belonged to the helicopter, and I would keep it as a memento of my dead family. The man who rescued me, however, grabbed the metal away from me. 'That's not from the helicopter,' he explained. He pointed to a symbol in the center. It was the insignia of the American Air Force. 'That metal must have belonged to the missile that shot down the helicopter,' he explained.

"I dropped the piece of metal as though it was burning my fingertips. I did not want to see it again. To me, that piece of metal symbolized the murderers. Ever since that day, I have hated America."

"How old were you then?"

"I was just eight years old," Ishmael said softly.

"And how old are you now?"

"Twenty-eight."

"How did you find our organization?" bin Laden asked, his eyes clearly sympathetic.

"The man who rescued me was a member. I think he was already associated with al Qaeda when he first met me. His connection deepened while I was living in his house and he influenced me to join." Ishmael's eyes glowed with fiery zeal. "I hope some day that the organization will send me to fight America."

Bin Laden suddenly became very serious. "Your hopes will be realized. I am choosing you to be Allah's messenger, to fight against the Americans. Yes, I will be able to assist you in revenging your family's death."

Ishmael fell to bin Laden's feet. "Please help me take revenge against the Americans," he begged, tears coursing down his face.

"Are you willing to sacrifice your life for this elevated goal?" bin Laden demanded, in a tone of voice that brooked no compromise.

"Yes," Ishmael-Yechezkel replied with utmost sincerity. "If I know that my death will cause them harm, just like they harmed me and my family."

Nine

September 11, 2001

The first rays of light from the east penetrated the wall of haze—a result of the pollution from millions of cars clogging the streets—that was the status quo in Los Angeles. Summer was drawing to an end, but the weather was still hot and humid.

Rachamim walked down the empty street. No one was out at this hour of the morning. Everyone was still fast asleep in comfortable, air-conditioned rooms.

He stopped at the end of the block, in front of an imposing edifice. Above the front door was an elegant marble sign with "The Yechezkel and Yosef Synagogue" inscribed in large black letters. This morning, like every other morning, Rachamim paused for a moment to look at the sign. As always, he thought about his two sons and how they had been tragically taken away from him. More than twenty years had passed since that day, but the pain was still as sharp as if it had happened yesterday.

Rachamim took a heavy keychain from his pocket. Using the largest key, he opened the ornate front gate. He was always the first one to arrive, so he was charged with opening the front door each morning. He came two hours before the prayers started so he would have enough time to recite the entire book of *Tehillim*.

He had thought about reciting *mishnayot* for the sake of his sons' souls, but could not bring himself to take such a step. That would be tantamount to admitting that they were dead, and that was something he refused to do, as long as there was no proof to that effect.

He told Naomi that each morning he prayed for the souls of their two young children who had been so tragically taken away from them. He did not want to cause her any more pain. He did not want to admit that somewhere deep inside of him, he still nurtured a spark of hope that his children were alive. He continued to pray for their welfare and beseech Hashem that someday he would have the privilege of being together with them.

The hall was dark. Just as every other morning, he waited a few seconds for his eyes to adjust to the darkness before turning on the light switch. But this morning, to his surprise, there was a streak of light coming from under the last door to the right, which led to the janitor's tiny cubbyhole.

That small room was the domain of Jamil, the synagogue's Kurdish janitor. The light should have been off. Rachamim knew that Jamil would never leave the light on. He had grown up in extreme poverty, and frugality was so ingrained in his nature that he would never waste a penny and leave the light burning all night like that.

Had something happened to Jamil? It seemed a small thing, but in twenty years Jamil had never deviated from his routine. Rachamim knew that Jamil often napped on the grungy old sofa that was in the room, and that he occasionally slept there instead of returning to his tiny one-room apartment in a rundown area of the city. But whether he stayed or left, he always made sure to turn off the light.

Rachamim turned on the hall light and silently walked across the heavy carpet to Jamil's room. He stood outside the door and tried to decide whether or not he should enter. A private person by nature, Rachamim never liked intruding on others' personal space. But maybe Jamil was in trouble. Rachamim owed it to Jamil to help him, if he needed it.

Jamil had saved him from the jaws of death when the helicopter that was carrying his family across the border had crashed. The events were still so vivid in Rachamim's mind that it seemed as if they had occurred yesterday. He recalled how the soldiers had forced him and his family onto the helicopter. He remembered the shouts of the pilots that the Americans were shooting at them, and how the helicopter had maneuvered wildly in the air.

Somehow he had struck his head and blacked out. When he woke up, he found himself sprawled out on a flea-bitten bed in Jamil's decrepit hut. The first thing he had seen was a bearded man, dressed in filthy rags, bent over him. The man's eyes lit up when he saw that Rachamim had finally waken up.

"My name is Jamil," the stranger had introduced himself in a strangely accented Persian. "I was afraid you wouldn't survive."

Jamil had sat next to Rachamim. He was holding a cup of muddy water and using it to wet Rachamim's lips every few minutes.

"Where am I?" he asked Jamil.

"Don't worry," Jamil reassured him. "You're in good hands. This is Turkey."

"Where are my children?" Rachamim asked. He could see Naomi lying on a bed across the room, but his two boys were nowhere in sight.

Jamil shook his head. "I had no idea that there were children in the aircraft."

In panic, Rachamim tried to sit up. A sharp pain knifed through his chest, causing him to lose consciousness for a moment.

Jamil slapped him across the face, forcing him to wake up again. "Don't move!" he ordered sternly. "You must have broken a few bones."

"But what about my children?" Rachamim started to cry. "I want to look for them."

"That's impossible." Jamil shook his head. "You can't even stand up by yourself. You'll collapse."

Rachamim realized that this man was right. But he could not lie there peacefully while his children suffered. "I have ten thousand dollars in my pocket," he offered.

He patted his jacket pocket. Naomi had sewn the package inside. Yes, it was still there.

Rachamim saw Jamil's eyes grow wide in amazement. "I will give you this money as a present if you can bring me my children," he insisted.

He knew that Jamil could easily take the money without doing anything. He had to rely on the strong Arab tradition of hospitality.

"I don't want your money," Jamil retorted. "But I'll leave right now to search for your children."

Jamil walked over to a dark corner of the room and picked up an old Army pistol. He placed the pistol on his belt and then concealed it under his ancient jacket. It was then that Rachamim noticed that there was someone else standing in the corner. "Come on, let's go see if there are any other survivors," Jamil said to his friend.

The two men left, and Rachamim fell into a light, troubled sleep.

Jamil and his friend returned two hours later. They told Rachamim that they could not find a living soul. There were no bodies. In fact, the debris from the helicopter was nowhere to be found.

"How did you discover us?" Rachamim asked, hoping that Jamil's answer would help him find out what had happened to his children.

Jamil told him that he had seen their helicopter explode over Turkey. He and his friend were standing nearby when it had happened, and they raced to the scene. Jamil pulled Rachamim out of the rubble and threw him over his shoulder, while his friend took care of Naomi. Jamil did not think that anyone else had survived.

They ran away the moment they saw additional helicopters coming from the Iranian side of the border. They assumed that the fallen helicopter must have been carrying important people from the Shah's government, and that the rebels had shot it down as it crossed the border into Turkey.

Jamil devotedly cared for Rachamim until his fractures had completely healed. Rachamim offered to pay him, but Jamil refused any monetary compensation. He shared his meager bread and water with his guests. Rachamim did not touch any other food.

During that time, Jamil and Rachamim became close friends. With tears in his eyes, Jamil asked Rachamim and his wife to remain, but Rachamim was determined to move to the United States. "I must go," Rachamim apologized. "I want to use the money that I smuggled out of Iran to search for my missing children."

As Rachamim was getting into the ancient car that Jamil had hired to drive him and Naomi to Ankara, the capital city, Rachamim suddenly asked, "Jamil, maybe you would like to travel with me to the United States? You can live with us."

Jamil was clearly taken aback by the offer. "I don't even know how to read or write Turkish, so how could I possibly travel to another country where I don't know the language? I can barely pronounce the word 'English,' let alone speak it. And what would I do for a living there? No, it's not for me!" He stared down at his muddy feet. "Go, Rachamim, go, and may you have success. But don't forget that you have a devoted friend living here, on this side of the world."

Rachamim got out of the automobile and grabbed Jamil's arm. "Come with me, Jamil," he urged him. "You know that there is no future here. If you come to the United States, I'll be there to help you."

Jamil was swayed by his friend's concern for him. Somewhat hesitantly, he agreed to come along. Rachamim bought Jamil a new wardrobe in Ankara and then arranged a tourist visa for him to enter the United States.

Rachamim settled in Los Angeles, California, which already had a large, well-established Iranian community. He opened a textile business, and before long he was nearly as wealthy as before.

The moment he could, he started searching for his lost children. He hired the best American detectives who, for a hefty fee, were willing to travel to the area where the helicopter had supposedly exploded. The detectives asked all the tribes living in the region if any of them had seen Rachamim's children.

The detectives never found the boys, but the information they supplied gave him the impetus to continue his search. He still held on to the hope that his children were alive.

Eventually, Rachamim became wealthy enough to build a synagogue and pay for its maintenance. He asked Jamil, who had never found a regular job, to become the synagogue's janitor.

Jamil was more than happy to accept the position. Rachamim provided him with a special room for his private use. He made the room as comfortable as possible, equipping it with a small refrigerator, electric burner and washing machine.

Now Rachamim carefully opened the door to Jamil's special room. He was greeted by a horrific sight. Jamil was lying on the bed in a drunken stupor. Rachamim saw an open bottle of whiskey on the floor next to the bed. Half of its contents had spilled out, creating an ugly stain on the carpet.

Rachamim was shocked. Jamil never drank alcoholic beverages. Over the past twenty years, he had never seen his friend in such a state.

Rachamim gingerly approached Jamil and started gruffly shaking his shoulders. "Jamil, Jamil, do you hear me?" he asked repeatedly.

Jamil did not answer. The moment Rachamim stopped shaking him, he fell back onto the bed like a lifeless doll.

Rachamim gave up and glanced at his watch. It was after four-thirty. The first members of the congregation would start arriving in an hour and a half—they were now saying *selichot*, and *davening* began an hour earlier than usual. He still had time to finish most of *sefer Tehillim*. Meanwhile, the effects of the alcohol would wear off. Maybe he would manage to speak with Jamil before he went to pray.

Shortly before six o'clock, Rachamim closed his *sefer Tehillim* and returned to Jamil's room. Jamil was awake now and sitting on his bed. He started violently when the door opened, and looked at Rachamim in terror. The two men stared at each other for a few moments without saying a word.

"When did you start drinking?" Rachamim asked, breaking the heavy silence.

Jamil did not respond. He simply continued staring at Rachamim.

"Jamil, are you in trouble?" Rachamim asked in Persian. Although twenty-two years had passed since they had arrived in America, they continued to speak to each other in Persian. Jamil had never learned to speak English properly.

Jamil lowered his eyes. Rachamim did not know if it was out of shame for having been caught drinking, or because he wanted to tell him something. When Jamil looked back up, Rachamim saw that there were tears on his cheeks.

"Did something happen?" Rachamim made his voice gentle. "Tell me what it is. Perhaps I'll be able to help you."

"Rachamim ..." Jamil's voice came out as a hoarse whisper. "Rachamim, this is important. You need to get away from Los Angeles. Run away as quickly as possible."

Rachamim stepped back in shock. "Leave Los Angeles? Jamil, are you still drunk?"

Rachamim stared into Jamil's eyes. They were bloodshot and

sunken, but his gaze was clear. He didn't appear to be drunk. What was apparent, however, was the fear in his eyes.

"What are you afraid of?" Rachamim demanded.

"Shh ..." Jamil looked around fearfully. "Don't talk so loud. But please, listen to me. Disappear for at least a short while."

"But why?" Rachamim said in exasperation.

"When you leave," Jamil went on, ignoring the question, "make sure no one knows where you are going. It should be done in such a way that no one realizes that you are leaving."

"I'm not going anywhere yet," Rachamim said sharply. "You haven't said anything to convince me to listen to you. Why should I disrupt my entire life? You're not used to drinking, Jamil, that's the whole problem. It's all in your imagination."

"I'm not drunk," Jamil said. "I'm also not illiterate and unsuccessful, like you think I am."

Rachamim stared at him, wide-eyed. Jamil was speaking in perfect English! But the Jamil he knew could barely string two sentences together in that language.

"How long have you been fluent in English?" Rachamim demanded.

"For years, even before we moved to the United States." Jamil continued to surprise him. He was speaking without a trace of an accent. His English was so good that he could have easily passed for a native American.

"That's not the only thing that I have kept hidden from you," Jamil went on. "I have kept many secrets throughout the years. You think that we have a simple friendship, but that's not at all true. Our relationship is actually very complicated. For the last twenty-two years I have been intentionally misrepresenting myself."

Jamil paused to take a deep breath. "We're going to have to go our separate ways. It's very possible that we'll never see each other again. But before we say goodbye ... I would like to ask for your forgiveness."

Too many surprises, coming all at once, made Rachamim curt in his response. "No, Jamil, I can't forgive you because I haven't got the slightest idea what it is that you've done. Besides, what could you have done to me already?" Rachamim softened his tone. "It must be the whiskey. I don't know why you've hidden your knowledge of English from me all these years, but there's no crime in pretending not to know English. There's no need to overreact. Wait for the effects of the alcohol to wear off, and then we'll talk again."

Jamil shook his head. "No, it's not the alcohol. This nightmare has been unfolding for the past twenty years. And now, when everything is finally coming to a head …"

Jamil suddenly became quiet. His entire body started shaking. He remained like that for a few minutes before getting out of bed. Completely ignoring Rachamim's presence, he quietly stripped the dirty sheet from his bed and threw it into the miniature washing machine in the corner of the room. He took a red plastic bottle of liquid detergent from the small closet next to the machine and poured some into the washing machine.

Jamil turned the washing machine on. He peered into the glass door to make sure that the laundry was covered with soapsuds. Then he started washing the floor—all the while ignoring Rachamim's presence.

Rachamim had remained standing in the doorway, unsure of what to do with himself. It was clear that Jamil wasn't ready to say any more right now. He heard the front door open and footsteps in the hallway. He glanced at his watch. It was seven-fifteen. The congregation had arrived to pray.

There was nothing more for him to do here. Jamil was ignoring him. He turned to leave the room, but glanced back just before closing the door. Jamil was leaning on the handle of the mop. His lips were moving, but he was not making a sound. His message, however, was clear: "For G-d's sake, I beg you, please do what I asked you to do."

Ten

"The seat belt light has been turned off," announced the captain on Flight 057.

The plane had departed from Ronald Reagan Washington National Airport in Washington, DC, and was on its way to San Francisco, California. It was nine-fifteen in the morning. Most of the passengers had rushed to catch their flight and had not yet managed to eat breakfast. The flight attendants stood up and went into the tiny kitchen to start preparing the breakfast carts.

"Don't move!" Four men stationed throughout the plane started yelling in unison.

The passengers and flight attendants stared wide-eyed at the four men. They looked Arabic and were speaking with thick accents.

"This plane has been hijacked," the leader announced. He was standing in the first-class section, brandishing an enormous sharp knife. To prove his intentions he pointed to his two companions, who were holding what looked like hand grenades.

The passengers were shocked into silence. The flight attendants raced out of the kitchen and stared in disbelief at the terrorists. Their worst nightmares were coming true.

"We will not hesitate to bomb the plane if we see anything suspicious on your part," the terrorists threatened.

The frightened passengers remained glued to their seats. The head flight attendant had gone through special training on how to react in this situation. Now he fought to keep calm and recall what he had learned.

"Never oppose the hijackers," he quietly told his fellow flight attendants. "They can be very serious about their threats. They are usually desperate people who have given up on life and are willing to act on what they say. Let the experts come to rescue you. Don't try to be a hero," he emphasized. "In a hijacking, your job is to keep the hijackers calm. Give them the feeling that you are willing to do whatever they ask and accept their conditions. In this way, they will begin to trust you, making it easier for people on the outside to do whatever is necessary to liberate you."

The other flight attendants did as they were told. They sat in their seats and watched as two terrorists walked down the aisle toward the cockpit. The two men holding the hand grenades remained standing in the first class section, watching the passengers intently to make sure they remained in their seats.

The head flight attendant glanced at the intercom above his head. Although he had warned his co-workers to obey the hijackers' orders, he felt it was his duty to alert the pilots. The moment the hijackers glanced away, he lifted his hand to pick up the intercom.

"Don't!" screamed the closest hijacker. He moved threateningly toward the flight attendants. The head flight attendant quickly dropped his hand.

The passengers could hear sounds of conflict taking place in the cockpit. The door to the cockpit flew open, and they saw the pilots trying to fight the hijackers. The hijackers, who had the advantage of surprise, were armed with long, sharp knives. It wasn't long before they overcame both the pilot and copilot and threw them out of the cockpit.

The two hijackers who had been left to guard the passengers grabbed the pilot and copilot and securely bound their hands and feet.

The plane made a sharp turn to the right and started to fly east. It almost seemed as though the plane was returning to the airport. The Boeing's main cabin was equipped with screens that showed the passengers the details of the flight. They saw the plane rapidly lose altitude while continuing to fly at the same speed as before—four hundred miles per hour.

Looking out the windows, the passengers were able to see the houses underneath them. The plane was rapidly approaching ground level. The Lincoln Memorial appeared to the right of their plane. They were flying so close that they felt as if they could touch it.

"We're about to crash!" people screamed in desperation.

There was the White House, directly in front of them. The plane was making a beeline toward the building.

"Watch out!" screamed the passengers closest to the cockpit. "We're going to crash into the White House!"

The two hijackers guarding them laughed.

"Twenty minutes before nine," Osama bin Laden murmured.

He was seated together with his commanders and assistants. With his white caftan and scarlet turban, bin Laden secretly felt like the prophet Muhammad. And now, like the prophet, he was going into battle against the infidels.

"Eighteen minutes before nine," he murmured again, as the hands of the large clock hanging on the wall opposite him moved slightly. The clock was designed in such a way that its hands swept across an enormous map of New York City. Important national monuments were marked with red circles. The minute hand was now pointing toward the World Trade Center.

"Throngs of workers are now entering the buildings," bin Laden said, his voice filled with anticipation. In just a few minutes, he would give a blow to the United States the likes of which it had never received before. "The battle is about to begin—the battle of the believers against the infidels."

The satellite television, tuned to the New York television station CBS, was in the middle of broadcasting a commercial for a fabric softener. The commercial was suddenly interrupted. "Stay tuned for an important announcement," a voice announced.

The Morning News announcer appeared on the screen, looking extremely serious. "We have just received information that a horrible accident has taken place in the World Trade Center located in downtown Manhattan. A passenger plane crashed into the upper floors of the northern tower. Our reporter, Lou Williams, is presently on his way to the site. Stay tuned to CBS as we continue to give you an up to the minute report."

The men crowded into al Qaeda's headquarters center, located in cave number five in the underground system of caves that bin Laden had constructed in the Tora Bora Mountains, burst into a spontaneous round of applause. "*Allah Akhbar, Allah Akhbar!*"

They watched the screen as enormous tongues of fire burst out of the building's top floors. "The northern tower is on fire," they heard Lou Williams report. In the background, they could hear hundreds of sirens as scores of emergency vehicles rushed to the scene. "Fire departments throughout New York and New Jersey were called in to assist the Manhattan Fire Department," Williams announced dramatically.

"There's more to come," bin Laden announced to his gleeful men. "Let them delude themselves for a few more minutes into thinking that this was only an accident."

Another huge gray airplane could be seen approaching the southern tower. The television camera was now focused on the incoming plane. The men watching could see the word "United" written across the plane's tail. They looked on in excitement as the second airliner flew straight into the south tower.

The announcer's face suddenly appeared on the screen. "It appears that the two collisions were not accidents. According to our most recent information, the collisions were terrorist attacks, stabbing at the very heart of our nation."

The broadcast quickly returned to the scene of the accident. The viewers watched, mesmerized, as flames licked at the sides and roofs of the Twin Towers. They were still sitting there an hour later when the announcer reported that there had been an attack on the Pentagon. He had barely finished announcing that tragedy when he received news of the plane crash outside of Pittsburgh.

"All civilian flights are grounded," the announcer continued. "Air Force fighter planes are patrolling the skies."

The television broadcast returned to the fire in the Twin Towers. Bin Laden's companion's mouths dropped open in shock when they saw the first tower start to collapse. They knew that they would be giving the United States a hard blow, but this was more than they had ever dreamed of.

Their initial shock quickly gave way to ecstatic shouts of *"Allah Akhbar!"* Bin Laden, however, did not join in their joyous celebration. A slight frown formed on his face, which deepened when the second tower collapsed.

"What is it?" his assistant, Abu Salim, whispered. "Is something wrong?"

"I didn't intend for that to happen," bin Laden admitted. "I had never expected such results."

"That's good, isn't it?" his assistant asked, unable to understand the problem. "The American nation has just received a fatal blow. Perhaps they will now understand that they do not rule the world."

"That's true. But it's not that simple."

Bin Laden stood up and started walking toward the door. He made his way along a narrow corridor toward his private office in the underground cavern. Abu Salim followed him.

"Why is it so terrible?" Abu Salim asked again, once they were alone inside the long corridor with its walls of natural stone. Bin Laden liked these roughly hewn walls; they made him feel ready to do battle. He refused to have them painted.

"You ask me what's so terrible?" Bin Laden turned around to face Abu Salim. "Don't you realize what's going to happen?" He spoke like a prophet. "America has received a terrible blow which will arouse the world's pity. All the nations will come to its aid."

Bin Laden paused for a moment to put the key in the lock. The alarm system went off, warning the guard inside the office that someone was opening the door. The guard appeared, moving aside in awe when he saw his revered leader.

Bin Laden sat cross-legged on a deeply piled rug that adorned the floor. Even here, in his own office, he scorned the luxuries that he could easily afford to buy. He lived simply, like his men, and that made them admire him all the more.

"We had better pack our bags and flee," he stated.

"But why?" Abu Salim asked. "Muhammad Omar would never hand us over to the Americans!"

"That may not be his choice," bin Laden said in a weary tone. "Muhammad will undoubtedly be forced out of power. I expect the world to form a coalition to fight against us within days. The Taliban do not have the resources to defeat such a force."

Bin Laden stood up. "We have to be ready for the future. I wouldn't want the United States to find us unprepared." He stood up and walked over to a television screen built into a cabinet in the wall, turned it on and returned to his position on the rug.

"Are you expecting more attacks?" Abu Salim asked, puzzled.

Abu Salim had been personally involved in planning the attacks on the Twin Towers, the Pentagon and the nuclear reactor in Pennsylvania. The attack on the nuclear reactor had failed. He had watched the news report show pictures of the crash outside Pittsburgh. He did not know of anything else that was planned.

"Yes, one more," bin Laden replied. "It's going to be a serious blow to the Americans, destroying their defense and providing us with time to find a secure shelter."

The two hijackers seated in the pilot and copilot's seats were serenely gazing at the land stretching beneath them like a green checkerboard carpet. The streets appeared to be black lines cutting back and forth through the lush greenery of the grassy capital. The plane was rapidly approaching ground level. The two men grasping the control sticks on the instrument panel were counting the minutes until the plane crashed into the White House.

Ishmael was seated in the pilot's seat. He glanced at his companion seated to his left. He knew he was called Essam, but he had no idea if that was his real name. Each of the terrorists had been trained in a different al Qaeda base in Afghanistan. Osama bin Laden was not about to take any chances with an operation that he had been planning for so many years. Neither of the hijackers knew the others' identity, nor did they know all the details of this mission. They were willing to perform their specific task and sacrifice themselves for a higher calling, trusting fully in their revered leader's judgment.

The two men sat together in silence. Ishmael eyed his companion from time to time; he thought he had seen him somewhere, and he debated asking him about it. But he changed his mind. *In a few moments there will be nothing left of either of us. So what difference does it make?*

The White House appeared on the horizon. The plane was flying toward it at a speed of three hundred and fifty miles per hour. Ishmael estimated that he had another three minutes before the crash.

His hands were shaking violently as he removed them from the control stick. Now, in these last few minutes before the end of his life, there was one thing he had to do.

Eleven

Rachamim came back to check on Jamil after his morning prayers, but Jamil was not in his room. In fact, the room was immaculate. Jamil had managed to clean the room and put everything back in place. It was as though nothing unusual had occurred earlier. Rachamim remained standing there for a few moments, trying to decide what to do.

Tired from standing so long, he sat down on one of the chairs in the sparsely furnished room. He decided to wait until Jamil returned and then ask him for an explanation. He wasn't about to leave home without more details about Jamil's warning.

Rachamim waited for over half an hour, but Jamil never showed up. Reluctantly, he stood and left the building. He knew that if he were to remain any longer, Naomi would become frantic with worry. Ever since their flight from Teheran, Naomi tended to become hysterical over every little thing. Rachamim slowly left Jamil's room and closed the door behind him.

Naomi heard her husband open the front door and ran to greet him. He saw that she was upset and worried. "What happened?" Rachamim asked in concern.

She hesitated, not sure what she should tell him. Meanwhile, Rachamim went over to a chair and started hanging his jacket over the back of it. That was when he noticed the three suitcases piled in the middle of the living room floor.

Rachamim strode into the living room. Naomi moved aside to allow him to enter. Two of the suitcases were already closed. They were so packed that they were almost bursting at the seams. The third suitcase was open, and he could see that it was filled with her wardrobe.

"What's going on here?" he asked, bewildered. "Are you planning to take a vacation now?"

"Why are you making jokes at a time like this?" she asked testily.

"What joke? What are you talking about?"

She looked at him, trying to decide if he was serious. "Don't you realize that we have to leave Los Angeles immediately?"

"Naomi, what's the matter with you? What are you talking about?"

"Jamil told me that he had warned you that we must leave immediately. Why are you pretending that you don't know?"

"Jamil!" Rachamim was thunderstruck. "You mean he talked to you too?"

Naomi ignored the question. "So if he warned you, why are you wasting your time asking useless questions instead of helping me pack?"

"He was drunk, Naomi. Don't pay attention to what he told you. If you would have seen the way he looked this morning, you would not be taking his warning seriously."

"He didn't sound drunk to me," Naomi retorted as she walked into the bedroom. A few minutes later, she returned, carrying another huge pile of clothes.

"Why are you taking Jamil so seriously?" he asked impatiently. "This morning I found him sprawled out on his bed, filthy and drunk. The floor was littered with bottles of whiskey. Anything he told you was just a delusion."

She plunked the pile of clothes on top of the closest chair. "He definitely was not drunk when he knocked on the door this morning." Rachamim could feel the color drain from his face. Jamil had actually come all the way to the house to warn her.

"He explained to me that you had not taken his warning seriously, so he came to speak with me personally," Naomi went on. "He convinced me that his intentions were sincere. Yes, he told me about how he looked when you found him this morning. He explained that his conscience was bothering him and he had gotten drunk to escape his inner battle."

"Did he explain why his conscience is bothering him?" Rachamim asked.

"He muttered something that was not really clear. He said that he had deceived you, well, basically both of us, throughout the years. He said that we had been so good to him, while he had misled us."

Rachamim thought back. Jamil had also apologized to him for having deceived him. "How has he betrayed me?" he asked aloud. "Jamil rescued me from certain death. And then, throughout all our years together, he has constantly proven his loyalty to me. What could be weighing on the man's conscience?"

"I don't know," Naomi admitted. "He didn't want to tell me. He just said that someday we will understand ourselves."

Rachamim's curiosity got the better of him. "What else did he say about this strange idea of his, that we should leave everything and flee?"

"Not much," she answered softly. "He raced down the hall without looking back."

Rachamim suddenly stood up. "Forget this business. We're not leaving." He started opening the suitcases. "Something must have happened to Jamil. I am not about to destroy my life because of some crazy psychopath. I'm going to put our clothes away."

Naomi watched him, uncertain for a moment, as he pulled his suit out of the suitcase and hung it back in the closet. But as he continued to remove clothing from the suitcase, she stepped forward to stop him.

"Please, Rachamim, I know this sounds crazy—but I have a bad feeling about this. I think we should go."

Rachamim stared at her, incredulous, as she went to the bedroom to resume her furious packing. Muttering in frustration, he sat on the armchair, helplessly observing his wife. He did not think they should run away from their peaceful life and beautiful home. They weren't young anymore. They were both over sixty. Rachamim would be eligible for social security benefits in less than a year.

The fact was that he really didn't need it. Using the money that he had managed to transfer out of Iran, he had succeeded in building an extremely successful textile business. But the mere fact that he would soon be eligible for a pension caused him to realize that it was time for him to slow down and take life a bit easier.

Naomi finished packing. "Can you help me carry the suitcases down to the car?" she asked. The question was posed in such a way that it sounded as if they were setting out on a pleasure trip. There were no signs of tension in her voice.

Rachamim was angry. "Don't you think this trip will be too difficult for us at our age?"

She stared at him, bewildered. "Our life is only lent to us; it doesn't really belong to us. The only reason we are still alive is because that is Hashem's decree."

"Then why run away?" he challenged her. "Whatever happens is Hashem's will."

"I must do this for Yechezkel and Yosef, for our beloved children. They may be alive somewhere, and maybe—at this very moment—they are looking for us. I don't want to disappoint them." Her voice was shaking.

He remained seated while she tried to pick up the suitcases by herself. They were too heavy for her frail body. Unable to lift them, she started dragging them toward the front door.

He did not have the heart to watch her. He realized that there was nothing he could do or say to make her change her mind. Rachamim stood up and took the heavy suitcase from her. Naomi ran to the front door and opened it a crack before peeking out to make sure that no one was standing in the hallway outside. Seeing that, Rachamim began to worry for her sanity.

The elevator was in the center of the stairwell. He helped her drag the suitcase to the elevator, then pressed the basement button for the parking lot. The numbers started flashing as the elevator made its swift descent.

When they reached the parking lot, Rachamim dragged the suitcases over to the parked car and piled them in the trunk. Naomi continued peering around as they got into the car and drove out of the parking lot. Her fear was contagious, and he found himself glancing into the rearview mirror to make sure no one was following them. He smiled to himself when he realized what he was doing. It was ridiculous to run away like this, allowing Jamil's warning to destroy their peace of mind.

Rachamim stopped at the end of the block. "Where are we going?" he asked Naomi.

"Where?" Her face was blank. "I ... I don't know ..."

"I'm not just going to drive around aimlessly," he pointed out to her. "We need a destination."

"The airport, then," she said firmly.

"The airport?"

"Yes. We'll decide on a final destination once we get there."

Rachamim shook his head, but he didn't argue. The streets were emptier than usual. Within a few minutes, they had reached La Cienega Boulevard and were headed for the 405 south.

The freeway was normally crowded at this time of day. Rachamim drove this way every morning on his way to work. Today, though, almost no cars were on the road.

"Something funny is going on," Rachamim whispered.

Naomi sat up straight. "What's the matter?"

"The road," he said, not knowing how to explain it to her.

Two police cars pulled up on either side of their car. They slowed down and one of the policemen peered into their car. He apparently saw something that he did not like—he blinked at them to go to the side of the road, while the other police car began flashing its lights.

"Were you driving too fast?" Naomi asked.

"No," Rachamim said, shaking his head as he pulled the car to the side of the road. "I have no idea why they stopped us."

A tall policeman walked over to Rachamim's window. His partner stood opposite him, on the passenger's side of the car.

"Your license, please," the officer ordered.

Rachamim bent forward to get to his wallet. "I wasn't speeding," he said, as he handed over his license. "What did I do wrong?"

"You didn't transgress any traffic law," the policeman replied, without elaborating. He silently returned to the police car.

"It interesting that they didn't ask to see our insurance papers," Rachamim wondered aloud. "That's usually the first thing they request."

"Something strange is definitely going on," Naomi responded fearfully. Jamil's warning was reverberating in her ears.

The policemen left them alone for about fifteen minutes. From the rearview mirror, Rachamim and Naomi could see them speaking into their radios. "They must suspect me of something," Rachamim muttered. That was the only way he could explain their strange behavior.

One of the policemen finally returned to their car. "How long have you been living at the address written on your license?" he asked sharply.

"Umm…" Rachamim scratched his forehead. He tried to remember exactly how long they had been living in their apartment. "Approximately seven years," he finally said.

"And where did you live before that?"

"3029 Livonia Avenue."

"How long did you live at 3029 Livonia Avenue?"

"Close to fifteen years." These strange questions worried Rachamim.

"And where did you live before that?" the policeman continued.

Beads of sweat appeared on Rachamim's forehead. "What do you suspect me of?" he asked in a strange voice.

"Just answer the questions," the policeman retorted. "I'll explain everything after you finish."

The policeman continued questioning Rachamim about his past. He finally seemed satisfied with Rachamim's answers and handed him back his license. "I'm sorry for the unpleasantness I caused you," he apologized. "I'm sure you realize that it's because of what happened this morning."

"What happened this morning?" Naomi asked after the policeman drove away.

"I have no idea," Rachamim said, turning back onto the road. He turned on the radio to listen to the news.

"I promise you that I will bring those responsible for this criminal act to justice. They will have to pay the price for their deeds." The President's voice thundered over the speakers. "I will guide our country during the darkest hour of our history."

"What's he talking about?" Naomi asked nervously. "What dark hour?"

"I have no idea," Rachamim repeated impatiently. "Let me listen so I can hear what's going on."

The speech was apparently finished. The next speaker introduced himself as the head of NATO. He said his name so quickly that Rachamim was not able to make it out. The speech was broadcast directly from the NATO's central command center, in Brussels, Belgium. "NATO's high command has unanimously agreed to activate paragraph five of the NATO regulations. All member nations will do their utmost to defend the security of the United States. In addition, all member nations are putting their armed forces at NATO's disposal."

"Why do they have to defend the United States?" Naomi demanded fearfully.

The radio announcer started speaking. In a dry, stern voice, he explained the significance of paragraph five, adding that this was the first time in NATO's existence that the paragraph had been invoked. "Throughout all the difficult years of the cold war between the United States and the Soviet Union," the announcer emphasized, "there was never a situation that warranted NATO's intervention by activating paragraph five."

"*Ribono shel Olam*, what is going on?" Naomi was hysterical. "Has another world war begun?" She had suffered enough from war. She had lost enough to war, and she couldn't stand the thought of another war.

"Please let me listen," Rachamim told her. "I don't think another world war has begun. Who would dare attack the United States?"

"It sure sounds like someone did," Naomi replied. "Don't you hear what they are saying, about defending the United States from its enemies?"

"And now, we'll repeat the events of this morning," they heard the announcer say. The two of them were quiet so they could pay attention to his words.

The announcer quickly reviewed the events of that morning, September eleventh. "At eight forty-six in Manhattan this morning..."

Rachamim and Naomi listened in shocked silence. They wanted to hear more details, but at this time of day, the announcer was certain that his audience had already heard about the morning's events. Instead, he started interviewing a famous security expert, whose name they could barely understand.

Rachamim turned off the radio and continued driving. He was overwhelmed with a feeling of sadness and depression. "Now I understand why the policemen stopped us. They are suspicious of anyone who looks like an Arab or appears to come from the Middle East."

Naomi was staring straight ahead. "Let's stop here," she suggested, pointing at a sign that indicated a turn off for a shopping mall. "Maybe we can find out what's happening."

Rachamim turned into the right lane and exited the freeway. The shopping mall, filled with various shops and restaurants, appeared deserted. Only one person was seated in the huge McDonald's, nervously devouring his hamburger while intently watching the news on the television set hanging from the restaurant's ceiling.

Rachamim guided his wife to a bench just outside the coffee shop. "Why don't you sit down for a few minutes," he suggested. "I'll get you something to drink."

As Rachamim stepped inside the shop, his eyes were drawn to the screen overhead. He shuddered as he watched the two aircraft crash into the Twin Towers. It was an effort to pull his attention away and focus on the coffee machine, which was nearly full.

Rachamim filled two disposable cups with coffee and went to pay at the cash register. The clerk didn't even notice his presence. He was staring at the enormous television screen, watching the news.

"How much do I owe you?" Rachamim asked, trying to draw his attention.

"Those wicked people," the clerk burst out, ignoring his question. "Why did they do such a horrible thing to us? Who knows how many tens of thousands were murdered when the building collapsed!"

Rachamim didn't want to get into a discussion right now. But he felt obligated to say something.

"There are people whose goal in life is to destroy other people's peace of mind," he commented, recalling his own private pain. He had lost his family, the best years of his life and his wealth because of wicked people, just like the ones who had attacked America that morning. And now, again, he was trying to escape from their wickedness.

"Yes, but why us? Our nation comes to the assistance of anyone who's in trouble. What are their complaints against us? What did the innocent people in the Twin Towers do to harm them?"

Rachamim sighed. There was nothing he could possibly say to answer these questions.

"I have a brother who works in the World Trade Center. I keep trying to contact him. I called his wife and some of his friends and none of them have been able to contact him either. I heard that all the cell phones in lower Manhattan have stopped working because of the accident," the clerk added, obviously searching for a ray of hope.

Rachamim sighed again in commiseration. He placed two dollar bills on the counter and walked away, holding the cups of coffee in his hand. He didn't have the emotional energy to listen to someone else's troubles. Now he himself was in desperate need of encouragement.

Just as he exited the coffee shop, a policeman appeared. "Can I see your identification, sir?" he barked. The policeman's hand was resting on his pistol, ready to use it at the slightest provocation.

Rachamim carefully placed the coffee on a nearby bench and then took out his driver's license. He confidently handed it to the officer, who examined it carefully. The policeman was also dark, and spoke with a heavy accent. Rachamim assumed that the policeman was Hispanic, probably from Puerto Rico or some other South American country. *He might even be from the Middle East,* Rachamim realized with a start. He stopped himself from asking the officer where he had been born.

The officer finished examining the driver's license and handed it back to Rachamim. It seemed to Rachamim that there was a glint of victory in his eyes, as though he had found what he was looking for.

"Okay, everything's fine," the officer said, before walking away. Rachamim watched him take a small cell phone out of his pocket and start dialing. That was unusual, Rachamim thought. Don't policemen use radios to communicate?

Rachamim dismissed his suspicions. He walked over to Naomi, who was still staring at the news through the windows of the coffee shop. She barely noticed when Rachamim stood next to her.

"Here, Naomi."

She turned to him with a start, and he handed her the coffee.

"Thank you," she said absently. "Did you see what they said? The airport is closed. They evacuated it until further notice."

"They did? Why? What happened at the airport here?"

"Nothing." Her voice was listless. "Come on, let's go. I can't sit around here any longer."

He sat next to her. "Drink your coffee first."

She stared at the cup in her hand as if she had never seen it before. Then she murmured a *bracha* and slowly started sipping the black liquid.

Rachamim also started drinking the bitter brew.

"I feel like we're being followed," Naomi said suddenly.

"Who's following us?" he asked.

Naomi slowly turned around so she was facing the large glass doors that served as the shopping plaza's main entrance. "He's still standing there," she said in a shaky voice. She needed both hands to keep her coffee from spilling.

"Who's still standing there?" he asked. He saw only a police car stationed in front of the shopping center.

"Don't you see that police car?" she whispered.

"So what?" he asked, unable to understand her fear. "It doesn't seem strange to me that on a day like today there would be police cars stationed throughout the city."

"The policeman who stopped you to check your identification…" She paused, trying to collect her thoughts so she could explain her suspicions.

"What's the matter with that policeman? He just wanted to make sure that I'm not a terrorist. Don't forget, in light of the present situation, any person who looks like an Arab is automatically under suspicion."

"That's not the problem." She shook her head impatiently. "The officer who stopped you is sitting in that car."

"And so?" He couldn't understand why that upset her.

"The officer suddenly appeared from that corner." She pointed to a dark area on the other side of the room. "It was almost as though he was waiting for you to arrive. And that police car was not there then.

The police car only showed up after he finished speaking with you."

"That's not a reason to be frightened," he tried to reassure her. But the chain of events was strange. He wondered why the police car was still there. They must have seen his wife point toward the corner.

"Let's get out of here now," Naomi suggested when Rachamim had finished drinking his coffee and had disposed of the Styrofoam cup in the nearest garbage can. She also threw her cup in the trash, although it was still half full.

"Where do you want to go from here?" he asked as they walked back to the car.

"Anywhere! I want to get away from here as quickly as possible. I have a strange feeling about the place."

They passed the police car on their way to the parking lot. Rachamim glanced inside and noticed that there were two policemen sitting there. They were staring at them and didn't even try to hide it.

"What do they want from us?" Naomi asked in a shaky voice. "What did we do wrong? Why are they staring at us?"

"I'll explain it again. Don't forget that we look like Arabs, and the people who just attacked our country were Arabs. Their suspicions are understandable."

When Rachamim reached the car, he was surprised to see that there was a car parked on either side of his. He hadn't noticed any cars entering the parking lot, and other than his car and the two cars on either side of him, the lot was completely empty. Why had the drivers decided to park next to him?

As he drove out of the parking lot, Rachamim looked around to see if the police car was following him. The car remained stationed in front of the mall.

Rachamim spent the next twenty minutes driving aimlessly along Interstate 405, which remained almost completely empty. Every once in a while he glanced into the rearview mirror to see if a car was following him. Everything seemed clear.

"We need to decide what we're doing," he said abruptly.

Naomi did not answer him.

"Do you have any idea where we're going?" he asked.

"No, I have no idea where to go." She burst into tears. "I just want to run away from the entire situation. I don't want to end up trapped in a war again. I have already lost my children; what else do I have left to lose? I can't live with what's going on. I just pray that I'll wake up soon and discover that this is a passing nightmare."

Rachamim wondered what he could possibly say. The easiest thing to do would be to reassure her that there was nothing to worry about. But he was also worried. He was petrified that the terrorist attack would result in another world war. The revolution in Iran was nothing compared to what could happen now.

He suddenly recalled Jamil's warning that morning. *Was there a connection between his warning and this morning's terrorist attacks?* He was terrified at the thought. Unable to contain himself, he asked Naomi, "Do you think that there's any relation between what Jamil said and this morning's events?"

"Yes," she replied immediately. She did not seem surprised. She had apparently already come to that conclusion.

"I think that we had better report it to the FBI," he said.

"Do you think that's a good idea?" Naomi wondered aloud.

"I have a feeling that Jamil knew about the attack before it happened. I found him completely drunk at four o'clock this morning. He must have gotten drunk a few hours before that. When it was four o'clock by us, it was seven o'clock in New York, two hours before the attack. Why did he get drunk then? That was the first time that he ever got drunk. And why, on such a fateful day, did he insist that we run away from our home?" Rachamim summarized his thoughts.

"Even if he knew about this evil deed, he probably couldn't do anything to stop it," Naomi pointed out, trying to defend their friend who had once saved them from certain death. "He probably couldn't stand up to the pressure and decided to drown his woes in alcohol. If you report this to the FBI, he'll be dragged into it even though he had nothing to do with the crime. So we'll end up hurting the person to whom we owe our lives."

"It's possible," Rachamim mumbled, forced to agree. He decided to wait to see what developed. He suspected that Jamil had disappeared the moment they left, so it wouldn't be easy for the FBI to find him, even if Rachamim informed the police of his suspicions.

Twelve

Ishmael quickly removed a piece of paper from his wallet. It was an old Iranian rial bill, faded and torn. He held the bill close to his face. "Abba, I am doing this for you … I am about to avenge your death."

He stared at the bill. In the middle was one word written in a language that he did not understand. The word seemed to jump out at him. Although he was unable to read it, he understood its meaning.

"Abba, I can still remember. On this bill you wrote the word, '*Echad.*' You begged me to always remember that I belong to one nation and that I believe in one G-d. Yes, Abba, I have followed your orders. At every opportunity, I found a way to be alone with this bill and repeat what you said to me before we left our home. I am only pretending to be a Muslim. In my heart, I have remained a Jew, just as you asked of me. Now that I am about to join you, I am declaring that I believe with a full heart that I belong to one nation and that there is only one G-d in the world."

The White House was looming ahead of them. In just another few seconds, the plane would crash into the western wing of the building, where the President's headquarters were located. It was there that the President had decided to abandon his ally, the Shah, in his hour of need. Over twenty years had gone by since that day, and many men had sat in the presidential chair. But to Ishmael, the President's chair had come to symbolize the source of his troubles. It did not matter who currently sat there; it represented all that he hated about America.

Ishmael looked out the window at the White House, braced himself for the crash ... but it never came. Instead, with a sudden lurch, the plane abruptly changed direction. The sun blinded him in a dazzling blue sky as the airline headed upward.

Aghast, Ishmael tried to grab the control stick. His companion's hand was locked in place, pulling back on the control stick, causing the airline to head straight upward—missing the White House with barely room to spare.

Ishmael was furious. His companion had betrayed him, betrayed their mission, betrayed bin Laden, their revered leader. He glared at his companion, brandishing his knife. "What are you doing?" he demanded.

Essam did not let go of the stick. He stared at Ishmael, hope and fear warring in his eyes.

"I don't know if you're a traitor," Ishmael said contemptuously, "or if you're simply afraid to die. But it doesn't matter. Let go of the stick."

Essam did not move.

"Let go," Ishmael said threateningly, "or I will stab you."

"Wait." His companion's voice was hoarse with some unnameable emotion. "Let me show you something first."

Silently, Essam handed Ishmael a folded piece of paper. Ishmael hesitated before taking it. Was this some sort of trick? Was his companion trying to distract his attention, so he could gain the upper hand? Ishmael kept a wary eye on his companion as he unfolded the paper to see what was inside.

Abu Salim remained with bin Laden for over an hour. Every few minutes bin Laden glanced impatiently at his watch. Abu Salim realized that his commander was on edge. Something must have gone wrong.

Bin Laden was unable to hide his worry. "The fifth attack was supposed to take place three quarters of an hour ago," he said after a long silence.

For the next fifteen minutes, they stared at the screen. The announcer reported the attack on the Twin Towers, the Pentagon, and the plane that crashed outside Pittsburgh. He never mentioned a word about an additional attack.

Bin Laden was extremely serious. "The Americans might get here quicker than I had originally thought."

There was an awkward silence in the room before bin Laden began speaking again. "I am now instructing you to immediately activate the Long Distance Contact Plan."

Abu Salim stared at him in shock. "The Long Distance Contact Plan? Whatever for? The hijackers were all killed, every single one of them. Why should we place ourselves in danger by activating that plan?"

"Didn't you hear my order?" bin Laden thundered.

"Yes," Abu Salim said quickly. This was clearly not the time to oppose bin Laden.

Bin Laden spoke more quietly. There was a strange glint to his eyes. "I don't have a choice. I'm going to play my last card."

"What are you going to do?"

"You'll have to wait and see."

Ishmael stared in shock at the piece of paper in his hand. It was a torn, worn out Iranian bill. Written in Hebrew letters across the center of the bill was the word "*Echad.*"

It was identical to the one he kept in his pocket.

"Where did you get this?" he shouted at his accomplice. His voice was shaking in rage.

"My father gave it to me," Essam whispered.

Ishmael looked at his companion, incredulous. "Your father?"

"Yes." Essam's voice faltered. "It's hard for me to remember—it was so many years ago …"

"But then—that would mean—*are you Yosef?*"

Ishmael leaped to his feet. He forgot that he was right in the middle of hijacking an airplane, that just minutes before he had been prepared to end his life in a fiery grave. Essam had the presence of mind to straighten out the airplane before Ishmael had grasped his arms and was hugging him tightly.

"Yosef!" Ishmael wept. For now he knew the truth.

Essam was his long lost brother.

Essam had been just four years old when he was torn away from his family, to be brought up by Islamic militants. Memories of his earlier life had faded, until they had seemed no more than an unreachable dream. But somehow, through all the hardships of the intervening years, he had managed to retain that one memento from his family—the torn bill that his father had given him, so long ago.

When his accomplice had pulled out a torn bill—when he had said the word "*Echad*"—all at once, the last scene with his father had come back to him. His father's last wish had been that if they lost contact with each other, they should constantly recite this word and recall its meaning. "That will remind you that you are Jews," he had said. "With that password, you'll be able to find each other someday." Only he and his brother knew that his father had written this word on each side of the bill.

Essam could not recall how his brother and father looked. But now, with his father's voice ringing in his ears, it was apparent that the man sitting next to him, his accomplice in this barbaric hijacking, was none other than his long lost brother.

Dazed, Essam had pulled out his own torn bill, which he had taken with him for his last journey on earth. The word "*Echad*" continued to reverberate in his ears. All at once, he knew that he wasn't ready to die.

With the White House rushing up to meet them, Essam had acted almost without thought. He pulled back on the stick, bringing the plane out of its dive and heading back into the clear blue sky.

"Yosef, Yosef," Ishmael repeated, crying tears of joy.

"Yosef," Essam said wonderingly. "It almost feels like a dream. I … I haven't heard that name in so many years."

He moved back slightly, gently pushing Ishmael away so he could see him clearly. The two men studied each other for a long moment.

"Look," Ishmael said finally. He was holding the two halves of the torn bill together, and Essam could see that they were a perfect fit.

"Yechezkel," Essam said suddenly. "You are Yechezkel! And I am Yosef!"

The two stared at each other, oblivious to the panicky transmissions coming over the radio. The navigation tower was desperately trying to contact the airplane. But the two brothers ignored the radio. They were hugging each other and crying in joy.

Yechezkel was the first to return to reality. He realized their situation was extremely precarious. They were in the cockpit of an airliner they didn't know how to land, with the United States Air Force undoubtedly on their way to shoot them from the sky. Not to mention the two terrorists guarding the passengers, who were certainly wondering what had gone wrong. Yechezkel knew that it was only a matter of time before they came into the cockpit to investigate.

"I think we had better contact the control tower," Yechezkel said, going back to the pilot's chair. "We don't want anyone to start shooting at us."

He keyed the radio transmitter. "This is United Flight 057. Can you hear me? Over." The intense training that he had received in the al Qaeda camps prepared him to remain outwardly calm in situations such as this one.

At least three navigation towers responded at once. "Yes, we hear you."

"Good," he replied forcefully. "The plane has been hijacked."

This time, the radio remained silent. The flight supervisors had no idea how to respond. Each was waiting for the other to go first.

"Are you interested in bargaining with me?" he asked. He turned the plane to the right, so it was heading back toward the White House.

"Am I speaking with the hijacker?" the chief supervisor in National Airport finally asked.

"Yes," Yechezkel said tersely. "I am asking you again. Are you willing to start bargaining with us?"

The men in the control tower watched the radar screens as the airplane flew closer to the White House. Several F-16 fighter jets were in the vicinity, but shooting the airliner down now would cause it to slam into the Capitol Building and rain debris down on the White House.

"What are your conditions?" the supervisor asked, keeping a wary eye on the screen. He motioned to his assistant to contact the FBI while he kept talking to the hijacker.

"I want to speak with the President of the United States," Yechezkel responded.

"Let me try to contact him," the supervisor replied. He glanced at his assistant, who nodded in his direction. The director of the FBI was on the phone. The supervisor felt a sense of relief—the responsibility was out of his hands.

As the plane continued circling the capitol, the radio remained silent. The Air Force fighter planes that had been called in to defend the region kept their distance, to avoid frightening the hijacker—as long as he was willing to bargain with them.

A different voice came on the radio. "This is the director of the FBI."

"I asked to speak with the President," Yechezkel insisted.

"I'm afraid that's impossible. The President is being kept hidden in a secure place, and we have no way to contact him there," the director explained.

Yechezkel believed him. He could well imagine what was going on in the government offices. "Okay," he agreed. "What can you offer me?"

"What are you asking for?"

Yechezkel fell silent for a moment, considering how to proceed. "Listen. I was just about to complete my mission for al Qaeda. If I had, your White House wouldn't be here any more. But at the very last minute I discovered that my brother is in the plane here, together with me. I realized then that the stories I had been told, that the Americans had murdered my entire family, were a bunch of lies. I have a feeling that my parents are still alive, somewhere."

The director shook his head in bewilderment. He had no idea what the hijacker was trying to get at. "So what do you want from us?" he asked.

"Two things," Yechezkel said firmly. "First, I am requesting immunity for my brother and me, a promise that we will not be punished for hijacking the plane."

"I give you my word," the director quickly responded.

"And second," Yechezkel continued, "promise me that the FBI will do everything in its power to discover what happened to my parents."

"I promise," the director replied, both relieved and perplexed at this second request.

"Okay. Let me speak to someone who can guide me in landing this plane."

"I'm on the frequency," the supervisor's voice was heard over the radio. "Make a fifty degree turn to the right. I'll be guiding you to National Airport, just across the Potomac River from downtown Washington."

Yechezkel obeyed the supervisor's directions and turned the wheel fifty degrees to the right. "Guard the door," he yelled to his brother. "The other two hijackers might push their way in here the minute they realize that I'm planning to land the plane."

Yosef released his safety belt and left the co-pilot's seat, while Yechezkel continued to guide the plane. National Airport appeared ahead of him. Yechezkel's heart was pounding. He wasn't sure if he knew how to land such a gigantic plane. While studying at the Hoffman Aviation School in South Carolina, he had not paid too much attention to learning how to land a plane, since that detail was not important for the mission.

"Runway number seven is ready," the supervisor informed him. "You're heading straight toward it."

In the distance, Yechezkel could see the flashing lights of emergency vehicles. "I don't know how to land a plane," Yechezkel admitted to the supervisor.

There was a short silence. "You've never landed an aircraft?" the supervisor asked in a strained voice.

"Nothing this big. I've flown small aircraft, single engine and multi-engine planes, and I've practiced turns in the 767 simulator…" His voice trailed off. Yechezkel could recall the surprise of his instructor that he only wanted to practice turns in the simulator—most students practiced takeoffs and landings.

The supervisor sounded dubious. "There's a big difference, although some experience is better than nothing. What about the pilots? Maybe they can land the plane for you."

"They're in the passenger section. The other hijackers are guarding them. If I leave the cockpit, they'll make sure that no one will land the plane."

"I see," the supervisor responded, though he wasn't sure if he fully understood. Apparently there was some sort of disagreement among the hijackers. "Circle the airport for a few minutes while I find an experienced pilot to guide you."

Yechezkel pulled the navigation stick to the right and started circling the airport. Beneath him he saw hundreds of grounded planes filling the runways, sparkling in the sun. They had barely managed to leave a runway open for him.

It took ten minutes. Yechezkel could imagine the panic that was taking place on the ground. An inexperienced pilot at the controls of a huge aircraft was a disaster in the making. They would need to find an experienced pilot with the ability to talk him down to the ground.

The supervisor finally came back and informed Yechezkel that he had found a pilot willing to guide him in landing the plane.

"Good morning. My name is Jim Stewart," the pilot began. "I'll be pleased to assist you in landing the plane."

"All right. I'm ready," Yechezkel responded, reassured by Stewart's calm voice.

"Turn west and continue flying straight for the next five miles. Then, turn around so you'll be heading straight back to the airport. That way you'll be flying directly toward the runway."

Yechezkel followed Stewart's orders. "I'm heading east now," he reported.

"Lower your speed to 120 knots and push the control stick down. On the right side of your instrument panel, there's a knob with a blue handle. Do you see it?"

"Yes."

"Pull the handle towards you," the pilot continued instructing him.

Yechezkel obeyed. They heard a strange noise. "You just set the landing gears in motion. What you're hearing are the wheels being lowered into place."

Yechezkel was breathing hard. Landing this aircraft wouldn't be easy. The 767 was enormous, and the technique, while similar in some ways, was very different from the smaller planes he had learned on.

"Do you see the flaps lever?"

Yechezkel peered at the instrument panel. "Yes."

"Push it to 25."

"Done," Yechezkel reported, as he slid the lever into place.

"Okay, now try to keep your height steady at one thousand feet. We'll wait until you come in a bit closer. You'll start descending in a few minutes."

Yechezkel listened intently, following the pilot's orders exactly as the plane continued to lose altitude. Within ten minutes, the plane's wheels touched ground.

"Slam on the brakes!" Stewart screamed.

"I am!" Yechezkel shouted back. He was panting from the effort of pressing on the brakes to stop the plane as it raced along the runway. He could see the end of the runway looming ahead of him. A few moments ago, he had looked forward to death. Now, his only desire was to live.

"Pull up the throttle, throw the engine in reverse and then hit the switches!"

Yechezkel quickly complied. The plane shuddered as it came to a stop, just inches away from the end of the runway.

Thirteen

The journalists had been arriving since early that morning, ever since the news had broken about the attacks on the Twin Towers. The club was crowded and the air was thick and heavy, filled with a combination of cigarette smoke and human sweat. The reporters working for the smaller papers crowded around the more experienced and influential journalists, the ones with the right government connections, who usually managed to access classified information.

The club served the journalists working in the American capital, and it had become a marketplace for information, similar to the stock exchange. It was common to see reporters arguing over the price of an exclusive scoop. The price, of course, was never monetary. One news report was exchanged for another with a similar value. To give the club a marketplace atmosphere, the owners had set up a huge screen in the center of the room, which was almost identical to the screens used in the New York stock exchange. Here, however, the screen was constantly transmitting worldwide news reports.

Within the confines of the club, international borders ceased to exist. Deals were made between impossible partners. A stranger would be astonished to find reporters from communist countries such as China and its satellites huddled in a corner exchanging information with a reporter from the *New York Times* or *Newsweek*, considered a banner of Western capitalism. Reporters from the various news agencies were constantly walking around, trying to pick up interesting tidbits of information.

The Beehive—that was the name the reporters used for their meeting place. From early morning until the late hours of the night, the Beehive was teeming with activity.

"Osama bin Laden was behind the attacks," one of the American reporters whispered, as he watched the second tower collapse on the enormous screen. "He'll have to pay for this."

For many of the reporters in the club, however, the tower's collapse was of minor importance. Earlier they had faced death squarely in the face—with a full view of the diving aircraft that had nearly ended all their lives.

Many of them had been on the White House lawn earlier that morning, soon after they had heard about the attack on the Twin Towers. They had been waiting for a White House representative to notify them of the government's official response and what actions would be taken. Suddenly an enormous plane had appeared, flying at a low altitude directly toward the White House. The noise had been deafening. There was no doubt that the plane was about to crash into the White House and that they would become the next victims.

At the last moment, the plane veered sharply upward and flew away, just missing the roof of the White House. Why had the pilot decided to change his course at the last second? Had the passengers gained control of the hijackers? What was going on?

A few minutes later, secret service agents had ordered minibuses to escort the reporters back to the Beehive. As the reporters left, they could see that two F-16s had been brought in to defend the White House. On their way back to the Beehive, they tried unsuccessfully to contact their offices. All their cell phones had stopped working. There was no way for them to report about the airplane that had barely missed crashing into the White House.

Inside the Beehive, dozens of FBI agents were standing there, preventing anyone from touching a telephone. Other FBI agents guarded the exits. They spent the time listening intently to every announcement that was made by the FAA, expecting to hear some mention of the plane that had almost plowed into the White House. But the television stations continued reporting on the two attacks without mentioning the incident.

The broadcast stopped abruptly. In a dramatic voice, the announcer stated, "A White House spokesman will soon appear to make an official statement to the media." The camera focused on the front lawn of the White House. The President's personal spokesman appeared on the screen.

"The President has been informed that the United States was attacked. The President is not able to respond personally, since according to emergency regulations he is presently in a secure location. The President has requested that I inform the nation that the authorities are in control of the situation, and that within the next few hours he will personally speak with the nation."

The announcer came back with a new development. "We have just been informed that a plane has crashed outside of Pittsburgh, Pennsylvania. Authorities assume that the plane was on its way to crash into the White House."

"That's a lie," whispered several of the journalists who were avidly watching the broadcast. They knew that there had been a completely different airplane which had nearly successfully destroyed the White House.

"Another possibility is that their target was the nuclear reactor located just outside Harrisburg, Pennsylvania," the announcer went on. "It appears that at some point the passengers revolted and succeeded in overwhelming the hijackers. They were unable to navigate the plane properly, and it crashed."

"Blah blah blah." William Clingford made a crooked face and laughed as he spilled his whiskey to the floor. William was the head of the *Time* magazine team of reporters who worked in Washington. He was a well-known journalist, and the other reporters trusted him. "Don't they realize that we ourselves saw the pilot heading straight into the White House?" he muttered angrily

William took a packet of cigarettes out of his front coat pocket. He was so upset that he completely forgot that he had been bragging to everyone he knew that he had decided to stop smoking.

The Beehive suddenly became quiet. Dozens of conservatively dressed men appeared and dispersed among the reporters. It was obvious that they were secret service agents, and that an important person was expected to show up soon. It took just a few minutes for the agents to take control of the entire room. Each one had a tiny earphone in one ear; their hands grasped their weapons, and it was clear that they were prepared to shoot at a moment's notice.

The reporters instinctively turned around to face the main door. Their mouths dropped open when they saw the Secretary of Defense standing there.

The Defense Secretary walked to the bar in the middle of the room, which was slightly raised above the rest of the hall. Deep worry lines had appeared on his face.

"Do you recall a time when such an important government official came here to speak with us?" the reporters whispered among themselves.

The Secretary of Defense banged a spoon against one of the crystal glasses on the counter in an attempt to quiet the crowd. "I understand that you have questions concerning the plane that crashed outside of Pittsburgh."

From every corner, he saw the reporters nodding their heads.

"You have every right not to accept the announcement," he said with the twinge of a smile. He realized that he now had their full attention. "The announcement was false," he continued.

"Are you telling us the government lied? And you're admitting it?" William Clingford's voice rose above the crowd.

The Secretary of Defense raised his voice and lifted his hands for quiet. "I ask you to work with us to keep silent about what actually happened near the White House this morning. For the interests of the United States—in fact, for the sake of the entire world—it is important that the public thinks that the story is true."

He paused again to observe the audience's reaction.

"I am turning to you, this time, for the sake of humanity." There was a trace of supplication in his voice. "Help us convince the world that the story is true, that this is what really happened to the plane that was on its way to crash into the White House."

The reporters' natural rebellious instincts were held in check. They realized that this situation was different. There was something much more important at stake than an exclusive news scoop.

"We still don't have exact numbers for the number of people injured in the Twin Towers," the Secretary continued in a confidential tone. "We have no doubt, however, that there are thousands of victims. Yes, thousands. The United States and the free world received a hard blow this morning. We have no idea what lies ahead of us, and I am asking that you do as I have requested."

The audience remained silent. This was the first time that they had been asked to keep their mouths shut. In the overwhelming silence, the Secretary continued in a clear voice, "I meant what I said. I want everyone here to give me his word."

In one voice, the men in the audience replied, "We give you our word. We promise."

The Secretary's eyes widened for a moment. He was clearly both surprised and touched by the spontaneous show of support by this sector, which stood at the helm of the freedom of the press.

"May G-d bless America and the free world," he declared, then turned and left the club.

Dozens of civilian cars followed the Boeing plane as it sped past the point on the runway where it was supposed to have come to a stop. The plane finally screeched to a halt right before the end of the runway, and the cars drove up quickly, surrounding it on all sides. Policemen dressed in civilian clothes, armed with automatic weapons, jumped out of their cars and quickly took cover behind them.

"Okay, the landing was a success," Jim Stewart said into the microphone. "I am handing the transmission over to the regional FBI agent."

There was no reply from inside the plane.

"Do you hear me?" he asked anxiously.

Again, there was no reply.

"Something's going on in there," Stewart pointed out to the FBI agent.

"I can see that myself," the FBI agent replied. He quickly picked up the phone and dialed a number. It was the personal phone number of the FBI director.

"There may be a problem here," the agent began.

"What's going on?" the director asked.

The director sounded tense, and for good reason. Everyone realized that once the initial shock dissipated, the public would point an accusatory finger at the FBI, CIA and every other organization involved with national security. The FBI director, who stood at the helm of the main organization in charge of the United State's security, would be mercilessly grilled for his part in allowing these attacks to take place on American soil.

"There's no reply from the airplane," the agent explained. "The hijackers stopped cooperating after the plane landed."

"What do they want? Why did they switch tactics? They got everything they requested," the FBI's director wondered aloud.

"It's possible that this is just another camouflage tactic," the agent suggested. "The hijacker wants us to be busy with this plane, so another one of bin Laden's units can work undisturbed."

The director thought about that. It did make sense. That was exactly the way bin Laden operated. He always tried to hit where least expected. But what could he be after now? They had almost destroyed the White House. The President was not there at the time, but how could they have known that?

The director knew that at the moment, the President was in midflight. He was on Air Force One, his personal plane. Perhaps they had prepared some type of ambush for the President's plane? That would be easy for them to accomplish when the entire security system was concentrating on the airplane that had just landed.

"Keep trying to communicate with them," he said finally. "I'll be back in another few minutes with instructions on how to continue."

As the agent on the scene continued to try to get through to the airplane, the director looked up Thomas Glickman's number, the officer in charge of the President's personal security.

"Where is the President right now?" the director asked.

Glickman didn't like the sound of the director's voice. "What's the matter?" Glickman demanded. "If there's a threat to the President's life, I need to know now."

"Answer my question first," the director countered.

"He's on Air Force One."

"Oh, that's great," the director snapped.

Glickman forced himself to stay calm. "If the President is in danger, it's important for me to know about it."

"Yes, you're right. Okay, here's what I think. I suspect there is a danger that a terrorist will try to crash into the President's plane. I suggest that we immediately change the plane's course."

"Obviously," Glickman answered. "I will contact the pilot on Air Force One and tell him to change course immediately."

"Another thing," the director interrupted him. "Keep the change a secret. Ask them to keep radio silence."

"Of course." Glickman hung up.

The President's plane, which was flying near Virginia, made a sharp turn. Instead of flying toward Washington, the plane headed toward the Texas-Louisiana border. The pilot closed all radar location markers and the plane disappeared from the radar screens in the navigation towers. The army assisted him in navigating the plane through a satellite connection.

About an hour later, the plane landed in a secret Army base in the heart of Louisiana. The President was rushed to an underground bunker. Only then were his security forces able to breathe a sigh of relief.

Fourteen

Loud banging could be heard on the cockpit's doors, together with screams of *"Eftach el bab*, open the door!"

The moment the plane touched ground, the two hijackers guarding the passengers realized that the plan had failed. They wondered if their comrades had betrayed them and changed the plane's course, or if someone had succeeded in entering the cockpit without their knowledge and had overcome the two hijackers. The hijackers in the passenger department discussed the problem in whispers and decided to take the risk of only one hijacker guarding the passengers while the other went to find out what was going on inside the cockpit.

Yosef was standing behind the door, grasping the Swiss Commando knife that he had managed to smuggle onto the plane. He was planning to surprise the other hijacker. Yechezkel continued slamming on the brakes with all his might. His hands were shaking from trying to keep the plane on course.

As the plane jerked to a stop, Yosef was thrown against the door, and from there back into the co-pilot seat.

The banging outside also stopped. Yosef realized that the other hijacker had been thrown by the sudden stop. Yechezkel quickly got up from his seat and raced to the door to assist his brother. Meanwhile, Yosef had returned to his post behind the door. The two men were ready to surprise the other hijackers the moment they broke into the cockpit.

It wasn't long before the inevitable occurred. They could hear the two hijackers speaking in a heavily accented English. Although they did not understand what was said, they realized that the two hijackers outside were threatening the passengers, explaining that if they tried to do anything suspicious, they would explode a bomb and destroy the entire plane. They had practiced this tactic often in the al Qaeda training camp. "Show them an imitation hand grenade, attached to some type of a mysterious instrument, and then threaten to blow up the plane if anyone tries to stop you," their teacher had taught them. Every step of the hijackers' behavior was as expected.

They could hear calls through the radio. The brothers knew that the officials outside would be wondering why they weren't responding. They refrained from answering because they didn't want the hijackers on the other side of the door to hear them, find out their exact location, and attack in that direction.

Yechezkel looked fearfully at the flashing lights of the police cars and fire trucks that surrounded the plane on all sides. He saw Army jeeps racing toward them. They might break into the plane at any moment, and if that happened, all his hopes would be dashed. The government would claim that the hijackers had not delivered the plane peacefully to them.

"We must contact the navigation tower immediately to tell them what's going on, before the rescue teams break into the plane," he hissed at Yosef.

The banging was now coming from two places on the door. That meant that the second hijacker had joined his friend in trying to break into the cockpit.

Yechezkel smiled. He had an idea on how to extricate himself from this situation.

"Okay, you can enter the plane," the FBI agent finally heard over the radio.

The supervisor raised his hand and made a "V" for victory sign. "We've regained contact!" he yelled, as he grabbed the microphone. The senior FBI agents standing around him were anxiously waiting to hear the conversation.

"I'm going to transfer you to someone from the FBI," the supervisor reported.

One of the federal agents stood up. Greg Miller was a senior member of the FBI's hostage rescue team. His training included a special emphasis on hostage rescue through negotiation. Miller had already spoken with the FBI director to get the full picture, and he was prepared to deal with the terrorists aboard the aircraft.

Miller's coworkers moved to the side to let him sit down next to the radio. He took the microphone in both hands and paused for a few moments to gather his thoughts.

"This is Greg Miller," he finally said. "Why did you wait until now to respond?"

"Because I had a difficult problem on my hands, and I had to take care of it," the hijacker calmly explained. "The other two hijackers were not willing to surrender, so we had to overcome their resistance before we could respond to your transmissions."

"So why didn't you respond to our attempts at contacting you?" Miller asked.

"We were located in the cockpit while they were in the passenger section. As soon as they discovered that we had betrayed them, they tried to break into the cockpit. If we had responded to your transmissions, they would have known our exact location. It was impossible for us to leave our posts to get to the microphone."

"I see you were taught to be cautious," was Miller's carefully worded response. Although the hijacker's story made sense, Miller was afraid that this might be a trap. He knew that he had to come up with a plan to gain control of the plane without endangering agents' lives.

"I'm about to bring the mobile staircase up to the plane's door. Will you allow the passengers to disembark before you, and before my agents board the plane?"

"Of course," the hijacker replied. "Don't we have an agreement between us that we won't be punished, and that you will cooperate in helping me find out what happened to my parents? Am I correct?"

"That's correct," Miller responded immediately, trying to reassure the hijacker.

"Don't worry. I'm not relying on your promises," the hijacker retorted. "I have valuable information about the terrorist organization that I know you'll be willing to pay for."

"We are anxiously waiting for the opportunity to hear about it," was Miller's candid reply.

Miller picked up the intercom and instructed the workers to drive the mobile staircase so it would be flush with the plane's door. He left the radio open so the hijackers could listen to his instructions. He didn't want to surprise them.

Using army binoculars, the people in the navigation tower watched as the mobile staircase slowly approached the plane. The truck moving the staircase was surrounded by a small group of FBI agents, which included members of the hostage rescue team who were trained in fighting terrorists.

The driver was so terrified that he was barely able to maneuver the staircase properly. The moment the stairs were in place, the plane's door opened and one of the stewards appeared in the doorway. Within seconds, a wave of passengers rushed to leave the plane as quickly as possible. The two stewards standing on either side of the door urged the passengers to be careful as they made their way down the steps.

Miller counted the passengers as they disembarked. Seventy-six passengers walked down the steps. That meant that there were four passengers missing. Muller assumed that they were the hijackers. After the passengers were all safely off the plane, the crew started to disembark. Six flight attendants and two pilots left the plane.

Two gray buses with "United Airlines" printed across the side drove up next to the plane and opened their doors wide. The passengers were the first to board. The crew was just about to climb onto the bus when a small car pulled up and an FBI agent jumped out and ran over to them. He requested that the two pilots and the head steward join him in the car. They sped away even before the pilot had a chance to close the back door.

"Are you positive that no one, except the hijackers, is left on the plane?" the agent in the car asked.

"Definitely," the head steward replied. "We were the last ones to disembark. Before I left, I checked to make sure that we didn't leave anyone behind."

"Good," the FBI agent responded. He turned to the pilot. "Are you positive that there were no explosives planted on the plane?"

The pilot shrugged. "No one placed any explosives after the plane was hijacked, at least not that I could see. They claimed they had placed explosives on board prior to takeoff, but I don't think it's true. I can't tell you for sure, though."

The agent nodded. "Good enough. I think we'll have to chance it." He spoke into his radio. "Everything seems clear."

"Move it!" Greg Miller ordered the hostage team.

Dozens of FBI agents wearing protective gear dashed onto the plane. Another half dozen agents stood just outside the door, ready to enter at a moment's notice.

"Halt!" someone yelled from inside the plane.

The agents standing outside trained their weapons on the plane's door. Two swarthy young men appeared in the doorway with their hands raised high above their heads. Four of the agents standing outside jumped on them and threw them to the floor, while two other agents stood with their guns trained on the terrorists. The four agents quickly tied the terrorists' hands behind their backs and then frisked them for concealed weapons. Once they were sure that they were not hiding anything suspicious, they assisted them in standing up and guided them down the stairs.

"That's two of them," Miller noted. "There should be two more."

A few seconds later, the agent in charge and his assistant appeared in the doorway, dragging the other two hijackers by their feet. Miller could see that the hijackers' hands and feet were tied.

"The first two must be the ones we negotiated with," he commented. "They somehow managed to tie up the other two."

It took just three minutes from the moment that the first agents had entered the plane before the agent in charge announced that the plane was empty. A few minutes later, a unit of Federal agents, together with trained dogs, entered the plane to check for hidden explosives.

Within thirty minutes they had determined that the plane was not booby-trapped, and that all the hijackers were in police custody. The passengers were released two hours later.

Before allowing them to return home, the assistant director of the FBI told them about the tragic events that had occurred earlier. He let them know how lucky they were to have survived. He concluded his speech with a heartfelt request that for the sake of national security, the passengers should refrain from telling others about their experience. "Only then will we succeed in taking revenge against the hijackers and the evil people who sent them."

The assistant director could see from the expressions on the passengers' faces that they would keep the story quiet. He realized that it might leak out, but he was relying on the promise that the Secretary of Defense had received from the members of the press to keep this entire episode a secret.

After walking out of the airport, one of the passengers—a dark, swarthy man carrying a Portuguese passport—decided to make a phone call. He walked to a public telephone and placed three coins in the slot before dialing a number.

"The pilots rebelled," he whispered.

"Are you sure?"

"Yes. The two hijackers who were guarding the passengers tried to regain control of the plane, but they were not successful."

"Contact me again in another half hour. By then, I should be able to instruct you on how to proceed."

Osama bin Laden left his private office and returned to the communications center. The men had mostly dispersed, though there were still a number of them watching the television screens and enjoying the sight of the Twin Towers tumbling to the ground, over and over again.

They stood in respect as bin Laden entered the room, but he ignored them. He made his way to the short wave radio that was installed near the bank of television screens. A radio operator was on duty at all times.

"Get me al Zawahiri," he ordered the young man on duty.

Ayman al Zawahiri was bin Laden's second in command. The two had met during the Afghan war in the 1980's, and they had soon discovered that they shared a dream of a strong, united Islamic world.

Al Zawahiri was currently in the military camp, two hours from command headquarters in the Tora Bora Mountains. Bin Laden was afraid of using satellite phones in his headquarters, since he knew they could be traced. He preferred directing all phone calls through al Zawahiri in the camp, and then relayed to him via radio, so his location would remain a secret.

"Do you have information on the fifth plane?" bin Laden asked tersely, as soon as he heard al Zawahiri's voice.

"Yes." The transmission crackled with static. "I have just received information from my sources in Washington that the plane has landed in Ronald Reagan National Airport, not far from the White House,"

"Do you know what happened?"

"The brothers rebelled."

Bin Laden hissed in anger and hatred. "Those Jews betrayed us ..."

It was several minutes before he was able to compose himself and continue speaking. "Did you contact our cell in Los Angeles?"

"Yes. I was just speaking with the leader of the cell. He told me that Rachamim and his wife have panicked. They left everything and ran away," al Zawahiri replied.

"Are you trying to tell me that they disappeared?" Bin Laden was furious. "Who keeps on trying to destroy my plans?"

"Don't worry. They ran away, but they did not disappear," al Zawahiri said reassuringly. "The members of the cell are carefully observing their every move."

Bin Laden was reassured. "Where are they trying to escape to?" he asked.

"Nowhere in particular. They seem to be driving around Los Angeles without any particular direction or goal."

"Tell the cell to watch them closely. At some point those traitors will discover that their parents are still alive and then they will start searching for them." Bin Laden's eyes sparkled with an unexplained emotion. "The day will come when those Jews will serve me again. And this time, there will be no opportunity for them to escape."

"Is there anything else you need me to do?" al Zawahiri asked.

Bin Laden paused a moment. "Yes," he said finally. "I need you here. I need your help to implement the next part of my plan. Call the cell leader, and then get ready. I'll send someone down for you."

As al Zawahiri signed off, bin Laden turned to Abu Salim, who was standing silently next to him. "Drive to the training camp and bring al Zawahiri back immediately," he ordered.

Abu Salim hurried out of command headquarters. The moment he stepped outside, his driver and personal bodyguards jumped to attention.

"Take me to the military camp," he ordered.

The driver took his seat behind the steering wheel in the latest model Land Rover, purchased by the generous proceeds of the bin Laden family business. Abu Salim sat down in the middle, while his two bodyguards, their machine guns poised, took their positions behind him.

The main camp was located about thirty miles south of headquarters—not that far in distance, but a long drive along the winding mountain roads. After a two hour wild drive along narrow, curving pathways in the Tora Bora Mountains, Abu Salim arrived at the camp's front gate. The guards recognized him and jumped to attention.

"I have to see al Zawahiri urgently," Abu Salim rapidly explained. They guided him to the back section of the camp, where al Zawahiri was, as usual, delivering a fiery speech to a group of new recruits.

The moment al Zawahiri saw Abu Salim, he started winding down his speech. Abu Salim leaned against the spiked fence that surrounded the base and listened patiently.

Within ten minutes of Abu Salim's arrival, al Zawahiri was comfortably seated in the Land Rover on the way to bin Laden's headquarters. The two men found themselves staring at the high mountain cliffs that surrounded them on all sides. Today they seemed threatening. The cliffs, so often their protectors, could easily turn into deathtraps.

As they rounded the mountain, two armed guards jumped in front of their Land Rover with drawn machine guns. The driver jammed on the brakes, and the car started to skid in the slippery mud. The moment the guards recognized the passengers they gestured for them to continue.

They drove in silence for the next few minutes. A few hundred feet later, the driver stopped in front of a steep mountain that looked identical to the surrounding mountains. They could hear a motor humming and patiently watched the mountain begin to split open.

When the opening was wide enough for a car to enter, the driver pressed on the accelerator and began navigating the twisting road leading down into the bowels of the earth.

The men were shivering from the drastic change in temperature, from the searing heat outside to the cool dampness underground. They eventually arrived at an underground parking lot. The driver parked the car and remained seated with the two passengers.

Within seconds, a group of bearded guards armed with submachine guns surrounded the car on all sides. Once they were certain of the passengers' identities, they guided them through one of the surrounding doorways and into a room lined with benches. The two men were familiar with their leader's headquarters. The commanding guard instructed Abu Salim to take a seat on one of the benches and wait. He asked al Zawahiri to accompany him.

The guard guided al Zawahiri through a narrow hallway into bin Laden's personal headquarters. Just in front of the door, the guard stopped. "You'll have to continue without me," he told al Zawahiri.

Al Zawahiri knocked on the door.

The door opened immediately. Bin Laden was standing there, waiting expectantly for him. Al Zawahiri felt uncomfortable. Bin Laden's face was lined with wrinkles, and he appeared to be extremely worried.

"Please, come inside," bin Laden invited him. He guided al Zawahiri to a set of plush cushions placed in a semicircle on the colorful Persian carpet and instructed him to take a seat. Once al Zawahiri was seated, he went over to the small kitchenette on the opposite wall and prepared two cups of strong Turkish coffee.

Al Zawahiri felt even more uncomfortable as bin Laden's towering figure bent over to serve him his coffee. Bin Laden settled down on the cushion opposite him and tucked his feet beneath him as he slowly started sipping his boiling brew. "Just the way I like it," he commented, "bitter and strong."

Al Zawahiri personally did not enjoy bitter coffee, but he was too polite to say so. He slowly turned the cup from side to side as if waiting for it to cool down a bit.

"The operation in the United States was only fifty percent successful," bin Laden reported, before taking another sip of the bitter brew.

"Why only fifty percent?" al Zawahiri asked. "In my opinion, it was a total success. It will take a long time before the Americans recover from the blow they received this morning. They'll remember us forever."

Al Zawahiri considered himself somewhat of an expert in military analysis and continued speaking enthusiastically. "There's one iron rule, and that is that no action will ever be one hundred percent successful. It is our duty to plan a variety of operations in the assumption that only a few will succeed. For that reason, we planned five terrorist attacks for September 11, hoping that one would be successful. So in reality, we were much more successful than we had expected. We managed to strike three lethal blows to the very heart of the United States."

"But what about the White House? That was our main goal."

"Yes, I am well aware that the White House was high on your list of priorities, and that was one of the reasons that I put such effort into assuring its success." *That was also the reason that I opposed sending the two Jewish brothers on that mission,* al Zawahiri thought to himself. But bin Laden had insisted.

"You're right about that," bin Laden admitted. "I can't blame you for the failure. It was completely my decision to send the two brothers, and I take full responsibility."

There was a short silence. "Still, even without the White House, the mission was by all counts a huge success," al Zawahiri went on. "We have struck a blow at America—"

"You said that before," bin Laden interrupted him. "The problem is that since the President was not killed, the United States is able to respond quickly. They will be attacking us soon, unless we come up with a way to stop them."

Al Zawahiri leaned forward in interest. It was clear that bin Laden had a plan in mind.

"Fortunately, I already considered this possibility," bin Laden went on. "I have a backup plan prepared. And as I said to you before, this time the brothers will not be able to avoid helping us succeed."

"So, what is the plan?" al Zawahiri asked.

Bin Laden rose to his feet. "Come, I will show you."

Fifteen

They had spent the last few hours aimlessly circling the streets of Los Angeles. Naomi had adamantly refused to return home, but with the airport closed, there really wasn't anywhere for them to go. She had been content to stay in the car and keep moving—even though they had no destination in mind—and Rachamim had reluctantly agreed.

As the sun began to set, Rachamim noticed that his gas gauge was almost on zero. "We have to stop in a gas station," Rachamim pointed out to Naomi, who was lost in her own private world.

"Are you sure?"

The question made him smile. "Yes. I think the car will refuse to travel any longer if it doesn't get some fuel."

"Oh." Naomi realized that she had asked a silly question. "So stop at the nearest gas station."

Rachamim got off at the closest exit. He had no idea where they were. He decided to look for a hotel where they could spend the night. Naomi would not allow him to return home.

He was shocked by the prices in the gas station. Two dollars for a gallon of gas? He never paid more than a dollar fifty. He pointed that out to the attendant who filled the tank.

"You're in Beverly Hills," the attendant retorted, "the most expensive place on earth. If you count your pennies, you can be sure that you don't belong here."

Rachamim had driven into the luxurious area where the movie stars made their homes. He wouldn't stay a moment longer than necessary.

He waited for the attendant to finish and then handed him a twenty-dollar bill.

"That's not enough, sir," the attendant retorted. "The bill came out to twenty-three dollars."

"Twenty-three dollars?" Rachamim shook his head in disbelief. He quickly handed the attendant another three dollars and drove away.

Naomi remained indifferent as Rachamim studied the street signs, trying to find his way out of the neighborhood. Once they were back on the freeway, he started to feel comfortable again. He kept glancing at the billboards, looking for a hotel where they could spend the night. He saw an advertisement for a Holiday Inn and took the exit leading to the hotel.

"We'll spend the night here," he said as he parked opposite the entrance and went inside to register. Naomi waited for him in the car.

The reception clerk examined his driver's license carefully. It was obvious that he felt extremely uncomfortable about something. He walked slowly back to the counter after Rachamim finished filling out the hotel's registration form and carefully checked all the details against Rachamim's driver's license. Only after he was sure that they matched was he willing to accept the credit card.

It looked as though the clerk was expecting the credit card company to refuse to honor Rachamim's card. But the company accepted it. He gave them a room on the top floor, room 319.

Rachamim tried to laugh it off as he left the lobby. "My dark complexion makes me suspect wherever I go," he told Naomi as he sat back down in the driver's seat. "He gave us a room on the third floor. He probably thought that in that way, I'll only explode the top floor and leave the rest of the hotel intact."

Rachamim brought the car right up to the hotel entrance and opened the trunk. "Can you help me bring our stuff upstairs?" he asked Naomi.

He took out a small overnight case and some of the food that Naomi had packed. Naomi took the smallest suitcase and started walking towards the hotel entrance, while he walked after her.

The reception clerk was speaking on the telephone. From the way he was gesturing, Rachamim realized that he was excitedly trying to describe something.

The clerk's conversation came to a sudden halt the moment the automatic doors opened. Rachamim noticed the clerk hurriedly whisper something into the telephone before he stopped talking. He just held the receiver close to his ear. The clerk had probably alerted someone to check out the suspicious characters who had checked into the hotel for the night.

By now Rachamim was getting angry. He had suffered enough from Islamist extremists during his life. Now others were lumping him together with the terrorists. It seemed completely unfair.

"Let's go up to our room already," Naomi pleaded with him. Apparently she, too, had noticed the uncomfortable atmosphere.

Naomi securely locked the door to their room. Only then did she feel safe enough to take out the food that she had packed earlier that morning. They were both hungry—they hadn't eaten the entire day. While Naomi prepared the meal, Rachamim stood up to *daven maariv*.

He had just finished *davening shemoneh esrei* when someone knocked on the door. Naomi was so startled that she dropped the can of corn she was holding and the kernels spilled all over the floor.

"Open the door. It's the FBI," a voice ordered.

Rachamim looked out the peekhole and saw two men standing outside. They knew that he was looking at them. One of them held up a plastic card. Rachamim could see the FBI logo on the card. The suspicious reception clerk had probably alerted the FBI.

"It's the FBI," he told Naomi. She was shivering in fright. The color drained from her face as he opened the door.

"Good evening, Mr. Roji," the agent standing to his left began. "Can we come in and speak with you?"

"Please," Rachamim replied with exaggerated friendliness, moving aside to allow the two men to enter.

The men entered the room but remained in front of the door, with their hands in their pockets. They stayed in that position for several minutes, examining the hotel room until they were certain that it was safe to step inside. There were two chairs and a small table in the room. Rachamim gestured the men to the chairs, while he and Naomi sat opposite them on the bed.

"Mr. Roji," one of them began, "don't you live in Los Angeles?"

"Yes. I live in Los Angeles," Rachamim replied. He anticipated the next question.

"Why did you leave your home and come to a hotel that is only eight miles away from where you live?"

Rachamim was startled. He had no idea that the hotel was located so close to his own home. It really did appear strange, and he did not have a logical explanation. He recalled that according to American law, he had the right to remain silent if there was no lawyer present, and he decided to take advantage of that right. "You forgot to remind me of my rights."

"No, we didn't forget," the agent responded. "This is not an interrogation. You could call it a clarification." The agent's expression changed from friendly to threatening. "Another thing. Even if this could be classified as an interrogation, we have every right to interrogate you without a lawyer present. The right to remain silent is for criminal acts during normal times. America is being threatened, and the President has declared a state of emergency. This interrogation is considered a matter of national security, and you have no right to remain silent."

"Do you suspect that I had something to do with the terror attacks that took place this morning?" Rachamim demanded.

"No, no," the agent said soothingly. He flashed an artificial smile. "But we must check anything that appears unusual. You must agree that your behavior is rather unusual. So please, answer the questions. Why did you leave your home to spend the night in a hotel located just a few miles away from your house?"

Rachamim opened his mouth to reply. But he stopped short. He knew that the moment he told the agents about Jamil's warning, Jamil would be in trouble with the law. What should he do?

"What were you about to say, Rachamim?" the agent asked, trying to encourage him. "Is it all right if I call you by your first name?" he politely added.

"Of course," Rachamim replied.

"My name's Harry," the agent continued, apparently trying to put Rachamim at ease. "So now, Rachamim, could you please tell me what caused you to circle the city the entire day and at the end check into a hotel just a few miles away from where you live?"

"I was warned this morning that I had better leave my house quickly," Rachamim admitted.

The agent's eyes grew big. He sensed that he had touched on dynamite.

"Did I hear you correctly? Someone warned you to leave your home?"

"Yes, that's what I said," Rachamim confirmed.

"Who warned you to leave?"

Rachamim had to swallow several times before he could reply. "The man's first name is Jamil."

"Who is Jamil? How are you connected to him? And why do you trust him?"

"Jamil saved my life when I escaped from Iran. The helicopter that was taking us across the border crashed. Jamil found us in the rubble, hovering between life and death. He brought us home and nursed us back to health until we were strong enough to immigrate to the United States. I arranged for Jamil to come with us."

"So you owe this Jamil a large personal debt for having saved your life," Harry noted.

"That's right!" Rachamim stood up in sudden agitation. "I don't want to talk about it anymore. I refuse to continue speaking without a lawyer's presence."

"Rachamim," Harry responded, trying to appease him. "I repeat, this is not an interrogation." He placed his hand on Rachamim's shoulder and guided him back to the armchair. He pulled up a chair next to him and started speaking in a low, soothing voice. "We have no reason to suspect you of having anything to do with those evil people who stuck a knife in the American people. You yourself admit, however, that after this morning's events, we must examine every possible avenue to discover who was behind these attacks." The agent looked directly into Rachamim's eyes, and saw that he was nodding in agreement.

"You also agree with me that the man who saved you so many years ago was behaving very strangely this morning. The fact that he told you to run away from the area just a few hours before the tragic attack took place is begging for an explanation," he continued.

The agent waited for Rachamim to nod again, but Rachamim refrained. He couldn't agree with a negative opinion of the person who had saved his life so many years ago. Yet at the same time, he could not refute their suspicions, especially since he had the same concerns.

"I know you owe Jamil a great debt. But you also owe something to your country. It's very important that we find Jamil as soon as possible."

Rachamim closed his eyes. He had no idea what he should do. On one hand, he owed his life to Jamil. If he were to inform on Jamil, they would arrest him, and since he was illegally living in the country, the government could imprison him without trial. At best, they would send him back to Turkey. But at the same time, Rachamim realized that it was in the country's interest to find Jamil as quickly as possible.

"Approximately six thousand people were killed today in the World Trade Center," the agent continued. "It is assumed that approximately two hundred people were murdered in the attack on the Pentagon. Who knows what else they are planning? It's very possible that every minute you refrain from handing over this information, you are allowing the terrorists to continue working on their next attack."

Rachamim was convinced. "He's in charge of our synagogue building's upkeep, and he sometimes sleeps in the back room there. But I doubt if he's there now."

The two agents started walking toward the door. Before leaving, one of them handed Rachamim a white business card. "Try to contact me if you have any additional information."

Rachamim stuffed the card into his inner pocket.

"Don't lose that card," the agent cautioned him. "I have a feeling that you will need my assistance. If that happens, don't hesitate to call the number that's on the bottom of the card. Tell the secretary your name and I'll make myself available for you."

With those words, the agents left and closed the door behind them.

Rachamim removed the business card from his pocket. It was made of cheap government paper. The agent's name—Harold Clark—was written in the right hand corner. To the left of his name was the FBI insignia, and underneath the insignia were the words, "Anti-terrorist Department."

Rachamim was tempted to throw the card into the garbage. But an inner voice told him not to. For some reason, he sensed that the agent's words were true. He would still need his assistance some day. His hand was trembling as he placed the card back in his pocket.

Sixteen

Bin Laden carefully pulled himself up to a standing position. He strode to the far end of the room and lifted the end of the rug. "Come here," he beckoned to al Zawahiri, who followed him curiously.

In the floor beneath the rug was the outline of what was clearly a trapdoor. Bin Laden felt along the side, and the trapdoor sprang open. The opening of the door must have also served as a light switch, because a dim bulb in the cavity beneath the floor began to glow.

Al Zawahiri peered into the hole. He could see a long, pointed object. To al Zawahiri, it looked like an American Mark 84 missile.

"What are you planning to do with that missile?" al Zawahiri asked in puzzlement. The American Mark 84 was very popular and was usually dropped by aircraft on various targets. It had been used throughout Operation Desert Storm in Iraq. But the missile, weighing around 2,000 pounds, was not that useful for terrorist operations—it was too difficult to hide and transport.

"This isn't what you think it is." Bin Laden pointed to the missile. "Look carefully, and you'll see some differences. It uses the same launching system as the Mark 84, but inside, it contains less than twenty pounds of something very, very powerful."

A chill gripped al Zawahiri's heart. "What is it?" he asked, his voice dropping to a whisper.

Bin Laden looked at him, a gleam of excitement in his eyes. "Plutonium," he said quietly.

Al Zawahiri instinctively backed away from the bomb. It was difficult to imagine how such a small piece of metal could cause such tremendous damage. He wondered what would happen if, as a result of some technical problem, the missile were to explode now. Although he had spent most of his life inciting young men to become martyrs for the sake of Jihad, he personally had no desire to sacrifice his life for the holy cause.

"How long ..." He cleared his throat. "How long has this missile been here?"

"Just over a year."

"You never said a word to me about it!" al Zawahiri exclaimed. "Last year you met with that Pakistani nuclear scientist, Sultan Bashiruddin Mahmoud. But you told me that he couldn't help you."

"Yes, I know I told you that," bin Laden said calmly. "I wanted to keep this secret. In fact, he was very helpful. Through his contacts I was able to obtain nuclear material that had been stolen from Uzbekistan, where the Soviets used to manufacture their weapons."

Al Zawahiri swallowed hard. "So why did you decide to say something now?" he finally asked.

"Because I will soon be getting rid of it," bin Laden responded.

"Where will it be going?" al Zawahiri asked.

Bin Laden smiled "How about Los Angeles?"

"You don't mean ..."

Al Zawahiri couldn't complete the sentence. This bomb contained sufficient explosives to destroy the entire city and kill the millions of people residing there. Was bin Laden capable of pulling it off? Had he considered how the United States would react to such an attack?

"Yes. I am planning to use it against the city of Los Angeles," bin Laden confirmed. His eyes were shining with an inner glow.

Al Zawahiri knew that bin Laden was serious—dead serious. He wondered what would happen to Afghanistan after the attack. Surely the Americans would retaliate and flatten the country with their atomic arsenal.

"So what do you think?" bin Laden broke the silence. He could see that al Zawahiri was frightened, but he also knew that eventually he would put his personal fear aside. The moment he recovered from his initial shock, he would regain his usual enthusiasm.

"How are you planning to bring the bomb into the United States?"

al Zawahiri asked quietly, struggling to recover his composure. "By boat? That will take a long time."

Bin Laden smiled. That was exactly how he had expected al Zawahiri to react. After recovering from his initial fright, he had resumed his role as military strategist. "I can be patient when I need to be," bin Laden told him. "But those traitorous Jews have given me another piece of the puzzle—a way to get the bomb into the United States, directly to where it needs to be."

Al Zawahiri waited for bin Laden to continue, hoping that he would explain exactly how the two brothers would be used for their cause. But bin Laden did not elaborate on the plan.

"Do you think Los Angeles will make an excellent target?" he asked instead.

"Why not New York?" Al Zawahiri asked. "That would cause even more destruction."

"I considered New York, but that city has already been devastated. It's time to attack another American city, this one on the west coast," bin Laden said enthusiastically. "The Americans will discover that no part of their country is safe from me."

"How will you get the bomb out of here?" al Zawahiri asked. He could hardly pull his eyes away from the missile. "For that matter, how did you get it in here?"

"Look up." Bin Laden gestured to the ceiling, where al Zawahiri now noticed a sling hanging from some sort of hook. A track led from the end of the room, where the bomb was hidden, and out the door.

"I will use the sling to place the bomb in a crate," bin Laden explained. "Then we'll put the case into the sling and have it taken outside. That track," bin Laden pointed overhead, "leads directly outside, where it can be loaded onto a truck."

"And then?"

"Then, you will see."

Yechezkel was sweaty and nervous. For the umpteenth time, an FBI agent was asking him if he could recall anything about his family's escape from Iran. "I can barely remember a thing," he said again. "I just remember that I was standing on top of a tall mountain when a group of soldiers appeared from out of nowhere and surrounded us. My parents were extremely nervous."

"When did your father give you that half bill?" The interrogating agent tried a new direction.

"It was earlier, before we had left our home. But I can't even recall what my father looked like. I just remember that he was standing next to us at the time. He was very worried. I recall that he told us many different things before tearing the bill in half." He moved about uncomfortably. "Ah, yes. I just remembered something else. He said something about a bank account, something about numbers and a bank." Yechezkel nervously pushed a lock of hair off his forehead as he tried to remember his father's last words.

The two brothers were sitting with a group that included the FBI director; Special Agent Greg Miller, who had accompanied them from the aircraft; and a staff psychologist, who until now had remained silent.

The director nodded at Miller, who took a deep breath. "Would you be willing to be interrogated under hypnosis?" Miller asked. The tension was palpable. This was his last card.

Yechezkel stared at him suspiciously. He didn't like the sound of that. "Once you hypnotize me, you'll have no problem finding out everything I know about al Qaeda. And then, once you have all the information you need, I doubt you'll be willing to make the effort to search for my family."

The director spoke up. "I am the leader of an organization charged with ensuring that the United States government abides by its own laws. I promise you that I can be trusted."

"I've heard plenty about how the FBI lies to people. Oh, yes, of course—it's always for a good reason," Yechezkel responded sarcastically.

"Are you taking what al Qaeda has told you as fact?" the director demanded. "They want you to mistrust us. But I give you my word. If we want to be trusted, we must be trustworthy."

"I prefer to see you take some steps to find out what happened to my parents before handing over all my information," Yechezkel replied.

"You still haven't told me if you're willing to be interrogated while under hypnosis," Miller interjected. "In order to find your parents, we will need additional information, and we'll only be able to obtain this information under hypnosis."

The agent's words made sense. It was impossible for the FBI to do anything with the few clues that he had provided for them. He thought quietly for a few moments while the FBI agents sat in silence, allowing him to think the matter over.

Yechezkel sighed and nodded. "Yes, I'm willing to be interrogated under hypnosis, but on condition that my brother will be present during the interrogation."

The director smiled. "That's fine. I have no qualms about your brother being present during the interrogation. He'll see that I mean exactly what I say. I am not planning to squeeze out additional information at this point. I just want to hear whatever is necessary to help us discover what happened to your parents."

Bin Laden carefully pressed a button. The sling, which had been placed around the missile, gently lifted it off the floor. When the missile was about twelve feet above ground, he pressed another button and the sling stopped. The two men carefully placed a long, well-padded crate directly underneath the missile. Bin Laden pressed the button again, and the crane slowly lowered the missile into the padded crate.

Al Zawahiri's eyes remained riveted on the bomb, his lips continually whispering a prayer. He could envision a huge mushroom cloud of smoke exploding inside the cave and destroying the entire mountain.

Al Zawahiri breathed a sigh of relief the moment the bomb was safely enclosed in the well-padded crate. He looked up to see bin Laden smiling at him. "Frightening, isn't it?" he commented.

Al Zawahiri did not deny his fear. "Yes, it is. What do you think? Don't you feel threatened?"

"I can't deny that this toy is definitely frightening. That's what it's made for, to frighten the evil people in this world," bin Laden agreed. "But it gives us power—beyond our wildest dreams. For such power, it is worth taking chances."

Bin Laden locked the crate and picked up the gold leaf bell that was on his desk. Achmad, bin Laden's personal valet, appeared in the doorway. "The package is ready to be sent," bin Laden informed him.

"The plane is also waiting to depart," Achmad announced. "The soldiers are awaiting your orders."

"Tell them to come into my office and load the package," bin Laden ordered.

"Plane?" al Zawahiri asked, as Achmad left the room.

"Yes, the truck will be driven out of the mountains to Pakistan, where I have ordered an airplane to stand by."

Bin Laden fell silent as four bearded soldiers entered the room. They were dressed in long white robes and had automatic rifles flung over their shoulders.

"Place the sling around the crate," bin Laden ordered.

The soldiers carefully placed the sling around one end of the crate, then slid the sling down so the crate was resting right in the middle. Bin Laden pressed the button to lift the crate in the air, then pushed a handle forward. The crate started moving slowly forward, down the track toward the door. The soldiers followed the crate, which was lifted just five feet in the air, allowing them to protectively balance it in the sling.

"Be careful with the cargo," bin Laden warned them. "It's extremely expensive, and can be easily ruined."

He watched for a moment as the soldiers and the crate slowly left the room, heading toward the outdoors.

"Shouldn't we go with them?" al Zawahiri asked uncertainly.

"The driver of the truck knows what to do," bin Laden told him. "I need to take care of something first."

Bin Laden picked up the telephone and dialed a three-digit number. "I need Abu Salim," he ordered.

It took less than two minutes for Abu Salim to get to the phone.

"You'll be leaving tonight to our base in Mexico," bin Laden said. "We're sending an extremely valuable package on the plane, and you're in charge of making sure it arrives safely."

"I'm happy to obey," Abu Salim answered quickly. He felt a surge of relief. What a perfect opportunity! He would be able to get out of

Afghanistan before the Americans started their attack.

It was close to midnight by the time the two-engine Russian plane took off from al Qaeda's secret airfield, located right on the border of Pakistan near the Tora Bora Mountains. Abu Salim was seated in the passenger section, together with his four bodyguards and a sour-faced steward. The cargo section contained the crate that had been brought from headquarters. The remainder of the cargo section had been converted into fuel tanks, enabling the plane to make the long flight to Mexico without stopping to refuel.

The flight took over fifteen hours. Just before morning, they were able to make out Mexico's coast on their radar screen. They lowered their altitude, flying as close to the ground as they could, far below the country's radar detectors. Below them was a desolate desert, with endless pale sand dunes as far as the eye could see.

The desert soon began to give way to a hilly region. Sparse vegetation covered the rolling hills, but it was otherwise just as desolate as the desert which surrounded it.

A small clearing appeared just ahead, with just enough space to land a small plane—though there were no overt signs of civilization. The plane began to descend, and a few minutes later, the wheels touched ground. As the plane came to a full stop, a group of soldiers raced out of the nearby hills and surrounded the plane on all sides.

An officer boarded the plane to check the newcomers' identity. Once he was certain that this was the group they had been expecting, he dismissed the majority of his soldiers, and divided the remaining soldiers into two groups. One group was charged with transferring the passengers to a large underground cave, while the second group used a crane to carefully transport the crate to an underground bunker. The plane quickly refueled and soon took off again. By then, any evidence of a terrorist base in this area was completely hidden from sight.

Seventeen

In the morning Rachamim had made up his mind. There was no purpose to this aimless wandering around the city. "We are going home now, Naomi," he told his wife firmly. "We are not accomplishing anything by trying to run away. If something was decreed from Above, it will happen no matter what we try to do to stop it."

Naomi was too exhausted to argue. She silently helped Rachamim take their things downstairs to the hotel's lobby. The clerk who had stared at them yesterday was gone. Today's clerk was friendly and greeted them with a smile.

They drove the short distance home in complete silence. By the time they arrived, it was close to eight o'clock in the morning. Rachamim would have liked to *daven shacharit* in *shul*, but he promised Naomi that first he would accompany her into the house and make sure that everything was as they had left it.

Rachamim patiently trailed along behind his wife as Naomi examined the entire house, checking to be sure that nothing had been moved. Although he was late for his usual *minyan*, he did not try to rush her. He would *daven* with a later *minyan*.

Fortunately, everything was as it should have been, and Rachamim was finally able to leave. On his way out, he warned Naomi that she shouldn't hesitate to call the police if she saw anything suspicious.

He arrived late for the second *minyan* and quickly donned *tefillin* to join them. He didn't notice the strange looks coming his way until the *chazan* began reciting the *shemoneh esrei*. He couldn't understand why his friends were looking at him like that. He had only been gone for one day. Maybe they were surprised that he had arrived late. This was the first time that he had come to *shul* late.

At the end of *davening*, some of his friends came over and asked if he had been sick. He realized that he must look terrible and that they were worried. "I feel fine, *baruch Hashem*," he tried to reassure them. "I've just arrived home from an exhausting trip."

"Thank G-d it's nothing worse," they responded.

After everyone left, he remained in the *shul*. Still wrapped in his *tallit* and *tefillin*, he began to recite his daily quota of *Tehillim*. When he finished he fervently recited the special prayer that he had been saying every single day for the last twenty years, beseeching Hashem to bring his sons home.

Rachamim realized that he was alone in the enormous synagogue. He usually came early to recite his *Tehillim* before *shacharit*; today, the other members of the congregation had rushed to work and left him to lock up. He slowly removed his *tallit* and *tefillin* before entering the tiny office that he had as president of the *shul*.

Rachamim opened the door to his office. At first, everything looked the way it always did. His desk was piled high with papers, as usual. Behind it was the executive chair that he had once bought for twenty dollars at a public auction. On the other side of the desk, directly opposite the executive chair, were the two chairs that he had upholstered in a fabric similar to the one on his own chair. He recalled that at the time that he had them re-covered, the upholsterer had suggested that he change the upholstery on all three chairs so they would be exactly alike.

With a start, Rachamim realized that he wasn't alone in his office. Someone was sitting in one of the visitor's chairs. The man had his back to his door, but as Rachamim walked in, he quickly turned to face him.

It was Jamil.

The room was silent. Rachamim and Jamil stared at one another without saying a word. Finally, Rachamim broke the silence. "What are you doing here, Jamil?" he asked uncomfortably.

"Maybe you can explain what you're doing here," Jamil responded.

"What do you mean? This is my office, isn't it?"

Jamil stood up. "I told you to get out of here! Was my warning only good enough to scare you for one day? You don't seem to understand the type of a danger you're putting yourself in!"

"You're right." Rachamim deliberately kept his voice calm and level. "I don't know what type of danger I'm putting myself in. You won't tell me, and as long as you won't tell me, I simply have no reason to listen to you."

"You know I'm your friend," Jamil said, his voice low. "Do you think our friendship is nothing more than an illusion? Haven't I done enough for you to earn your trust?"

Rachamim shifted uncomfortably. "It's not that ..." He tried to think of what to say. "I've already had to leave my life behind, to flee with my family from the only home I had known, and start again in a strange country. I'm not ready to do that again, Jamil—not unless I have more information to convince me that it's needed. Even your word, my friend, is not enough to make me flee once again from my home."

"What will it take to convince you?" Jamil wondered out loud.

"Tell me one thing, at least," Rachamim said anxiously. "Does this have anything to do with what happened yesterday?"

Jamil stared at him. His eyes were filled with pain, and the mournful expression on his face brought Rachamim to tears. It took a few moments before Rachamim realized that while Jamil was staring straight at him, he was actually looking through him.

Jamil suddenly started mumbling. "Achmad ... don't be so calm ... let's attack them ..." He thrashed his arms about. "They'll kill us if we don't do something ..." Jamil suddenly started screaming loudly. "Achmad, why are you standing there like a helpless lump of clay? Help me! Please help me!"

Jamil suddenly started pounding his fists against head. "No! *No!*" he screamed, then burst into tears.

Frightened, Rachamim ran to Jamil, grabbed him around the shoulders and started shaking him back and forth. "Wake up, Jamil!" It was clear that Jamil was reliving a painful episode from his past. Rachamim needed to bring him back to the present. "Jamil, you're here, sitting next to me. We're in Los Angeles."

Jamil looked startled as he woke up from his nightmare. He stared at Rachamim as though he had no idea what he was doing there. "I'm sorry," he muttered. He looked down in embarrassment. "There's no reason for you to have to suffer because of what I've gone through."

"No, Jamil. It's important for you to talk about it. Why should you carry all that pain around with you? You've been suffering for years because you've kept it bottled up like that."

Jamil looked at his watch. It was a simple wristwatch that Rachamim had given him after returning home from a business trip to New York. "It's late," he said sharply. "I must get out of here."

"No, Jamil. Please don't leave," Rachamim pleaded with him. "I can help you. You need help."

Jamil threw him a quick glance before walking to the door. "No, Rachamim. There's nothing you can do for me. The truth is, you can't even help yourself."

Jamil opened the door and peered into the empty corridor. Before stepping out into the hallway, he turned his head and stared hard at Rachamim. "I'm warning you for the last time: leave Los Angeles fast! Something terrible is about to happen here."

"My father took out an Iranian bill from his pocket and wrote the word *Echad* on it." The hypnotist had put Yechezkel into a trance, and he was now describing his family's escape from Iran. "He said that if we are ever separated from him, we must remember that we have one Father in heaven who is always watching over us. He asked us to always remember that we are members of the Jewish nation."

Yechezkel started trembling from emotion. "Abba tore the bill down the middle, and showed us the numbers on either half. 'This is the number of our bank account in Switzerland,' he told us. 'The account contains a small fortune. You will need the entire number to take money out of the account.' My father gave one half of the bill to me, and the other half to my brother. 'You need both halves of this bill to take money out of the account,' he explained. 'I am giving each of you only half the number. Only when you are together will you be able to take the money out of the account. Divide it equally and use it well. My only request is that when that happens, you'll return to the faith of your fathers.'"

Yosef listened, entranced by Yechezkel's story. He wanted to hear more, but the director turned to the hypnotist. "I think we have enough information to continue. Bring him out of it."

"Don't you want a description of his father?"

"Do you think you'll be able to get it for us?"

"No problem," the hypnotist said confidently.

An FBI artist was already there, his pencil poised to begin. He handed the hypnotist a list of questions that would provide him with the necessary information to sketch the portrait.

"Can you describe your father's appearance?" the hypnotist asked Yechezkel.

"Of course. I can see him clearly in front of me."

The hypnotist slowly started asking the artist's questions. Yechezkel answered them as if his father was standing there, in front of him. When the portrait was complete, everyone was astounded to see that Yechezkel's father looked like a combination of the two brothers.

The hypnotist slowly brought Yechezkel out of his trance. When he woke up, he could not remember what had transpired. But he was exhausted from the emotional trauma that he had undergone.

Geneva's main streets were relatively empty that morning, the thirteenth of September. The city's financial district was almost completely closed. Most of the establishments were lifeless. New York's stock market was closed, causing all the stock markets around the world to shut down as they tried to recover from the heavy blow they had received just two days before, on September 11.

Lou Swiss's main branch was one of the few financial establishments to open the day after the tragedy. The manager had decided not to close the bank, although there were few transactions. The bored clerks listened to the latest news on the radio, nervously changing stations every few minutes.

A tall, middle-aged man accompanied by a younger man entered the bank. They were wearing expensive business suits, appropriate outfits for such an exclusive establishment. The two men walked rapidly past the rows of clerks, straight to the bank manager's office.

The manager was listening to the latest news from New York and Washington over his transistor radio. He looked up when they entered and quickly turned off the radio.

"What can I do for you?" the bank manager asked.

"We have to speak with the bank's executive director immediately," the older one explained in heavily accented German. The younger man's eyes never left the bank manager's face.

The bank manager looked at the two men carefully. Every once in a while people told him that they had come to speak with the bank's executive director. But they always made an appointment first.

"Did you make an appointment?" he politely asked. He knew they hadn't.

"I'm Louis Felder," the older man said, without answering the manager's question. "I'm the American embassy's security attaché in Geneva."

Louis waited for the bank manager to digest these words before continuing. "I must speak to the bank's executive director urgently. The matter that I want to discuss directly affects the security of the United States and Europe."

The manager's demeanor changed immediately. He picked up the intercom and dialed the director's extension to tell him about his unexpected guests.

The director agreed to see them, though he knew why they had come. On any other day, it wouldn't have bothered him. He was used to politely refusing requests made by officials of various countries, asking for protected information about suspects. Now, however, the situation was different. The world was shocked by the brutal attack against the United States. Yet did he have any right to breach the confidentiality of his clients?

The bank manager stood and asked the two men to accompany him upstairs. They entered the elevator and rode up to the fifth floor.

The bank manager knocked lightly on the director's door. "Come in, please," the director said.

The bank manager entered, accompanied by the two men from the American embassy. The director politely asked them to take a seat. The manager lingered next to the door, listening to the conversation.

"My name is Louis Felder," the older man began. "And this is my assistant, Queen." He pointed toward the younger man sitting next to him.

"So how can I help you?" the director asked.

Louis removed a folded paper from his suit jacket's inner pocket. "I have a number of a bank account here. I'd like to know who the account belongs to."

It was obvious from the expression on the director's face that he was not about to give them this information.

"I realize that you have an ironclad rule never to provide information about the people who have accounts in your bank. This time, however, the situation is different." Louis looked the director squarely in the eye. "You have to realize that Tuesday's attack was completely unprecedented, a vicious attack against the free world. This information is necessary to continue our investigation. I am begging you, in the name of the American nation and the free world, not to refuse this request."

The director lowered his eyes for a few moments. He almost wished he could give the Americans the information they wanted. But he had no choice—he had to refuse. Otherwise, he would be breaching the bank's hundred-year-old tradition of trust, and that would cause the bank enormous damage.

"I'm really very sorry," the director whispered. "I am not allowed to hand over information concerning one of our customers."

Louis gave him a piercing look. "Do you realize how many people were murdered in the Twin Towers?"

The director squirmed uncomfortably in his seat.

"In fact, no one knows how many people lost their lives in that attack," Louis answered his own question. "But this we do know—thousands of people, including at least forty-seven Swiss citizens, were killed. They did nothing wrong, yet their lives were brutally cut off. Doesn't that touch your heart? One of those people might be a friend of yours, or even a relative."

"That certainly is a possibility," the director responded brusquely. "And it's also possible that I am making the wrong decision by refusing to provide you with this information. But I have a responsibility toward our customers. I am not about to break the trust that has been given to me."

The director's voice brooked no compromise, and Louis realized that it would be impossible to persuade him to change his mind. The two men stood up and walked toward the door. The director made a great show of putting on his reading glasses and turning his attention to one of the letters on his desk, ignoring his guests completely.

The bank manager silently accompanied them to the elevator. When the three of them were alone in the elevator, he handed Louis his business card.

"I finish work at five," the manager whispered. "Call me on my cell phone at five-thirty. The number's here, on the card." His voice was quivering and Louis saw that his cheeks were wet. The manager removed a tissue from his pocket and wiped away a stray tear. "I am able to help you," he said simply.

Louis glanced at the bank manager's business card. His name, Hans Weiss, was printed in large letters, and underneath it, in smaller letters, his position in the bank. His cell phone number was printed in the lower right hand corner.

The elevator opened onto the lobby and Louis quickly buried the card in his pocket. The bank manager suddenly appeared tough and businesslike. He coldly showed them the way to the door. Anyone watching would have concluded that Hans hoped that he would never see them again.

The search beneath the ruins of the World Trade Center continued. Two days had gone by since the attack, and the rescue workers were starting to lose hope. The American nation was nervous and demanding revenge. The world was eager for someone to pay the price.

Osama bin Laden was not waiting patiently. He knew that it was just a matter of time before he was attacked, and he was taking full advantage of this lull before the coming storm. Al Qaeda quickly moved most of its men and equipment into the villages inhabited by the wild tribes that dotted the chain of high mountains bordering

Afghanistan and Pakistan. The tribes admired him and he knew that they would protect him and his men.

The weapons were divided into two categories. The less important ones were shipped to southern Yemen, while the more valuable weapons were sent to the base located in Mexico. Bin Laden felt that it was best to keep those weapons as close as possible to the enemy, so he could attack quickly if necessary. Fortunately, Abu Salim was already at the site. He took charge of the growing arsenal and expanded the training facilities in Mexico.

Eighteen

Hans Weiss was seated in the elegant car that he had purchased just two months ago, nervously glancing around him. The people walking by looked curiously at the expensive auto that was completely out of place in this area, a working class neighborhood inhabited mainly by new immigrants. Many of them tried to peer into the darkened windows.

Hans was beginning to regret that he had chosen this spot. He had originally decided on this neighborhood, rather than an upper class suburb, because he was frightened that the bank director or one of the workers at the bank might notice him meeting with the Americans.

At exactly five-thirty, Hans's cell phone started ringing. His hands were trembling as he opened the tiny device and brought it up to his ear.

"Mr. Weiss," he heard someone whisper.

"Yes," he replied, sounding distracted. That white car over there. Hadn't he seen it drive past at least three times? He watched the suspicious car enter one of the parking lots.

"Are you ready to meet with me?" the man asked. He spoke German with a strong American accent.

Hans was staring at the building above the parking lot that the suspicious car had just entered. He saw a light go on in one of the apartments on the third floor. He was relieved. *That car belongs to a resident.* Hans felt more confident. "Yes," he replied in a strong, even voice.

"Where do you want to meet?" the man asked.

"In the White Swan pub. It's located…"

"I know where the pub's located," the man interrupted him brusquely. "I'll be there in five minutes."

"Five minutes?" Hans repeated. "Where are you? How can you get there so fast?"

"I'm near the pub. I'll be there in five minutes."

"Okay," Hans agreed. He was near the pub himself, since he had chosen to meet in this neighborhood. But the Americans didn't know about that yet.

Or did they?

With a chill, Hans realized that he must have been followed. The Americans were almost certainly nearby.

For a moment, he was tempted to call the whole thing off. Why risk his career and the bank's reputation just to please two American spies? But the thought was fleeting, for Hans had his own personal reasons for cooperating with the Americans.

The pub was right across the street. He got out of his car and locked it. Five minutes after hanging up the cell phone, Hans was sitting on an old, peeling chair next to a wobbly table, waiting to be served.

"A bottle of Bok beer, please," he told the waiter.

"I'll bring it right away," the waiter replied. He disappeared for a few minutes, only to return carrying a bottle of cheap beer. "I'm sorry, sir, all the Bok's finished," he apologized. "But I promise you that this brand is just as good, if not better."

Hans glanced at the waiter, trying to decide if he was making fun of him. Hans was just about to say something when he noticed a tall man approaching the table. "Can I join you?" the man asked.

"Of course," Hans replied. He recognized Louis immediately.

The waiter understood that he was not wanted and left to take care of the other customers. Hans leaned across the table. "I understand that you are trying to obtain information that will help you capture the criminals who masterminded that horrible attack." Hans's voice was quivering with emotion.

"Yes," Louis replied. "Can you help us with that?"

"Definitely. I have free access to the bank's database."

Louis examined Hans closely to see if he was telling the truth. He had never met anyone working for a Swiss bank who was willing to provide information about the bank's clients. "Why are you so interested in helping us?" Louis asked curiously.

Hans glanced around the pub. "The waiter standing to the right of us is making me nervous," he whispered. Louis glanced to the right. Yes, the waiter was too curious. "I would prefer that we speak outside," Hans added.

"I have no problem with that," Louis agreed.

Hans quickly finished his beer and gestured to the curious waiter to bring the bill.

"Wasn't I right about that beer? It's just as good as the more expensive brand."

Hans did not feel like arguing with him. "You're always correct," he responded. He handed the waiter a ten franc bill and stood up. "Keep the change," he called back, as the two men left the pub.

"Let's sit in the car," Hans suggested. He crossed the street and opened the door for Louis before coming around to the driver's seat. The car was silent for a few minutes as Hans composed his thoughts, considering where to begin.

"My brother Johan suffered his entire life. He was dyslexic, and was never successful in school. My parents did not understand his problem, so they never gave him the attention he so desperately needed. Instead, they criticized his low grades and poked fun at him. His classmates would make jokes at his expense. Johan was always miserable and lonely.

"When Johan finished high school, no university would accept him. He worked hard as a construction worker, while the rest of us were professionals. My brothers and sisters could not understand him, and they started avoiding him. He was an embarrassment to them. They never visited him, nor did they invite him to visit them. Even when they met him on the street, they tried to make it look as if he was an acquaintance, not a relative.

"I was the only one who had anything to do with him. He would pour out his heart to me and ask me why he had to suffer like this. I tried to encourage him, and reassured him that there were better days ahead."

Hans's shoulders heaved in emotion. Louis placed a hand on his arm to reassure him. "Calm down. You don't have to tell me everything now."

Hans took a handkerchief out of his pocket and wiped his nose. "No, it's better for me to get this off my chest."

He took a deep breath before continuing. "When Johan was thirty years old, he finally got married. He was the happiest man in the entire world. He stopped complaining about how hard he worked or how little he earned. He was grateful to have someone in the world who understood him.

"One year after his wedding, Johan's wife gave birth to a little girl. Their joy knew no bounds. They spoiled that baby rotten. My brother insisted that his wife leave her job to stay home and care for their child. He started working extra hours so she could be with the baby twenty-four hours a day.

"All this was destroyed on a beautiful sunny morning, the fifth of October. My sister-in-law was taking her daughter for her regular checkup when a drunk driver plowed into them as they were crossing the street. They were hospitalized in critical condition and passed away a few days later.

"My brother had a nervous breakdown. He closeted himself in his house and refused to speak with anyone. I had a key and would force myself into the house and try to get him to talk about his feelings. At first he completely ignored me. My siblings felt sorry for him and were willing to help. They helped me locate an excellent psychologist who worked with him until he was willing to leave his house.

"I advised my brother to go on a trip and see the world. I felt that he needed a vacation, and I was willing to pay for it. I arranged for him to join a tour of the United States.

"Before my brother left, I gave him a cell phone so we could remain in constant contact. We had been in almost constant contact since his wife and baby were killed.

"My brother called me often. They flew straight to Los Angeles to tour the West Coast. Afterwards, they spent the next twenty-one days traveling by bus across the entire country. New York was their last stop. They had two days to spend touring the city and shopping before returning to Geneva.

"My brother visited all the city's attractions. His favorite spot was in Windows on the World, the restaurant near the top of the Twin Towers. He was so excited that he even phoned me from the restaurant to describe the view. It was a beautiful, sunny day, and he could see far into the distance.

"When I heard the excitement in his voice, I was grateful that I had convinced him to go on the trip. 'Just to give you an idea of the height of this building,' he said, 'I see an airplane flying so close to the building that it looks as if it's about to crash into it.'

"Two minutes later, the American Airlines plane crashed into the tower. No one in the restaurant survived."

Hans stopped. Louis remained silent—there was nothing he could really say.

"That's why I'm doing this for you," Hans finally managed to say. "I want you to get those who were responsible! I want you to teach them a lesson they will never forget! I will do everything in my power to assist those who are bringing the murderers to justice."

Louis's face turned serious. "You can help us," he whispered. He was sure now that Hans could be trusted.

"What do you need?" Hans asked succinctly.

"Here, let's get out of the car for a minute."

Louis and Hans left the car and walked a few steps, until they were standing directly underneath a street light. Louis removed a folded paper from his pocket and opened it. It was plain white stationery. In the middle, there was a line with nine numbers written on it. "This is one of the accounts in your bank," he whispered into Hans's ear. "It's important for us to know who this account belongs to, as well as any additional details that you have."

Hans looked thoughtfully at the paper in Louis's hand. "I'll need a few days for this. I don't want anyone to suspect what I'm doing, so I want to work slowly. Let's meet again in exactly three days." He took the paper with the account number. "Then I'll give you all the information on the account in the bank's database."

Hans turned around and walked back his car. Louis tried to thank him, but Hans had already gone.

Rachamim had not touched his Swiss bank account for over twenty years. He had decided long ago that this money would be for his children. If he were to take the money out of the account, it would be an admission that he had given up hope. And that was something he refused to do.

When he first arrived in the United States, Rachamim had withdrawn a small amount to start his business, but he had returned it to the account many years ago. Over the years, the money in the account had quadrupled in value. Every once in a while he checked to see if anyone had withdrawn money from the account. But the answer was always no. Finally, he had given up hope and had stopped checking.

But now, the experience of the past week had reopened a painful wound. Although he did not admit it to his wife, ever since the day they had spent wandering aimlessly through the city, petrified of their own shadows, he was constantly reliving the horror that he had experienced when escaping Iran. His pain was so deep that every once in a while he had to find a private corner to cry about the tragic loss of his beloved children.

The two of them had spent a pensive week, followed by a soul-searching *Rosh Hashanah*. They weren't the only ones in a serious mood—everyone had been affected by the attack on the Twin Towers, and the *tefilot* that year had been even more intense than usual. But Rachamim had his personal history to torment him, as well. He had reached the point where he knew that he had to do something about it.

Rachamim realized that calling the bank would reopen the wound even further. But he couldn't stop himself. He needed to pursue every possible avenue. If there was hope, he needed to know about it.

Rachamim opened his wallet and looked through his credit cards until he found it—a faded card containing two rows of numbers. It had obviously been written a long time ago. His hands were trembling violently by the time he picked up the phone and dialed the first row of numbers. He glanced at his watch. It was 7:37 AM, making it 4:37 PM in Geneva. The Swiss bank clerks should still be at their desks.

A woman's voice answered in German. "Lou Swiss Bank. How can I help you?"

"I would like to check the balance in my account," Rachamim replied in English.

The clerk immediately changed to heavily accented English. She asked Rachamim to wait on the line.

A few minutes later, a male voice got on the phone. "Hans speaking. How can I help you?"

Rachamim repeated his request. Hans asked for the account number. Rachamim read the numbers and was greeted by a heavy silence.

"Hello?" Rachamim said finally. "Are you there?"

"Oh! Yes, I'm here," Hans said quickly.

Rachamim listened in puzzlement. There was an undercurrent of excitement in Hans's voice.

"Can you check the balance?" he asked again.

"Yes, yes I can ... just a moment."

Rachamim could hear keys clicking in the background. "Tell me," he said abruptly, "has someone taken money out of this account recently?"

"No, no," Hans quickly replied. "The last time someone accessed this account was over thirty years ago."

"Has anyone asked you about the account lately?" Rachamim persisted.

Again, there was a sudden silence. *What's going on?* Rachamim wondered.

"Not recently, no," Hans finally responded.

Rachamim wasn't convinced. The man sounded nervous, and the long silences made him think that Hans was hiding something.

"Are you sure?" he said.

"Of course!"

Now Hans sounded indignant. Rachamim gave up. He knew he wouldn't be able to persuade the manager to tell him the truth—if, indeed, he was being dishonest at all. *I'm probably imagining it*, Rachamim thought glumly as he hung up the phone. He realized that he was willing to grasp at practically anything that would give him hope that his children were still alive.

That evening Hans handed Louis a large brown envelope containing several pages of text. "I'm sorry it took so long. I didn't want to take any chances."

"I understand," Louis murmured.

"I printed all the information contained in the database," Hans explained. "And here's something interesting… the account holder called the bank today to check the balance."

"Is that unusual?" Louis asked.

"Normally, no. But in this case, no one has inquired about the account in several years. No one has touched the account for over twenty years."

"I want to thank you, in the name of the American people, for your assistance," Louis said sincerely.

"Don't bother thanking me," Hans told him. "The only payment I want is revenge for my brother's death."

"That's exactly what we're trying to do," Louis assured him.

"Good," Hans replied. "I just hope that you'll treat the terrorists with the same brutality that they showed my dear brother."

"We will not treat them with kid gloves," Louis answered. "You can be sure of that."

Hans stared out into the distance. "According to American law, criminals can be punished with death. I certainly hope that in this case, the criminal will receive capital punishment."

"I never thought otherwise."

Hans gave a curt nod, then went back to his car and quickly drove away.

The next day, Rachamim forced himself to go back to work. It was difficult for him to concentrate on the job. But there were suppliers waiting to be paid, workers who needed their salaries, and other matters that were awaiting his attention. He knew it was time to move forward.

The iron shutters that covered the front of the warehouse were closed, just as he had left them over a week ago. As Rachamim left his car, Joey, who owned the wholesale shoe store next to his warehouse, ran over to him.

"Hey, Rachamim, good to see you. Is everything okay?"

Rachamim was startled. "What do you mean?"

"Well, when I saw you yesterday, you ran away pretty quickly," Joey explained. "I was wondering if there was some sort of emergency."

"Yesterday!" Rachamim stared at him. "I wasn't here yesterday!"

"But I saw you! You parked your car right in front and went inside. I was about to come over to say hello, but then I saw you run outside and drive away. I figured you needed to leave in a hurry."

"When did you see me enter the warehouse?" Rachamim asked. It was obvious that Joey was telling the truth. Someone had gone into his warehouse and Joey had assumed that it was him.

Joey scratched his forehead and thought for a few seconds. "At around five-forty."

"Are you sure it was my car?" Rachamim asked.

Joey looked taken aback. "I'm not sure, to tell you the truth. I just assumed … do you mean it wasn't you after all?"

"No, it wasn't me. I didn't come to work yesterday."

Joey looked completely confused. "So who was it?"

"Good question." Rachamim slowly started walking towards his warehouse. He placed the key in the bulky lock that was hanging to the right of the heavy iron bars covering the front door. He carefully removed the lock and held it in his hands while opening the second lock.

"Do you want me to go with you into the warehouse?" Joey suggested as Rachamim bent down to lift up the heavy iron bars covering the inner door.

Rachamim stopped. He really would prefer to have Joey go in with him. "If you don't mind, I really would like it if you came with me. Just in case. Unless you're afraid?" Rachmim looked at Joey anxiously.

"Afraid?" Joey laughed. "Don't forget, I fought in Vietnam, and I really do think the jungles were much more dangerous than your warehouse. And even if I am afraid, what are friends for if not to help out at times like this?"

Joey helped Rachamim lift the iron shutters up over the door. Rachamim placed the key in the lock and cautiously opened the warehouse door.

The two men hesitantly entered the dark room. Rachamim felt along the wall until he found the light switch and turned on the fluorescent lights lining the ceiling.

The warehouse looked exactly as he had left it.

"Let's double check to make sure that everything is in its place," Joey suggested. "Then I'll leave so you can get down to work."

The two men examined the entire warehouse, but they did not find anything suspicious. "I wonder what he was looking for?" Rachamim mumbled. "It doesn't look as if anything's missing."

"Maybe he was looking for money?" Joey suggested.

"Hmm." Rachamim frowned in thought. "Whoever came here probably knows that I never carry cash. Don't forget, the person let himself in. That means he must have had a key, which means, of course, that he was probably one of the workers. They're the only ones who have keys, and they know that I never keep cash on hand."

"I don't think it was one of the workers." Joey lowered his eyes. "The person who entered looked like you. Ah, what I mean to say is …" It was hard for Joey to express himself. "I don't want to insult you, but … he was dark. He looked like an Arab. That's why I assumed it was you."

"I see," Rachamim murmured.

"I'll let you get back to work." Joey turned around to leave. "Everything looks okay."

Rachamim waited until Joey had left before walking into his small office in the corner of the enormous warehouse. He stopped for a moment before opening the door. He should have had Joey wait while he checked in here, too. He felt a sense of trepidation as he unlocked the door.

Everything looked exactly as he had left it a few days ago. When he walked over to his desk, however, he saw an envelope lying on top. He didn't recognize the handwriting, but the letter was clearly addressed to him.

Frowning, Rachamim lifted the envelope, turning it over carefully. There was nothing to identify the sender. But it was unstamped, so someone had obviously hand delivered it while he was away.

The mysterious visitor? It seemed probable.

Rachamim ripped open the envelope with a quick movement and unfolded the single piece of paper inside.

Rachamim, how many times do I have to beg you to leave the city? I cannot keep endangering myself for your sake. This is your final warning. Leave the city immediately. Get as far away from Los Angeles as possible.

There was no signature, but Rachamim knew it was from Jamil.

Now what? Rachamim knew what he ought to do. He should call back that FBI agent and tell him about Jamil's latest warning. He wavered between loyalty to Jamil and loyalty to his country, but the thought of the thousands killed in the terrorist attack in New York finally decided it for him. His debt to a single individual was outweighed by the need to bring the criminals to justice. If Rachamim could help in any way, he had a duty to do so.

Rachamim reached into his pocket for his wallet. He opened it and took out the card that he had hoped he would never need, with the name "Harold Clark" written in bold letters. There was a telephone number under the name. Rachamim forced himself to dial the number.

"FBI, how can I help you?" A woman with a strong foreign accent answered the phone.

"I must speak urgently with the FBI," Rachamim replied, feeling somewhat confused. He had expected Harold to answer.

"You've reached the FBI," the secretary replied. "Is there anyone specific you would like to speak with?"

"Yes. I'd like to speak with Harold Clark."

"Please wait on the line for a few moments. I'm going to look for him right now."

Rachamim heard a click and then, a few minutes later, an authoritative male voice got on the line. "This is Harold Clark speaking, from the FBI anti-terrorist department. How can I help you?"

"Um ... I have information that might help you in finding the terrorists belonging to the ..." Rachamim fumbled for the words. He could not recall the name al Qaeda, although he had heard it mentioned repeatedly on the radio.

"Who's speaking?" Harold asked in a businesslike voice.

"Oh, I was so nervous that I forgot to identify myself," Rachamim apologized. "My name is Rachamim Roji. I'm not sure if you remember me."

"Of course I remember you," the agent interrupted him. "I must apologize for that very impolite visit we made to your room at the Holiday Inn." Harold was now warm and friendly.

"I have some information for you," Rachamim repeated.

"What type of information?" Harold asked carefully. He signaled to his assistant to trace the call, in case Rachamim would have second thoughts and hang up the phone.

"I'm not sure if this is what you are looking for, but it looks strange enough for me to bring it to your attention."

"What do you want to tell me?" Harold asked again. Recent events had taught the FBI that every tidbit of information could be important.

"My good friend keeps on returning and warning me over and over again that I must get out of the city quickly, before something terrible happens."

"Would you be willing for me to send someone to speak with you? I think it's best to discuss this personally."

"No problem," Rachamim replied. "But the agent shouldn't show up here with flashing lights."

"No one was planning on using flashing lights," Harold reassured him. "Are you at home?"

"No, I'm in the office."

"Oh, you're speaking from your business? What type of business do you have?"

"Textiles."

"No problem. No one will know it's an FBI agent. What's your address?"

Rachamim gave the address, then hung up. He couldn't help wondering if he had done the right thing.

Nineteen

Ten minutes later Rachamim heard a truck pull up in front of the warehouse. He ran outside to see who had arrived. A white truck with the name "Johnny's Textiles" written in red letters across the side was parked in front of the main door. A middle-aged man wearing blue overalls jumped out of the driver's seat, while a younger man in khaki overalls opened the door on the opposite side. The two men ran around to the back of the truck and removed an enormous roll of material. They started carrying it to the front door.

It took a few minutes for Rachamim to recognize Harold, who was dressed in overalls with the words "Johnny's Textiles" printed across the front. "We have clothes for every occasion," Harold smiled. The younger man accompanying Harold placed the roll of textiles next to the front door, then joined Rachamim and Harold in the office.

The office was furnished simply. There was a black leather executive chair on one side of the desk, and two simple wooden chairs on the other. Harold did not wait for an invitation. He sat down on one of the wooden chairs and waited for Rachamim to take his own seat. The younger man remained standing in the doorway, his back to Rachamim and Harold, blocking the entrance while observing the warehouse to make sure no one was there.

"You phoned to tell us that you have important information concerning the recent terror attacks," Harold began.

"Yes," Rachamim replied hesitantly. He handed Harold the paper that he had found on his desk.

Harold leaned over and took the paper from Rachamim's hand. It had been torn from a notebook. He slowly read the message.

"Can you think of anyone who would want to make you nervous?" Harold lifted his eyes from the paper.

"No." Rachamim shook his head. "None of my friends like to play practical jokes. I told you over the phone that I know who wrote this letter."

"Who wrote the letter?"

"Jamil."

"Is that the same Jamil you told me about in the hotel?"

Rachamim nodded his head.

"Do you know his last name?" Harold asked.

"Abu Chakim," Rachamim replied. He never called Jamil by his last name, but it was on the checks the synagogue paid him for his work.

"Do you know where Jamil lives?"

"He often stays in a small room next to our synagogue. The community provides him with this room as part of his salary for keeping the synagogue clean. He has an apartment somewhere …" Rachamim tried to think. "I can't remember," he said finally. "I'm sure there's a record of it somewhere in the synagogue, though."

"And where is your synagogue located?"

"1500 Cardiff Drive."

Harold jotted the synagogue's address down in a notebook. After the interrogation, he would check the synagogue closely. He would need to go through the records and check Jamil's room, though he doubted he would find anything there.

"How did you and Jamil meet?" Harold asked.

"Our friendship began in Turkey, over twenty years ago. Jamil saved my life."

"Turkey? I thought you were from Iran. Isn't that what you told me? When were you in Turkey?"

Rachamim had never told Harold that he was originally from Iran. He decided to ignore the fact that in the amount of time it had taken Harold to get to the warehouse, he had managed to check Rachamim's personal history. "It was when I was escaping Iran after the revolution against the Shah. Our escape was not successful."

Harold listened attentively to the chain of events, starting with Rachamim's escape from Iran until the present. Harold tried to write every detail in his notebook. Later, he would enter the information into the FBI's database, so all the agents involved in anti-terror activities would have access to it.

"Thank you for the information," Harold said politely. "I will pass it on to the proper authorities. I'm certain that the information you provided will be used to prevent further attacks on the United States."

Harold was standing in the doorway, ready to leave, when Rachamim stopped him. "Jamil is a wonderful person. He's not a terrorist. I'm positive of that. He's had a miserable life. If you find him, please have mercy on him. Don't make his life even more bitter than it already is."

"How is his life bitter?" Harold asked curiously.

"He has had a terrible life," Rachamim said somberly. "He has no family—no brothers or sisters or children. He has no one. I was the closest person to him, and yet, he always kept a certain distance from me. He has always been quiet, a real loner."

"Is that so?" Harold stepped back into the office. "Do you know that people like that are the best candidates to become suicide bombers? Just think for a moment. His life is already worthless, so why shouldn't he sacrifice it to merit the wonders of the next world, which the imams so willingly promise?"

Rachamim was beginning to regret that he had told the FBI about Jamil. "I can promise you that Jamil is not like that. He couldn't even kill a fly."

"I see," Harold said noncommittally. Rachamim knew that Harold wasn't impressed with his statement. "I'll contact you the moment we find him," Harold added. "Maybe you can help us pump him for information."

"Take my cell phone number," Rachamim suggested. "It's very possible that I won't be home for the next few days."

"I have it already, thank you," Harold replied. He and his assistant hurried through the warehouse. Rachamim followed them, watching as they stepped out the front door.

The moment they were outside, Harold leaned against the side of the truck and took a deep breath of fresh air. "I think we've just touched the tip of the iceberg," he said to his assistant.

"You really think so?" the younger agent asked.

"I don't think so. I know it." Harold paused, thinking. "Let's get going. I'd like to get this information sorted through, and then we'll have to seriously investigate this Jamil fellow."

The two men jumped into the truck and quickly drove away.

The fax machine emitted page after page of printed material. Two senior agents, one from the FBI and the other from the CIA, watched intently as the pages emerged from the machine. This was one of the few times the two agencies had joined forces. After the unprecedented terrorist attacks, the government had concluded that only through working together would they be able to prevent another attack in the future.

"Do you want to read the material first?" CIA agent Sam Wolford asked the FBI agent, Ralph Waterman.

"Sure." Ralph picked up the first sheet and scanned it quickly. The information from Switzerland was written in German. Both men had been chosen for this stage of the operation because of their fluency in the language.

Sam put on his reading glasses and took the first page from Ralph, who was already up to the second page of the fax. Sam had served for two years as a special agent in East Germany under the communists, and was completely fluent in German. By the time he was halfway down the first page, his face was glowing with excitement.

"Did you see this?" he exclaimed.

"It gets better," Ralph noted, as he handed the second page to Sam and started on the third.

"It looks like we have a lead here," Sam remarked, as he read through the last page of the fax.

"I agree," Ralph nodded. "Let's call it in."

Ralph had already started dialing the FBI director's office number in Washington, DC.

"Is the director in, please? It's urgent."

"Hold on a moment."

Minutes later the director's voice came on the line.

"It's Ralph," the agent identified himself, "with Sam Wolford from the CIA. We got good information from Switzerland."

"Give me the details," the director said tersely.

"The account number that the hijacker gave us still exists. It was first opened in 1977 by an Iranian, which fits the information we already have. No money has been removed from the account in over twenty years, though periodically inquiries are made about the status of the account.

"Just yesterday, someone called to ask about the balance of the account."

"Where does the owner live?" the director demanded.

"Los Angeles. The owner has a company called Rachamim Textiles," Ralph replied.

"You have an address?"

"3104 Santa Monica," Ralph answered.

"Good. Stay where you are. We might need you later. Meanwhile, let me pass this information to our agents in Los Angeles."

Harold had been silent since leaving the warehouse fifteen minutes ago. For the umpteenth time, he reviewed the conversation that he had had with Rachamim. *Who is this Jamil?* he wondered. *How is he connected with al Qaeda? He's been living in the United States for years!* Harold wondered if Jamil had been planted by al Qaeda—a perfect sleeper agent, put in place and left for years until needed by the organization.

Harold's cell phone began ringing just as he stopped at a red light. His supervisor was on the line. They had worked together for years, and Harold could tell that he was very nervous about something. "Weren't you supposed to be at the textile warehouse?"

"Yes. I'm coming from there right now," Harold replied.

Harold heard his supervisor take a deep breath. "The owner is now on the top of the FBI's most wanted list, in connection with the events of September 11."

"What?" Harold could not believe his ears. "That elderly Jewish businessman is suspected of collaborating with al Qaeda?"

"No one thinks he is directly connected to the terrorist organization," his supervisor reassured him. "The impression I get is that he has some important information that could help us."

"I probably already have that information," Harold said. "But I must admit that I wouldn't build on it. There are plenty of things missing."

"Okay. I'll let the director know that you have the information they're looking for."

Harold hung up the phone, but it rang again a few minutes later. "I guessed wrong," his supervisor admitted. "The director doesn't want information. He wants the warehouse owner himself. Apparently they need him desperately. How far away are you from the warehouse?"

Harold glanced down at his watch. Twenty minutes had gone by since he had left the warehouse. He had been driving slowly, though. If he drove fast, he could be there quickly. "I can be there within ten minutes," he replied.

"Okay, get there fast. I'll send reinforcements. They'll be there within half an hour. Do everything in your power to keep the warehouse owner in custody until I arrive. I'm about two hours out of the city."

Harold made a U-turn and started speeding in the direction he had just come from. In ten minutes he was back, parking his truck outside the warehouse.

"Do you think he's still here?" his assistant asked.

"His car's still there," Harold pointed. "Okay, let's go get him."

He was about to open the door of the truck when another car drove up and came to a sudden stop in front of the warehouse. Harold stopped. He sensed that something was wrong even before the car's doors were thrown open and four men jumped out.

"Uh-oh!" he muttered.

The four dark-complexioned men started running toward the warehouse.

"We've got to stop them!" Harold gasped.

"But there's only two of us," his assistant pointed out.

"Doesn't matter. Come on!"

Harold leaped out of the truck, fumbling for his gun. He quickly ducked behind the truck for cover. In the meantime, three of the attackers stood just outside the door while the fourth man kicked the door open. The four men raced into the warehouse, their guns drawn.

Harold bent down as he raced toward the warehouse, staying under cover of the other buildings. He fumbled for the on button of his cell phone, then pressed the speed-dial button for his supervisor. "We've got competition," Harold snapped as soon as his supervisor got on the phone. "Send reinforcements quickly. Someone has gotten here before us."

"Who are they?"

"They look like Arabs, I think. Definitely Middle Eastern."

Harold stood at the edge of the doorway and peered inside. The four men were roaming through the warehouse, clearly looking for someone. It was only a question of time before they found the office in the far corner.

"Halt! FBI!"

Listening on the cell phone, Harold's supervisor could hear a single shot being fired.

"Harold!" he said sharply. "Don't go in there if it's dangerous!"

"We're outnumbered," Harold reported, sounding breathless. "I'm waiting right outside the warehouse. Don't worry, they missed me."

Just then, there was another shot. Harold hadn't seen a fifth man, who had been waiting in the car. The man was also armed, and he had finally noticed the FBI agent near the building. This one didn't miss.

The bullet had entered Harold's shoulder. His pistol fell out of his hand, onto the sidewalk. A second later, the cell phone had dropped out of his other hand. Just then, another shot rang out. The man shooting at him quickly darted away.

Struggling to get away, Harold fell to his knees.

"Are you okay?"

It was the welcome voice of his assistant. "Cell phone ..." Harold said feebly.

The assistant quickly scooped up both the cell phone and the pistol from the sidewalk.

"What's going on?" Harold's supervisor was still on the line, nearly frantic by this time.

"Send reinforcements and an ambulance," the assistant said rapidly. "Harold's been shot. Looks like a shoulder wound. He should get medical attention immediately."

"Get out of there now!" the supervisor ordered. "Wait in your car until reinforcements arrive."

The assistant helped Harold stand up and walk carefully to their truck. From a distance, Harold could hear the sirens of approaching police cars and ambulances.

Watching from inside their vehicle, the FBI agents saw the four men forcefully drag Rachamim to their car. "They're taking Rachamim with them," Harold's assistant reported to their supervisor. He watched them brutally throw Rachamim into the back of the car. Three of the men jumped into the back with him, while the other one took his seat in the front, next to the driver.

The car sped away. The first ambulance arrived a moment later, and immediately afterwards, a Los Angeles police car appeared at the scene. Harold's assistant jumped from the truck and beckoned to the emergency medical technicians, who came racing over to him. Harold was lying down on the floor in the back of the truck.

A few minutes later Harold was inside the ambulance, speeding to the hospital.

With their guns drawn, the police surrounded the warehouse. The FBI agents who arrived a few minutes later entered the warehouse, then left again. "He was kidnapped from the warehouse," the lead agent reported. "There are signs of a struggle. It doesn't look as if the owner left of his own free will."

"Maybe someone witnessed the kidnapping?" the police officers asked.

"We had two agents at the scene," the FBI agent said. "The problem is that one was shot and lost consciousness on the way to the hospital, while the other was too busy helping the first one to notice what was happening. According to the medics, the injured agent's situation is stable. It's possible that he'll be able to provide us with additional information once he regains consciousness."

Another group of FBI agents rushed to Rachamim's residence. There were signs of a struggle ... and Naomi had disappeared.

Twenty

"Your parents were just kidnapped."

Yosef and Yechezkel stared at the FBI director in shock.

"They literally slipped through our fingers." The director sounded both saddened and angry.

"I don't understand," Yechezkel said, bewildered. "Where did you find them? Who would have kidnapped them?"

"How do we know you're not trying to evade your responsibility?" Yosef demanded.

"I assure you, we've been doing everything in our power to discover your parents' whereabouts. Just an hour ago, we had found them! We were actually on our way to bring them here when they were kidnapped, literally before our eyes."

"Do you have any idea who kidnapped my parents?" Yechezkel asked again.

"We don't have too many details. One of the agents who witnessed the kidnapping was shot and lost consciousness. The other was taking care of his injured partner, so he wasn't paying that much attention. We do know that there were four kidnappers, plus a driver, and that they looked like Arabs." The director hesitated. "We're not dismissing the possibility that they were kidnapped by members of al Qaeda."

Yechezkel drew in his breath sharply. "How did they know?" he said, almost speaking to himself.

The director had been wondering the same thing. Had the kidnappers known that the FBI was on the trail—or was the timing coincidental?

"I think they've been tracking your father for years," the director told Yechezkel. "Apparently your father has a close relationship with a Turkish man named Jamil, who has been warning him to leave the city of Los Angeles. I strongly suspect that Jamil has ties to al Qaeda, and that part of his task has been to keep track of your father. After all, it's pretty clear that bin Laden knew who you were. Your kidnapping when you left Iran was part of an elaborate plot to bring you into the terrorist organization."

"It doesn't matter." Yechezkel stood up and started pacing across the room. "Bin Laden is mistaken if he thinks that this will break me. I have enough knowledge to badly damage him and his organization, and I will use it!" Yechezkel's cheeks were flushed crimson and his eyes were blazing with fury.

"You know bin Laden," the director said. "What do you think he will do with your parents?"

Yechezkel forced himself to calm down and think. "He will probably bring my parents to Afghanistan. That will be sending me a clear message that he expects me to return there, where we will almost certainly be forced to stand before a military court."

The director looked skeptical. "How will he know that you understood this so-called message?"

Yechezkel's eyes glinted in amusement. "Bin Laden isn't taking any chances that his message will be misunderstood. He'll make sure that I understand him perfectly."

It was a quiet evening in the exclusive aviation club located in Los Angeles, California. The number of flights made by members of the club had dwindled by seventy percent since the events of September 11. The bored guard had fallen asleep on duty when he was startled awake by the sound of a van's motor. He looked out of the guardhouse window and saw a pair of headlights stabbing through the darkness.

The guard activated the searchlight to illuminate the approaching van. It was a commercial Club Model Ford. The driver shaded his eyes to keep from being blinded by the searchlight.

When the van pulled up next to the guardhouse, the guard recognized the driver—Faraj Atrak's pilot. Faraj was a Saudi millionaire living in Los Angeles who kept his executive plane in one of the club's hangars.

"Good evening, John," the pilot smiled. "This is Faraj's cousin. I'll be taking him for a spin."

The guard nodded in greeting to the man sitting next to the driver. The pilot was about to hand over his pilot's license, as required by the club's regulations, but the guard stopped him. Faraj always sent him nice presents, so he didn't see any reason to stand on formalities. "There's no reason for you to identify yourself. After all, I know you well."

The guard opened the gate to let the van through.

The van drove the length of the field and stopped in front of the hangar where Faraj's plane was kept. The man sitting next to the driver jumped out of the van and opened the hangar's door. Once the van was inside, the man closed the door behind them.

A small executive airplane was parked in the middle of the hangar. The van was parked in such a way that its back door faced the ramp leading up to the plane's door. The driver and his helper opened the van's two back doors and removed a stretcher. The doctor sitting next to the stretcher also got out of the van and held a plastic intravenous bag, which was attached to a limp figure who did not stir.

The three men transferred the stretcher to the plane and placed it on the floor. They waited until the doctor finished placing the intravenous bag on a pole before transferring the second stretcher to the plane, this one occupied by another limp figure.

The men returned to the van and cleaned it carefully to remove any incriminating evidence.

Within half an hour, the plane was waiting on the runway for permission to take off. The pilot notified the navigation tower of his flight plan. "I'm flying to Hawaii. Permission requested for takeoff."

The moment permission was granted, the plane took off and headed westward.

The doctor made sure that Rachamim and Naomi were well sedated during the flight. He attached them to respirators and provided them with intravenous nourishment. Bin Laden's personal instructions had been very clear. Rachamim and Naomi must be healthy upon their arrival in Afghanistan.

The plane landed in Hawaii to take on fuel. Here, too, it landed at an exclusive flight club. While the plane was fueling, the pilot went into the office and filled out the necessary forms for continuing on to Hong Kong. Permission was immediately granted. Above the ocean, he changed direction and started flying toward Afghanistan.

The pilot knew how to evade the radar detectors of the different countries they passed as he flew toward Afghanistan. About seven hours later, he landed the plane in a rundown airport that had been built by al Qaeda in a deserted area. After taking on more fuel and food for the pilots and doctor, the plane took off again and continued west.

It was about midnight when the pilot started lowering his altitude. He landed the plane in a tiny airport in Pakistan, right at the edge of the Tora Bora Mountains. The moment the plane touched the tarmac, a group of fighters dressed in white robes and long white headscarves surrounded the aircraft. They spread out, keeping their weapons trained on the plane.

The pilot let down the stairs. The co-pilot appeared in the doorway and shouted, "*Salim aleikhum!*"

The group's officer gave the traditional reply, "*Aleikhum salim.*" Although he recognized the co-pilot's voice, he could not rely on that. Bin Laden had taught his followers to be cautious. He instructed his men to tighten their ring around the plane before ordering the two soldiers at his side to enter.

The soldiers climbed into the plane and started examining it thoroughly. Fifteen minutes later, they appeared in the doorway and announced that everything was clear.

The officer instructed the pilot, co-pilot and doctor to exit the plane. He greeted them warmly on the tarmac before several of the soldiers climbed into the plane and started removing the stretchers.

"The Sheikh himself is waiting to see you," the officer said with obvious pride as he accompanied them out of the airport.

They heard the sound of a vehicle coming towards them. A large Land Rover appeared and stopped right next to them. "Come with me," the officer ordered while climbing into the parked jeep.

The three men obeyed and climbed into the jeep. The jeep sped away and drove wildly along the narrow, curving roads toward an unknown destination. The three men were exhausted, and within fifteen minutes they were sound asleep.

Before dawn, the jeep came to a sudden stop. Opposite them was a small military camp made up of tents surrounding a dilapidated old shack. Soldiers suddenly appeared and surrounded them on all sides. The officer who had accompanied them left the jeep and started speaking with one of the soldiers. The soldier motioned to the others to let them through.

Inside the camp, a different group of soldiers greeted them warmly. They must have understood why they had come. One of the soldiers asked the four men to accompany him.

They entered the dilapidated old shack, which was illuminated by a gasoline lantern. The walls were made of wood. The building consisted of one large room, tastefully furnished with good quality Middle Eastern furniture. The floor was covered with lush Persian carpets.

They recognized bin Laden sitting quietly on the carpet. He greeted them with the traditional "*Salim aleikhum.*"

"*Aleikhum salim,*" they replied respectfully.

Bin Laden instructed them to sit down next to him on the rug. He spent the next hour questioning them about their mission. He listened carefully when they told him that there had almost been a mishap as they dragged Rachamim out of his warehouse. "The FBI arrived earlier than we thought they would," the pilot explained dramatically. "We had to put one of the agents out of commission. The other agents who arrived later probably saved their lives."

"You have done a great service to Muhammad and his servants," bin Laden praised them. "The day will soon come when you will understand what you have accomplished for the good of Islam."

"Can I use the computer?" Yechezkel asked Robert Shipper, the FBI agent who remained with the two of them. The director had excused himself to take care of an urgent matter, leaving the two brothers under Robert's supervision. "I need to check if I received a message from al Qaeda."

"How could that be?" Robert was taken aback. "They don't know that you're with us. We asked the media not to mention the plane that was about to crash into the White House, and so far they've complied with our request. How would bin Laden know where to contact you?"

"Al Qaeda is the most sophisticated and cunning organization in existence," Yechezkel said seriously. "It has unlimited funding, which it has used to purchase the most advanced technology available. Never underestimate them." Yechezkel paused. "I'm sure some of those reporters who saw the plane fly above the White House were members of al Qaeda. Aside from that, bin Laden knows that he sent me here. The lack of news about that plane is proof that something strange is going on, and he would immediately suspect government intervention."

"I guess you're right," Robert admitted. "All right, come with me."

Robert led them to a spacious office and gestured to one of the computers. "You can use that one."

Yechezkel sat down and clicked on Internet Explorer. He typed something in the address bar. Robert watched with interest as a new page appeared. "Vintage Cars," the title proclaimed, with an antique 1933 Ford pictured on the home page.

Yechezkel pointed to the screen. "There's a message waiting for me."

"Where?" Robert was puzzled.

"Two days ago, there was a different car on the home page. A 1939 Ford is my password. Each member of the group has a different model."

"So where's the message?"

"I'll find out in a few minutes." Yechezkel turned his attention back to the computer. He right-clicked on the picture and transferred it to a file.

"Do you have a graphics program?"

"Sure. How sophisticated do you need? Will Photoshop Elements do the trick?"

"Yes, that'll be fine."

Robert showed him the icon for Photoshop Elements. Yechezkel started the program, opened up the picture he had saved, then started carefully peeling away parts of the picture as if it was a puzzle. Robert watched, mesmerized, as the picture underwent a complete metamorphosis.

Twenty minutes later, the picture of an antique car had turned into a three-line letter. Each line contained only a few words. The first line stated, "Your parents are in our hands." The second line said, "We know you failed in your task," and the third line said, "If you want to see your parents, come and take them from us."

Yechezkel looked up from the computer screen. "Well, there's the message," he said quietly.

"What are you planning on doing?" Robert asked.

"I am returning to Afghanistan," Yechezkel said firmly.

"What?" Robert's eyebrows shot up. "Did I hear you correctly?"

"Yes, you heard correctly." Yechezkel nodded decisively. "We're going back there to rescue our parents."

"Don't you realize that you'll never see your father? They just want you to return so they can take revenge on your traitorous behavior. They'll murder you as soon as you show up."

"You don't think I realize that?" Yechezkel retorted. "I know perfectly well that they're planning on setting up a trap for me. I will obviously need to plan this out before I go there."

"What options do you have?" Robert wondered. "It'll be impossible for you to retaliate against bin Laden, especially on his territory."

Yechezkel shook his head. "Not so fast. I am much more familiar with the organization than you are. I've been part of al Qaeda. I know their plans. And I know their weaknesses. They don't realize that I know how to ruin their plans."

A spark of hope appeared in Robert's eyes. "Really?"

"Yes," Yechezkel responded with confidence. "I know how to destroy their plans. At the same time, I'll take revenge for what they did to me and my family."

Robert did not look completely convinced. "How can I be sure that by returning to Afghanistan you're not trying to get away from us?"

"There is no need to convince you of that. It's up to you to decide if you want to assist me or not. If you do, that's fine. And if not, I'll find a way to go without you."

"And what happens if we stop you from going back there?"

"You'll just be harming your efforts to fight terror." Yechezkel looked Robert squarely in the eyes. "My brother and I will refuse to cooperate with you as long as our parents are not with us."

Robert heard the ironclad determination in Yechezkel's voice. One look at Yosef told him that he was in complete agreement.

"Okay," Robert ceded. "We'll have to run it by the director, of course, but I suppose he'll have to agree. How are you planning to go back there?"

"Simple." Yechezkel was smiling widely now. "You'll bring us back."

Twenty One

Rachamim was the first to wake up. He was lying on an old, filthy mattress, covered with a torn blanket. Looking around, he realized that he was in a tent made out of dark green canvas. He wondered where he was and how he had gotten there.

His head felt fuzzy. He noticed an intravenous pole next to his mattress. Why was it there? A plastic tube was leading into the vein of his right hand. Had he been in a traffic accident? Was he taken to a military hospital, for some reason? Rachamim's mind was blank.

He was shivering. He wasn't sure if it was because of the weather, or if it was because he was so weak. He pulled the blanket tightly around him. He saw it was filthy, and knew he was not in an American hospital.

Someone entered the tent, pushing the canvas to the side. The sun was so strong that Rachamim couldn't see who had entered until the flap fell back in place. The man was young and bearded, and wearing a long white robe. There was a purple turban perched on his head. His eyes had a certain gentleness and softness that was in complete contrast to his appearance. He looked just like one of the fanatical Shiites whom Rachamim remembered from before the revolution in Iran.

"Oh, so you've finally woke up." The man was speaking Persian. Rachamim was now certain that he was a Shiite. His accent, however, was different from the one used in Iran.

"Where am I?" Rachamim's lips were so dry that he could barely speak. He also spoke Persian.

"Afghanistan."

Rachamim shivered in terror. It took him a few seconds to compose himself. "Who are you? How did I get here? Why did you bring me here?" The questions poured out in a torrent.

The man held up his hand to stop the flow of questions. "One at a time," he proclaimed in a mocking tone. "First, who brought you here. Who do you think?"

"The … the al Qaeda?"

"Very good," he complimented Rachamim.

Despite his sardonic tone, Rachamim thought he noticed a spark of pity in the man's eyes, something that he had not expected to find in a member of that murderous organization. He wondered if he could trust his instincts. "Why did you bring me to Afghanistan? What use am I to you?"

The man did not respond immediately. He crossed to the other side of the tent and bent over, clearly examining something or someone.

With great effort, Rachamim managed to lift his head and look in that direction. He was horrified to see Naomi lying on another mattress.

"Why did you bring her here?" he screamed. "What use is my poor, fragile wife to you?"

Naomi woke up from Rachamim's screams. She turned her head from side to side as she tried to figure out where she was.

"You can help us," the man stated. "We'll give you a wonderful present if you collaborate with us."

"If that means you want us to carry out a terrorist attack, you can forget about it before you even begin!" Rachamim said scathingly. "I am not about to assist you in murdering innocent civilians. Especially since there is nothing you could possibly give us that would compensate for such an act. Our lives are worthless."

The man listened attentively. It seemed that Rachamim's words had an effect on him. He continued speaking gently. "And what if I can bring back your two lost sons?"

Rachamim jerked upright, ignoring his spinning head and protesting muscles. "You're lying," he hissed. "You're just trying to toy with my emotions."

"No, I am not lying. I can prove to you that I know where your children are."

Rachamim moistened his lips. "How?" he whispered.

"The code word ..."

"What code word?"

"*Echad.*" The man pronounced it with an Arabic accent. "Does that word mean anything to you?"

Rachamim fell back on his mattress as a sense of shock flooded through him.

"Isn't that the word you told your children to always remember?"

Rachamim could only nod his head dumbly. This was the first sign he had received from his children since he had parted from them, over twenty years before. It was obvious that this man had been in close contact with at least one of his sons.

"Your two children are alive and well," the man reassured him. He looked at Naomi and saw the tears sliding down her cheeks. "If you cooperate, I'll help you get out of here together with your children. And do not be too concerned—I will not ask you to take part in a terrorist attack."

"How can we help you?" It was difficult for Rachamim to speak. "What do you want us to do?"

"When the time is ripe, I'll tell you. Meanwhile, I want you to try to forget this conversation. Sometimes, for appearance's sake, I'll have to behave brutally. Please try to ignore that. I have to make sure my friends never realize that there is a secret agreement between us."

Rachamim nodded. The man glanced at Naomi. She also nodded her head.

The man turned and left the room without saying another word.

A group of men quietly gathered around the monstrous figure of a UH-60A Blackhawk combat helicopter, parked on the deck of the aircraft carrier Kitty Hawk. Kitty Hawk was stationed on the Pacific Ocean, about two hundred nautical miles from the coast of Pakistan. The night was quieter than usual. Other than the sound of the waves breaking against the side of the ship, and the murmuring of the group of men standing on deck, everything was silent. The sailors and marines readying themselves to attack Afghanistan had been instructed to remain in their rooms.

The pilot, already wearing his helmet, stuck his head out the window of the helicopter. "Ready for takeoff," he announced.

"We're also ready," answered the tall black man standing directly below. He was the commanding officer of the elite unit that was about to set out on a dangerous journey.

The tall black man was the first to climb into the helicopter. Another soldier, wearing the unit's special combat gear, jumped in after him. Then it was Yechezkel's turn. "Are you ready?" the commanding officer asked, extending a helping hand.

"I can climb in by myself," Yechezkel snorted. He turned around to speak with the FBI agent who had accompanied him to the aircraft carrier. "I don't know if I'll survive this mission. I hope to succeed, but if not …"

Yechezkel paused for a moment, then continued. "Tell the FBI director that I am grateful for everything he did for us. I hope to return, but if I fail, please ask him, in my name, to take good care of my younger brother."

"I will relay every word," the agent promised.

"Did you take care of the message I asked you to send?"

The agent nodded. "Yes, it's been done."

"Thanks," Yechezkel said, before jumping into the helicopter. The commander quickly closed the door behind him.

The pilot had already turned on the motor. The commanding officer had to shout to be heard. "We're ready."

The helicopter quickly gained altitude and started flying to the west. It continued flying parallel to the coast of Pakistan for seven miles before making a sharp turn and flying directly toward the coast.

About fifty miles from the coast, the helicopter lowered its altitude so it was just a few meters above the ocean. Pakistan blocked the nautical approach to Afghanistan and refused to allow the United States to operate within its borders, although the country's president, General Musharaf, recently stated that he was inclined to permit the American invasion to operate within the country.

They left the open sea and flew inland. The helicopter slowed down. The region was extremely hilly, making navigation very complicated. The pilot placed the helicopter on automatic pilot, so it would maintain a constant altitude of fifty meters above ground level.

Seven hours after takeoff, the pilot announced that they were now flying above the Tora Bora Mountains. He turned around to look at Yechezkel. "Where do you want us to drop you off?"

Yechezkel was sitting in the helicopter, bent over a map of the region. He looked up. "Seventy-two miles from the Pakistani border, on a straight line with the city of El Zahvil."

The pilot checked the electronic map on the control panel opposite him. "We're located twenty miles from the site. Are you ready?"

"Definitely," Yechezkel responded, his eyes bright with anticipation.

"Be prepared to move quickly," the pilot cautioned him. "We'll touch down for just two minutes, long enough for you to run out and get clear of the rotor while we take off again. As soon as you leave the door, run to the left and then throw yourself on the ground. Understand?"

Yechezkel nodded. He had been given these instructions already.

"Five minutes," the pilot announced.

The men were silent, waiting as the minutes ticked away. Yechezkel stood near the door, next to a crewmember who would be opening the door as soon as they landed.

"Two minutes."

The helicopter began to lose altitude. Yechezkel took a deep breath in anticipation.

"One minute."

The helicopter came to a full stop on the ground. The door slid open.

"Go!"

The crewmember slapped Yechezkel on the shoulder. He leaped out the door, turned to the left and ran several paces forward. He could hear the helicopter rotor turning, and he could feel the sting of sand being thrown up by the air.

Yechezkel threw himself down on the ground just as the helicopter moved forward again, lifting into the air. Within a minute, it had disappeared from view in the inky night sky, though the sound continued to fade for several more minutes.

Everything was silent. Yechezkel scrambled to his feet. He looked around and took a deep breath of the crisp September air. In another few weeks, the weather would change and it would be freezing cold. In the high mountains, the temperatures often dropped to several degrees below zero.

He had asked the pilot to drop him here because he knew that this particular mountaintop was clear of terrorists. The mountain was so steep that it was almost impossible to climb to the top, preventing the organization from bringing equipment or building a military camp here.

But there was another reason he wanted to land there. Someone else knew about this mountaintop. Long ago, he had told his friend Achmad about this lonely spot. Every once in a while the two men would come here together, to have some quiet time to think. They would sit on the stones and dream about their own individual worlds.

Yechezkel had asked the FBI director to post a message to Achmad via the "Vintage Cars" web site, telling Achmad that they needed to meet. He wasn't able to specify a location, but he knew Achmad would understand that this would be their meeting spot.

Yechezkel sat down to wait. He glanced at his watch. It was two o'clock in the morning, local time. He would wait outside until daybreak, at the very least. The darkness protected him from discovery. At dawn, he would climb into the cave he had discovered years ago, and spend the day sleeping until the following night, when he would wait on the mountaintop for Achmad to arrive.

He heard an owl screeching in the distance. Yechezkel smiled. There were no owls at this altitude. It was Achmad calling him. In the past, they had called to each other by imitating the sounds of different birds. He still wanted to be certain, however, that it really was Achmad. Yechezkel screeched like a hawk, then threw himself on the ground and crawled away a few feet to hide behind a large rock nearby.

Again he heard the screech of an owl. This time Yechezkel stood up.

The silhouette of another figure appeared from behind a huge rock and started walking toward him. It was impossible to make out the other person's features in the all-pervading darkness, but from the way he walked, Yechezkel had no doubt that it was his good friend

Achmad. He ran to meet him. The two men fell on each other's shoulders in greeting.

"My brother, how were you saved from your mission?" Achmad asked Yechezkel.

"I found my brother." Yechezkel was smiling widely now.

"You found your brother?" Achmad repeated in astonishment. "Tell me. Tell me more!"

"My brother was also in an al Qaeda training camp. I have a feeling that al Qaeda had originally kidnapped us from our parents."

"I believe that," Achmad interrupted him. "I suspect that they did the same thing to me. I think they use the same tactics with everyone."

"You think so?" Yechezkel was surprised. Until this moment, Achmad had never mentioned a word to him about his past.

"Right now, let's concentrate on your story." Achmad brushed aside his own history.

Yechezkel sighed. His smile was gone now. "I found my brother, and I almost found my parents. At the last moment they were kidnapped from under the noses of the Americans agents, who were trying to bring us together. I am certain that they were brought here. My brother and I received a message to that effect from the organization."

"Yes, they were brought here," Achmad confirmed. "I even know where they are."

Yechezkel looked at him in disbelief. "Can you bring me to them?" he gasped.

"I could," Achmad admitted, "but it would be extremely dangerous."

Yechezkel stood up straight. "I want to take them out of here. I promised my brother, who is waiting for me with the American navy, that I'll bring them back."

"What about the organization? Are you finished with them?"

Yechezkel looked closely at Achmad to see if the question was serious. He could not read his expression. "Yes. My connection with the organization has ended. I have nothing more to do with al Qaeda."

"I also want to get out," Achmad said softly. "But I don't think the time has come for me to leave yet."

"Perhaps you could come back with me!" Yechezkel's eyes sparkled. "I have always thought of you as a brother, and it hurt me to think that I might have to leave you and that I would probably never see you again."

Achmad was more pragmatic. "Let's not discuss this now. We must begin making plans for your parents' escape. Perhaps you can also contact the Americans and ask if I can join you."

"Of course you can. They'll be happy to have you."

"Don't be so certain," Achmad replied, putting a damper on Yechezkel's enthusiasm. "The Americans might suspect that I am a double agent." He fell silent for several minutes. "I have an idea," he said finally. "Contact the Americans and tell them that I am willing to lead them to Abu Salim, in exchange for political asylum."

Yechezkel's eyes grew wide in disbelief. "You can lead them to Abu Salim, bin Laden's assistant? Isn't he the number three man in the organization?"

Achmad smiled. "Yes. Abu Salim is still the Sheikh's assistant, the number three man in the organization."

"How is it that you are able to lead them to such an important person?" Yechezkel wanted to know.

"Much has happened since you left Afghanistan," Achmad said seriously. "While you were training to crash into the White House, I was advancing within the organization. Today I am very close to bin Laden, and I am privy to many of his closely kept secrets. I would be exaggerating if I said that I have Abu Salim. But he is in a place where he can easily be captured, with the help of your American friends, that is."

Yechezkel was skeptical. Everyone knew that bin Laden was extremely careful and trusted very few individuals. While Achmad had been a part of the organization for a long time, he had never been a part of bin Laden's inner circle. What had changed?

By now, the first rays of the sun could be seen on the horizon. Achmad approached the edge of the cliff and looked down onto the deserted rocks that had become visible. "Let me tell you what happened one night, about two years ago. It was a small thing—but it changed everything."

PLAN B

Twenty Two

Achmad had come to this isolated mountaintop to think, as he often did since his friend Ishmael had left on his mission. That night, as he made his way home from the mountaintop, he heard a moaning sound coming from a tiny footpath that wound along the mountainside.

Cautiously, Achmad began walking toward the source of the noise. He saw a glimmer of white ahead on the path. As he grew closer, he realized that a tall, bearded man wearing a white robe was lying in the dirt, obviously in pain. It was only after Achmad offered his assistance to the injured man that he realized he was speaking to the Sheikh himself, Osama bin Laden.

Bin Laden did not explain why he was there. He simply stated that he had stumbled while walking along the path, and he asked Achmad to assist him as he stood and returned to their base. Bin Laden leaned his entire weight on Achmad. Somehow they managed to walk two miles back to the base. Achmad nearly collapsed from the effort.

Upon their return, bin Laden asked Achmad for his name and the name of his unit. The next morning, his commander excitedly told him that he had been invited to a private meeting with their esteemed leader. "I don't know exactly when," the commander admitted. "You will be told at the proper time."

That evening, bin Laden's messenger arrived in a dusty army jeep. "Come here," he ordered. "I need to put this on you." He held out a frayed white cloth. Achmad approached hesitantly, but allowed the messenger to place a blindfold over his eyes. The man then helped Achmad climb in the jeep.

Achmad sat, disoriented from his inability to see where they were going, as the jeep drove along twisted roads for about an hour. The jeep jerked to a sudden stop. Achmad felt a hand grip his elbow as his companion assisted him in climbing out of the jeep. He began walking, careful to keep from stumbling as the man guided him through what seemed like endless twisted corridors.

Suddenly the guide grabbed him by the shoulders and forced him to stand still. The blindfold was removed. Achmad blinked, trying to get used to the sudden light.

Once his vision cleared, he could see a beautiful wooden paneled door right in front of him. "From here on, you'll have to walk alone," the guide said. "I am not allowed to go any further."

Achmad stepped forward. With a sense of trepidation, he turned the doorknob and pushed the door slowly open. But an innocuous sight met his eyes—a long corridor, with the far end shrouded in shadow.

Achmad's back prickled as he walked down the hall. He could sense hidden eyes watching every move. He reached the end of the hallway, only to discover yet another door, similarly paneled in wood.

Achmad drew in his breath sharply as he swung the second door open. He had reached his destination. Osama bin Laden was seated on an exquisite Persian carpet—the only sign of luxury in the austerely furnished room.

"Come, sit next to me," bin Laden invited him warmly.

Tongue-tied, Achmad sat down next to his hero and revered leader. Bin Laden quickly put him at his ease. Before long, Achmad found himself telling bin Laden of his innermost feelings, including his fervent belief in al Qaeda.

"I have a new job for you," bin Laden told him, after they had been speaking for nearly an hour. "I need a personal assistant, someone who can help me with day-to-day tasks, someone I can count on."

Achmad caught his breath. "I would be honored," he finally managed to say.

In his new position, Achmad learned much about al Qaeda, its methods and its goals. He became privy to a great deal of confidential information as bin Laden's trust in him grew. And finally, just the day before, bin Laden had entrusted Achmad with an extremely sensitive task: caring for a couple who had been mysteriously brought into the camp.

The couple, Achmad quickly discovered, were none other than the parents of his dear friend, Ishmael.

Yechezkel stared at Achmad in shock. "My parents are in your hands?"

Achmad nodded his head.

"I want to see them." Yechezkel pleaded.

Achmad shook his head. "Not yet. It's still too early. It will endanger me, you and them."

Yechezkel's eyes filled with tears. "At least let them know that their son is well, and that I am nearby."

"That is also impossible," Achmad said firmly. "They would not be able to hide their knowledge—their excitement will be too great. One of the guards might realize what's going on, and that will destroy any hope we have for their rescue."

"So how will I be able to see them?"

"Tell the Americans that the helicopter should return here at midnight tomorrow. I'll make sure your parents will be here, and together we'll escape."

Yechezkel removed a tiny satellite phone from his belt and prepared to transmit Achmad's request. Achmad placed his hand over the phone and stopped him from dialing. "Promise your American friends that after they take me out of here, I'll hand Abu Salim to them," he told him.

"All right." Yechezkel turned on the telephone and dialed the number that the helicopter's commanding officer had given him. Before he finished dialing, he realized that Achmad had already started climbing down the cliff. "Wait for me here," Achmad called up to him. "Hide here during the day, and tomorrow at midnight I'll be back here with your parents."

"Don't you want to wait to hear the American's response?"

Achmad's expression was hidden by the darkness. "Your contact man will not be able to give an immediate response. He'll have to discuss it first with people higher up in the government hierarchy. By tomorrow night, though, you'll have a positive answer."

Achmad was gone by the time the helicopter's commanding officer got on the line. Yechezkel quickly told him about the conditions that Achmad had made for rescuing his parents, as well as the prize that he would be giving them for his own rescue. He recognized from the officer's reaction that he was excited at the mention of Abu Salim's name.

In the end, his response was exactly as Achmad had predicted. "I'll call you later to confirm. I have to discuss this with my superiors."

After finishing the conversation, Yechezkel looked around at the mountaintop where he had spent so much time throughout his teenage years. He stood at the edge of the cliff and gazed nostalgically into the darkened valley. In just one more day, he'd be leaving this region forever. He couldn't wait to be reunited with his parents.

The dark, camouflaged helicopter blended into the inky darkness of the moonless night. The crew had been ordered to keep radio silence while flying this close to al Qaeda's hunting grounds. Ken Caron, the pilot, was wearing a special helmet with built-in low-light goggles. The green and gray display showed the mountain peaks surrounding them, as they flew just several hundred feet above the treetops.

Caron jerked the stick back to climb over a dangerously high peak, then immediately lowered his altitude to avoid any nearby unfriendly radar detectors. Alex Kyle, the co-pilot, was busily adjusting one of the instruments on the control panel while he kept track of the helicopter's altitude.

"We've crossed the border into Pakistan," Caron announced. The soldiers sitting in the back were relieved. While the danger had not yet completely passed, here they were in relatively friendly territory. They were also happy that the region was becoming less hilly. They were growing seasick from the constant movement of the helicopter as it traveled right above the changing landscape.

Still, it would be another four hours before they reached the Pacific Ocean. Only then would they be able to start flying at a normal altitude.

The helicopter landed on Kitty Hawk just before dawn. The exhausted crew was surprised to see the ship's captain standing there as they climbed down from the helicopter. "Great job," he congratulated each one. "Yechezkel has already contacted us. So far, everything is on track." The captain hesitated. "Do you think you'll be ready to make the trip again tonight? We'll need to get Yechezkel and his parents back here."

The pilot nodded. "Sure, we'll do it. But how confident are we that this isn't a trap? How much faith do we have in Yechezkel's contact man? He might let bin Laden know that we're on our way."

"It's a risk," the captain agreed. "You'll have backup, though. After Yechezkel called us, I sent another Blackhawk with several troops from the Delta unit. They're watching the hills where you dropped Yechezkel off. As of now, they have not reported any unusual activity in the area."

At eight-thirty in the morning, Achmad gently knocked on the door of the room where Rachamim and his wife were imprisoned. They had been moved here from the tent the day before, after the doctor had pronounced them to be in perfect health. The hinges screamed in protest as he pushed the door open. The hinges were fairly new, but the dampness of this underground cave had caused them to quickly rust through.

Rachamim was in the middle of *davening*, the tears coursing down his cheeks. He did not respond to Achmad's arrival, though he could not have missed the door opening. Naomi looked up, apathetic, but quickly stared back down at the ground.

Achmad cleared his throat. "How are you this morning?"

Rachamim raised his tear-stained face. His eyes were deadened, expressing his deep despair. He was a strong man who had survived many tragedies. But now, he felt certain, there was no hope left. He had no idea why the al Qaeda had brought him here to begin with, but he had no illusions that they would ever let him go.

Achmad stood there, looking indecisive. He seemed to struggle with an inner decision. He finally spoke again. "I had an important visitor last night."

Rachamim just stared at him.

"You'll be happy to meet him," Achmad went on.

Neither one responded. After all, who would they possibly want to meet out here in the Tora Bora Mountains?

"It's time for you to be reunited with your son."

That finally got a reaction. Both Rachamim and Naomi leaped to their feet. Naomi's eyes were filled with sudden hope. But Rachamim was more wary.

"Don't toy with our emotions," he said harshly. "Tell me what you mean."

"I mean it," Achmad insisted. "Your son has come to visit you."

Rachamim did not believe him. It was true that Achmad had given them a sign that their son was alive, but perhaps it was because he had tortured one of them until he finally learned the secret. Rachamim had spent dozens of years searching for his son, without finding a single clue. He was unable to believe that his search had finally ended.

"You're lying," Rachamim hissed.

"I am telling the truth," Achmad stated. "To prove it, I will give you another sign from your children." Achmad paused. "Didn't you tear an Iranian bill and tell them that the numbers across the bottom are the numbers of your Swiss bank account?"

Rachamim's eyes widened in surprise and wonder. He knew that if al Qaeda had known about the Swiss bank account, they would have removed the money from it long before. Rachamim was now convinced.

"Where are they?" he demanded. His voice rose, until he was nearly shouting. "Where are my children?"

Achmad placed the palm of his hand over Rachamim's mouth to keep him quiet. "We must be extremely cautious," he whispered.

Achmad slowly removed his hand from Rachamim's mouth. Rachamim remained silent, but his pleading gaze spoke volumes. From the corner of his eye, Achmad could see Naomi sitting in the corner and sobbing.

"We must be cautious," Achmad said again, supporting Rachamim as they walked across the room to sit next to Naomi. "Your son has come here to rescue you. The two of you will have to wait another day before I can bring you to him. Tonight I'll come here to take you to the meeting place. An American rescue force will be waiting there for us, and it will take us out of Afghanistan and back to the United States."

"May Hashem's name be blessed, now and forever," Rachamim whispered in Hebrew.

"What did you just say?" Achmad asked.

"Just a verse of thanksgiving, thanking G-d for returning my lost son."

"Instead of reciting prayers of thanksgiving, pray to your G-d that He help us get out of here," Achmad suggested. "There is still plenty of danger ahead of us."

Achmad walked to the door. "I'm going to leave you now. Remember, you must continue to act as if you don't know anything about your son, and that there is no connection between us."

"We will," Rachamim assured him.

Achmad slipped out, and the door banged shut behind him.

Instructions came into Kitty Hawk at two-thirty in the afternoon. The crew would be heading back into Afghanistan to rescue Yechezkel. This time, however, a second helicopter would be coming along. In addition to retrieving the Delta unit, the helicopters would be taking out three additional people. The helicopter would enter Afghanistan that night at midnight. Yechezkel, his parents and his contact man would be waiting at the same spot where they had been dropped off the day before.

The officers in command of the two helicopters spent the rest of the day discussing the details of the operation. It was obvious that they would have to retain radio silence throughout the flight. The communication men on both flights reviewed the signs they had agreed upon, using infrared lights to signal in Morse code.

At nightfall, the two helicopters lifted off Kitty Hawk and began flying toward Pakistan. They penetrated Pakistan at low altitude and flew directly toward Afghanistan.

The screeching made by the hinges as the door was pushed open rudely pulled Rachamim and Naomi out of their sleep. They jumped up in confusion. Achmad was standing in the middle of the room, dressed in black overalls. His head was encased in a black hood, leaving just his face showing.

"Put these on quickly." Achmad handed them two pairs of black overalls, similar to the ones he was wearing.

Rachamim and Naomi quickly put the overalls over their clothes. Achmad handed them two black hoods. "Place these over your heads. I don't want you to stand out in the darkness."

As the two complied, Achmad stuck his head out the door and peered around the empty hallway. He put his head back in. "Follow me." He quickly crossed the hallway, with Rachamim and his wife trailing close behind.

When they reached the end of the hall, Achmad turned off the light switch. The hall was enveloped in an inky blackness. "I had to turn off the lights," he whispered. "Otherwise the guards might notice the light when I open the door." They heard a door open, and felt an icy wind on their faces. They had spent the last few days breathing the stale air in the cave, and without thinking, they automatically took a deep breath of the fresh night air.

"The area's clear. Follow me," they heard Achmad whisper. It was too dark for them to see his figure. It was so dark outside that if not for the fresh air and wind, they would have thought they were still in the building. The stars were completely concealed by heavy clouds.

Once their eyes were used to the inky blackness, they were able to discern Achmad's figure. He looked like a shadow moving ahead of them. Achmad walked slowly, taking into account Rachamim and Naomi's age and health.

Achmad stopped in front of a black mass. When they got closer, they saw it was a jeep which had been painted black for camouflage. Rachamim felt a firm hand grasping his own. "Let me help you climb into the jeep," Achmad whispered.

Rachamim gladly accepted the offer. He was exhausted by the events of the last few days. Achmad also helped Naomi climb into the back seat, next to her husband. Then he jumped into the driver's seat and sped off.

They drove along the twisting mountain paths. Achmad wore a special helmet with night goggles—a replica, in fact, of the helmets used by the helicopter pilots. He was the only one who could see the narrow twisting paths they were driving along, with steep cliffs on either side.

The car came to a sudden halt. "We're here," Achmad said loudly. "We'll have to proceed by foot. Will you be able to manage?"

Rachamim was frightened. "Why are you talking so loudly? Don't you think someone might hear you?"

Achmad laughed. "Yes, I'm sure someone's listening to us. These mountains are crawling with soldiers."

Rachamim shuddered. Had Achmad been playing a game with them? Had he rescued them from prison to lead them into another trap?

"Don't worry," Achmad said reassuringly. "The soldiers surrounding us are American troops, though they don't know that I can see them."

"Raise your hands," they heard someone behind them order in fluent English.

For Rachamim, the English language was like a breath of fresh air. Delighted that safety was close at hand, he instinctively turned his head to see the person who was speaking to them.

He was stopped by the click of a gun. "Stand still. Don't move." The order was given by someone standing just a few feet away.

Rachamim obeyed. He understood that the soldiers had to be cautious. Strong hands checked his pockets.

"He's clean," said the man.

"So is mine," said another voice just a few feet away.

"What's your name?" the man standing behind Rachamim asked.

"Rachamim Roji."

The man standing behind Rachamim turned on a small two-way radio. "We've got group number two," he announced. "They're alone."

"I'm directly above you," a choppy voice said on the radio. "I'm lowering the penetrator."

Rachamim could hear the rotors beat against the air. But it was too dark for him to see a thing.

Rachamim felt, rather than heard, something descend through the air and land next to him. "Please sit down," one of the soldiers said. He did not wait for Rachamim to sit down—he carefully guided him to what seemed to be a small metal seat on the end of a chain. A hook secured Rachamim in place. Within seconds, he was being lifted up toward the sky.

A strong arm reached out and pulled him into the helicopter. "Recovery complete," a voice announced. The helicopter door was banged shut.

"Naomi, are you here?" Rachamim asked. It was so dark that he could not even see his own hands.

"Yes, I'm here," she responded.

"But where is my son?" he screamed. They were leaving Afghanistan without him!

"You'll see him soon," one of the soldiers replied. "He was taken out earlier, on a different helicopter. You'll have to wait patiently for another seven hours or so."

Twenty Three

"**I must speak to al Zawahiri** immediately," Yassin told the guard, who was trying to prevent him from entering the command base. "Something terrible has happened. I must inform al Zawahiri right now. It can't wait."

The guard looked at his watch. "It's four o'clock in the morning! Al Zawahiri is sound asleep at this hour."

"You don't understand. Time is precious. You'll regret it if you don't let me speak with him immediately."

The guard wasn't completely convinced, but he let Yassin inside. "I am letting you in on condition that you accept complete responsibility for this," he warned. "Wait here."

The guard entered the hallway leading to the bedrooms reserved for the organization's elite. He stopped in front of the last door and knocked lightly.

"Who's there?" he heard a sleepy voice ask.

"It's me, Mustapha."

With half-closed eyes, al Zawahiri glanced at the alarm clock next to his bed. It was 4:17 in the morning. "Can't it wait?" he asked, hoping to catch a few more hours of sleep.

"No," Mustapha replied hesitantly. "Yassin is here and he says he must speak with you urgently. He told me that it's of utmost importance and that it can't wait."

"Okay. Give me a few minutes."

Growing impatient, Yassin had stalked down the hallway after the guard. He was in time to catch al Zawahiri's final words.

"Every moment is precious!" Yassin shouted.

"Who's that?" al Zawahiri asked from the other side of the door.

"It's Yassin. Rachamim's guard."

"Okay, okay. I'm coming." Al Zawahiri opened the door, barefoot and still trying to tie his kefiya. He looked half-asleep and confused.

Yassin fell to al Zawahiri's feet. "I'm not to blame!" he gasped in terror. "I did everything I could!"

"What in the world are you talking about?" al Zawahiri asked impatiently, pushing the crying Yassin with his foot.

Al Zawahiri was exhausted. Bin Laden had kept him in a meeting until after one o'clock this morning, discussing the expected American attack. And now here was Yassin, whining like a sick cat. "Get off the floor," al Zawahiri snapped, this time kicking the groveling Yassin with more force. "Tell me exactly what happened."

Al Zawahiri's anger intensified Yassin's fear, but he made a massive effort to pull himself together. Stuttering in his nervousness, he managed to say, "Th … they ran away. The A … Americans escaped."

"They did?" Al Zawahiri became very still. When he spoke next, the coldness of his voice chilled Yassin's blood. "And how did they escape?"

Yassin felt faint. "I don't know! I know I locked their cell. I also locked the section of the cave where their cell was located. I noticed just twenty minutes ago that the section was open and realized that something dreadful must have happened. I raced to their cell. The door was unlocked and the cell was empty."

Al Zawahiri stared at him. "Did someone else come to visit the section after you locked it?"

"Um … no."

He was not convincing. Al Zawahiri knew that Yassin was lying. "Tell me, who visited the section after you locked it?"

"Um … I … I don't know." Yassin was quivering in fright.

Al Zawahiri slapped him hard across the face. Yassin tumbled to the ground. "If you value your life, then stop lying to me."

Shaking his head groggily, Yassin managed to sit up and lean against the wall. "He forbade me to tell anyone about his visit," he muttered, gingerly feeling his bruised cheek.

"Who forbade you to say something? Is there someone above me who you've begun listening to?" Al Zawahiri glared down at Yassin.

Yassin glanced toward the guard, who was still standing there, to let al Zawahiri know that he couldn't speak as long as the guard was present.

"Leave us alone," al Zawahiri commanded the guard, who quickly retreated down the hall.

"It was Achmad," Yassin whispered the moment the guard was out of hearing range. He continued looking around to make sure no one else was listening.

"Achmad?" Al Zawahiri looked startled.

"Yes, Achmad. The Sheikh's personal assistant."

"I know which Achmad you are referring to," al Zawahiri said impatiently. "What was Achmad doing there?"

"I don't know," Yassin answered hesitantly, trying to sound as trustworthy as possible. "He told me that he had been sent by our revered leader, and that no one is allowed to know of his visit. He warned me that our revered leader will hang me if he finds out that I told anyone about his visit."

Al Zawahiri had no idea how to react. If bin Laden had ordered it … but on the other hand, something did not make sense to him. "What do you mean that you don't know what he did when he was there? You were there, and you're not blind. At least I don't think you're blind."

"He commanded me to remain in headquarters until dawn."

Al Zawahiri nodded grimly. All the evidence seemed to point toward Achmad. As far as he knew, Achmad was the only one who visited the cell that night. There was no legitimate reason for him to go there at such a late hour.

Still, that left open the question of Achmad's motives. He could not believe that bin Laden had sent him. Achmad must be a traitor. But what interest did he have in the Americans? What was he trying to accomplish?

One immediately following the other, the two helicopters landed on Kitty Hawk's enormous landing pad. Yechezkel was the first to leave the aircraft, together with the soldiers who had rescued him. The second helicopter carried Achmad, Rachamim and Naomi.

The ship's commander, Rick Newhouse, approached the helicopters the moment the rotors stopped. He warmly greeted each of the soldiers as they disembarked, thanking them individually for their part in making this mission a success. After that, he went over to Rachamim, who was pale and trembling from exhaustion as he assisted Naomi in getting out of the aircraft.

Newhouse beckoned to Rachamim. "Come, join me in my office," he invited him. "There's someone waiting to meet you."

Rachamim felt as if a bolt of electricity had coursed through his body. He looked anxiously at Naomi. He didn't know how she would react to meeting her long-lost sons. It would have to be done gradually.

Naomi looked up at her husband questioningly. He nodded at her reassuringly as the commander led them off the deck and into a corridor. "Watch your step," he cautioned. The doorsills were high, making it necessary to lift their feet as they hurried after the commander.

"Do you know if my children are here, on this ship?" Naomi called to the commander.

Rachamim and Rick Newhouse exchanged glances. Rachamim was relieved to see that Newhouse also recognized the need to be cautious. Neither wanted Naomi to be overcome with shock at the moment of reunion.

"Possibly," Newhouse said finally. "Come to my office, relax a little, and then we'll talk."

Naomi had to be content with that.

Up on deck, Achmad was still standing next to the helicopter. No one seemed to be paying any attention; it almost appeared as if he could wander around at will. But Achmad realized that he was being closely watched. The two pilots had remained in the cockpit, and he suspected that they were keeping a close eye on his movements.

A young officer walked up to him. "Come with me, please."

Achmad followed the officer down ladders and through narrow corridors, into the bowels of the ship. He stopped in front of an unassuming steel door and knocked lightly.

The room was simply furnished. A middle-aged officer wearing a light gray uniform was sitting behind a desk. He was holding a gold pen and doodling on a notepad.

The officer stood up and greeted him warmly. "Jim Wilson," he introduced himself, extending his hand. Achmad blinked in amazement at the officer's height. He must have been at least six and a half feet tall. The palm of his hand was so huge that it almost swallowed Achmad's.

"Take a seat, please," Wilson said in fluent Arabic.

As Achmad gingerly sat down, the soldier who had accompanied him retreated to the corner and stood, watching him intently. Achmad realized that he was still considered a dangerous member of a terrorist group. He knew he would have to earn the Americans' trust.

"According to what we've heard, you've become one of bin Laden's close confidants," the officer began. "Is that correct?"

"Yes, that is so." Achmad replied.

"What can you tell us about al Qaeda?"

"A lot," Achmad responded, hoping to impress him.

Jim Wilson nodded noncommittally. This wasn't the first time he had interrogated prisoners, and Achmad's reaction was typical. It indicated that the prisoner was interested in striking a deal. While under normal circumstances he would wait a few days, trying to get the information without having to give anything in return, the circumstances now were anything but normal. Al Qaeda had struck a terrible blow to the United States, and they needed to know what else was being planned. His superiors were pressuring him to obtain information as quickly as possible.

"Give me an example. What type of information can you give us?" Wilson asked.

"I know bin Laden's location, at least until this morning. I also know where the next in command, al Zawahiri, can be found."

"That information is of limited value," Wilson noted.

"You're right," Achmad admitted. "By now they are almost certainly on their way to a different location. However, what they don't know is that I can find Abu Salim."

"Oh?" Wilson said, masking his excitement.

"Yes." Achmad leaned forward eagerly. "That information is secret, but I managed to find it out, thanks to my close association with Osama bin Laden. They have no reason to tell him to hide. So I will be able to lead you right to him."

"I see. So what would you want in return? Are you asking for political amnesty?"

"That's not enough for me," Achmad replied. "I'm really not sure that I even need political amnesty. After all, I never did anything to harm the United States."

"So what are your conditions?"

"Twenty-five million dollars. You promised a twenty-five million dollar reward to anyone providing information that will lead to the arrest of Abu Salim."

"That was the amount offered," Wilson admitted. He disliked the idea of rewarding a member of al Qaeda. But he realized that he could not play games with Achmad. "Give me a few minutes to phone Washington and get permission."

"No problem. I have all the time in the world. Oh, by the way, when you call your superiors in Washington, don't forget to ask them to provide me with a new identity, in addition to an American passport."

"Don't worry. Once you become a part of our protected program, all the details will be taken care of."

Wilson motioned to the soldier standing guard, who had been silent throughout the exchange. The man came to attention.

"Could you wait outside for a few minutes, please?" Wilson requested.

Achmad shrugged. "Of course." He allowed the soldier to lead him out of the office. They were waiting in the corridor less than five minutes when Wilson's raised voice called them back in.

"My superiors in Washington accept your conditions. They are willing to give you the reward."

"Wonderful," Achmad responded eagerly. "Here is the information you need. Abu Salim is presently in Mexico, not far from the American border."

"In Mexico?" Wilson's astonishment quickly turned to fear. The United States had been concerned that al Qaeda would try to create a base in Mexico. The border between the United States and Mexico was nearly impossible to police, and illegal crossings were common. Now al Qaeda had an easy, convenient entry point into the United States.

"Yes, in Mexico. He was sent there to build a military camp to be used in missions against the United States. After the events of September 11, bin Laden realized that it would be difficult for terrorists to enter the United States through the airports. Mexico provides an easy way to get into the country."

"Where in Mexico?"

"Do you have a map?" Achmad asked.

Wilson reached into a drawer and pulled out a package of maps. He sorted through them quickly, finally choosing one and unfolding it on the desk. Achmad leaned over the map and studied it carefully before pointing at one spot near the Mexican-American border.

"Here. Abu Salim created a military camp right at this location. The base is still small. But it is developing rapidly, and the next attack will go out from this base."

Wilson had difficulty containing his excitement. "How large is the base?"

"At the moment, there are less than twenty soldiers, including Abu Salim. There's a small airport and helicopter pad. As soon as everything is finished, they will start transporting additional soldiers and equipment from Afghanistan to Mexico."

"Do you have any information about the planned attacked?"

Achmad looked about fearfully, and his voice dropped to a whisper. "They are planning to attack the United States with a nuclear missile."

Wilson forced himself to remain impassive. For some time, the military had been concerned that bin Laden was trying to get his hands on weapons of mass destruction. This was the first time they had received confirmation of that from a reliable source.

"Is there any more information you can give me?"

Wilson tried to play it cool, but Achmad knew that he had struck the jackpot. A small smile played on his lips as he removed a piece of paper from his pocket. "I photocopied this document that I found on our leader's desk."

Wilson put on his reading glasses and unfolded the paper. The document contained a detailed map of the Mexican desert bordering the United States. There was a red star drawn in the center. The map looked as if it had been photocopied from another document, while the red star appeared to have been drawn in by hand.

"That's the location of the al Qaeda base," Achmad explained, pointing to the red star.

Wilson raised his eyes and asked, "Who added the red star?"

"Me. That's the way it looked in the original document. For some reason, it didn't come out properly when I copied it."

"Okay. I'll send the document straight to Washington."

Twenty Four

Osama bin Laden folded his legs beneath his body as he sat back down on the rug. Al Zawahiri was too nervous to sit; he stood, shifting from foot to foot as bin Laden closed his eyes and breathed deeply for a moment. Finally he raised his head and gazed squarely into al Zawahiri's eyes.

"Achmad knows the exact location of our base in Mexico." His tone was serene.

"What!" Al Zawahiri clutched at his head. "This is even worse than I thought. He will tell all this to the Americans! How does he know about it?"

Bin Laden smiled slightly. "I made sure he remained alone in my office while the document was on my desk. He took advantage of the time that I wasn't in the room to make a copy of the document."

Al Zawahiri stared at bin Laden. Something strange was going on. Bin Laden was always very careful about security. Why was he taking such risks now, at this critical time? It almost seemed as if he was glad that Achmad knew the location of their secret base. "How did he know that the document was referring to the base in Mexico?" he asked.

"He was here with me when I told Abu Salim about the base."

"Wasn't Abu Salim concerned about the young soldier's presence?"

"Of course it bothered him. But he had to rely on me when I told him that I trusted this young man implicitly."

"And now you realize that you made a mistake," al Zawahiri responded hesitantly. Even as he said the words, he realized that he was wrong. There was something, a vital piece of knowledge, that he was missing which would enable him to piece it all together.

Bin Laden's smile deepened. "No, I did not make a mistake. I assure you, I knew exactly what I was doing." He laughed. "I realized the entire time that Achmad could not be trusted."

Al Zawahiri was totally confused. "You knew that he could not be trusted, and yet you left him alone with a top secret document!"

"And that's exactly why I left him there. I even gave him enough time to copy the document. I did not come back into my office until I saw with my hidden television camera that he had finished copying the document and returned it to its place."

The puzzle seemed to have no solution. Al Zawahiri knew that bin Laden had a scheme up his sleeve. "Am I allowed to know what you're planning?" he asked.

"Of course. I think it's about time to bring you into the picture."

With a wave of his hand, bin Laden invited al Zawahiri to join him on the rug. His nervousness gone, al Zawahiri was finally able to sit down comfortably. Apparently, whatever had happened was somehow according to plan.

Bin Laden started speaking very softly. Al Zawahiri had to lean forward to be able to hear him clearly. "I don't think you know the entire history of the people we kidnapped. You already know that the two pilots who were supposed to fly into the White House, Ishmael and Essam, are brothers.

"The two brothers came under my wing when their family was trying to escape Iran. They had arranged with a smuggler to get their family across the border into Turkey." Bin Laden smiled. "They didn't know that their smuggler was actually working for me.

"I arranged to have a helicopter pick them up. Once in the air, the pilot announced that they were being shot at by the Americans. In the confusion that followed, my men knocked all the family members unconscious. Then the pilot crossed the border and landed the helicopter in a mountainous region of Turkey.

"The brothers were sent to live with separate members of our organization. A member of the organization also took in the parents and told them that the helicopter had crashed, and that he had found the two of them half-dead. A similar story was told to each of the brothers, so each thought he was the only one to survive the crash. By blaming the crash on the Americans, we began training the children to hate the United States.

"This cover story worked well for many years. The man who had supposedly saved the couple from certain death has remained in close contact with them for over twenty years, and I have asked him to continue keeping a close eye on the couple. Since the father is paying my agent a decent living wage, there is no need for me to finance this dormant cell's living expenses.

"The two children were later transferred to Afghanistan, where they were converted to Islam and recruited into al Qaeda when the organization was still in its beginning stages.

"As we began planning the tremendous events of September 11, I came to the conclusion that these two brothers were the best candidates for striking a lethal blow to the United States. I planned to have them destroy the White House. Imagine the irony!" Bin Laden nodded in satisfaction. "The Jews themselves would destroy the source of their strength."

"But it didn't happen," al Zawahiri dared to say.

Bin Laden sighed. "True. It never occurred to me that during the hijacking these two brothers would discover that they were related. After all, they had not seen each other since they had been taken away from their parents. For years, each had assumed that he was the only one to survive."

"How did the two brothers discover that they were related?" al Zawahiri asked.

Bin Laden extended his hands. "I have no idea. But that is almost certainly why they ended up refusing to complete their mission."

"How does Achmad fit into the picture?"

"Simple. Achmad was Ishmael's closest friend. Throughout the years of their training, the two men would often spend their free time together. I knew that if Ishmael would ever need something from within the organization, he would turn to Achmad for help.

"I deliberately chose Achmad as my personal assistant. I wanted him to be privy to all our secrets—at least, the ones that I chose to share with him. I made sure he knew how to find Abu Salim. When I kidnapped Ishmael's parents, I let the brothers know that their parents had been taken back to Afghanistan, then gave Achmad full access to the prisoners."

Again bin Laden smiled. "The bait worked even better than I had planned. The two brothers contacted Achmad, and the older one came here to rescue his parents."

Al Zawahiri was flabbergasted. "You knew that Ishmael was here, in Afghanistan, and you allowed him to slip through our fingers without forcing him to give an account for his traitorous behavior?"

"Oh, don't worry. He'll still have to give an account for his betrayal," bin Laden laughed. "He'll certainly have to give an account."

"I don't understand," al Zawahiri protested. "It sounds as if you wanted Ishmael to come here to rescue his parents. Why, if not to capture and punish him?"

"Because I have a much better punishment in mind." Bin Laden suddenly became serious. "Remember the nuclear missile?"

"How can I forget?" al Zawahiri muttered with a shudder.

"As you know, we sent it to the Mexican base with Abu Salim—though he isn't aware of it, of course."

Al Zawahiri waited. He knew there was more to the story.

"Abu Salim has no idea that he was chosen to be the *shahid* (martyr) who will explode this missile in a heavily populated city in the United States," bin Laden went on, "becoming the tool for Islam's revenge against the American infidels."

"But won't Achmad ruin your plan?" Al Zawahiri still could not fathom why bin Laden had allowed Achmad to discover Abu Salim's whereabouts. "Won't he tell the Americans how to find Abu Salim and the nuclear missile?"

"I'm counting on it, in fact," bin Laden told him. "This will solve the problem we discussed before—how we will bring the bomb into the United States."

Al Zawahiri nodded. He remembered broaching this subject as soon as bin Laden had told him about the missile.

"I asked you to come up with a solution," bin Laden went on, "but I actually already had an idea of my own."

"And that is?" al Zawahiri asked.

"The Americans themselves will bring the bomb into the United States."

Al Zawahiri blinked in surprise. "How will that ever happen?"

"They're about to capture Abu Salim, right?"

"Yes ..." Al Zawahiri let his voice trail off as he began to understand the plan. Of course! That was why bin Laden had made Achmad his confidant, and why he had allowed him to photocopy the map showing the exact location of their Mexican base. "Does Abu Salim know anything about this?"

"What do you think?" bin Laden retorted.

"That he doesn't know a thing," al Zawahiri smiled.

"Exactly. While Abu Salim is talented at convincing recruits to become *shahids* for our holy cause, he would hardly consider such a drastic step for himself. I, however, feel differently. Therefore, without his knowledge, I have given him the privilege of performing the greatest mission in history for the good of Islam. As a result of his personal sacrifice, the world will finally show Islam the respect it deserves."

Al Zawahiri suddenly went very still. *Who knows what bin Laden has planned for me?*

"Don't worry," bin Laden said, as if reading al Zawahiri's mind. "You are more important to me alive than dead."

Al Zawahiri took a deep breath. "So the Americans capture Abu Salim. How will that bring the bomb into the United States?"

"Oh, very simple. The Americans will enter Mexico with some sort of military aircraft, undoubtedly one that can carry missiles. In order to invade the military base, they'll land the aircraft."

Al Zawahiri was an expert in military strategy. It was difficult for him to understand how bin Laden could be so confident. "Why are you so certain that they'll land? Maybe they'll just parachute the troops?"

"The forces will have to return to the United States with their prisoners. This is meant to be a two-way trip. They'll need to have the aircraft nearby, so why not land?"

Al Zawahiri wasn't convinced. "They may just parachute the troops, then come back for the troops and the prisoner," he argued. "Leaving aircraft on the ground is an extra risk for discovery, and they'll want to avoid that."

"Perhaps," bin Laden agreed. "This isn't foolproof. But it's certainly worth a try. If it doesn't work out, I will make sure that the Americans do not escape with their prize."

"What are your plans?"

"I already have a special squad keeping the area under constant observation. The moment the aircraft arrives and the troops leave, the squad will sneak up to the helicopter and pump in sleeping gas. While the pilots are sleeping, they'll exchange one of the missiles with our nuclear weapon, which looks the same. When the invading troops return, they'll have no idea that the bombs were exchanged. No security guard is about to check an American military helicopter on its return flight from a military operation. It will never occur to them that the helicopter is carrying deadly cargo."

"And what about the pilots? When they wake up, won't they suspect that something happened?"

"When they wake up, they'll discover two Mexicans emptying their pockets and stuffing a torn suitcase with anything of value that they find. They'll apprehend them. They might even bring them back to the United States to keep them from talking about what they saw."

Al Zawahiri still looked doubtful. "You're building the entire operation on the premise that the American forces will arrive there with a helicopter, and that it will be carrying two identical missiles. What if they don't land the helicopter, or they use different missiles, or—"

"Enough!" bin Laden snapped. "As I said, if that happens the American force will be completely destroyed. Abu Salim will be transferred to a different base, and I'll find a different way to bring the bomb into the United States."

Naomi was beginning to feel claustrophobic—the narrow corridors and steep steps, almost like ladders, led deeper and deeper into the bowels of the huge ship. The aircraft constantly taking off on deck overhead punctuated their journey with thunderous roars. Finally, the captain pushed open a door at the end of a corridor and invited Naomi and Rachamim inside.

As Naomi passed through the open door, she realized that the room was already occupied. Two young men sitting near a table in the small room slowly rose to their feet. She could hear Rachamim gasp, and she looked at her husband in puzzlement. His gaze was locked on the older of the two men standing there.

There was a long, frozen silence. No one seemed to want to speak first.

"Naomi," Rachamim finally said in a whisper, "do you know who these men are?"

Naomi's eyes widened in shock. Logically, she knew that her lost children had long since grown into adulthood. But in her mind they had remained little boys, still in their childhood years. She fought to connect these two men with the trusting little boys who had been so brutally ripped away from her.

Naomi could feel herself sway, and she leaned against the wall for support. Her heart was beating wildly and her throat felt dry. "Yechezkel?" Her voice came out in a croak. "Yosef?"

As if released by the sound of her voice, the two men ran toward them. "Abba, Ima!"

And suddenly they were all together, laughing and crying, tears of sorrow for the lost years indistinguishable from tears of joy at their astounding reunion.

After several minutes Naomi loosened her grip on the boys and stepped back, staring at them, trying to find a comparison between these men in their late twenties and the two children she had known. These two men looked alike, and she was pleased to see a striking resemblance between them and her husband.

"Thank you, Hashem," she whispered, "for making my dream finally come true."

"Ima, it's not a dream," the older son assured her. "The long nightmare is finally over, and now this is reality."

The ship's commander tactfully stayed out of the room for a short while, giving the four of them privacy for their emotional reconciliation. After half an hour, the commander knocked on the door and came in with several soldiers. "I've prepared the guest suite for you," he explained, "where you can have privacy and be more comfortable. Please follow my men and they'll take you there."

Rachamim, Naomi and the two boys walked silently after the cadet as he led them to the suite. The room was tastefully furnished. The walls were covered with cream colored wallpaper and most of the floor with a beautiful hand-woven rug. White sofas were placed strategically at either end of the room, with a glass coffee table in the center. The cadet pointed to a telephone hanging on the wall. "If you need anything, you can use this phone to call me," he explained. "There's no need to dial, just pick up the receiver and it will automatically dial my extension."

The cadet gave a slight bow and left the room. Naomi and Rachamim remained standing, wondering how to begin the conversation.

"Let's sit down," Yechezkel suggested.

They all sat on the same sofa. "Abba, how were you saved when the helicopter crashed?" Yosef asked.

"I really don't know. Ima and I must have been unconscious for some time. I have no idea what happened while we were unconscious. Actually, I can't even remember that the helicopter crashed. I got knocked out somehow when the pilot was trying to get away from the Americans—I must have banged my head on something."

Yosef threw his brother a meaningful glance, which was not lost on Rachamim. "I am not sure that you are correct," Yosef noted.

"What do you mean?" Rachamim tried to understand.

"I'll explain soon. Meanwhile, continue telling me what happened. You said that you were unconscious for some time. What happened after that?"

The brothers listened intently as Rachamim related everything that had happened when he had woken up in Jamil's home, after the supposed helicopter crash. Just as he was finishing his story, someone knocked lightly on the door. The cadet waited for them to respond and then pushed the door open. He was standing in the doorway holding a tray with sandwiches, a thermos, several cups, coffee, sugar and milk.

"Can I offer you a sandwich and something hot to drink?" the cadet politely asked.

"Um … is it kosher?" Rachamim asked, looking askance at the tray.

The cadet looked blank. "I have no idea." He brought the tray closer and placed it on the coffee table. "Can you tell by looking at it?"

Rachamim took one look at the bologna and cheese sandwich and shook his head. "This is definitely not kosher, I'm afraid."

Yechezkel and Yosef were looking at him in puzzlement. It was clear that they didn't have the slightest idea of what he was talking about. With a heavy heart, Rachamim realized that they had undoubtedly forgotten nearly everything they had once known. He silently prayed that he would find the way to reach their hearts and bring them back to their Jewish heritage.

"I'm sure we have kosher food available on the ship," the cadet exclaimed. "I'm going to speak with the chaplain. He'll know what we have that we can serve you."

"You don't have to put yourself out like that," Rachamim said, trying to reassure him. But the cadet was already out the door.

"What did you tell him?" Yosef and Yechezkel asked together. "Why did you refuse to eat the sandwich? What's the connection between the sandwich and the chaplain?"

Rachamim carefully worded his response. "You realize, I'm sure, that we're Jews."

"Jews are only allowed to eat meat that has been slaughtered according to the laws of Islam?" Yosef wondered.

"No," Rachamim explained. "Muslims call slaughtered meat *halel*. We call it kosher. The Islamic laws and the Jewish laws pertaining to how meat is slaughtered are very different." He tried, as much as possible, not to make light of Islam. He had no idea how they felt about the religion. "In addition, Jews are not allowed to eat meat together with foods containing milk."

"Oh, we had no idea," the two of them apologized. "I'm sure we once knew about these laws, but over the years we forgot."

"I understand," Rachamim reassured them. "I am not blaming you. They spent years brainwashing you, and don't forget, you were very little when we were separated."

"Now that we've escaped bin Laden's clutches," Yechezkel added, "we're ready to learn about being Jewish."

"You were with bin Laden?" Rachamim suddenly paled. He started crying, "My children, my beloved children, you've had such a difficult life."

"Abba, don't cry over the past. What was, was, and is over and finished," the older son tried to console him.

Rachamim managed to smile through his tears. "Are you truly willing to return to Judaism?"

The two brothers did not respond. They looked into each other's eyes for a long moment. This time, it was Yechezkel who broke the silence. "Abba, Judaism must be the most beautiful religion in the world, and I am willing to return to my heritage with my entire heart and soul."

Twenty Five

Bin Laden pulled out a satellite phone. Al Zawahiri looked at him in surprise.

"I thought you weren't going to use that anymore, in case the Americans are tracking you."

"You're right," bin Laden admitted. "But I'm taking a chance just this once."

Al Zawahiri watched as bin Laden removed a small instrument from his pocket and attached it to the phone's mouthpiece. "This is a sound mixer," he explained. "It will help disguise my voice, for the benefit of any Americans who might be listening."

Bin Laden quickly dialed a number. Al Zawahiri instinctively leaned forward, though he was unable to hear anything.

"Western Star," bin Laden murmured into the phone. "The time has come for you to take action."

Bin Laden placed his hand over the mouthpiece and commented to al Zawahiri, "He needs time to recover. He has been dormant for the last twenty years."

He put the phone back to his ear. "In another week, perhaps a bit longer," bin Laden said to the person at the other end. "I'll inform you of the exact time."

Bin Laden disconnected the phone "This agent was dormant for close to twenty years," he explained. "I revived him a few weeks ago. To be more precise, two days before September 11. At that time, I told him what will be expected of him and why I broke off contact for twenty years."

"Does he know the entire plan?" al Zawahiri wondered out loud.

"Certainly not." Bin Laden smiled grimly. "No one knows the entire plan—except for me."

The message was clear. As much as al Zawahiri knew, he, too, did not know everything.

One by one, the long line of black limousines, the typical vehicle used by people in the government's hierarchy, passed through the guarded gates of the White House. The newspaper reporters watched them enter and wondered what was going on. Several rushed to report back to their editors that the attack against Afghanistan would most likely begin that evening.

The limousines entered the underground parking lot. Instead of entering the western wing of the building and heading upstairs to the President's office, the subdued group quietly made its way downstairs to the basement, into the strategy meeting room.

The National Security Advisor (NSA) was sitting at the head of the table, with the Secretary of State to her right and the Secretary of Defense on her left. The NSA looked around the long table, waiting for all the seats to be occupied before beginning the meeting.

She began with a thunderbolt. "I have received reliable information about a high ranking member of al Qaeda who is presently located in this part of the world."

The room became charged with excitement. The implication was clear: another attack was imminent.

"There is no immediate danger," she cautioned. "According to the information we have, he is just in the beginning stages of creating a terrorist base."

"That's not enough," the FBI director said angrily. The events of September 11 had taught him not to rely on information provided by informants. He had learned the hard way that every piece of information must be thoroughly investigated. "This information could be six months out of date. An attack could be on its way here already!"

The NSA kept her cool. She turned to the soldier standing at her side, holding a heavy folder. "Distribute the documents," she ordered.

The soldier removed a stack of white files with the insignia of the

National Security Council embossed on their covers. Underneath the insignia was printed the words "Top Secret" in large red letters. The soldier handed a folder to each person at the table.

After giving everyone a chance to leaf through the documents, the NSA opened her folder. "The first page," she began, "contains a satellite picture of the military base. It was taken just a few hours ago."

It was a colored picture, obviously taken from a great distance. It was difficult to make out what was in the picture. The region was hilly. The green blotches scattered throughout the picture showed that there was some vegetation. Here and there, they could see white fissures in the greenery. These signified rocks. In the center was a large level area.

"This picture will provide you with a general idea of the region where the base is located," she explained. "It is safe to assume that our satellite capability is known, and that al Qaeda has taken steps to hide their existence from our satellites. In addition, we have had no reason to closely examine this area of Mexico. As you will see in the following pages, we would never have discovered this base if we hadn't received information about its existence."

The statement was greeted by silence. No one could find anything suspicious in the picture.

"The next page contains an enlarged photograph of the base." The room echoed with the sound of pages being turned. "In this photograph, we can see people. Notice that they are all wearing wide rimmed straw cowboy hats. Several of them are also riding horses.

"Thanks to the wide rims of their hats, their faces are completely hidden. From above, they appear to be typical Mexican peasants. Since it's impossible for the satellite to catch a picture of their faces, there would never be a reason for us to suspect that they are really Arabs."

"They thought out every last detail," the Secretary of Defense muttered.

"Definitely," the NSA confirmed. "Take a good look at the photograph. Do you see any buildings?"

Everyone started carefully examining the photograph. There was a tense silence as each person tried to find some detail that might conceal a building. One by one, they raised their eyes in defeat.

The NSA smiled. She knew they would never succeed in identifying a building.

"The rocks are artificial. Turn the page to see a photo of the same location taken two years ago."

The rustling of pages being turned was heard. The third page contained a photograph of a hilly region, without any of the details that existed in the previous two photographs.

"This photograph was stored in our computerized database. As I said before, our experts did not invest their time in examining the photos of Mexico, so they never noticed the differences. After we received information about a Mexican terrorist base, they reviewed the photos and noticed the differences between the pictures taken two years ago and the present photographs. They focused the satellite camera on the area, and discerned openings leading into artificial caves that must have been built in the last one and a half years. Please turn the page to see something interesting."

The room was once again filled with the sound of turning pages. Several people let out a spontaneous yelp of surprise when they saw how the openings to the caves were constructed. The white lines were in the same spot as in the previous photographs, but there was a difference in one detail. In the white areas showing the artificial rocks, the white was darker in four separate spots. It looked like a shadow.

"The openings were built under a stone overhang," the NSA explained. "That way, it fits in perfectly with the other artificial rocks. Someone looking at this photograph would assume that the white lines were natural stones. It was only after we received the information about the military base being built here that we noticed the openings. The terrorists must have invested a tremendous amount of time and energy in concealing this base from our satellite, and, as I explained before, they knew how to go about doing it."

"There's no doubt," the Secretary of Defense added, "that these people are extremely dangerous. They invested tremendous time, energy and thought into creating this terrorist stronghold."

"In that case," the FBI director said, trying to keep his voice calm, "how can you be so certain that they aren't yet ready to strike?"

The mixture of pressure and public criticism had taken a heavy toll on the FBI director. He was beginning to lose his patience. For the last few days, all his thoughts and efforts had been centered on how to prevent another terrorist attack against the United States. His staff had detained over a thousand people for various minor offenses—which, under normal circumstances, would almost certainly have been overlooked. Now, however, any affiliation to Islam and possible connection to al Qaeda was considered suspect and investigated thoroughly.

"We're keeping the base under constant surveillance," the NSA said coolly, "to prevent any surprises. I'm not that concerned about it. I am far more concerned about the military bases that we do not know about."

A sharp retort was on the tip of the FBI director's tongue. He felt she was treating the problem much too lightly.

"That, of course, brings us to the purpose of this meeting," the NSA went on. "We need to decide on a course of action concerning this base." She turned around to face the Secretary of Defense. "I'll let the Defense Secretary finish chairing this session, to let you in on his plan."

The Defense Secretary was on his feet even before the NSA sat down. "I have here a detailed plan to destroy this terrorist cell. Obviously, a major part of the plan is to capture Abu Salim and bring him here alive so he can provide us with crucial information."

"Abu Salim?" The cry erupted from everyone in the room. They all knew he was bin Laden's chief assistant, second only to al Zawahiri.

"Abu Salim is presently in charge of the Mexican base," the Secretary of Defense confirmed. "We were given this information by our informant, a former high-ranking member of al Qaeda, and it was later confirmed through photographs taken by the Global Hawk surveillance aircraft. Abu Salim grew careless." He smiled slightly. "He removed his hat just in time for the pilotless Global Hawk to snap his picture. We were clearly able to identify Abu Salim among the terrorists."

"So what's the next step?" the FBI director asked.

"A team of twenty hand-picked soldiers from one of our elite units is currently undergoing specialized training. The primary objective is to abduct Abu Salim and bring him safely back to the United States.

Once that's accomplished, we'll destroy the base."

"Why don't we tell the Mexicans about the operation, or at the very least, ask them for permission to operate in their country?" asked Martin Okner, an aide to the Secretary of State.

The FBI director and the Defense Secretary traded glances that spoke volumes. "This is a black operation," the Defense Secretary finally said, leaning forward for emphasis. "Under no circumstances will I tell the Mexicans about our plans."

The Secretary of State wasn't surprised. He and the Secretary of Defense were at opposite ends of the political spectrum. The Defense Secretary felt that American interests were of prime importance and that the government should not concern itself with other countries if their interests collided with American interests. The Secretary of State insisted that the United States, as the leader of the Free World, had a moral obligation to protect the interests of the less powerful countries.

"Martin is correct," the Secretary of State defended his assistant. "We have no right to take military action in another country without first receiving their permission, or at the very least, informing the other government of what we're about to do."

"And did Osama bin Laden ask anyone's permission before taking military action on American soil?" the Defense Secretary asked sardonically.

"Does bin Laden give you the right to break all diplomatic agreements?" the Secretary of State retorted hotly. "Are you entitled to break international law? Is there any justification to stooping to that level? Then you will be assisting bin Laden in his task of promoting anarchy and terror in the world!"

The Defense Secretary responded quietly, trying to contain his fury. "No. I am not planning to break international law. I am not about to assist bin Ladin, as you so aptly described it. Mexico will undoubtedly express their gratitude when they discover that we removed this cancerous growth from their midst."

The Secretary of State decided to put a stop to their argument before it escalated and got completely out of hand. "I suggest we let the President decide," he quickly stated.

"Acceptable," the Defense Secretary agreed. He knew the President well, and he was certain that his view would prevail.

A military helicopter was waiting on Kitty Hawk's deck with the first rays of morning light. Rachamim and Naomi were led up to the deck. The soldiers accompanying them glanced toward the opposite end of the deck, as if they were waiting for someone to appear.

Rachamim followed their gaze. In the dim predawn light, he could discern four figures approaching. The four men were involved in a heated discussion about something. As they came closer, he realized that it was his two sons accompanied by two men in street clothes.

The man walking next to Yosef extended his hand to Rachamim. "I'm Bruce Weisel. I work for the Central Intelligence Agency, commonly known as the CIA."

"Nice to meet you," Rachamim responded with forced friendliness. He felt uncomfortable being in close contact with people in government service. Fear of the government was an ingrained trait from the time he was a child living under the corrupted officials of the Shah.

"Your sons were a real help to us," Bruce said enthusiastically. "The information they gave us in the short time that we have been together will prevent many future terrorist attacks."

"One night is not enough. We've been members of the organization for years," Yechezkel pointed out.

Rachamim noticed the exhaustion on his sons' faces. "I apologize for keeping them the entire night," Bruce continued. "We need to take advantage of every possible moment to get the most information in the least amount of time. Most of the information that they gave me has already been transferred to Washington."

The soldier accompanying them to the helicopter looked pointedly at his watch, then gestured toward the helicopter to let them know that it was time to get going. The helicopter's pilot helped them climb into the aircraft, then showed them how to fasten their seatbelts and put their helmets on properly.

"Throughout the flight, all communication will be through the earphones located inside your helmets," the officer explained.

Bruce sat down between the two brothers. "I want to take advantage of every possible moment," he commented with a smile.

The helicopter gained altitude and started flying west. "We'll land in another hour," the pilot informed them.

Rachamim looked out the window. He was worried that by the time they'd land it would be too late to *daven shacharit*. He was reassured to see that it was still half-dark outside. He had planned to *daven* before leaving, but it had been dark outside. Now, with the noise and constant bumping of the aircraft, it was impossible.

The aircraft entered a thick cloud and they were surrounded by grayness on all sides. Upon leaving the cloud, they were greeted by a magnificent sight. The mountains had abruptly ended, and a green plain spread out beneath them. Flowers nodded their heads in the morning sunlight. The helicopter came to a stop in the center of the valley and rapidly started losing altitude.

The helicopter rocked violently as it touched ground. The pilot opened the door and they were greeted by a cold gust of wind. Rachamim shivered.

"Here we are," the pilot announced, removing his helmet. "From now on, you'll be traveling by plane."

Rachamim gazed in amazement at the endless field of grass surrounding them. They could not see any airport in the vicinity. It looked like a natural wilderness.

"Look over there." The pilot pointed to the southeast.

They could now see a green building that blended in almost perfectly with their surroundings. A large door opened in the wall facing them, and a silver airplane appeared. There was a roar as the plane's engines came to life. It dazzled in the bright morning sun as it drove toward them and came to a stop in front of the helicopter.

The plane's door opened, and the sound of the engines died away. The man standing in the opening waved in greeting, then murmured something into a microphone clipped to his shirt. Rachamim could hear the helicopter pilot respond—clearly giving the agreed upon password. Then he turned to his passengers. "Climb in. This plane will take you back to the United States."

"Thank you so much for everything you've done for us." Rachamim expressed his gratitude to the helicopter's pilot, who remained standing, watching him climb into the airplane. Naomi and the two brothers followed Rachamim inside. Bruce and his assistant remained below, standing next to the helicopter and speaking enthusiastically into a large cell phone. The pilot waited patiently for them to finish their conversation and enter the plane.

The plane's door closed the moment Bruce and his assistant were inside. The plane started speeding along the grass, swinging violently from side to side. "I apologize for the uncomfortable takeoff," the pilot shouted. "We're leaving from a temporary airport, which was made for emergency use only. In just a few minutes we'll be in the air, and then the flight will be much more comfortable."

Ten minutes later, they gained altitude and the plane stopped careening from side to side. Once the plane reached proper altitude and the pilot announced that they could release their seatbelts, Bruce turned to Rachamim, Naomi and their two sons. "I understand that you have a lot to discuss between yourselves."

Yosef and Yechezkel nodded. They were exhausted, but forced themselves to remain awake so they could get to know their parents.

"Enjoy yourselves. We'll talk more after we arrive in the United States." With those words, Bruce and his assistant put back their seats, stretched out their legs and closed their eyes to catch some sleep.

The first thing Rachamim requested was that the two men stop using their non-Jewish names. "Your Jewish name is Yechezkel," said Rachamim, turning to his firstborn son. Speaking to the younger brother, he continued, "And your name is Yosef. That's the name I'd like you to use from now on."

The two brothers readily agreed. Within minutes, they were so engrossed in a deep discussion that they completely lost track of time. Rachamim wanted to hear about what they had gone through over the years. He and Naomi cried bitter tears as they listened to their children talk about their difficult lives.

The two brothers discovered that many times they had been in close physical proximity to each other, and they had even served on the same military base. Was that part of the cruel game that bin Laden had played with their lives? Rachamim also told them how he had sent people to search for them, but had never discovered a trace of their whereabouts.

The sun was slowly moving towards its peak. Rachamim told the boys that he had to take a break and *daven*. The present situation reminded him of how Yaakov Avinu must have felt when he first met his son, Yosef, after twenty-two years of not knowing that he was alive. Rachamim wanted to ask his sons to join him, but he was afraid of pressuring them. He realized that he'd have to proceed slowly.

"It's no problem," his two sons reassured him, apparently recognizing his hesitation. "In fact, we want to learn how a Jew is supposed to pray."

"I'm afraid that I can't show you how Jews are supposed to pray. I was abducted without my *tallit* and *tefillin*," Rachamim sighed. "A *tallit* is a special shawl that Jews wear while praying, and *tefillin* are small black leather boxes containing words of Torah confirming our belief in G-d. We place them on our foreheads and upper arms during prayer. I'll also have to pray by heart since I don't have my prayer book."

Rachamim said the morning blessings aloud. Afterward, he started praying the *pasukei d'zimra* in the beautiful melody that had been handed down from father to son by Iranian Jews. The two brothers listened carefully to their father's prayers. The haunting melody reawakened long forgotten memories.

Naomi looked at them with joy tinged with sadness. It was obvious that they did not understand what Rachamim was reciting, but she could see that they appreciated the fact that he was praying. She silently asked G-d to help them return to their heritage after so many years of being completely cut off from anything Jewish.

Twenty Six

Sunset. Just a small wedge of sunlight could be seen peeping over the horizon. The two sweaty Mexicans slowly climbed to the peak of the last mountaintop in the range. Behind them was a small valley, overgrown with natural desert foliage.

This hilltop was the last they would be climbing until it was safely dark. The two men lay on the grass and pulled their wide brimmed Mexican hats over their faces to keep the last rays of the setting sun from blinding them. One of them took a small short wave radio out of his pocket and brought it to close to his mouth.

"Mike, this is Rafael, over." He spoke perfect English, without any trace of a foreign accent, although he appeared to be a typical Mexican peasant.

"Rafael, this is Mike. I hear you perfectly," came the reply.

"We're at the end of the mountain range. There's just a small hilltop separating us from the valley."

"Wonderful," his officer complimented him. "Wait there until it's dark, and then use your night binoculars to observe the valley. Tell me what you see before continuing."

"Okay," the Mexican responded.

"One more thing, Rafael."

"Yes."

"Proceed with caution," the officer warned him. "The information you gather will be critical to the success of our mission. Don't take any chances."

"Roger, Mike, will do," Rafael responded, before signing off.

Rafael had been raised by his mother in the crime filled slums of Mexico City. His father had died when he was an infant, a victim of the gang wars that filled the streets of his neighborhood. As a young child, he had been forced to steal for survival. Daily he witnessed people being murdered for a few pesos.

At the age of thirteen, Rafael made up his mind that he could not continue living like this. He decided to smuggle himself into the United States to start a new life.

His mother sobbed hysterically when he took leave of her and tried to stop him. He was, after all, the family's only source of income. But he refused to give in. Instead, he gave her the money that he had saved up to take with him. "This money is enough for you to survive until I get settled in the United States. Once I'm settled, I'll send you money to leave this place."

Rafael set out to begin a new life without a penny to his name. He walked from Mexico City to the United States-Mexican border, managing to survive by eating fruit he picked along the way. When he was close to the border, he hid in the enormous sand dunes. Rafael spent the night alone in the desert, carefully observing the border guards. He watched hundreds of people try to cross the border illegally. Some of them succeeded, while others were caught.

Finally, he was able to accurately predict the timing of the different patrols. Rafael stole out of his hiding place the moment one of the patrols had passed. He now had twenty minutes until the next patrol arrived. He raced north, toward the American border. Every once in a while he glanced down at his watch. Exactly eighteen minutes after he started crossing the border, Rafael dropped down and covered himself with sand, so only his face was protruding.

The patrols used sophisticated equipment to catch illegal immigrants and Rafael was petrified that they would see him. He shuddered at the noise of the jeeps and the sounds of the soldiers talking in the peaceful night.

They did not find him. Rafael continued on, stopping every eighteen minutes to hide in the desert sand, until he was in Texas. With the help of a map that he bought at a gas station, he spent the entire night walking toward Houston, Texas.

He found the immigrant Mexican community in Houston. They were happy to help one of their own. The Organization for the Protection of Mexican Immigrants found him a job working in a cheap restaurant that paid less than two dollars an hour. The job, however, did provide him with a bed in the storage room and all the leftover food he could eat. Rafael supplemented his meager paycheck with tips.

Rafael was a devoted worker who put away every penny he earned. After one month in the United States, he proudly sent a fifty-dollar money order to his mother in Mexico.

Two weeks later, he received a letter from home. His boss, Carlos, who was also from Mexico, called him over in the middle of work and handed him a letter with Mexican stamps on it.

"This is addressed to you," he said, smiling. Carlos had several immigrant workers, and understood the emotional impact of that first letter from home.

Rafael's hands were trembling when he took the envelope from Carlos's hands.

"Go to your room and read your mother's letter," Carlos said in a fatherly voice. "Take as much time as you need."

Rafael muttered a few undecipherable worlds in gratitude. Carlos gave him a gentle nudge and Rafael ran to his private corner in the storage room.

Rafael tore the envelope open. It was difficult for him to decipher his mother's handwriting. She thanked him profusely for the money and gave him a detailed list of how she had used every cent.

Lying on the mountaintop and hearing his officer's warning reminded Rafael of how he had hidden in the sand dunes while trying to leave Mexico. This was the first time he had returned to Mexico since leaving the country fifteen years before. He had enlisted in the American army when he turned twenty, and now his allegiance to his adopted country was even greater than that of the country of his birth.

Rafael's thoughts were interrupted by the sound of a motor on the next mountaintop. He took out his night binoculars, which were covered with green and yellow camouflage paint to blend in with the surrounding desert vegetation, and peered toward the source of the sound.

Clearly visible to his infrared night binoculars was the entrance to a cave. Just outside the opening was an army jeep, with several people seated inside. It looked as if they were waiting for something.

Another jeep appeared, carrying cages similar to the type used by veterinarians to hold stray dogs. Rafael counted five cages, each one of them containing a fully-grown dog.

The two jeeps drove to the center of the next mountaintop. Rafael continued observing them with his night binoculars. He lowered his eyes for a moment. "Kohn," he whispered to the soldier crouching next to him, "take a look at what's going on over there."

Kohn looked through his own binoculars. "What in the world are they doing?" he asked.

"I think I know, but I don't want to rush to any conclusions. We'll continue watching them."

The two jeeps stopped. The driver of the jeep carrying the animals climbed into the back of the jeep and lifted one of the cages. The dog yelped in fright, scratching uselessly against the metal bars of the cage. The driver carried it over to the second jeep, which had a sturdy metal box in the back, slightly larger than the cage holding the dog. The box was opened, and the driver carefully placed the cage inside.

Rafael watched closely. He saw the second driver lift an oblong object, about the size of a book, from the floor of the jeep. He twisted something on the side, threw it into the metal box, then slammed the cover of the box shut. The two drivers then quickly leaped into the second jeep and began driving rapidly away.

Kohn watched, puzzled, as the jeep came to a halt about two miles away from the first jeep. Nothing seemed to happen for several minutes. Finally, after ten minutes, the jeep reversed and slowly returned to where the jeep with the metal box was parked.

The two drivers conferred for a few minutes. Then one of them gingerly reached over to the metal box and opened the cover. Again the jeep drove away, while the two hidden American soldiers watched in puzzlement.

Finally, the jeep drove back for the second time. The driver stepped over to the metal box. As he reached inside, Rafael realized that the man was wearing a gas mask.

The cage was lifted out of the box. Even from this distance, Rafael could see that the dog inside appeared limp and unresponsive.

"They're trying out chemical warfare," the two men exclaimed at once. Rafael placed the night binoculars on the ground and carefully removed the short wave radio from his backpack.

"Mike, this is Rafael, over," he whispered, his voice shaking.

"Rafael, this is Mike, over," came the reply.

"Chemical weapons," he said tersely. "They're experimenting with chemical weapons."

There was a short silence. When he spoke, the officer's voice was panicky. "To the pickup point, Rafael. Respond!"

When Rafael did not reply, the officer repeated his order. "Rafael, this is an order. To the pickup point now!"

The private plane landed on a side airstrip in Los Angeles International Airport. Rachamim and Naomi watched with relief as the runway rose up to meet them. They were exhausted from their long, harrowing journey and couldn't wait to go back to their normal routine, to return to their own home and get a few hours of sleep in their own beds.

They stared out the plane's window and watched as a minibus drove up to the door. A car with a flashing yellow light on its roof also stopped next to the plane. The pilot, who had barely said a word to them during the long trip, opened the door and removed steps that were folded inside the plane. "You can go down now," he said.

Rachamim and Naomi heaved themselves up from their seats. Yechezkel and Yosef jumped up. The long journey had not affected them. Physically fit from the long years of military training, they assisted their parents in disembarking from the plane.

Several people were waiting at the bottom of the stairs. One of them went up to Rachamim and warmly shook his hand. "Arthur Singer. I am the agent charged with your welfare." He gestured to the group of men standing nearby. "These are my devoted assistants."

"Can our family remain together?" Rachamim asked.

"Of course," Arthur responded, his smile growing even wider. "I am not about to separate you again."

"That's wonderful!" Naomi was excited. "I can barely wait to show my children our home."

"Um…" Arthur looked uncomfortable. "I don't think that will be possible. You'll be together, but for now, at least, it's too dangerous for you to return home. Al Qaeda knows your address."

"I understand." Rachamim responded in disappointment. He would have liked to show his children the synagogue that he had built in their memory. He also wanted to bring them back into the Jewish community as quickly as possible.

"Can I ask a favor?" Rachamim asked.

"I'll be happy to help you if I can," Arthur responded graciously.

"Since I was abducted by al Qaeda, I have not been able to put on my *tallit* and *tefillin*." He realized with a start that Arthur probably had no idea what he was talking about. "A *tallit* and *tefillin* are religious articles that we wear during prayer," he explained.

Arthur smiled. He gestured to one of his assistants, who removed Rachamim's *tallit* and *tefillin* from the back of the jeep. Rachamim was amazed. "We found these when we searched your home after you were abducted. We had no idea what they were. We eventually contacted a Jewish chaplain, who explained their importance. Since we knew how much they meant to you, we made sure to bring them along with us."

Rachamim was speechless.

A black Lincoln with a taxi sign on its roof pulled up next to them. Arthur opened the back door and told Naomi to get inside. Rachamim and Yosef followed her into the back seat, while Yechezkel sat in front, next to the driver. The moment all the doors were closed, the driver stepped on the gas and sped toward the exit.

Yechezkel noticed that several cars were following them. All the cars stopped for a few seconds in front of the airport's main gate, while the guard looked inside and exchanged passwords with the driver.

Rachamim sat in the taxi observing the traffic signs. He became hopeful when he saw that the driver was heading toward his own neighborhood. Although he realized that it was too dangerous to return home, he hoped that at least he'd be in the vicinity of his synagogue and the Jewish community.

The conversation was so interesting that Rachamim forgot to keep an eye on the street signs. When he looked out the window again, he realized that he was now in an unfamiliar neighborhood.

They stopped in front of a decorative cement fence surrounding a suburban home. The front garden was well cared for. "You'll stay here for the next few days until we can find a better place for you," the driver said.

Arthur was already standing outside the taxi's back door. He opened the door from the outside and waited until Rachamim, Naomi and Yosef were out. A different agent stood next to the front door and covered Yechezkel with his own body as he exited the car. Other agents surrounded Rachamim and Naomi. Rachamim noticed people walking up and down the street, their hands in their pockets. They were obviously armed agents, making sure that the area was secure.

Once everyone was safely out of the car, Arthur guided them toward the fenced-in yard, while several agents trailed behind them. They stopped in front of the locked gate. Arthur took an enormous key out of his pocket and placed it in the keyhole. The hinges squeaked when he pushed the door open. Inside was a mailbox placed on a wooden pole. Arthur opened the box and removed a few letters, then pressed a button inside the mailbox to turn off the digital security system that sounded an alarm several seconds after the gate was opened.

"Follow me," Arthur murmured as he started slowly walking along the path leading to the house, which was hidden by the trees.

Most of the other agents spread out among the foliage, while one remained behind to close the gate and reset the button inside the mailbox. They crossed a path leading through a magnificent flower garden. The fragrance was intoxicating. Every corner contained a different type of flower or plant, some of which Rachamim had never seen before.

The house appeared suddenly, as if it had sprouted from the flowers. The building was covered with vines and shrubs.

Arthur opened the front door and guided them into a round entry hall. The walls were covered with elegant gold embossed wallpaper and the floor was colored marble. The architect had used the combination of colors in the marble to create the figure of an eagle holding an olive branch in one claw and arrows in the other.

"That is the Presidential Seal," Arthur explained when he saw them staring at the figure. "This house was supposed to be President Ronald Reagan's private home, to be used during his visits to California. But by the time it was finished, Reagan's term of presidency was up, and the next president, President George Bush, preferred to make his summer residence in Texas, his home state. That's why the FBI was granted this safe house."

Arthur started showing them around the house. The first floor contained an enormous kitchen, a huge dining room, and a palatial living room. Marble steps led up to the second floor, which contained six bedrooms, each one tastefully decorated in a different style. The adjoining wing contained two bedrooms the size of a small auditorium, and a library without books.

Finally, Arthur brought them back down to the modern kitchen. "The kitchen is not kosher," he explained. "We'll provide you with readymade food from one of the kosher restaurants in the city. This evening, we ordered a meal from Nathan's. The kosher supervisor personally signed the boxes so you can check that it meets your standards."

Arthur walked across the kitchen and stopped before the door to the back yard. Before leaving, he showed them a small button just above the lock. "This button is for the alarm," he explained. "We're located just outside the house the entire time. If you ever feel threatened, don't hesitate to press the alarm and we'll be here immediately."

Arthur opened the door and wished them a good night. Just before he stepped out into the surrounding darkness, Rachamim stopped him. "I would like to ask you one last favor," he said.

"Yes, what can I do for you?" Arthur replied graciously.

"I see that you understand something about Judaism," Rachamim began hesitantly. "You realized that the kitchen is not kosher."

"No, not exactly," Arthur explained. "I didn't realize it myself. The chaplain pointed that out to me."

"Anyway," Rachamim went on, "It's important that I pray with a *minyan*." He understood that Arthur had no idea what he was referring to. "A *minyan* is a group of ten men who pray together. I would be grateful if someone could take me tomorrow morning to pray in the synagogue where I always pray."

Arthur had no idea what to do. He didn't want to refuse Rachamim. He realized that this was important for him. He felt close to this elderly gentleman who had suffered for so many years while dreaming of the day he would be reunited with his children. He had also been instructed to do whatever was necessary to gain the family's trust, so they could pump them for information on al Qaeda.

"I first have to get permission from my commanding officer," Arthur said, to explain his long silence. "But before I contact him, I want to carefully consider if this is the correct thing to do. It's very possible that al Qaeda is searching for you this very minute."

"I am no longer frightened of them. G-d, who has miraculously saved me from their hands, will continue to guard over me," Rachamim replied.

"Maybe we'll bring you to a different synagogue, where there's less of a chance that al Qaeda will find you?" Arthur suggested.

"No! I want to pray, at least one more time, in the synagogue where I have been praying for the last twenty years." Rachamim looked straight into Arthur's eyes. "I want you to understand. In that synagogue, I have been begging our Father in heaven for the last twenty years to bring me my children. That was where G-d hearkened to my pleas, and now I want to go back to the same place to express my gratitude that G-d has given me back my beloved children."

Twenty Seven

Arthur was an experienced agent, who had seen the worst of what life had to offer. Yet Rachamim's emotional request touched a chord deep within him, awakening feelings that he didn't know he still possessed.

"I'll speak to my superior officer," he promised Rachamim. "Give me a few minutes."

Arthur stepped outside into the surrounding darkness. He walked twenty feet away from the house before turning on his short wave radio. "Play Bird, this is Jaywalk, over."

"Jaywalk, this is Play Bird, over."

"Could you please call me on my cell phone?" Arthur asked his commanding officer.

"I'll call immediately."

The cell phone started ringing before Arthur had a chance to put the short wave radio back in his pocket. "What's the problem?" the commanding officer asked worriedly.

"There's no problem," Arthur reassured him. "Simply..." He stopped, at a loss for words. He really had no idea how to word his request.

Now the officer was really worried. He knew that it would take something very serious to leave a seasoned agent like Arthur speechless.

"Oh, everything's really fine," Arthur tried to reassure him. "I just want to ask you something. But before I do, I'd like to ask you not to dismiss the request even if it seems completely impractical."

"Okay. I promise."

"Tomorrow morning, Rachamim would like to pray in his synagogue where he's prayed every morning for the last twenty years."

"What? Are you seriously considering this?" the officer asked in disbelief.

"You promised not to dismiss my request completely."

"Okay. I'm not dismissing your request. I'm just putting it off for now."

"Come on," Arthur coaxed him. "Dismissing the request and putting it off for now are really one and the same. Think a moment. If Rachamim decides that he wants to go to the synagogue, there is no way that we'll be able to stop him. Isn't it better that we cooperate with him so we can protect him, at least to a certain extent? If we cannot protect him, at least we'll be nearby if something does happen."

After a moment's hesitation, the other man replied, "Have you thought this through? Do you have a plan of action?"

"Give me five additional agents. We'll keep the synagogue surrounded."

"Okay. When do you need the reinforcements?"

"I don't know. I have to go inside to ask him when he would like to go. I'll call you back in a few minutes."

Arthur turned off the phone and went back to the kitchen. The minute he opened the door, he could see that everyone was upset. It seemed that there had been some type of an argument between Rachamim and his two sons. The moment they noticed him, they became quiet and looked at him expectantly, waiting to hear the commanding officer's decision.

"I convinced my commanding officer to allow you to pray in your synagogue."

Rachamim was overwhelmed with joy. "I thank you from the depths of my heart."

"Are you certain that you made the right decision?" Yechezkel asked. "I certainly hope you realize what a tremendous responsibility you are taking on yourself."

Arthur was surprised that Yechezkel opposed the idea.

"I wonder if you really understand who you are dealing with," Yosef added. "Osama bin Laden's organization has deep roots here in the

United States. I wouldn't be surprised if there was an al Qaeda agent already stationed at the synagogue, waiting for my father to appear."

"We are aware of that. In case you haven't forgotten, less than fifteen minutes ago I was trying to stop your father from taking this step. But he's stubborn, and I respect his wishes. We'll do whatever we can to protect him from any danger."

Yechezkel gave him a threatening look. "And if you fail, if you don't bring my father back, you can forget about me cooperating with you."

"I understand that." Turning to Rachamim, Arthur asked, "What time do you want to leave tomorrow?"

"It depends on how long it takes to get there. The prayer service starts at seven o'clock, on the dot. I would like to be there fifteen minutes earlier."

"Be ready at six." With those words, Arthur stepped out the door to give them some privacy.

The reunited family continued talking until it was impossible to speak any longer, and they had to collapse into bed to get some rest.

Though the hour was late, the sidewalks were crowded. Men staggered along the street, weaving in and out of the pubs lining the streets of this rundown area in Los Angeles. Broken whiskey bottles rolled about in the gutters. Drug addicts also found a refuge here. The street corners were occupied with surreptitious figures; astounding sums of money changed hands, with high quantities of drugs being given in exchange.

Dressed in tattered rags, Jamil sidled just outside one of the cheap pubs. His commanding officer had ordered him to look like one of the many homeless who made this neighborhood their home. He loitered near the doorway, trying to appear inconspicuous.

The shabby pub door was pushed opened and Jamil found himself engulfed in a cloud of whiskey and human sweat. The bartender was leading a wobbly drunk out of the bar. The man was so inebriated that he could barely walk, and he had to lean heavily on the bartender's arm. The bartender threw the drunk outside and raced back into the pub, slamming the door behind him.

The drunk swayed back and forth just a few feet away from where Jamil was standing. Jamil moved slightly away, trying to avoid the worst of the stench. He wished he could walk away, but he was supposed to be meeting his commanding officer at this location.

To his immense annoyance, the drunk started walking toward him. Jamil looked around wildly. The last thing he wanted was to be accosted by the foul-smelling drunk. But he was afraid to move too far away—he might miss his rendezvous.

"What is your name?" the drunk slurred. He was leaning heavily against the wall.

Jamil tried to ignore him.

Broken pieces of furniture were scattered about on the street. The drunk picked up a broken table leg and used it to support himself as he walked closer to Jamil.

"Oh, this is wonderful," Jamil muttered under his breath.

He held his breath as the drunk stopped, less than two feet away. The man leaned close to Jamil and whispered, "Jamil."

Jamil stared at him in astonishment.

"At the end of the street there's a deserted store with boarded up windows. The door's open. Go in and wait for me," the drunk whispered. "I'll come in a few minutes."

Jamil stumbled off in a daze, wondering why his commanding officer had decided to meet with him in such a humiliating way. He quickly found the store and, like the officer had said, the door was open.

Jamil pushed the door open and was greeted by a sharp musty smell. He quickly closed the door behind him, and the room was shrouded in dusky blackness. Jamil could hear someone walking on the sidewalk just outside the door. Each step was accompanied by the heavy thumping of wood against the pavement. The door opened, and he could see the officer standing there. The drunk entered the store and closed the door behind him.

"Jamil, it's time for you to take action," the drunk began in perfect Arabic. He was speaking clearly now.

The officer removed a small flashlight from his pocket and turned it on. By the dim light, Jamil was able to see his commanding officer's face for the first time. He had only known him by voice until now.

The man's face was wrinkled and framed by a thin, straggly beard. His hair was long and tangled, and it was obvious that it had not been combed in years. A mixture of black and white, it hung down on either side of his face, resembling steel wool rather than human hair. It was difficult for Jamil to accept that this wretched looking creature was really his commanding officer.

Staring at the man, Jamil recalled the conversation he'd had earlier with his commanding officer—the conversation that had brought him back to life from his dormant state, just two days before September 11.

His cell phone had rung unexpectedly that afternoon. "Western Star," a voice had murmured into the phone. "The time has come."

Jamil had reacted in shock. This was the first communication he'd had from the organization in over twenty years.

"Our leader, Osama bin Laden, has declared a jihad, a holy war, against the Western world," his officer had declared. "Now your turn has come to contribute your part to this great undertaking. This is the moment you have been waiting for. Our leader is honoring you with a part in the greatest operation that has ever been planned against the Western world."

Jamil had remained silent.

"Aren't you willing to contribute to this great effort?" the officer demanded, affronted by his lack of response. "Have your ideas changed during all the years that you were dormant? Have the luxuries of America blinded you to the truth?"

Jamil was stung. Luxuries? What luxuries? He had not known a moment of peace or prosperity since he had arrived in the United States. Jamil quickly reassured his commanding officer, "Oh, no. I am more than willing to do my part in our leader's fight against the Western world, even at the cost of my life."

After telling Jamil that he would be getting in touch with him soon, the officer had hung up. Now it was time for Jamil to discover what part he was to play in this immense operation.

The officer showed Jamil an instrument that, at first glance, looked like a satellite phone, though it was slightly larger than a typical cell phone. He directed the flashlight toward it. "Take it," he ordered.

Jamil's hand was trembling as he took the device from his commanding officer. "Guard this like the apple of your eye," the commanding officer ordered. "This device contains the detonator, which will activate an explosion. When you're told to press the red button, the United States will experience a holocaust that they have never dreamed of in their worst dreams. After that, the entire Western world, with the United States at its head, will fall to our feet begging us to leave them alone. They will be delighted to hand us Palestine on a silver platter."

Jamil understood. He would be the one to activate the nuclear explosion that would destroy America. It was obvious that he would be sacrificing his own life at the same time.

Strangely, the loss of his own life did not worry Jamil unduly. He had had almost no happiness in his lifetime; he was ready to leave this miserable world behind him. But the thought that an entire city would be annihilated ... that was difficult to accept. He visualized the children in his neighborhood, and he broke out in a cold sweat at the thought of a huge mushroom cloud rising above the city, destroying everything.

"I want you to move to this address by eleven o'clock tomorrow morning." His commanding officer handed him a sheet of paper and illuminated it with his flashlight. Jamil could see an address written on top. Beneath the address was a hand drawn map with a star in the center. "Go there with the device, and leave your cell phone on. I will call you tomorrow with further instructions."

"I understand," Jamil responded. It was easier for him to obey knowing that his benefactor, Rachamim, was out of the danger zone.

He had been watching when Rachamim was abducted from the warehouse. Later, when he went to tell Naomi about the kidnapping, he noticed that their home was surrounded by police officers. Lurking nearby, he overheard the police commenting that the woman living there had been kidnapped, and he had understood that they were talking about Naomi.

True, they were probably being held by al Qaeda—a dubious safety at best. Yet under the circumstances, they were probably better off than anyone still in Los Angeles. With both Rachamim and Naomi safely away, Jamil knew that he was ready to proceed with his mission.

Jamil straightened up where he stood. "I am ready and willing to sacrifice my life for the sake of Islam!"

His commanding officer did not bother to hide his pleasure. "That's wonderful," he responded enthusiastically. Jamil's response was exactly as he had expected it would be. The officer was in charge of rejuvenating dormant cells dispersed throughout the United States, and he had seen this reaction many times before. The moment the psychological counseling went into effect, they all reacted the same way, displaying enthusiasm for the upcoming mission.

"May Allah be with you," his commanding officer blessed him, before slipping outside into the surrounding darkness.

Jamil remained in the store for a few more minutes. When he left, there was no sign of the drunk. Jamil turned around and crossed several narrow and neglected alleyways, stepping over dozens of homeless who were sleeping on the sidewalks. On the main street he stood waiting at the bus stop.

The bus arrived after twenty minutes. Jamil got on and took it several stops to the place where he had left his car. It was almost daybreak by the time he sat down in his car. He knew he would never be able to fall asleep now.

As Jamil gripped the steering wheel, a strange thought popped into his head. Before ending his life, he would like to pray one more time in the synagogue where he had served for so many years. Throughout those years, he would often listen to the morning prayers from his tiny niche outside the main synagogue. Although he prayed in Arabic, he liked to say his prayers together with the congregation.

Jamil decided to hide in the empty women's section, which was never occupied during the week. That way he would be as close as possible to the congregation.

By the time he arrived at the synagogue, it was almost four o'clock in the morning. Everything was dark and quiet. He fingered his key chain. Would his key still work, or had Rachamim changed the locks to prevent Jamil from entering?

The door opened easily—a positive sign. His tiny room was exactly as he had left it, another encouraging sign. No one had bothered to move his belongings. The room was located opposite the women's section. He decided that as soon as he heard the service begin, he would slip inside. Meanwhile, he would try to get some sleep in his own bed.

Rachamim was up at five. By five to six, he was already waiting by the front door. At six o'clock, when Arthur knocked, he was surprised to find Rachamim waiting impatiently for him.

Arthur nervously guided him through the backyard to where a brown sports car was parked outside the gate. Arthur opened the front passenger door and invited Rachamim to take a seat. Changing gears, he started through the back alleys and side streets, avoiding the famous Los Angeles traffic. He kept glancing into his rearview mirror. Ten minutes before arriving at the synagogue, he left the alleyways and entered the main streets.

Arthur pulled up to the synagogue at six-forty. He handed Rachamim a small cube of black plastic, about half an inch square. "Keep this in your pocket," Arthur ordered. "If you feel threatened, press on any one of the sides."

Rachamim tried it out and heard a ringing sound coming from Arthur's pocket. "That's my alarm. Make sure no one realizes you have this. In addition to acting as an alarm, it's also a homing device. If someone tries to abduct you, we'll be able to find you."

"Let's hope I won't need it," Rachamim murmured, speaking almost to himself as he left Arthur's car.

Jamil had finally fallen asleep out of sheer exhaustion. He woke with a start to the sound of the first *minyan* reciting the morning blessings. Jamil jumped up and raced to the sink in the corner of his room to wash his hands, feet and face, as commanded by the Koran. Then he quickly slipped into the women's section.

Jamil moved aside the curtain that divided the women's section from the main synagogue and peered inside. *Am I dreaming?* he wondered, rubbing his eyes. There was Rachamim standing in his regular place, praying as usual.

Jamil closed his eyes tightly, then looked again. Rachamim was wrapped in his *tallit*, so it was impossible for Jamil to see his face. But he was certain that it was Rachamim. His stance, his build, everything about him left no room for doubt.

How is this possible? Did the al Qaeda let him go? Impossible. The al Qaeda never let anyone go! How on earth had Rachamim escaped their clutches? Jamil had witnessed the kidnapping himself; he had seen how the FBI agents had been left helpless by the trained al Qaeda terrorists.

Jamil started praying. He simply didn't know what to do. He had been willing to obey orders, as long as he knew that Rachamim, who had been so kind to him over the years, would not be harmed. Now he had to find some way to warn Rachamim to escape as quickly as possible.

The service ended. The congregation, hurrying to their places of employment, quickly left the building. The second *minyan* had not yet arrived. The last one to leave reminded Rachamim to lock the door if he would be leaving before the second *minyan* showed up.

Jamil knew that he had only a few minutes to warn Rachamim. The second *minyan* would begin shortly. He didn't want to waste time walking around the building to the main entrance, so he jumped over the low wall separating the women's section from the main synagogue.

The noise startled Rachamim and he quickly turned around. His gaze locked with Jamil's. For one long moment, neither of them said a word.

Jamil broke the silence. "I must speak with you urgently. Follow me to my room."

Twenty Eight

"Mike, this is Rafael. Hold off on the pickup," Rafael said tersely. "There is some activity right below us."

The radio fell silent. Rafael and his companion subsided into the sand atop the hilltop, barely breathing but watching carefully as a tall man sporting a black beard, probably in his late thirties, appeared in the cave's opening. He was wearing a white gown that contrasted with the surrounding inky darkness, and on his head was a very wide rimmed Mexican hat. He was dressed in a mixture of Middle East and Mexican clothes.

Rafael stared at the man. He looked familiar to him. He knew him from somewhere. Rafael focused the night binocular on the man's face, and then enlarged the view.

Just then the man raised his head toward the sky. As his face came out from under the shadow of the hat, Rafael abruptly realized where he had seen him before.

"Abu Salim!" he muttered.

Next to him, Kohn barely held back an audible gasp. "Are you sure?" he murmured, careful to keep his voice barely above a whisper.

Rafael gave a short, curt nod. He knew he had to report this back as quickly as possible, but it was too dangerous to use the radio at such close proximity to the group below them. He motioned downward to indicate that he wanted to go down the hill, back where they had come from. He waited until Kohn nodded in comprehension before carefully picking his way down the hill, using his night goggles to guide his footing.

It wasn't until he reached the base of the hill that Rafael spoke into the radio again.

"Mike, this is Rafael, over."

"I read you, Rafael. What was that all about?"

"Abu Salim."

"What about him?" Rafael could hear an undercurrent of excitement in his commanding officer's voice.

"He's there, right at the entrance to the cave."

"Are you certain?"

"Absolutely. He was just half a mile away. I could see his face clearly."

There was a short pause as his commanding officer assimilated the information. "Good job, Rafael. That's one important thing we needed to confirm. Are you willing to stay longer to keep him under observation?"

"Roger that," Rafael replied immediately.

"I'm offering you a choice," the officer told him. "You saw what those chemical weapons are capable of doing. We will benefit from continued surveillance, but you should take safety precautions and return to the pickup point to equip yourself with gas masks first."

Rafael knew that this would be the most prudent choice. But to leave now would be taking a chance—Abu Salim might slip through their fingers.

"I would hate to have Abu Salim slip away before reinforcements were brought in," Rafael demurred. "We'll stay upwind, and the experiments have stopped for now."

"Okay, Rafael. Continue the surveillance. Call me every half hour if feasible."

"Roger," Rafael agreed, before breaking off contact.

The call went up the chain of command, through the communications van set up just inside the Mexican border, uplinked by satellite to the Pentagon's command center, and finally reaching the highest echelons of the Defense Department. The Secretary of Defense lost no time in conferring with his colleagues, including the National Security Advisor and the FBI director. Abu Salim's presence in the region was now a proven fact.

The Delta team was ready to move in—as soon as the President gave the go-ahead.

"We must speak with the President immediately," the Defense Secretary insisted. "I want to take Abu Salim out of Mexico this evening. He is a valuable source of information."

As the President's personal advisor, the NSA was the one to inform him about recent events. She was already in the White House, at a meeting with the National Security Council which she quickly cut short. Walking swiftly from the conference room, she took the elevator to the second floor, to the President's Oval Office.

The Secret Service agent standing in the doorway blocked her entry. "I must speak with the President immediately. It's urgent," she explained. "It's concerning a matter of great national importance."

Without moving out of the doorway, the agent picked up the intercom. "The National Security Advisor is here."

The door opened wide and the president appeared, pale and nervous. "What news do you have for me?" he asked.

"Good news."

"Well, that's a nice change," the President commented, as he sat down in his custom-made chair. The NSA was surprised at how much the President had aged since September 11. Just a few weeks ago, he had been young and full of enthusiasm. Now, he seemed like a tired old man.

The President leaned forward, listening closely.

"It appears that we've conclusively identified Abu Salim, and we'll be able to capture him—tonight, if we do it fast."

"Bin Laden's assistant?"

"Yes. He's in Mexico. We need the go-ahead for the operation."

The President became thoughtful. His advisor was asking him to take a very difficult and dangerous step, an operation that could cause serious diplomatic problems between the United States and Mexico. He had always been careful to maintain a good relationship with Mexico. The Hispanic vote had been a main factor in his road to the Presidency, and he made a point of developing a good relationship with the United States' southern neighbor.

But the stakes were too high this time. He could not lose an opportunity to capture an al Qaeda leader, especially since he would be able to provide them with valuable information. He also could not ask the Mexicans for permission. He was aware of the corruption in the government hierarchy, and it was out of the question to endanger such a crucial mission.

The President nodded his head sharply. "Do it," he said decisively.

"Thank you, sir," the NSA said, rising to her feet. "I'll set things in motion immediately."

She raced through the corridor back to the elevator, then down to the conference room in the basement, where she picked up a secure line to the Pentagon.

"It's a go," she ordered.

The troops were on their way.

Rachamim looked warily at Jamil. Was this an innocent invitation to speak—or did Jamil have sinister intentions? His hand slid into his pocket and he fingered the alarm that Arthur had given him.

Rachamim knew that he would have to remain on his guard. He removed his *tallit* and *tefillin* before following Jamil to his room, but kept his hand close by the alarm in his pocket.

"Haven't I repeatedly warned you to get out of this city?" Jamil demanded the moment they entered his room.

"You haven't given me any reason to listen to you," Rachamim told him. "My life was already completely disrupted once before. Do you think that I can just get up and leave everything, that I can destroy my life because of some figment of your imagination?"

"I am not imagining anything," Jamil said insistently. "I know what I am talking about! Here I am, trying to save your life, but you won't listen to anything I tell you!"

"Then explain it to me!" Rachamim said in exasperation. "Why don't you speak clearly?"

Jamil averted his gaze. "I did not speak clearly because I didn't know exactly what was going to take place. I only knew that something terrible would happen. And then … I saw that they had kidnapped you.

I was happy that you were safe from the tragedy that would be taking place in this city."

A shadow of a smile crossed Rachamim's face. "Actually, the kidnapping was good for me. In the end, I recovered the treasure that had been taken from me over twenty years ago."

"What do you mean?" Jamil asked in confusion.

"I found my lost children," Rachamim announced joyfully.

Jamil gasped in astonishment. He stared at Rachamim's beaming face. Found his children? Did that mean that they had been reunited in Afghanistan? The world seemed to spin for a moment, as everything Jamil thought he knew was suddenly turned on its head.

Jamil grabbed Rachamim's hand and shook it to bring him back to reality. "Listen to me!" he said urgently. "Don't you realize you're dealing with al Qaeda? If they let you escape with your children, it's because they want you to be destroyed here, in Los Angeles."

Rachamim shook his head stubbornly. "We escaped from under their noses. They didn't know about it until we were safely away."

"Don't believe it!" Jamil shouted. "Something terrible is going to happen, something that will destroy your family. If you've been reunited, then don't risk your family—escape now, you, Naomi and your children!"

Rachamim stared at Jamil. He seemed so certain, and yet …

"Tell me," Rachamim implored him. "Tell me what it is that is going to happen. Don't keep hinting at it! I need to know!"

Jamil shrank back. He did not reply.

"Why can't you tell me what's going to happen?" Rachamim whispered insistently.

Jamil remained silent.

"I will not leave the city if you don't tell me what's going to happen," Rachamim said with finality.

As he turned to leave, Jamil put out a hand to stop him. "Wait!" He fumbled in his pocket and pulled out a cell phone. "Here. At least keep this cell phone with you. I'll call you to let you know that it's time to escape. It's the most I can do."

Rachamim was left staring at the phone as Jamil walked quietly down the hall and out the back door.

"Here," Abdul whispered to Hakim, pointing to the two dark figures crawling along the opposite slope. These two men were part of the observation squad placed by al Qaeda throughout the region. Hakim focused his night binoculars on the two figures. The binoculars were made in the United States. The al Qaeda had paid plenty of money to obtain them.

"Those aren't Americans. They're typical Mexicans." The men were short and Hakim was not able to make out their faces.

"That's what they appear to be. But they actually are Americans, probably of Mexican origin." Abdul, who had been trained by Soviet specialists in the al Qaeda, knew a lot about military strategy. His teachers had brought a tremendous amount of knowledge from the former Soviet Union, and they taught their students well.

The two men watched the two Americans, who were lying perfectly still on the top of the mountain. Abdul and Hakim waited patiently. Finally, they saw one of the Americans take a thin pipe and lift it up so it protruded about ten inches above the bushes.

"He's using a periscope," Abdul explained. He watched the American placed one end to his eye and slowly start turning the periscope around in all directions. Abdul gently took the night binoculars from his assistant and handed him the regular pair of binoculars. "What does the periscope look like through a conventional pair of binoculars?" he asked Hakim.

Hakim peered through the lenses. "Like a reed sticking up out of the desert foliage."

"That's right. The Americans are intelligent. If anyone were to notice that pipe, he would assume it was just a part of that plant. The chance that anyone would realize it's a periscope is almost zero."

"This is the first time I've seen anyone use a periscope on land," Hakim admitted.

"Once you've spent a lot of time with us, you'll discover many things that you've never heard of before."

They watched the American fold the periscope and place it inside his backpack. The two Americans proceeded to the next mountaintop to continue observing the area through the periscope. This time, they saw the Americans use a short wave radio to report back to their superiors.

Abdul lowered the binoculars. "It's time for us to report what we just saw to our leader."

Hakim looked inquiringly at Abdul. "Should I come with you?"

Abdul considered it for a moment. "Perhaps not," he said finally. "Continue observing the men. I will contact our leader."

Hakim picked up the binoculars and continued watching the two Americans while Abdul slid down the mountaintop, away from the Americans. When he judged that he was far enough away, he took a short wave radio out of his backpack.

"The Americans are here," he reported.

There was a burst of static. Abdul strained to hear the response.

"Continue watching," he finally made out. "Make sure you are not seen."

In command headquarters in Afghanistan, bin Laden nodded in satisfaction as he turned away from the short wave radio. "Everything is in place," he said to al Zawahiri. "It's time to take the next step. Begin the second stage of the operation."

Twenty Nine

Abu Salim slowly sipped his orange juice while staring at the unpainted walls inside the cave-like structure. In ten minutes his cadets would be sent to the fields, and he would be going out together with them, to supervise their training.

The door opened suddenly and he jumped up in surprise. Two men entered, their faces almost completely covered by *kefiyas*. They ran over to where he was sitting. From the expression in their eyes it was clear that they were out to harm him. He tried to leap to his feet, but a heavy hand grasped his shoulder. He tried to twist away, but two strong hands held him tightly in place.

Another man entered the room, carrying a doctor's bag. His entire face—except his eyes—was also covered by a *kefiya*. Placing his bag on a nearby stool, he opened it and removed a syringe. Abu Salim struggled as one of the men holding him stretched out his arm and clamped it in a vise-like grip. The doctor took a cotton ball from his bag, poured on some alcohol, and pushed up the sleeve of Abu Salim's robe. He delicately swabbed Abu Salim's upper arm with the cotton swab, then lifted the syringe.

Abu Salim tried to struggle as the point of the syringe touched his skin, but the two men held him immobile. There was a sharp pinch on his arm that quickly faded as the syringe was withdrawn. A minute later, the doctor was bandaging his arm.

The two men who had been holding him in place released their grasp. Abu Salim painfully tried to move his shoulders. The doctor packed up his bag, and the three men left the room as abruptly as they had arrived.

What was that all about? What had they done to him?

The short wave radio in the corner suddenly crackled to life. "Abu Salim?"

Abu Salim leaped to the radio. He recognized his leader's voice. "I am here," he responded, his voice quavering.

"Abu Salim, how are you?" Abu Salim heard bin Laden chuckle.

Abu Salem stiffened. *Bin Laden is behind this. He knows what just happened. But why did he do this?*

"I'm fine," Abu Salim managed to reply.

"Are you sure?" Bin Laden asked politely.

"I believe so." Abu Salim could not restrain himself any longer. "Perhaps I wasn't feeling well before this treatment, but now, I must say, the treatment has already helped me."

"I am sending you on important mission," bin Laden explained, "and I expect it to be a success. That's why I placed an insurance policy inside you."

Abu Salim broke out in a cold sweat. He had once heard about the different insurance policies that bin Laden used to make sure his operations would be successful. Usually, these policies were extremely brutal. He wondered what policy he had invested in him.

Bin Laden did not give him time to wonder. "The computer chip that was placed in your arm contains two things. One—a tracking device, so I can know your location at all times. And two—a very small amount, just one tiny milligram, of cyanide."

Abu Salim felt his heart start pounding in fear. He had been personally involved in developing the al Qaeda's store of chemical weapons. He knew what these poisons were capable of doing. One milligram of cyanide was enough to kill a rhinoceros in just a few seconds.

"The cyanide is wrapped in a special plastic, and it's completely safe," bin Laden reassured him in a fatherly voice. "The cyanide can remain in its plastic wrapping for years without causing you any problems. That is, of course, if no one does anything to it. The problem is that the chip also contains a tiny mechanism that is designed to burst the capsule and release the poison."

Bin Laden fell silent, giving Abu Salim time to digest this information.

"When will the mechanism release the poison?"

Bin Laden's voice was as cold as ice. "In another twenty-four hours, unless …"

"Unless what?" Abu Salim asked hoarsely.

"Unless you do exactly what I ask of you."

"I would have done that, even without this extra insurance!" Abu Salim protested.

"I prefer to be absolutely certain," bin Laden said smoothly. "A little encouragement certainly won't hurt."

"What do you want me to do?"

"It's fairly simple, actually. I need you to allow the Americans to capture you in the next few hours."

"What!" Abu Salim shook his head to clear it. "What do you mean?"

"Yes, you heard me correctly. You are to allow yourself to fall into the Americans' hands. They're on their way to capture you now."

"Then we should destroy the camp and leave immediately!" Abu Salim gasped.

"No!" bin Laden said sharply. "You do not have the breadth of vision to understand my plan. You will remain where you are. I *want* you to fall into their hands. Once you're captured, I want you to panic. Plead with them to lighten your punishment. In exchange, tell them that I am planning a massive attack against the United States, and that you are willing to ruin my plan if they promise to keep you alive.

"The Americans will agree. Once they've promised not to kill you, tell them that I am planning to explode a dirty nuclear bomb. Ask that they fly you directly to Los Angeles. Tell them that you will recognize the two people arriving from the Far East who will be carrying out the operation. Convince them that only your personal intervention will prevent the two from carrying out their mission."

Abu Salim barely heard. He was fixated on the poison implanted in his arm. "What about the cyanide? When will you stop it?"

"The computer chip contains a tiny transmitter. Once you've arrived in Los Angeles, one of my agents will use a short wave radio to neutralize the mechanism. He has a small group of agents with him, and they are responsible to release you from the Americans and smuggle you out of the United States."

Abu Salim was skeptical that bin Laden would try to free him. He realized that bin Laden had been right—only the poisonous insurance that had been planted in his skin would ensure that he would allow himself to fall into American hands. He knew enough of al Qaeda's technological prowess to recognize that bin Laden's description of the computer chip was certainly plausible.

His life lay in his leader's hands—and he knew how delicate a grasp that was.

"I will do as you command," he said finally, his heart heavy with fear.

"I knew you would. Now, repeat your instructions to me."

Eleven soldiers of the elite Delta One squad were assembled next to a Chinook helicopter on a tiny landing strip among the sand dunes of the Mojave Desert in California, not far from the Mexican border. These soldiers were among the best the army had to offer—trained to steal though the night, to strike with stealth, to escape into darkness before the other side could react.

Like all professional soldiers, they did not need to know the why's of their mission. But they knew enough to make them all eager to take on this task. Their country was under attack—the terrorist acts of September 11 were undoubtedly acts of war—and now they were eager for a chance to strike back against an ephemeral enemy.

The men looked at their commanding officer expectantly, their eyes filled with enthusiasm. In a confident voice, the officer asked, "Is there anyone here who hesitates to take part in this mission?"

"No," the soldiers shouted in one voice. "We're ready and willing to go!"

"So let's *go!*" the commander ordered.

The troops got on board and the helicopter immediately gained altitude, sending a cloud of desert sand in every direction. The camp commander watched the aircraft fly away until it was swallowed by the surrounding darkness.

The soldiers were sitting on the helicopter's floor, leaning against the sides. Their supplies were packed into rucksacks on their backs and their weapons, M-2 machine guns, were slung across their knees.

"We just crossed the border," the pilot announced over the intercom. "We're flying eighty feet above ground level."

He was flying at this low altitude to evade the American and Mexican radar screens that had been set up in this region to prevent drug smuggling, which was usually done by lightweight airplanes. The Defense Department had made sure that the Ivax aircraft that was used to search for low flying aircraft would not be out this evening.

At two o'clock in the morning, the pilot notified the military base in the Mojave Desert that he was hovering above the designated area.

"Continue hovering for a few more minutes," the camp commander ordered. He immediately put in a call to General Mirce, who was supervising this operation from the Pentagon.

General Mirce of the Joint Chiefs of Staff was waiting in the Pentagon war room with the Secretary of Defense. The FBI director, the National Security Advisor, and the President were all listening in from the communications room in the White House.

"What's the situation on the ground?" the camp commander asked.

"There's no change," Mirce responded. "The landing area is clear. The terrorists are having a night training session, seven fighters plus Abu Salim. No sentries are posted nearby."

"Okay. Land the helicopter."

The camp commander transmitted the order.

The helicopter hovered for a few more minutes above a flat area tucked away between the mountaintops, then slowly settled to the ground.

The helicopter door burst opened. The commanding officer emerged from the opening and raced to the left, the other soldiers following close behind. Behind them, the helicopter's rotors slowed and finally came to a complete halt. The pilots inside remained on alert—they knew they might have to take off in a hurry.

The Delta troops were aware that they had assets in the area—Rafael and his men. At this point, Rafael was their best guide to where the al Qaeda terrorists were training. A technician in the Pentagon connected Rafael's transmission with the unit's commanding officer.

Following Rafael's direction, the soldiers quickly crossed the ridge separating the area where they had landed from the cadets' training camp. At the end of the ridge, they stopped for a moment to evaluate the region. The commanding officer used his night binoculars to peer around him. He could see the opening to the cave in the center of the valley. There was Abu Salim sitting in the entrance, holding a transmitter to his mouth—undoubtedly giving orders to the recruits.

The commanding officer crawled back to his men and whispered instructions. "I think we'll be able to capture Abu Salim without going into battle. We'll silently crawl into the camp and surprise him from behind. I don't think it will take more than fifteen minutes for me to reach the cave."

The commanding officer chose one soldier to accompany him. The rest were ordered to remain, keeping cover under the protection of the mountain while observing the operation. They would take part only if they saw that the two men needed reinforcements.

The two soldiers moved slowly, placing one foot deliberately in front of the other, maintaining a steady movement in the inky blackness. Their eyes swiveled around constantly, keeping a wary lookout for guards or booby traps. The other soldiers strained to watch as the two men seemed to disappear into the dark night.

Rachamim slowly left the synagogue building, deep in troubled thought. There was no question that Jamil was somehow directly involved with al Qaeda. For years, Rachamim had tried to make Jamil's miserable life more pleasant. Now he felt as if he had been slapped in the face. On the other hand, Rachamim knew that it was the least he could have done for Jamil, who had saved his life …

Or had he? Suddenly Rachamim realized that there probably hadn't been a helicopter crash, that the entire episode had been staged in order to kidnap his two sons, and that Jamil had been a part of the plot from the beginning. That must have been what Yosef had tried to tell him earlier. A feeling of fury began to burn inside him.

But then why was Jamil trying to save his life? Why was he trying so desperately to send Rachamim out of the city? As quickly as it had ignited, his anger cooled. It was clear that he still didn't know the entire story.

Rachamim fingered the cellular phone that Jamil had handed him. Jamil planned to call him soon, he knew. What would he tell him? If he left the city, then Jamil would feel free to carry out a terrorist attack that would undoubtedly kill many people. On the other hand, perhaps Jamil had no control over the coming attack—perhaps it would happen regardless of Rachamim's presence, and Jamil was merely trying to warn him in time. Did Rachamim have the right to risk his life on the chance that he *might* be able to save others?

Perhaps he could leave the city, but tell Jamil that he had remained. That way he would be safe, but Jamil would think he was still in danger—and call off the attack.

Arthur was waiting outside, leaning on the open car door. He looked relieved when Rachamim appeared. As Rachamim settled into the front seat of the car, he noticed several agents emerging from the shrubs surrounding the synagogue, wearing bulletproof vests and carrying heavy guns. They quickly disappeared into their cars and sped away from the area.

Arthur pressed on the gas. They drove several blocks in silence. When they reached La Cienega Boulevard, Arthur commented, "You almost caused me a heart attack."

"Why?"

"We saw someone sneak out of the synagogue's back door. He was so fast that by the time our agents realized what was going on, he was gone. All one agent noticed was that he appeared to be an Arab. You can imagine that we did not find that description exactly reassuring. We were just about ready to burst into the building when you walked out."

"He contacted me," Rachamim spoke quietly, as if to himself, staring blindly at the heavy morning traffic. He did not see the cars. Instead he went back in time, watching the mountains disappearing under the helicopter as he tried to escape Iran.

The traffic came to a complete stop as Arthur slammed on the brakes. "What are you talking about?" he demanded.

Rachamim looked up. "Jamil," he clarified. "I now realize that he's deceived me for all these years." Rachamim took a deep breath. "A terrible tragedy is going to occur here in this city. I think that it's important for me to inform the FBI."

"I *am* the FBI," Arthur pointed out. "And what in the world does Jamil have to do with this?"

"Jamil has everything to do with it," Rachamim said impatiently. "There's no time to explain. I'm warning you that a catastrophe will soon take place here, in Los Angeles. Contact the FBI immediately!"

"I *am* the FBI," Arthur said again.

"Then call your boss," Rachamim insisted. "You need to get working on this!"

Arthur stared in astonishment at Rachamim before turning his attention back to the freeway. He couldn't decide if Rachamim had a valid reason to worry, or if the difficult events of the past week had finally taken their toll. Either way, there was no point in taking chances. He stepped on the gas and started weaving in and out of traffic, eager to reach the safe house as soon as possible.

"We'll be back at the house soon," he told Rachamim, while keeping his eye on the road. "In the meantime, tell me what you know."

"The man who you saw sneaking out of the synagogue's back entrance warned me to leave the city as quickly as possible." Rachamim tried to control his emotions so he could speak calmly. "That man was Jamil, my friend for the last twenty years. He once saved my life, and ever since then I have been nice to him and have tried to do whatever I could to make his life better." Rachamim let out a breath. "All those years, I never ever realized that he was a terrorist."

"What makes you think he's a terrorist now?"

"It was the cell phone."

"Cell phone?"

"Here." Rachamim fumbled in his pocket. "Jamil gave me a cell phone. He told me that he would call to warn me to leave the city before the attack."

Arthur shook his head in resignation, then reached for his own cell phone. This whole story was getting stranger by the minute. Jamil was probably a poor beggar with delusions of belonging to al Qaeda. Still, with everything on high alert since September 11, he knew he couldn't afford to ignore this.

"All right. I'll call this into headquarters, and we'll track the cell phone down."

Arthur quickly dialed a number. "Hey, John, it's Arthur."

"What's up on your side of the world?" John asked. "I hope you're taking advantage of the warm California sun to get a nice suntan."

"Not right now," Arthur admitted. "I need to get through to the director. We have a warning of a major terrorist attack in the L.A. region, starting immediately."

"Say that again?"

Arthur rapidly explained the circumstances. "I'm going to track down this mysterious cell phone," he concluded. "In the meantime, get the director informed. We'll need some technical assistance from your end."

"Will do," John said immediately, then hung up.

Thirty

The four figures hiding in the thin shrubbery on the hilltop overlooking the landing pad waited until the soldiers were five miles away. They had spent years in America, becoming United States citizens and then joining the army. After years of training on American army bases they knew exactly what they would find on the landing pad below.

The radio clicked twice. The squad leader along the soldiers' route had seen them pass by. It was time to move.

The fighters began walking forward, moving slowly but steadily toward their goal. When they were about ten feet away from the helicopter, they came to a stop and lay flat on the ground. Here, they divided into two groups to surround the helicopter. The commander, wearing special night glasses, crawled up to the helicopter's door, while his assistant followed close behind.

One of the two pilots was inside, checking through the weapons systems, while the other was on the ground—looking, as it so happened, in the wrong direction. Neither noticed the four terrorists creeping up on them. But the pilot outside did hear a faint hissing sound as the terrorist leader took a can from his pocket and twisted the cap open, releasing a gas into the air.

Feeling for his weapon, the pilot on the ground began turning toward the sound. But it was too late. His legs were already feeling rubbery from the effects of the chemicals. Two minutes later, he was lying on the ground, completely unconscious.

The second group of two forced open the helicopter door and threw the open gas can inside. The pilot, who had jumped up at the sound of the door opening, was able to take no more than two steps forward before he, too, slumped to the ground.

The terrorists were careful to keep their gas masks in place as they clambered aboard the helicopter. The commander secured the pilot's hands with special iron cuffs attached to his belt. The second pilot was carried on board, and he too had his hands tied. The commander went back into the cargo section, checking to make sure it was empty, then reappeared in the helicopter's doorway. He lifted his radio and pressed the transmit button. "Let's go!"

Two jeeps appeared, seemingly out of nowhere. One was carrying something that appeared to be a missile. The second jeep contained two soldiers, their weapons ready. The jeeps approached the helicopter and parked next to the right hand missile on the helicopter's underside. The soldiers immediately began removing that missile from the helicopter's belly.

It took just a few minutes to remove the missile, using a special sling attached to the jeep. The missile was deposited on the back seat of the jeep, then the sling was carefully placed around the missile they had brought with them. It appeared identical to the one they had removed. Working carefully, they securely attached the new missile to the helicopter.

The entire operation took less than seven minutes. The jeeps sped off into the surrounding mountains, leaving behind a trail of dust.

The commander returned to the helicopter. He and his assistant started opening drawers and removing papers, making no effort to be silent. The effects of the gas were beginning to wear off. They could see the pilots stirring, then begin looking around, trying to recall what had happened.

When they had gained full consciousness, the pilots could see their captors looking at each other in consternation. "There are no important papers here," the pilots heard the terrorists mutter to each other. The terrorists ignored the fact that the pilots were now awake and continued their search. The helpless pilots could only watch, while trying to find some way to warn their comrades of the danger.

Two shadowy figures, barely visible in the dark night, came closer to the cave entrance. The Delta soldiers had managed to elude detection. There was enough noise coming from the al Qaeda training camp to mask any inadvertent sounds, since the terrorists were practicing with live ammunition. That also insured that the trainees' activities had Abu Salim's full attention—he didn't want any unnecessary casualties.

Abu Salim had just put down his radio when he felt cold, hard steel pressed against his neck.

"Don't move," a voice said in Arabic.

Abu Salim sat perfectly still.

"I want you to stand up very, very slowly. There are four of us here, so if you make any sudden moves, you are dead at least four times. Now."

Slowly, moving inch by inch, Abu Salim got carefully to his feet. He could feel hands expertly pat him down for weapons. The gun on his neck never moved from its position.

"Turn around, and start walking," the voice instructed him. "Don't worry about your men. They're doing fine without you."

Stiffly, his steps jerky, Abu Salim began walking. He looked longingly at his men—but no one had even noticed that he was gone.

"Call for the FBI director," Captain Stevens announced, putting the caller on hold.

The FBI director looked up. Captain Stevens was manning the switchboard in the communications room in the White House basement. While the President himself was no longer in the room, his entire security team was still there, waiting to hear the results of the covert operation in Mexico. Even though it was impossible to communicate with the soldiers in the field until they were back aboard the helicopter, everyone was too tense to leave. The waiting was difficult, but at least they would hear the news as quickly as possible.

"I'll take it here," the director said quickly.

As the director began speaking quietly on the phone, a call finally came in from the secure communications links on the aircraft. The Defense Secretary leaped over to Captain Stevens, who was taking down the transmission.

"Trouble aboard the helicopter, sir," the captain said tersely.

"What sort of the trouble?" the secretary demanded. "What's going on?"

The Delta unit advanced along the ridge as it made its way back to the helicopter. The commanding officer took personal charge of Abu Salim. The other soldiers surrounded their officer and the captive, protecting them from attack.

They could see the helicopter in the distance. Just then, the officer stopped. He held up his hand to bring his men to a halt. Something was wrong.

He could see light coming from the helicopter's front window. He couldn't imagine that the pilots could be careless enough to leave the light on inside the aircraft. Anyone passing by in the stark desert darkness would notice it immediately.

The officer handed the captive over to his assistant and motioned to him to wait there. He took the rest of the unit and proceeded quietly toward the waiting aircraft. They peered cautiously through the window—and noticed two men riffling through documents and exploring the aircraft, while the two pilots lay bound on the floor, their mouths taped shut.

The door was half ajar. The officer kicked open the door and leaped inside.

"Stop or I'll shoot!"

The two men froze in place. The soldiers who were covering for him kicked away the terrorists' weapons to the opposite side of the aircraft.

The officer waved his soldiers on board. "Search the back!" he ordered. "You two, secure the prisoners."

Two soldiers came forward and roughly grabbed the two terrorists, while another two released the pilots. In the meantime, the rest of the squad checked out both the outside and the cargo area of the helicopter before joining the commander in the front.

"All clear," they reported.

The pilots had gotten to their feet. They were groggily shaking their heads and rubbing their hands to restore the circulation.

"Will you be able to fly the helicopter back to base?" the commanding officer asked worriedly. Now was not the time to start asking about what had happened. His first priority was to leave the area as quickly as possible.

"Yes," they responded, although it would not be easy. They were still sleepy from the anesthesia, and the cramping in their muscles made movement difficult.

"Let's go!" the commanding officer ordered.

The pilots took their seats and began to prepare for takeoff.

The radio crackled again. "All is clear. Say again, all is clear. Aircraft is safe. We're taking off now, and we have Abu Salim with us."

A cheer went up from the room. The National Security Advisor exchanged smiles with the Defense Secretary. Their gamble had paid off! The threat in Mexico was neutralized, and they had Abu Salim, the notorious right-hand man of bin Laden.

In all the excitement, no one noticed the worried expression on the FBI director's face. He was hearing some very troublesome news from Los Angeles.

"Rachamim tells me that a huge terrorist attack is planned against L.A.," Arthur reported.

"Do you think this is reliable information?" the director asked.

Arthur hesitated. "It's possible. Apparently, Rachamim just met the al Qaeda agent who had been his close friend for many years. The terrorist is trying everything in his power to convince Rachamim to leave the city quickly. He's warned him that a major attack will occur very soon."

"Hang on, I can't hear you." In the background, Arthur could hear people cheering and talking loudly. He waited patiently for the noise to subside.

"Okay." The noise was still going on, but it was noticeably quieter. The FBI director had gone to a corner of the room, as far as he could get from the celebrants. "Now give me the details."

"One moment," Abu Salim blurted out.

The commanding officer stared at him. He was trembling and pale from fear. "I would like to make a deal with you," he pleaded. The other two terrorists were glaring angrily at him, but Abu Salim ignored their stares. "The United States is about to be attacked," he said in a desperate voice. "If you promise not to kill me, I will cooperate and do everything in my power to prevent a terror attack that is scheduled to take place very soon in Los Angeles."

The other two terrorists were staring at him with open hatred, hissing in Arabic, "Traitor, traitor."

Abu Salim turned away from his comrades, his cheeks burning in shame. "You will not be able to evade giving an account for your behavior," one of the terrorists threatened. "The Americans will not be able to prevent bin Laden from finding you, if you go back on the oath that you took."

There was total silence. Abu Salim lifted his gaze. "I'm willing to do whatever I can to prevent the attack."

"Aren't you concerned that bin Laden will take revenge?" the commanding officer asked.

"Obviously I expect protection." Abu Salim spoke with confidence. "You want to know everything, but I am planning to provide you with the information very, very slowly, so my life insurance will last a long time."

"Let me discuss this with my superiors," the officer said.

"You don't have much time to discuss things," Abu Salim warned him. "There's just a few hours left. We had better get to Los Angeles quickly before the city is destroyed."

"I understand." The commanding officer nodded to the pilots, who opened the secure link to the communications room in the White House.

"Sir, the commander of the Delta force is calling from the aircraft," Captain Stevens called to the Secretary of Defense.

"Anything wrong?" he asked in concern.

"Abu Salim is willing to make a deal with us," the officer related. "He says that there will be a major attack in Los Angeles within the next few hours. He is willing to help us stop it."

"Los Angeles?"

From his corner of the room, the FBI director looked up sharply. "Los Angeles? Who just said Los Angeles?"

"I did," the Defense Secretary responded.

"What about Los Angeles?" the director demanded.

"We have word from Abu Salim. He's willing to make a deal," the Defense Secretary explained. "He claims that a major attack is planned for Los Angeles."

"Are you willing to make a deal with him?" the officer asked over the radio.

The FBI director leaped to his feet. "Tell him yes!" he shouted. "I've just gotten confirmation from another source. There is an attack planned for L.A., and we need to find out as much as possible!"

The two men stared at each other for a long moment. "I think it's time to call the President," the Secretary of Defense said quietly.

The director nodded. They would need to move on this fast, if they hoped to prevent another disaster.

The radio crackled again. "Abu Salim warned me that with every passing minute, the chance of preventing the attack becomes less. The terrorists are already in Los Angeles. Abu Salim's the only one who knows their identity and is able to stop them."

"I don't think we should wait for the President," the FBI director said quickly. "I'll give the okay for providing him with clemency."

"Okay." The Defense Secretary leaned over the radio link. "Tell him I accept his conditions, as long as the information he gives us is reliable. If we find out that he's lying, then we don't owe him a thing. Tell him that if he's playing games with us, I will personally make sure that he receives the death sentence."

The FBI director turned back to his phone call. "We just got independent corroboration on the L.A. attack," he said urgently. "You need to take this one seriously. What have you got?"

"We have a name, and a cell phone that may belong to the alleged terrorist," Arthur reported. "The terrorist claims that he will be calling Rachamim on the cell phone shortly."

"Get things set up in place," the FBI director ordered. "When that call comes in, we'll want to track it down immediately."

Thirty One

"Nextel, may I help you?"

"Arthur Singer from the FBI," Arthur identified himself. "We have a cell phone here and we need to identify the owner."

"I'm not allowed to give out that information," the clerk retorted. "All customer information is confidential. It's illegal and against company policy for me to provide you with that information."

"I'm an FBI agent," Arthur tried to explain. "We need this information urgently."

"First of all, I have no way of knowing if you really are who you say you are. And even if you are an FBI agent, you have to bring me a court permit before I can provide you with the information."

"Excuse me. Did you ever hear of September 11?"

"Yes, but what does that have to do with your request?"

Arthur spoke in a threatening tone. "It can happen again, because of people like you who refuse to assist us. You know what? Osama bin Laden couldn't care less about your customers' right to privacy. If we continue to act so fanatically, then the chances of being saved from another terrorist attack are negligible."

The clerk lost his confidence, and apparently decided to take the easy way out. "I'll transfer you to my supervisor," he said quickly. He put Arthur on hold without waiting for a reply.

It took just a minute for the supervisor to pick up the phone. Arthur repeated his request for information. This time, he immediately emphasized the seriousness of the present situation. The supervisor was ready to assist him. "I'm willing to provide the FBI with any information they need. But first I have to be sure that you are an FBI agent and not a criminal trying to take advantage of the chaotic situation."

"Call the local FBI office and ask them to transfer your call to Arthur Singer."

"Okay," the supervisor agreed. He understood that the present security situation justified breaking the rules.

Less than two minutes later, Arthur's cell phone rang. He immediately recognized the supervisor's voice. "Okay," he said. "How can I help you?"

"I have a cell phone and I want to know who owns it."

"The serial number is on the inside of the plastic battery covering. Read it to me," the supervisor instructed him.

Arthur used his shoulder to wedge his own phone in place while opening the cover on Jamil's cell phone. He managed to remove the cover and find the serial number. "The number is five, two, three, seven, one, nine, nine, zero, one, one. The phone's a Nokia 8325." Arthur heard the supervisor type the numbers into a computer while he was reading them to him.

"The telephone is registered as belonging to Jamil Abu Chakim," the supervisor responded.

"Where does he live?"

"2113 Rexford Drive, Los Angeles, California."

Arthur repeated the address out loud, while glancing at Rachamim to see his reaction.

"That address can't be right," Rachamim exclaimed. "Rexford Drive is in an exclusive neighborhood. Jamil rented a one room apartment in a run down area."

"If he's a member of al Qaeda, money will pose no problem," Arthur pointed out. "All the terrorists who hijacked the planes on September 11 were traveling first class. The al Qaeda has unlimited financial resources."

"But I know he didn't live there! His address is on the checks he was given for his services in the synagogue, they were on his tax forms ..."

"He obviously had another center for his al Qaeda operations. You knew him for over twenty years, but you never realized that he was a member of al Qaeda," Arthur pointed out.

"You're right," Rachamim admitted. "But then it's just a front. You won't find him there."

"I don't think it would hurt if we sent a couple of agents to check out the address."

Rachamim shrugged his shoulders. He was sure it would be a waste of time.

Jamil's cell phone suddenly sprang to life. Arthur and Rachamim were caught by surprise.

Arthur quickly considered who should take the call. At the third ring, Arthur handed the cell phone to Rachamim. "You answer it!" he ordered.

Rachamim's hand was shaking so violently that he was barely able to press the green button to accept the call. "Rachamim."

Rachamim immediately recognized Jamil's voice. It was quivering from emotion. "Tell me that you've listened to me. Tell me that you've left Los Angeles." Rachamim could hear Jamil crying.

"No, I haven't. I'm here, smack in the middle of the city."

Jamil, breathing heavily, did not reply, though he did not hang up.

In the meantime, Arthur had activated the FBI's communications network. "Jamil's on the line right now. Find out where he's calling from, and do it fast!"

"Rachamim..." Jamil's voice broke. Rachamim could hear him sobbing. He remained silent while Jamil cried. He could hear Arthur whisper, "Keep him on the line as long as possible."

"Rachamim, your time is almost up. This is your last chance to leave the city before it is too late. Rachamim, it breaks my heart. It's hard for me to accept that I will have to hurt you."

"So don't hurt me!" Rachamim almost yelled back at him. "You don't need to hurt anyone!"

"No. It's impossible. I must end this conversation now. I've stilled my conscience. I did everything in my power to save you."

"You didn't do anything to save me," Rachamim insisted. "I am not going to leave the city. I will remain here." Rachamim waited for a reply, but the line was dead.

Arthur's cell phone started ringing. It was the FBI calling back. "We found out where he's calling from," the technician declared. "He's in the Gateway Center in Union Station, downtown Los Angeles."

"He's hung up the phone now," Arthur reported.

"It's okay. As long as he doesn't turn the cell phone off we can trace him. He's still in the Gateway Center."

"Great. Keep tracking it and tell me if anything changes." Arthur hung up, then activated his radio. "We need units to surround Union Station immediately! Don't let anyone leave before we arrive."

Arthur turned to Rachamim. "I prefer that you stay here. Do you think I'll be able to identify him on my own?"

"I believe so. You can definitely tell that he's an Arab. He's not tall, and he's around seventy-five years old. He has no identifying marks on him. Oh, yes … I forgot. He does. He has a brown birthmark under his eye, and there's a scar on the left side of his chin. The marks are difficult to notice. If you look at him carefully, though, you'll be able to find them."

Arthur frowned. "You know what? Maybe you should come with us. Under the circumstances, since he is so emotionally involved with you, this might be our best chance to get through to him."

Rachamim did not resist. He quietly went with Arthur, who helped him get into the car waiting for them outside. The moment Rachamim was safely in his seat, Arthur jumped into the driver's seat and sped away.

"Okay, we got permission to grant you clemency," the officer told Abu Salim.

"Wonderful. Of course, there's also the reward."

"What reward?" the officer asked suspiciously.

"The twenty-five million dollar prize that was promised to anyone who helped capture bin Laden or one of his three main assistants, of whom I am one," Abu Salim said confidently.

The officer stared at him. "You mean, you captured yourself?"

"Right!"

It sounded strange to him, but the officer just shrugged. "You'll probably get it. If your information is good enough, then that's probably the least they'll be willing to give you."

"Fine," Abu Salim said briskly. "There's a lot to do. We must get as quickly as possible to Los Angeles International Airport. That's where the al Qaeda terrorist is located. He's controlling a nuclear weapon, and he plans to detonate it within two hours."

A short, shocked silence descended on the helicopter. The soldiers hadn't expected anything of this magnitude. The pilot was the first to move, turning on his radio and shouting into his microphone.

In the communications room at the White House, it was as if a bomb had suddenly exploded. "Nuclear attack!" they heard the pilot say tersely. "Bin Laden has a nuclear attack planned for L.A.!"

The room fell silent as the import of the pilot's words sank in. Just then, the President walked into the room, eager to hear the latest from the Mexican operation.

"Mr. President," the Secretary of Defense turned to him. "I have upsetting news for you."

He quickly related what the soldiers had discovered from Abu Salim.

"That's impossible. That's absolutely impossible." The President's voice was panicky. "Maybe he's making it up, just to get clemency?"

"That's possible," the Defense Secretary admitted. "But we've had corroborating evidence from the FBI that an attack is planned for L.A. Too many pieces are fitting together for this to be completely made up."

"May I add something?" the commanding officer in Mexico interrupted. He could hear the President clearly over the radio.

"Of course," the Defense Secretary replied.

"Abu Salim is acting in a way that shows he is desperate. He decided to collaborate only as we were about to take off, when he realized that there was no chance of rescue. He's expecting to receive money and a new identity after providing us with additional information. If you were to ask me, I would say that we should take his words very seriously."

"I agree," responded the Secretary of Defense. "Especially since we received a similar warning from a different source."

"I think we had better tell the governor of California what's going on. Can the city be evacuated quickly?" the President asked, trying to control his panic.

"In two hours?" The Secretary shook his head. "It's out of the question to evacuate so many people in such a small amount of time."

"How did they ever get a nuclear weapon?" the President demanded.

"It's not as difficult as you think. With money and connections, it's easy to obtain one of the many nuclear bombs that disappeared with the fall of the Iron Curtain."

"Abu Salim says that we're losing valuable time. We have to fly at maximum speed to get there in time," the commander warned them.

"Okay. Get moving," the Secretary of Defense commanded. "Get there as fast as you can."

The helicopter slowly gained altitude. It was now carrying three extra men. At one hundred and fifty feet it made a sharp turn to the west before continuing to gain altitude. A few minutes later, the helicopter had disappeared from the horizon.

A dark figure rose out of the bushes growing on the ridge at the far end of the valley. He stood up and straightened his back before carefully returning a pair of night binoculars into the dusty bag on his belt. From a different bag he removed a short wave radio.

"Abdullah speaking," he identified himself into the radio. "The helicopter just took off. It's flying westward. Everything's going exactly according to plan," he announced joyfully to his leader, Osama bin Laden.

"Excellent. I want to compliment you and your men for a job well done."

The words were positive, but Abdullah was surprised at the lack of euphoria in his leader's voice.

"Is everything all right?" he asked hesitantly.

"Yes, as I said, the operation went even better than expected. But the operation is still far from finished. I cannot be happy until it has ended successfully. Too many operations have been successful up to the final stage, and then, for some reason, they failed. Within the next few hours, I hope to join in your rejoicing."

Abdullah understood.

"The time has come to leave. Take the military base apart immediately," bin Laden ordered Abdullah. "The Americans will return to take revenge for what we're about to do to them."

"Okay," Abdullah confirmed the order. He jumped onto his desert motorcycle, which was hidden underneath one of the bushes, and raced off to the training area, leaving behind a trail of desert sand.

He came to a stop in the middle of the training area. The recruits were still working on their maneuvers. Abdullah placed two fingers in his mouth and gave a loud whistle.

The shooting stopped immediately. Some twenty-five recruits threw down their weapons and ran over to where he was standing in the center of the field. They waited respectfully to hear what he had to say.

"Our mission in Mexico is over," Abdullah announced with high spirits. "We have succeeded in what we set out to do."

The recruits looked at each other in confusion. *What is he talking about? After all, we've done nothing the whole time except practice.*

"Leave everything exactly as it is," Abdullah continued. "Get in the jeeps. We're driving to Mexico City. There, we'll disperse and blend into the local population. Each of us will have to find his own way out of the country."

He glanced around to see if the soldiers understood their orders. They were nodding in agreement. "I want you to understand that in a few hours, the Mexican government is going to be doing everything in their power to discover your whereabouts."

"We're ready," they responded in one voice.

Thirty Two

Dozens of police units surrounded the enormous building housing the bus terminal in the Gateway Center, blocking off all the entrances and exits. It was past the morning rush hour, so the terminal wasn't completely crowded, but there were still plenty of people around who were demanding an explanation from the police. The police weren't able to respond, since they had no idea why the building was cordoned off.

About fifteen minutes after the first police car arrived, Arthur drove up to the narrow road leading to the southern entrance. A police car was blocking the road so no cars could get through. The policeman manning the barrier approached the open window to tell the driver to turn around and leave. Arthur noticed a second policeman standing behind him, his gun drawn, providing coverage for the officer as he approached the car.

"Arthur Singer, FBI agent," Arthur identified himself to the police officer before the officer had a chance to tell him to turn around. The policeman carefully examined Arthur's identity card before deciding it was authentic. He told the second policeman to move the car and let them through.

"Tell the officer in charge of this operation that I'm here," Arthur ordered. "Tell him that I'm on my way to the southern entrance, and that I expect him to be there, waiting for me."

"Yes, sir."

Arthur changed gears and drove toward the entrance. "Are you ready?" he asked Rachamim, who was staring at his feet, without saying a word.

"Yes," Rachamim responded, slowly lifting his head.

Rachamim opened the car door and got out on his own. He felt dizzy. His heart was breaking at the thought of causing harm to Jamil, who had been a part of his life for so many years.

They entered the terminal. There were only a few people inside the main area—the rest had been shepherded out of the way of the police. Each of the men standing nervously in the corner had olive skin and appeared to be of Middle Eastern descent.

Rachamim looked closely at each of the people standing there. "Jamil is not here," he said.

"But he must be here," Arthur insisted. "His telephone is on, and it's inside the terminal."

"Maybe he's hiding somewhere."

"That's possible. We'll find out in a few moments. A technician from Nextel is on his way to the terminal, and he's bringing a hand-held searching device. He'll be able to find the cell phone's exact location."

A man wearing a brown uniform with the insignia of Nextel clearly visible on his lapel entered the terminal. He was holding a small briefcase that looked like it held a laptop computer. Arthur hurried over to him, dragging Rachamim behind.

"I'm Arthur Singer," Arthur said, extending his hand in greeting. "I'm the agent in charge of this operation."

The technician placed the briefcase on one of the benches and removed a device that looked like a large radio. He held the device in the crook of his arm and turned it on. "Okay. Are you ready?" he asked.

"Of course."

The device's right side looked like a calculator. The technician entered a nine digit number and the device buzzed several times before its screen turned green. In the center of the screen was an arrow pointing toward the terminal's southeast corner.

The technician started following the arrow, with Arthur and

Rachamim trailing close behind. The arrow continued pointing the same way. It started buzzing loudly next to a trash can.

"The telephone is inside the trash can," the technician announced.

Arthur looked around in disappointment. There was no one there.

The technician started digging through the trash. "Here it is," he said, holding a cell phone high in the air. "This is it!"

"He played a trick on us!" Arthur was furious. "He left the cell phone here on purpose."

Rachamim was astonished that the simple-seeming Jamil could be so cunning.

"There's no point in staying here any longer," Arthur admitted in defeat. "We'll remove the police cordon around the terminal. In the meantime, let's get back to the car so we can plan our next step."

They dragged themselves to the entrance. Their car was parked exactly where they had left it. Arthur looked for the keys in his pocket. They weren't there.

"You left them inside the car," Rachamim pointed out. He noticed that the motor was running and the door was unlocked. Arthur had been in such a hurry to get into the terminal that he had forgotten to turn off the car motor.

As soon as Arthur got into the car, he radioed FBI headquarters. "The subject dropped the cell phone into a trash can before leaving," he reported. "We found the phone, still on."

"No one ever accused al Qaeda of stupidity," the FBI dispatcher commented. "Call this into the director. He's been asking me for an update."

"Okay." Arthur felt reluctant as he dialed the director's direct line. He hated admitting to failure.

A strange voice answered the call. "Who's this?" Arthur asked suspiciously.

"Sharon Browne, executive secretary to the FBI director," the woman said promptly. "Who's calling, please?"

"Arthur Singer, from the L.A. field office. I need to speak to the director urgently."

"I'm sorry, but the director is unable to come to the phone. He's on another call."

"He's probably trying to call the L.A. office again," Arthur said in exasperation. "Please tell him that Arthur Singer from Los Angeles would like to tell him what happened in the terminal."

"Hold on, please."

Sure enough, the director immediately took the call. "Did you find him?"

"Not exactly. I found his cell phone instead."

He related what had happened. There was an ominous silence for several minutes when he had finished. "This isn't good," the director said finally. "We have a grand total of two hours to get to the bottom of this. Put a tracer on that cell phone that Jamil gave Rachamim. We have to hope that he'll call again. In the meantime, we'll get Abu Salim to L.A. as fast as possible. But I hate to take such close chances."

"Abu Salim?" Arthur asked in puzzlement.

"Never mind." The director was abrupt. "I can't explain it all now. I'll talk to you later. Let me know when you have something important to tell me."

The phone went dead.

There was a bitter taste of failure in Arthur's mouth. He did not exchange a word with Rachamim the entire drive home, and they entered the house in silence. Naomi was sitting in the living room, also in silence despite the three agents in the room with her. The moment she saw Rachamim and Arthur, she came alive again.

"Did you find Jamil?" she asked, a tinge of hope in her voice.

Rachamim shook his head. "No. No, we didn't find him. He outwitted us. He left the open cell phone in a trash can, hidden away in a bunch of old wrappings. He dragged us there so he could get away."

"Are you sure it was Jamil?" Naomi asked in disbelief.

"Yes. It was Jamil," Rachamim assured her. "I spoke to him myself."

Just then, the cell phone started ringing again. Everyone stared at the small device in Rachamim's hands. He looked at it, then glanced at Arthur. "Take the call," Arthur whispered.

As Rachamim slowly brought the phone to his ear, Arthur hastily dialed the number of the Nextel technician. "He's on the phone now. Start tracking the call!"

"Jamil." Rachamim's voice cracked. "I can't take it any longer. I can't watch my wife suffer emotionally like this. Why are you doing this to me? What have we done to harm you?"

"The call is coming from a location about two miles from the airport," the technician informed Arthur. "The telephone is stationary. So it's possible that he's playing a game with us, and the same thing will happen as at the Gateway Center."

"Okay, hang on." Arthur activated his radio. "I need as many units as we can find to converge on the following location." He gave the coordinates near the airport. "Any agents near the area?"

His radio squawked. "Roger that, Willis and Jones are five miles out."

"Get there as fast as you can. Backup is on the way."

"What are we looking for?"

"A man, an Arab, talking on a cell phone."

"Any danger?"

Arthur hesitated. He didn't think Jamil was dangerous, but still …

"Negative information on that. A single man, he could possibly be armed but we do not know."

"Roger. We're on our way."

Arthur looked up from his radio. Rachamim still had the phone pressed to his ear, though he wasn't speaking now. Tears were trickling down his face.

"Is the phone call still going?" Arthur asked the technician.

"Yes."

"Okay. Keep tracking the call," Arthur instructed the technician. "We've got people on the way there. Let me know if the location changes."

Arthur called the director again to keep him informed of the latest developments. Again he got the executive secretary, who eventually got the director on the phone.

"Jamil has called again, and we have pinpointed his location," Arthur reported.

"How do you know he hasn't done the same thing he did before? Maybe he's dumped the phone."

"He's still on the line with Rachamim."

"What are they talking about?" the director asked curiously.

"They aren't talking. They're crying."

"What did you say?"

"They're crying," Arthur repeated. "At least Rachamim is. I suspect Jamil is doing the same thing."

"Doesn't sound like a run-of-the-mill terrorist," the director commented.

Arthur frowned. The director wasn't taking this too seriously, that was clear. "Our units have already been alerted, and they're converging on him now."

"Where is he?" the director asked, his voice devoid of any real interest.

"Not far from the airport."

"What! Did you say that he's near Los Angeles International Airport?"

Arthur could not understand the director's excitement. "Yes, that's exactly what I said."

"That's him! That's him!" the director yelled. "He's the guy who's threatening L.A.!"

"What are you talking about?"

The director ignored Arthur's question. "Hang on a minute. I'm going to pass this on. I'll be right back."

Arthur heard the receiver drop to the floor. A few minutes later, the director was back on the line. "Okay. Here's what you need to do. Forget about your plan to capture Jamil. Divert everyone who's heading for his current location and surround the airport instead. He'll be heading toward the airport shortly. But be discreet. We don't want to scare him off."

The tiny light bulb burning in the corner of the huge warehouse provided just enough light to illuminate the entranceway. Jamil did not want to turn on the main lights. He preferred the darkness now, during the last few hours of his life.

What should I do about Rachamim? The question gave him no rest. How could he convince him to leave before it was too late? He would do anything to help Rachamim survive. Anything, that is, except go against orders.

Yet an inner voice refused to give him peace. He could not harm his close friends, Rachamim and Naomi. They had treated him like the family he had never had, and they were a part of him now. He couldn't destroy the city until Rachamim was safely gone.

Jamil slowly began pacing across the empty room, recalling events from the past. The room was chilly, and he wrapped his tattered coat tightly around himself. He was struck by the irony: al Qaeda was willing to spend millions to murder innocent citizens, but was unwilling to invest an extra fifty dollars to buy a decent coat for one of its devoted soldiers.

Almost automatically, he pushed these thoughts away. The rigorous mental training that he had received over twenty years ago created a mental block that prevented him from thinking rationally. Taught by the al Qaeda that the ideals of the movement were absolute truth, that they would lead to his salvation, that the American way was corrupt and destructive, and that murder in the name of Islam would lead to paradise—Jamil was now incapable of shedding this mindset. He could not criticize the movement or its leader, even in the recesses of his own mind.

But this did not affect his relationship with Rachamim and Naomi. Somehow, they had slipped past his defenses. They had become more precious to him than anything in the world. The expert psychologists who had programmed his way of thinking had not prepared him for such a close relationship.

Jamil recalled their twenty years of friendship. Aside from these two wonderful people, he had no one in the entire world. He couldn't bear the thought that they would be among the victims—and that he would be the one to destroy them.

Jamil tried to push these thoughts away. Instead, he focused on the device that represented his task. The large, red button in the center beckoned to him. Just one push on that button, and his work would finally be complete …

But it was too soon. It wasn't supposed to be pressed until he heard the device start buzzing. Three minutes before, he had been told, the device would make a buzzing sound. That would be his final warning. Then, when the light on the device lit up, it would be his holy duty to press the button. Jamil knew that he still had to wait.

The longer you wait, a voice whispered inside of him, *the greater chance Rachamim has to escape.*

Angrily, Jamil pushed the thought away again. He looked again at the device in his hand. Why did it need his intervention? Why didn't it just go off by itself?

Perhaps, he decided, he didn't really need to press anything. The device simply had to be in the right location for it to work. The detonator had to be here so the bomb would explode when it came within a certain radius of the device.

All that really didn't make a difference, however. The main problem was that Rachamim refused to leave the city.

Back to Rachamim! My thoughts keep going around in circles! Jamil kept pacing up and down the dark, empty warehouse. *Can I destroy the city if Rachamim and his wife are in it? How? How?*

Once again, Jamil removed the cell phone from his belt. He had to call. He had to make sure that Rachamim was safe.

Before he could turn the phone on, it started to ring. Startled, Jamil nearly dropped the phone. He grabbed it and stared at the tiny screen to see who was calling him, but no name was visible.

Jamil pressed the receive button and brought the tiny phone to his ear.

"Jamil," a voice announced, "your time has come."

"I hear," Jamil responded automatically. "What do you want me to do?"

"Go to warehouse number twenty-six, just outside the airport, and wait until the device begins to buzz. The rest, you know …"

"Yes, I know," Jamil answered. "I'm leaving immediately."

Jamil hung up the phone and took a deep breath. His time had come. For twenty years, he had waited for this moment. All thoughts of Rachamim were banished from his mind as he savored the knowledge that he, Jamil, had been chosen to bring this great glory to Islam.

The street in front of the warehouse was empty. Jamil carefully slipped out of the warehouse and into his car, parked opposite the doorway. He slowly drove away, stopping every few blocks for a red light. He was extremely careful so there would be no reason for the police to stop him.

Jamil drove about twenty minutes before stopping on a deserted corner two miles from the airport. His hand was trembling as he took the cell phone and dialed Rachamim's number.

As Rachamim started sobbing, Jamil felt the tears slide down his own cheeks.

"Why are you doing this to us?" Rachamim repeated.

Why? Why? Jamil wondered. *Why am I harming these wonderful people?*

"I'm not," Jamil finally managed to whisper through his tears. "I am not doing this to you. You are doing it to yourself! I've warned you, I've told you to leave. Why won't you listen to me?"

"Tell me, Jamil. What happens if I listen to you, if I leave the city?"

"Then I am free," Jamil sighed. "I am free to do my duty."

"Your duty?" Rachamim whispered.

"Yes. It is the task that I have been waiting to do for twenty years."

Abruptly everything became clear to Rachamim. He realized that he—and he alone—could save the city of Los Angeles. It was only his presence here that was keeping Jamil from taking the final step toward the city's destruction. If he left, then Jamil was free to perform his deathly task.

"Listen to me, Jamil," Rachamim said urgently. "I am not leaving. Do you hear me? If you destroy the city, you've destroyed me as well."

"Rachamim, I'm not about to argue now. I just want to let you know that within the next hour, Los Angeles will disappear off the face of the earth. This is your final opportunity to escape. Goodbye, Rachamim. We will never see each other again. Remember that I always loved you."

"No! No! Jamil, I will not leave Los Angeles. Naomi and I will be here, together with all the other innocent people who live in this city. I promise you, by everything I hold holy, that I will not leave the city."

His only response was a click. Jamil had hung up.

Thirty Three

Jamil left Interstate 405 shortly before the airport exit, entering an industrial zone that was filled with dilapidated warehouses. He drove slowly, trying to make out the faded building numbers in the bright afternoon sunlight.

Finally he spotted it—number 26. Jamil stopped and turned the steering wheel toward the garage door. He left the motor running while he pulled the garage door open. Then he jumped back into his car and drove into the dark warehouse.

The headlights illuminated the garage, but the area was quickly plunged into darkness as Jamil parked the car and shut the lights. He left, closing the garage door behind him.

The door leading into the building was unlocked. Using a high-powered flashlight, Jamil carefully examined the cavernous room. It was empty. He quickly spotted the door to the office where he had been told to wait. Pushing the door open, Jamil discovered a rusty old metal desk and a torn office chair.

He placed the detonator on the table, next to his cell phone. Then he settled down to wait.

"Alpha Seven, Alpha Seven, can you read me?"

The sudden noise startled the soldier on duty, who had just dozed off while manning the radar screen on the California-Mexican border.

"Alpha Seven, Alpha Seven," the voice sounded a second time over the short wave radio, before the soldier had a chance to respond.

"I read you five-by-five."

"Alpha Seven, this is General Brand, commander of the Northern Air Front."

The name caused the soldier to jump to attention.

"In twenty minutes, a helicopter will be flying over the border. It's coming from Mexico," the general continued. "It'll be flying at an altitude of five thousand feet. Ignore it."

"Acknowledged," the soldier said, before signing off. *What's going on?* he wondered. He quickly notified his commanding officer, who insisted on contacting General Brand himself to confirm the order.

"That's confirmed. Do not contact the aircraft, do not ask the aircraft to identify itself."

"Roger," the officer said. It was his turn to wonder what was going on.

Osama bin Laden was in his headquarters in the Tora Bora Mountains. He knew this was the safest location for him at this time. Even if the Americans succeeded in overpowering the Taliban, they would be hard-pressed to find anything in these mountains—as the Russians had learned, to their great cost.

Bin Laden was sitting cross-legged on several pillows, surrounded by his close advisors—including al Zawahiri. The wall opposite them held seven television screens, all receiving satellite transmissions from United States stations located on the west coast. The center screen was set to CBS Los Angeles. This transmission would stop the moment the bomb, presently on its way to Los Angeles International Airport, exploded.

The room was deathly quiet. All eyes were riveted to the television screens.

The short wave radio sitting next to bin Laden crackled to life. Bin Laden donned his headset and listened carefully for a long moment before putting the headset down.

"The helicopter has just passed our observation post," he announced. "It's presently about fifteen miles inside the United States. It's flying in a straight line to the airport. The bomb has successfully crossed the border."

The room erupted in cheers. Only bin Laden himself and al

Zawahiri held themselves back from rejoicing. They knew that the mission would not be complete until the final moments of success.

"It will still be almost another hour before the helicopter gets close enough to the bomb trigger, which is right near the airport," he said to al Zawahiri in low tones.

The men caught their leader's mood, and a feeling of tension slowly settled on the room. Al Zawahiri's eyes flickered nervously between the television screens and the clock on the wall.

Fifty-five minutes to go.

Jamil's hand was shaking as he wiped the sweat off his brow. He was alternately consumed by chills, then covered with sweat. His head felt feverish as his mind kept considering and rejecting the possibilities. *Should he go ahead with it? How could he not? Wasn't this his duty? But what about Rachamim?*

Circles, tortured circles of thought. And even as he tortured his brain, he was aware of the minutes ticking away. Soon, he knew, it would be too late for them all.

He was startled by the ringing of his phone. Jamil managed to still his shaking hands and bring the receiver to his ear.

"Are you in place?" his commanding officer asked without preamble.

"I am here," Jamil confirmed.

"This is your thirty minute warning," the officer announced. "In just thirty minutes, you will fulfill your glorious mission and enter paradise."

Thirty minutes. Jamil didn't think he could hold out another thirty minutes.

"Can't you make it happen earlier?" he demanded feverishly.

His commanding officer sounded startled. "Earlier? I'm afraid that it's really not in my hands. A military helicopter is transporting the bomb to the airport. The helicopter is flying at maximum speed, so you'll have to wait a bit longer."

"I understand." Jamil's voice was hoarse. He was ashamed at his outburst. "In the meantime, I will pray."

"Yes, that would be fitting. A glorious future awaits you. I envy your sacrifice."

Sure you do, Jamil thought with a tinge of contempt. If he really envied him that much, no doubt the officer would have found a way to do this himself.

Jamil hung up the phone, then stared at the device on the decrepit old desk. Almost automatically, he started dialing the first three numbers of the cell phone he had given Rachamim. Realizing what he was doing, he angrily turned the phone off, then forced himself to put it down on the desk, next to the device.

He would wait. Ten minutes before the explosion—in just another fifteen minutes, now—he would call Rachamim for the last time.

The clock showed twenty-five minutes. Bin Laden took advantage of the quiet in the room to recite a few words of prayer from the Koran, while his disciples repeated the words after him.

"Twenty-three minutes," al Zawahiri raised his voice above the prayers.

Bin Laden got up and stood in front of his followers. With fiery enthusiasm, he began, "My beloved brothers, in another twenty-three minutes we will be giving a deadly blow to the Americans. This will teach the evil ones not to start up with the Muslim world. This blow will cause them to leave the holy land of Saudi Arabia.

"But before that happens, they will try to take revenge against us. We must disperse to the four winds. Only in that way will we be able to unite again to bring about the ultimate victory.

"I know they will succeed in capturing some of us who are here. They must, to save face. Therefore, I want each of you to swear that if he is caught, he will refuse to provide the enemy with information. Will you give me your word?"

"We promise. We give our word!" they answered in one voice.

That was not enough. Bin Laden walked around the room, individually shaking each person's hand, while looking directly into his eyes. He did not release his grasp until each person had repeated his promise.

"Eighteen minutes to the explosion," al Zawahiri announced.

The room became alive with shouts of *"Allah Akhbar!"*

Back in the FBI's safe house, Arthur paced the living room in frustration. There were hundreds of FBI agents and police officers surrounding the L.A. airport, but so far there was no sign of Jamil.

After decades as an FBI special agent, Arthur had developed good instincts. Now his instincts were telling him that they were going about this the wrong way. The director had told him not to track Jamil at his current location, but Arthur had a strong feeling that this was a mistake.

What if he's wrong? What if he's setting the bomb off somewhere else? What if, what if ...

Abruptly, Arthur made a decision. He grabbed his cell phone and punched in the number of the Nextel technician.

"Do you have a track on the phone now?" he asked.

"Hang on, let's see." The technician was silent for several minutes. "Okay, the phone isn't in use right now, but it is turned on. It's currently just outside the L.A. airport."

"Can you get me a location?"

"Let me map it ... okay." The technician rattled off an address.

"Got it?"

"Yeah, I got it, thanks. Look, I'm giving you my cell phone number. If that phone moves outside that area, let me know."

"Gotcha."

Arthur hung up the phone, then turned to Rachamim. "Come on. We're going to try to find Jamil."

"But I thought you said—"

"I know what I said," Arthur interrupted. He frowned in indecision. "I just have a bad feeling about sitting here and waiting for Jamil to walk into the airport. What if he gets through somehow?"

Rachamim nodded. Without another word, he followed Arthur to the car. Arthur wasted no time in getting on the freeway and heading for the airport.

Jamil watched the minute hand on his watch move slowly. *I'll call in ten minutes,* he thought. *Just ten more minutes!* But it was actually only two minutes later that he lifted the phone and called Rachamim's cell phone.

It rang twice before Rachamim answered. "Jamil?"

Rachamim's voice was muffled. Jamil instantly realized that he was traveling in a car.

"You listened!" Jamil said joyfully. "You are leaving L.A.!"

"No, I'm not," Rachamim said forcefully.

"Then are you at least getting far away from the airport?" Jamil asked fearfully.

"No. In fact, I'm heading for the airport right this minute."

"Why, Rachamim, why?" Jamil couldn't stop the tears that choked his throat. "Tell me why you are doing this to me!"

"Listen, Jamil." Rachamim forced his voice to be gentle. "If you want to destroy this city, I can't stop you. But I'll be here, in the city. I'm not about to leave. Whatever happens to the city will happen to me too! I want you to understand that."

From the corner of his eye, Rachamim saw Arthur dial his cell phone. "Is he still in the same location?" he asked the Nextel technician.

"Still hasn't moved," the technician confirmed.

"So be it," Jamil said finally. "In just eighteen minutes, a military helicopter will be coming here with the bomb. The bomb will go off, and that will be the end of everything."

"A military helicopter?" Rachamim repeated.

"Yes."

"A military helicopter." Rachamim's words caught Arthur's attention. Arthur tried to focus on Rachamim's conversation as he skillfully wove around the traffic on the freeway.

"And it will be here in just eighteen minutes?" he heard Rachamim say.

"Eighteen minutes!" Arthur reached for his cell phone. "I'd better pass that on."

Rachamim, concentrating on his conversation with Jamil, took no notice of Arthur's comment. "So what is your part in this?" he asked Jamil. "Can you stop it or not?"

"It is my task to bring the activator to the right place. As soon as it senses the bomb, I will press the button and the bomb will explode."

Rachamim felt a chill. *This is for real*, he realized. With the press of a button, the entire city will be destroyed.

"Don't do it," Rachamim whispered.

Arthur reached the director on the first try. "I have more information from the terrorist. He gives an estimated time of eighteen minutes to the explosion."

"Eighteen minutes!"

The FBI director set off at a run to the communications room, where the Defense Secretary and the National Security Advisor were still monitoring the flight of the helicopter.

"Eighteen minutes," he gasped. "That's the warning from L.A. We've got an agent in communication with the alleged terrorist there."

The room erupted in chaos, which was quickly stilled by the Defense Secretary. "Okay, settle down. We don't have time to panic." As quiet fell over the room, he turned back to the FBI director. "Tell me what you know," he ordered.

The FBI director took a deep breath. "My agent is currently guarding an Iranian Jew, who has a close connection with an alleged al Qaeda terrorist. Presumably he was planted as a dormant cell many years ago. According to the Jew, this man has repeatedly warned him of an attack that will be taking place in Los Angeles. He called him just a few minutes ago to tell him that the attack will happen in eighteen minutes."

"Why is he giving the Jew this information?" the President demanded. "How do we know this is a trustworthy source?"

"We don't know for certain," the director admitted. "But the details dovetail perfectly with the information we just received from Abu Salim. Why is he warning the Jew? Apparently, the terrorist saved the Jew's life when he escaped from Iran in 1979. The Jew returned the favor by adopting him as one of the family. Over the years, they developed a deep and caring relationship.

"The terrorist is doing everything in his power to convince the Jewish family to leave the city. He told the Jew that this massive attack will make the attack on September 11 seem like child's play."

"Do we know the terrorist's location?" the President asked.

"Last time I spoke to my agent, he said that the terrorist was a few miles from the airport. That's how I realized that his suspect was probably the terrorist who Abu Salim offered to identify for us."

"So how are you trying to stop him?"

"I've ordered agents to surround the airport," the FBI director said, trying to project an air of confidence that he didn't feel. "If he tries to get there, we'll have him."

"And maybe he isn't trying to get to the airport?" the President said sharply. "I don't want to rely on Abu Salim's word."

"Yes, but if he's wrong, he also gets blown up," the FBI director pointed out. "I can't believe he'd do that ..."

The director's voice trailed off as he belatedly remembered that logic didn't necessarily apply to al Qaeda terrorists, who had so far shown a willingness to be killed out of dedication to their cause.

"Yes," the President said finally. "Let's see if your agent has any more information for us. In the meantime, get Abu Salim there as quickly as we can."

"Estimated arrival in thirteen minutes," the Defense Secretary reported, from where he was monitoring the helicopter's progress.

Thirteen minutes. Would it be enough?

Arthur's car careened off the exit ramp. He was entering a small area filled with warehouses, right on the outskirts of the airport. This area, he realized, was just outside the cordon of agents guarding the entrance to LAX. It was as close as Jamil could get to the airport without encountering the police.

"This is it," he muttered. He slowed the car, searching for the address the Nextel technician had given him.

Just then, his phone rang. "Arthur Singer," he announced, his mind still on the addresses outside.

It was the director on the phone. "Any update on the terrorist?" he asked.

Arthur hesitated. He hadn't been told to track down Jamil—if anything, he was going against orders to be doing this. But still ...

"I'm right outside the location he last called from," Arthur said finally.

"Wonderful," the director said fervently. "Any information?"

Arthur glanced at Rachamim, who still had Jamil's cell phone pressed to his ear, though he had fallen silent some time before. "The last I heard from the terrorist was that the bomb would be exploding in eighteen minutes. That's when I called you. It was, oh, about eight minutes ago."

Ten minutes left.

"How much more time until Abu Salim's helicopter arrives in Los Angeles?" the President asked the Secretary of Defense.

"Approximately ten minutes," the Secretary whispered.

So close! Would the helicopter get there in time to stop the attack?

"Contact the helicopter pilot and ask him to fly at maximum speed."

"That's exactly what I was about to do," the Secretary of Defense declared.

"I'm already flying at maximum speed according to safety regulations," the pilot responded uncomfortably.

"Forget the safety precautions. Just get here as fast as you can!"

"Did he give you any other information?" the FBI director asked, as Arthur stopped the car in front of warehouse number 26.

"Look, I'm in front of the warehouse now," Arthur said, preoccupied. "I need to plan this out, sir, if that's okay. The only other thing he mentioned is that the bomb is being transported here in a military helicopter."

Thirty Four

A military helicopter... the bomb is being transported by a military helicopter....

The FBI director frowned and shook his head. Why was that fact significant? He tried to dismiss it from his mind as he turned to the more pressing issue: was there any way Arthur could keep the terrorist from carrying out his plan, or at least delay him long enough for Abu Salim to arrive?

"Do you need backup?" he asked Arthur.

"I've ordered two squads to come here, but to keep it quiet. I don't want to shock the terrorist into doing anything prematurely."

"Good idea. How are you going to confront him?"

"I don't know," Arthur admitted. "I have Rachamim here with me. We'll have to come up with something fast, though, so if you have any ideas, tell them to me now."

Jamil left the office and started pacing across the cavernous room, empty except for a few broken pieces of furniture. Oddly, he still had his cell phone pressed to his ear. Somehow he had never disconnected that last call with Rachamim. Neither man said a word, but Jamil knew that Rachamim was still there. It was as if they were both under a spell. Neither wanted to be the one to break the silence.

Jamil jerked to a stop as the door to the warehouse slowly swung open. The cell phone fell from his hand and clattered to the floor.

Rachamim stood in the doorway, outlined in the last rays of the setting sun.

Six minutes left.
Bin Laden sat tranquilly in front of the television screens. He had spent fifteen years dreaming of this day, fifteen years since he had first set in motion the plan to send a nuclear bomb against America. Now, at last, victory was in his grasp.

The men surrounding him shared in his hopes and dreams. But only he knew the true extent of his vision. With this one blow, bin Laden would usher in a new era for Islam and the entire world.

Al Zawahiri looked at the clock on the wall. "Five minutes," he murmured.

As Jamil stared at Rachamim, something seemed to explode in his brain. The powerful psychological training he had undergone decades before crumbled before the onslaught of emotion evoked by the sight of his old friend. All at once, he knew that he could not take this fatal step.

"Rachamim ..." Jamil whispered, taking a step forward.

He swayed where he stood. And then, as Rachamim rushed forward in alarm, he fell to the floor in a dead faint.

Rachamim stared at his fallen friend as Arthur elbowed past him into the warehouse.

"What happened?" Arthur demanded.

"I think he fainted," Rachamim said. He knelt by Jamil, and was reassured to see that he was still breathing, though his eyes remained closed.

"I think he's okay," Rachamim reported.

"That's wonderful," Arthur snapped, "but if we don't find that detonator fast, no one is going to be okay!"

Arthur spied the open door to the office. Just as he got inside, an ominous buzzing began to fill the room. Arthur's shocked gaze took in the detonator sitting on the table. The sound was coming from there, and a red light was flashing on the device's surface.

"What's that?" Rachamim had followed Arthur to the doorway.

"It's the detonator." Arthur grabbed the device and turned it over feverishly. "Three minutes left. I guess this is the warning signal.

There's got to be a way to stop this thing!"

"But Jamil isn't pressing the button," Rachamim protested.

"I don't think that matters. I can't believe bin Laden would take chances with this. I'm virtually certain that Jamil's job was to bring the detonator to the right location where the bomb will sense it, but that it will go off on its own."

Rachamim stared at the buzzing detonator. "So does this mean it's already started sensing the bomb?"

"Yes!" Arthur practically shouted. "We have almost no time left!"

"What about the batteries?" Rachamim suggested.

Arthur poked and prodded at the device, but there was no battery compartment.

"It's sealed," he muttered. His face was covered in sweat.

Arthur glanced frantically around the room. His eyes lit up when he spotted a rusty sink in the corner. "Water! I'll submerge it in the sink! Water should destroy the mechanism!"

Rachamim watched as Arthur rushed to the sink. He tried to turn on the water, but the handle was stuck. Back and forth he twisted it, exerting all his strength—until the handle snapped off in his hand.

Two minutes left.

"**ETA to LAX,** two minutes," the helicopter pilot reported. He twisted a dial on his radio. "Tower, this is special flight X Alpha Zulu 86, requesting permission to land, over."

"X Alpha Zulu, runway fifteen has been cleared for you." That runway was closest to the terminal. It had been closed for the past fifteen minutes.

"I'm beginning to lower my altitude," the pilot announced to both the White House communications room and the flight controller. "I'm approaching the airport from the southeast, at an altitude of nine thousand feet."

"X Alpha Zulu, land right next to the terminal," the controller radioed. "There are security forces standing by for your, ah, special passengers."

"Roger."

Slowly, the helicopter began its descent.

Arthur had dropped his cell phone on the desk in his mad rush to deactivate the device. He was staring, dumbstruck, at the broken handle in his hand when his phone began to ring.

Rachamim looked at Arthur, who made no move toward the desk to get his phone. He hesitated a moment, then picked it up himself. "Hello?"

"**Who is this?**" the FBI director demanded. "Where's Arthur?"

"It's Rachamim. Arthur is ... Arthur is ..."

"What's wrong?"

Arthur leaped across the room and grabbed the phone. "It's all over! Do you understand? It's finished! We're all going to die! One minute left!"

"What are you talking about, Arthur?"

"I can't deactivate the detonator! It's going to go off! That bomb is going to explode in exactly one minute!"

"One minute?" the FBI director repeated.

"One minute," the Defense Secretary said, intent on the radio link to the aircraft. "One minute until they land."

One minute left ... a military aircraft ... one minute ...

Abruptly the pieces came together in the director's mind. He suddenly realized exactly where the bomb was—and how it was getting into the United States.

"*Stop the helicopter!* Did you hear me? *STOP!*"

Silence. Everyone stared at him in shock.

The FBI director spoke quickly. "I know where the bomb is. Stop that helicopter, have it turn around and get as far away from the airport as possible."

When no one moved, the FBI director dashed across the room and grabbed the microphone from the captain who was monitoring the radio link to the helicopter. "Stop descending immediately and get away from the airport!"

"Wait a minute. Who is this?" the pilot demanded. He had already started preparing for landing.

The Secretary of Defense finally moved. "You'd better know what you're doing," he muttered, before taking the microphone from the FBI director. "This is the Secretary of Defense. Do what he said."

The order was greeted with silence. For the last few hours the pilot had been pushing his aircraft to fly at top speed, breaking all safety rules, so he could arrive at the airport quickly. Now, at the very last moment, he was being given orders to do the exact opposite.

"Are you sure?" the pilot asked incredulously.

"Yes, I'm sure. Acknowledge!"

"Acknowledged," the pilot said.

He related the orders to his copilot, and together they made the dangerous midair turn.

The Defense Secretary turned to the FBI director. "Okay. Now explain it to me."

"It was something Arthur said," the director said, still breathing heavily from his sprint across the room.

"Who's Arthur?"

"My agent in L.A. He found the terrorist, but he was unable to deactivate the detonator. The bomb was set to explode in one minute—and it was one minute until the helicopter reached the airport."

"I don't understand," the Defense Secretary said impatiently.

"The helicopter is carrying the bomb," the director said quietly. "The detonator is designed to set it off as soon as it reaches the airport."

"Are you crazy?" the Defense Secretary said incredulously. "Our helicopter is carrying bin Laden's bomb? How on earth could that have happened?"

"I don't know," the FBI director said stubbornly, "but it's the only thing that fits."

The pilot radioed in. "We've turned around," he reported. "I'm out of L.A. airspace. Now what are we supposed to do?"

The two men looked at each other. The FBI director took a deep breath. "Tell the pilots to land gently at a military airbase as far from L.A. as possible."

"If your hypothesis is right," the President interjected, "they should stay far away from any population center, just in case."

"I don't have that much fuel," the pilot reported. "I can go another half hour or so, tops."

The Defense Secretary called over one of his staff. "Find somewhere they can land, and do it fast."

Two minutes later, he was radioing coordinates to the pilot. "Head for Mackney's Airbase. We've got the staff there to deal with this. I'll let them know you're coming."

"So is that it?" the President asked. "Are you sure that this is the bomb?"

"Everything fits," the FBI director insisted.

"But what if you're wrong?" The President looked at his watch. "According to your terrorist friend, the bomb should have exploded one minute ago." He looked up at the now-silent room. "Do we know if L.A. is still there?"

Arthur was still babbling into the phone, rambling on about how they were going to die in less than a minute. Rachamim had his eyes shut tight, and was whispering *viduy*.

"Arthur! Arthur! What's happening? Will you stop the hysterics! Arthur, talk to me!"

The director's voice finally penetrated Arthur's consciousness. "What—what?" he gasped.

"Arthur, it's been a minute since the deadline. Sounds like you're still there," the director said sarcastically.

"I'm here," Arthur said wonderingly. He looked around at the room, at Rachamim sitting in the chair, at the detonator still in his grasp. The flashing light had faded, and the detonator was silent. "You're right. We're all still here!"

"I think we identified the bomb. It was aboard the military helicopter that was on its way to LAX."

"That's what Jamil said!" Arthur interrupted. "A military aircraft!"

"You're right," the director admitted. He paused. "In all honesty, it's because of Jamil and Rachamim that I managed to figure this out just in time. I've sent the helicopter away from L.A., and it's safely out of the detonator's range."

"Really?" Arthur couldn't believe it. His life was not going to end here, in this drab room, right next to L.A. airport.

"Really," the director reassured him. "I'll tell the field office in L.A. to have our agents stand down the alert around the airport. We'll continue to be on our guard, but it looks as if the danger has passed."

In a cave in the Tora Bora Mountains, bin Laden continued watching the television screen, his eyes intent on the CBS broadcast. Al Zawahiri coughed slightly.

"The bomb should have been there a minute ago," he said softly, his voice slightly questioning.

Bin Laden's face remained serene, though al Zawahiri could see the tightening in his shoulders. All he said, though, was, "We will continue to wait."

Thirty Five

The helicopter cautiously touched down on the landing pad. It was immediately surrounded by a group of soldiers, their machine guns ready. They had been given instructions to shoot without warning if anyone tried to approach the aircraft.

The doors opened the moment the helicopter touched ground and the commanding officer jumped out. Next were two soldiers surrounding Abu Salim, who was blindfolded. Behind him were more soldiers, surrounding the other captives.

"I can't help you when I'm blindfolded like this," Abu Salim argued, gesturing rapidly.

"Then we'll just have to forgo your assistance," the commanding officer responded sarcastically.

Abu Salim was at a loss. He didn't know what was supposed to happen next. Surely this was part of bin Laden's plan ... or was it? Had the plan failed? He had not been given instructions beyond this point. He had expected the Americans to take off his blindfold so he could identify the supposed terrorist in the Los Angeles airport. At that point, he had assumed, he would understand what his next steps should be.

Perhaps the plan had failed. Perhaps the Americans had somehow discovered the plot. Then and there, Abu Salim decided that it was better not to go back to al Qaeda. He would collaborate with the Americans. Perhaps they would be able to deactivate the poisonous capsule that had been planted in his arm.

"Listen," he begged, "I was forced to do what I did. They planted a poisonous capsule inside my arm. If you can get it out of me, I'll be happy to assist you."

The commanding officer looked skeptical, but he waved over the airbase commander and conferred with him quietly. Within a few minutes, the soldiers and their captive had been taken inside the building, where the doctor on duty would be able to check out Abu Salim's claim.

"He's not important now, anyway," the airbase commander said. "We've got to get rid of this bomb. There's a Hazmat unit waiting for us right there."

"Okay, stand back." The commander of the Hazmat unit strode up, surrounded by his men. They were completely covered in white protective clothes, with masks over their faces.

The unit's commander was carrying a black box with flashing lights. As he got closer to the helicopter, an electronic voice announced, "Positive… Positive…"

Everyone took a step back as the unit came closer. The device began to beep.

"Well, you've got some radioactive material in there," the Hazmat commander observed, "but not dangerous at this stage. Part of a nuclear weapon."

"What if the bomb goes off?" the airbase commander demanded, ashen-faced.

The Hazmat commander looked at him. "Then it's dangerous," he said dryly.

There was a short silence.

"I'd recommend evacuating all nonessential personnel from the base," the Hazmat commander added. "Just in case. This could be a big one."

The soldiers started evacuating the airbase. The airbase commander remained, but nearly everyone else was taken at least fifty miles from the site.

"All right, we've got our instructions. That bomb may be in delicate shape, so work carefully," the Hazmat commander ordered.

The unit surrounded the aircraft. The radioactive sensing device led them to the underbelly of the right-hand side of the helicopter, which was holding what appeared to be a Mark 84 missile. The soldiers moved aside to allow their commander to get a closer look at the missile.

"Okay, looks like a Mark 84, but there's something different …" He bent down and looked at the back of the missile, shining his flashlight down the length of it. When he straightened, there were beads of sweat on his forehead.

"It's a Mark 1a fission bomb," he said quietly.

"One of our bombs?" a soldier asked incredulously.

"I doubt it. Probably a Russian copy. But it's just as powerful. We need to get this to a safe location."

The commander carefully looked over the bomb, checking to see if there was anything connecting the missile to the helicopter that could cause the bomb to explode while they were in the process of detaching it. "Nothing," the commander reported. "It apparently never occurred to them that their plan might fail."

A special crane was set up, with a sling to catch the missile when it was released from the aircraft. The men worked carefully, and the missile soon came free. They brought it into an armored truck that was waiting nearby.

After securing the bomb to the vehicle, the driver drove, slowly and carefully, to an army testing location deep within the Mojave Desert. There, in an area far from habitation, they would use a special robot to dismantle the bomb. If something went wrong, the bomb would be far enough from civilization to avoid the danger of radioactive fallout to innocent citizens.

"Jamil!" Rachamim exclaimed. "We forgot about Jamil!"

Rachamim rushed into the cavernous room, with Arthur following slowly behind. Jamil was still on the floor, though he was sitting up now. His eyes looked dazed.

"Rachamim?" he croaked out. "Is that really you? Did I dream all this?"

"Yes, it's me," Rachamim said reassuringly.

Jamil looked past Rachamim, at the FBI agent who was emerging from the office. His expression contorted with fear.

"Who is that?" He pointed a shaking finger at Arthur.

"That's Arthur Singer, an FBI agent."

"FBI!" Jamil shrank back. "Are you going to arrest me?"

Rachamim turned to look at Arthur. "What are you planning to do with Jamil?" he asked worriedly. "Are you going to bring him to trial?"

Arthur looked thoughtful. "Actually, if you think about it, Jamil did not break any laws. In fact, if he hadn't called you and given you information about the bomb, we probably would not be here right now." Arthur's voice became gentle as he spoke directly to Jamil. "I understand that you were a dormant cell. Is that right?"

Jamil nodded mutely.

Rachamim was puzzled. "What does that mean, to be a dormant cell?"

"It means that your actions aren't really your own," Arthur explained. "From the constant training and beliefs that were planted in Jamil's brain years ago, certain thoughts and acts became almost automatic. For example, he probably has a fervent belief in al Qaeda, and finds it difficult to think badly of them." Arthur looked inquiringly at Jamil, who nodded. "It also means that it would be virtually impossible for him not to carry out his mission."

"I see," Rachamim said. He looked horrified at the thought.

"What the al Qaeda trainers didn't foresee was that Jamil would develop such a close relationship with you and your family. It was stronger than all those psychological barriers that were in place, and were enough to make him hesitate—at least until he thought you were safe. It was because he communicated with you that we were able to stop the bomb in time."

"So Jamil is the one who saved us!"

Jamil looked startled at this. He looked quickly at Arthur, who smiled. "I suppose so," the FBI agent agreed.

A spark of hope appeared in Jamil's eyes. "Is it possible?" he murmured. "Do you really understand me, and what I have gone through?"

"Yes, definitely," Rachamim said reassuringly. "You heard what Arthur just said. You had almost no control over your actions."

"In fact," Arthur interjected, "it's amazing that you were able to break through the psychological bonds at all."

Arthur looked thoughtfully at Rachamim. He realized that Rachamim had displayed real heroism that day. It would have been easy for him to leave the L.A. area to a place of safety. Instead, he had chosen to stay here, where he had the chance to save the lives of thousands of people. It no longer seemed so remarkable that Rachamim and his wife were capable of inspiring such loyalty within Jamil.

Fifteen minutes. The bomb should have exploded fifteen minutes before.

Bin Laden stood up. The men around him looked tense and fearful. Even before he announced it, they knew what he would say.

"We have failed."

Bin Laden's followers bowed their heads in disgrace as their leader quietly left the room. He wanted to be alone, to deal with the sharp pain of failure away from the eyes of others. Months, years, decades of hard work had been for naught.

"I don't think everything's lost." Al Zawahiri followed him out of the room. "Perhaps the helicopter has been delayed."

"No." Bin Laden stared unseeingly ahead of him. "We have failed. I can sense it."

Al Zawahiri watched in silence as bin Laden continued walking away, toward his office. He seemed to have aged several decades in the last few minutes. He reached for the doorknob, then hesitated. "Al Zawahiri," he said, without turning around.

"Yes."

"We will need to leave, you and I. We will go into hiding. The Americans will be seeking our destruction, and we cannot give them that satisfaction."

"What about the men?" al Zawahiri asked.

Bin Laden shook his head. "They will have to disperse. We must live on the run, and too many companions will slow us down. We have the technology and resources to set up a communications system—I already have the plans in place.

"The men are loyal; they will want to stay with me. You will have to convince them that their place now is to be elsewhere."

Bin Laden turned around. The look of defeat in his eyes was fading, replaced by a growing determination. "This is merely a setback. We will continue to strive, to persevere, and to strike at the Americans until we have achieved our goal."

Al Zawahiri bowed his head in acceptance. Then he went to speak to their loyal followers. A long road lay ahead of all of them. He could only hope that glory did, indeed, lie somewhere at the end of it.

Jamil was exhausted, shivering from emotion. "Come," Arthur urged them, "it's time to go. Let's get out of here."

Rachamim supported Jamil as the three men left the warehouse. Arthur gently helped him get into his car, parked right in front.

"My car is in there," Jamil managed to whisper, pointing to the garage.

"Don't worry," Arthur reassured him. "I'll have one of my agents bring it to you later."

The car drove down the street, but stopped short at the corner. Two police cars were blocking the street. As Arthur slammed on the brakes, several police officers emerged from their parked cars.

"FBI," Arthur said, showing his badge. "It's okay."

"We were told to cordon off this area," the officer explained.

"Yes, I know, I'm the one who asked you to do it," Arthur said. "I forgot to call the office to tell them to contact you. Everything is taken care of. The terrorist is in our custody, and the threat is neutralized."

The police officer looked curiously at the two men in the back of the car, but he didn't ask any further questions. The two police cars were quickly moved out of the way, and Arthur was waved through.

The drive back to the FBI safe house passed quickly. The ride was silent. Rachamim kept reliving the terror of that moment—when it seemed that their destruction was imminent, and that there was nothing they could do to stop it. From the look on Arthur's face, it appeared that his mind was similarly occupied.

And Jamil? Rachamim stole a look at his friend. He was staring down at his hands, which remained clenched in his lap. What was he thinking? What was he feeling? Impulsively, Rachamim reached out and touched Jamil's hands.

"It will be fine," he whispered.

Jamil looked up and tried to smile. But he quickly dropped his gaze.

The car pulled up in front of the lush garden that surrounded the house. Rachamim wasted no time in getting out of the car. He pulled Jamil to his feet, encouraging him to walk with him into the house.

Naomi, Yechezkel and Yosef had obviously been waiting for his return. They hurried forward as soon as the door opened.

"Is everything okay?" Naomi exclaimed.

Rachamim looked at his wife and his two sons. His family was here, whole again, and the danger was past. He looked at his friend Jamil, who had proven his loyalty despite everything the al Qaeda had tried to do to him.

Rachamim took a deep breath, and smiled. "Yes," he said softly. "Everything is absolutely perfect. *Baruch Hashem!*"